Within These Wicked Walls

⚔ A Novel ⚔

LAUREN
BLACKWOOD

WEDNESDAY BOOKS
NEW YORK

To my parents
who have never stopped believing in me

Published in the United States by Wednesday Books, an imprint of St. Martin's Publishing Group

WITHIN THESE WICKED WALLS. Copyright © 2021 by Lauren Blackwood. All rights reserved. Printed in the United States of America. For information, address St. Martin's Publishing Group, 120 Broadway, New York, NY 10271.

www.wednesdaybooks.com

Designed by Devan Norman

Excerpt from *Wildblood* copyright © 2023 by Lauren Blackwood

The Library of Congress has cataloged the hardcover edition as follows:

Names: Blackwood, Lauren, author.
Title: Within these wicked walls: a novel / Lauren Blackwood.
Description: First edition. | New York: Wednesday Books, an imprint of St. Martin's Publishing Group 2021.
Identifiers: LCCN 2021017544 | ISBN 9781250787101 (hardcover) | ISBN 9781250787118 (ebook)
Subjects: LCSH: Exorcism—Juvenile fiction. | Evil eye—Juvenile fiction. | Magic—Juvenile fiction. | Secrecy—Juvenile fiction. | Interpersonal relations—Juvenile fiction. | Horror tales. | Paranormal fiction. | CYAC: Exorcism—Fiction. | Magic—Fiction. | Secrets—Fiction. | Supernatural—Fiction. | Blacks—Fiction. | Horror stories. | LCGFT: Paranormal fiction. | Horror fiction.
Classification: LCC PZ7.1.B57 Wi 2021 | DDC 813.6 [Fic]—dc23
LC record available at https://lccn.loc.gov/2021017544

ISBN 978-1-250-78712-5 (trade paperback)

Our books may be purchased in bulk for promotional, educational, or business use. Please contact your local bookseller or the Macmillan Corporate and Premium Sales Department at 1-800-221-7945, extension 5442, or by email at MacmillanSpecialMarkets@macmillan.com.

First Wednesday Books Trade Paperback Edition: 2023

10 9 8 7 6 5 4 3 2 1

CHAPTER
1

Sweltering heat hit me like the sudden leap of a bonfire when I traded the protection of the mule-drawn cart's tarp for burning sand. I clutched my satchel, squinting against the dying sun. Heat waves created illusions of life out on the sand. Sometimes they came as ripples on a pool of water. Others, a snake looking to escape under a rock. Or an Afar caravan carting slabs of salt cut from the desert's floor to be sold in the market.

They were all just the desert's cruel trick. There was nothing out here. Nothing but me, the merchant I'd caught a ride with in town, and that towering mass of structured stone in the distance that was to be my new home.

My frizzy curls stuck to my temples and the back of my neck as I fished a sweaty bill from my pocket, but the merchant held up his hand against it like I was offering him a spider. "No charge."

"To show my appreciation," I insisted.

I should've just kept my mouth shut. The cart had been a godsend after six others had vehemently refused. A simple sheet of wood raised between two sturdy wheels on the back end and a sweating mule hitched to the front. Plenty of room for me to curl up and rest, even if I had to share the space with the merchant and his clay pots of spices. And it had a tarp to lie under for shade. A *tarp*. Even so, it was my last bit of money, at least until this new job paid. Besides, if I was going to pay him, the least he could do was drop me closer to the door.

But, God bless him, the merchant insisted more frantically, his raised hand turning into an aggressive shooing motion. "God have mercy on your soul," he said, and smacked the mule into a sudden run, kicking sand into the air as the cart circled back the way we came to take the long way through the desert.

The cloud of dust left behind stuck to every sweaty inch of me. I licked the salt from my lips and crunched on it.

Sand didn't bother me. My insides were so coated with it, at this point I was immune. But I wasn't so sure my employer would appreciate my appearance.

I hopefully he'd be forgiving. I needed this job. *Badly*. I couldn't remember the last time I'd eaten a proper meal. I mostly relied on the sand to coat my stomach, to trick my mind into thinking I was full. This job supplied a room and food. And a future patronage, which would ensure work for the rest of my life.

But one step at a time.

I waited until I was sure the merchant wasn't coming back, then held the collar of my dress open to pull my amulet out from where it was hiding, holding it up to examine it for damage. The thin, pure silver, carved by the heat of my welding pen into the shape of a Coptic cross, was wrapped along the edges with various colors of thread. Each welded line and curve, each row of color, built up protection against Manifestations of the Evil Eye. Any imperfection could throw off the design and ruin the effectiveness of the shield. It was the first real amulet I'd ever made—the only one I'd ever made, since there's no way Jember would've ever let me waste something as precious as silver for multiple tries.

Not to mention that this much silver could feed someone for a month, longer if they were frugal.

I hid my amulet under my dress again, adjusting the collar so the metal chain wouldn't show.

It was a survival habit Jember had taught me to live by since the age of five: *Protect your amulet better than it protects you.*

I spent part of the three-mile walk to Thorne Manor dusting myself off with one of my clean dresses, and the rest of it gaping at the castle itself. It looked like something from a fairy tale—brown stone ground down unevenly and undefined by dust storms, parapets where ancient emperors might have stood, carved-out windows with glass added to them. There were castles like that in grassier lands, I knew, but here? Who would want to be emperor of the hottest desert on the planet?

Some foreign travelers called it "exotic." Others called it "hell." The second was accurate, heat-wise. But to look at it? Heaven. Salt and iron crusted the land in yellow and rust, making the desert look alive with magic. But even a wonder like that wasn't enough to get travelers to pass this way, not anymore.

The Evil Eye had made sure of that.

It's said the Evil Eye was the first Manifestation of sin—namely jealousy and greed. In a constant state of longing, it latches on to any human who desires the same thing it does. Thriving crops, a random string of good luck, even receiving too many compliments could draw unwanted attention.

But material possessions, especially too much money, seemed to be the worst offender. Most of the clients Jember and I saw were people who insisted on having too many nice things in their house. Or, in the case of the man I was on my way to see, more money than any one human should be allowed to possess.

It didn't matter that the curse was confined to the walls of the castle, that the desert was perfectly safe if you knew how to traverse it. When it came to the Evil Eye, it was better to be safe rather than sorry.

Evening was settling, the sun peeking over the horizon before it said good night, when I finally made it to the castle. I lifted my fist to knock, then went for the sand-crusted rope hanging beside the door instead. Inside, an ominous bell echoed my arrival.

I waited, maybe thirty seconds, probably less—I don't know, my aching feet were impatient to get off the ground and into a proper bed. Only the sound of footsteps stopped me from pulling it again. The door opened, splashing me with a gust of cold air like a pail of icy water. I shivered and clutched at the amulet around my neck, nearly second-guessing its power to protect me from what was inside.

A white woman with greying hair and a sagging frown scrutinized me from behind small wire-framed glasses. She wore a wool sweater and a long, heavy skirt—an odd outfit for inside, let alone in the desert. Her pale face and hands stuck out like chipped spots on a dark painted wall against her grey clothes and the stone foyer behind her.

She raised her eyebrows, her gaze lingering too long on my face, but not looking me in the eye. *My scar.* I rubbed my cheek like I was soothing a sudden itch, wishing I could take the long mark on my skin with it. I always forgot it was there until I met someone new, and they stared at it like I'd grown a third eye.

"Andromeda, I take it?"

With just those few words I could tell she wasn't from around here. Amharic didn't leave her mouth comfortably—it stuck in all the wrong places.

That is, unless she'd intended to spit the words at me like a curse.

I bowed slightly, trying not to wobble on my exhausted feet. "Yes."

"The exorcist?"

Exorcist. I forced myself not to roll my eyes at the word. It was vague, limited. We debtera led the worship services with hymns and chants, as well as performed all the duties of the priests, without benefiting from being ordained or esteemed. We were healers. Artisans. Trained to attune ourselves to the spirit world deeper than anyone else would dare to. But, I supposed, for the purpose of my employer . . . "That's correct. The *exorcist.*"

The woman bit her lip. "You look awful young."

"I look it," I agreed, but left it there.

"This is not a job for a child."

"Would you like to see my identification?"

I held the woman's skeptical gaze firmly, secretly praying she wouldn't ask for it. Nineteen was an adult, according to law. Old enough to live on the streets, to starve daily. But not, in my experience, old enough to be taken seriously by the elder generation. The less she could judge me on, the better.

"Well . . . you're a skinny little thing," she said, as if the fact was both important and relevant. She opened the door wider and I stepped inside the frigid castle, forcing myself not to rub my shivering arms. "Then again, the grander-looking debtera didn't do us much good, did they?"

So, she *did* know my true title, though she pronounced it so strangely I barely recognized the word—*deb-TAIR-a*, with the accent on the second syllable instead of the first.

The woman shut us inside and, instinctively, I glanced around for an alternative exit. "I'm Peggy, Mr. Rochester's caretaker. Mr. Rochester will insist you call me that, even though I'm your elder and it should be improper. No, keep your shoes on, child. You never know what you'll step on around here."

I stood on one foot to hook the heel of my sandal back on, a violent chill-like pain running through my hand as I leaned against the wall for support. The stone felt like ice. The presence of evil spirits tended to cool down a room, but I'd never felt it to this extent.

Peggy led me through the dim, candlelit hall, the filmy windows only offering a bit more visual aid with the faded sun. I rubbed my arms, then gripped the silver amulet around my neck. It tended to gently pulse when there was an excess of Manifestations nearby—physical proof of the Evil Eye—but it'd never done it as consistently as today. I could practically feel the movement of Manifestations on the high, shadowed ceiling, like a mass of roosting bats, shifting away from the pulse.

"We only have a few hours to get you accustomed to things before curfew," Peggy said, leading me up the stairs. I slowed to match her pace. "The Waking begins at ten o'clock sharp, and everyone must be locked in their room by then. No exceptions. If you aren't, only God can help you."

I supposed the idea of a cursed house was scary to someone who didn't know how to cleanse it, but I'd never met a Manifestation that could withstand even one of my weaker amulets. "Late at night is when I can do my best work. It's easier to gauge the Evil Eye when I can see it in action."

Peggy dipped her chin, peering over her glasses. "You said you've done this before?"

"Many times." To rooms. Not an entire house, let alone a castle. But God knows when—or if—I'd ever get another job offer, not without a debtera license. A little lying was warranted.

"Well, you can take that up with Mr. Rochester. Until then, don't turn yourself into some great lady and start making your own rules." She opened a door a few feet from the top of the stairs. "This will be your room. You really should be downstairs with the servants, but Mr. Rochester wanted you down the hall from him. It's small, but you don't seem to have much, anyway."

A woman working for a man whose house was cursed by the Evil Eye didn't seem like someone who should be judging a poor girl and her lack of possessions . . . but it wasn't worth fighting over. I had a room to sleep in. I had food to eat. I didn't have Jember ordering me to steal drugs for him.

I took a deep breath, shoving the memory back.

Count your blessings, Andi. You're safe.

"Thank you," I said, and stepped into the room.

"Dinner will be served in an hour," she said, looking over my simple, sandy dress. "I trust you have something better to change into?"

I hid my cringe by pretending to adjust my bag. Stupid, frantic merchant.

She let out a short sound, like a scoff, and left me alone without another word.

CHAPTER
2

The barrel of water in the corner of the room must have been recently filled, because I broke the thin layer of ice easily with the bottom of a bucket and filled it, hanging it over the fire to heat. Then I found a rag in the dresser by the bed and scrubbed myself until the water went from scalding to chilled. I hadn't been clean in so long, I nearly forgot there was skin underneath all the grit. I used some of the tiny bit of butter I'd bartered for last week to moisturize my loose curls and dark, ruddy skin, then braided my hair in two neat French braids down my shoulders. I didn't have anything *better* to change into, but I did have a dress that hadn't been in the sand and sweat. It would have to do.

There was a large full-length mirror, and I hadn't looked at myself in so long I felt a bit distressed at seeing my reflection. There was no improving my face—my lips seemed too big for my tiny chin, which seemed too round for my thin nose, which would never settle evenly between my not-quite-round-not-quite-high cheekbones. And worst of all, the slightly raised scar on my face, an ugly nick in my top lip that ran all the way up my cheek. Not the purposeful show of beauty from scarification, but the aftermath of a brutal mistake on display.

I looked like a homely, misshapen doll. But at least I didn't look homeless. The last thing I wanted was Mr. Rochester to know he'd pulled me directly from the street.

If there was a clock in the room, I didn't bother looking for it—years of being charged by the hour for my work, even if most of it had just been tagging along with Jember, had helped me develop an internal one that worked just as well. So, at ten minutes to the hour I headed downstairs to find the dining room.

There were fireplaces blazing in every room, but otherwise there was no light or warmth. I'd never seen a house decorated so colorfully lack so much . . . color. There were rugs and pillows, baskets and tapestries, woven in traditional green, yellow, and red. But they were all lifeless, dulled by the sun and age. All that beautiful handmade craftsmanship was paired with walls and furniture that seemed like they were from another world. Too much gold and filigree and embellishments, excessively crowded patterns that left little room for the design to breathe. Not to mention, everything seemed a bit, well, off. A tapestry wasn't on the wall straight, a couple rugs weren't centered, furniture sat in strange places . . . whomever had decorated didn't care at all about the order and aesthetic of the rooms.

The main hall was one large square, and when I finished wandering and made it to the other side of the stairs Peggy and three others were standing at the bottom, whispering. One of the people—an older man with a mustache—saw me coming and nudged Peggy, prompting the other three to look at me. For a split second I bristled, feeling for the knife under my dress, but logic quickly calmed me down. They were standing with Peggy, which meant they probably worked here, same as me.

I could tell instantly that Peggy was the only one who didn't do any work out of doors, because her face was the color of concrete while the faces of the other three were rosy from the sun. Never in my life had I seen so many white people in one place. We hadn't been colonized like other countries, so my experience was limited to the occasional missionary or activist, who were all nice enough.

But I supposed it made sense. No local would dare step foot in a house so saturated by the Evil Eye. Hiring foreigners who were unfamiliar with the curse guaranteed employees would stay, as long as they were paid well.

"This is Andromeda," Peggy said. "The debtera."

"You finally picked the right one." The middle-aged man with grey on the temples of his black hair slapped Peggy on the back—maybe too hard, because she scowled and shooed at him.

"You say that every single time, Tom." The woman with bright orange hair and bizarrely blue eyes frowned at me. "She can't be older than sixteen."

"Yes, but she's seen war," he said, pointing to my scar. I fought the urge to cover it with my hand.

I'd thought Peggy just preferred her clothing to match her grim demeanor, but the three others wore that same dark grey to match the bleak walls. To be fair, it was probably less a fashion choice and more a matter of dyeing all the wool in one barrel. Even so, it was strange how well they matched the house. Like ghosts dressed in shadows.

"This is Tom," Peggy said. "He takes care of maintenance around the house. Emma here, the two of us share the task of cooking and mending. And Edward"—the old man nodded at me with a small smile, his eyes glistening kindness—"he keeps the horses. We all clean around here." She gave me a pointed look. "That includes you."

I was getting paid to cleanse the house of the Evil Eye, not of dirt, but I would argue that point with Mr. Rochester. "Four people taking care of such an enormous house?"

"We're all that's left," Emma said.

A somber silence fell over the group. Of course, it was obvious without even asking—the rest of the staff had left. Emma leaned against Tom, and he cradled her head comfortingly. When Edward cleared his throat it sounded harsh against the silence.

"Why doesn't anyone here wear an amulet?" I asked.

"Superstitious nonsense," Peggy said, waving away my words as if they stank. "Our God protects us."

I looked at the others, but they seemed to be deliberately avoiding eye contact with me. I took a deep breath, trying not to sound annoyed. "We worship the same God. He created the doctors to prescribe medicine, just as he created the debtera to craft amulets."

"Just folksy hogwash," she said gruffly, and I bit my tongue to keep from lashing back. She pointed to an entryway, glowing brighter than the rest. "Dinner is in the dining room."

"Good luck," Tom said, offering an encouraging smile.

"There is no good luck," Emma said to him as the four of them headed down a hall, "that's the entire point."

Entering the dining room was like walking into a séance—there were candles on every surface but the floor. The hardwood table was long with extravagantly ornate chairs. It was a room built for a dinner party, and yet a single man, dressed in a dark Nehru-collared shirt and a long coat, sat at the head of the table. He must've heard me come in, because he turned around in his chair, his white smile brighter than any candle in the room.

Even in the dim I could tell he was handsome. His tight curls were cropped close, even closer on the sides and the back, and edged carefully along the hairline. He had cheekbones like smoothed stone, a nose wide and symmetrical, laugh lines that seemed to worship the smile they graced. And if his rich brown skin was as angelic in daylight as by the simple highlight of a candle, I was almost afraid I wouldn't survive the next few months.

He was beautiful, and it suddenly struck me that maybe he would care that I wasn't.

"Andromeda?" The man pushed a few scrolls aside and stood. "Welcome. Come, sit."

"Will others be joining us?" I asked.

"Soon, I hope. But it's all right, we can start without them." He gestured to the table of steaming food. "You must be hungry from your journey."

I approached the table, stopping an appropriate few feet away. He wore a silver amulet around his neck, similar to mine—thin and flat with all the usual etchings and colorful thread wraps one would expect on an all-purpose amulet. He was wiser than Peggy, at least.

We stood like that for a few long seconds, his warm smile slowly slipping to stiff and polite, and I suddenly realized that a respectable man didn't just presume to touch a woman he didn't know. I stuck out my hand, and he shook it gently, and then I sidestepped defensively, my muscles tight but ready to act as he . . . pulled out my chair for me. I swallowed, my face warm with embarrassment. *You're not on the streets anymore. No one wants to attack you. No one wants to take your things.* I quickly sat, bowing my head so he wouldn't see my blush, and let him push my seat in. I even managed to hold still as he placed a wool blanket across my shoulders.

"We'll have to attend to our own needs tonight." The man—who had to be none other than Mr. Rochester—took his seat again and shifted a small basin in front of me. I held my palms over it silently as he poured water over them. "There aren't many servants, despite the size. Not many people are willing to work for a cursed household."

Servants. I'd never even had a mother. But I nodded politely as he handed me a small towel. "I'm adaptable."

"Good. You never know what will happen in this— Oh." He looked a little surprised, and then there was that dazzling smile as I shifted the basin in front of him. Guests didn't normally wash the hands of the host, but we had limited options. "Thank you."

I washed his hands, he dried them, and then he prayed over the food.

"I hope you don't mind my asking," Mr. Rochester said, "but why is it that Jember didn't send you away with a reference letter?"

It was a valid question, but not one I would ever answer honestly. Jember may have raised me and trained me to be a debtera, but he'd also first bought me from my birth parents. People who bought children could never hold them in high enough regard to write a letter designed to praise their accomplishments. Besides, even if by some miracle he had the heart to, he couldn't be bothered.

"He was too busy to meet my deadline," I said, trying not to stuff too much food in my mouth at once. I hadn't eaten in two days, but no one had to know that.

"Is that so?" Mr. Rochester watched me for a moment, and only then did I realize this was my fourth fingerful of food since I'd last spoken. *Slow down.* "It's not that I doubt your ability— your résumé is strong. But I don't seem to know anyone who's familiar with your work."

He wouldn't. Just stepping into the house, it was obvious that we moved in very different social circles. People like him hired people like Jember, who was the best debtera of his generation, licensed and supported by a highly respected church. People like him passed people like me—unlicensed and unrecognized by the church because a bitter mentor had thrown her out before she could earn it—on the street without a second glance.

"Jember and I traveled to many different villages to see clients. You may not be familiar with the ones who live further away."

He looked a bit embarrassed. "Yes, of course. I didn't mean to imply anything." He took a folder from his briefcase and laid it in front of me, removing a few pages and placing them on top. "This is your contract. Take your time reading before you sign, of course. Most of it is standard—free room and board, meals, amenities. I know your line of work is normally paid by the hour, but I believe I've settled on a flat weekly rate that'll better serve the both of us. And—not so standard—there's a list of rules that you'll be required to abide by."

He centered a numbered list in front of me, gesturing to the first line. "The first two rules are the most relevant to you: Don't leave your room after ten o'clock at night, and social time after dinner is mandatory. The rest are a bit trivial, but Magnus gets very bent out of shape if they aren't followed to the letter."

Peggy had warned me about the curfew, but mandatory socials? "Who is this Magnus?"

"Magnus Rochester, the owner of Thorne Manor."

"I'm sorry, sir. You're not . . . ?" I cleared my throat. "I thought you were the owner of this castle."

"Oh." He laughed lightly. "No. I'm sorry, I could've sworn I'd introduced myself. Call me Esjay. I'm the Rochester family's attorney."

"Then where is Mr. Rochester?"

"I'm sure he'll be down soon. However, he prefers 'Magnus.' No sirs or ma'ams necessary, as stated in rule twenty-three of your contract."

A bang like a slamming door echoed down the stairs, and I heard distant shouting.

Esjay folded his hands politely, taking a deep breath in and out through his nose, and then smiled at me. "It doesn't look like Magnus will be joining us tonight after all. But I'll gladly talk through the contract with you and answer any questions you—" Another bang, this one more like a gunshot. Esjay stood up quickly, his chair screeching against the hardwood. "Would you excuse me for a moment?" He rushed out of the room.

I listened to his dress shoes pound up the stairs, licked my fingers clean, then went after him.

The shouting made me pause at the top of the stairs to listen. Peggy and Esjay stood a little way down the hall, talking through a half-opened door while someone yelled at them from the other side. The argument ended with the door slamming, echoing in their faces.

Esjay patted Peggy's shoulder, then turned in my direction. He seemed almost startled to see me standing there, then smiled and made his way over. "I'm afraid this isn't a good night to talk business. Why don't you read over the contract tonight, and I'll be over tomorrow so we can discuss it?"

"Is he always this unreasonable?" I asked.

"He's . . ." Esjay's smile faded. "He's not doing well tonight. Normally he's in better spirits, but sometimes the curse, the evil in the house . . ."

"It takes a toll," I finished. That was true of every household I'd cleansed—the host always felt it the worst.

He nodded, then cleared his throat. "Tomorrow will be better. It always is."

"Esjay?" I said. He'd been heading down the stairs, but he turned slightly at my voice. "The gunshot?"

His features curved down, and he examined the rail of the stairs, as if to hide it. "No one was hurt."

"And believe you me, child," Peggy said, shoving by me—despite the hall being wide enough that she shouldn't have had to. "Guns aren't what you should be worried about around here."

"Peggy," Esjay said quietly, like a plea, and then looked at me. "With a résumé like yours, I doubt you'll have any issues. I'll be back tomorrow evening, before dinner."

"Don't bother Mr. Rochester this evening," Peggy snapped as she began to descend the stairs. I squeezed my fists against her biting tone. I'd been in this castle for less than two hours and already I hated the woman.

I waited until they had both disappeared around the corner before approaching the door and knocking.

I heard a sound of frustration, heavy footsteps accompanied by some sort of soft jangling, and then the door cracked open with a creak. I winced against the chill that came from inside, and my amulet pulsed heavily against my chest. "I told you I'm not hungry, Peggy," a voice growled from behind the door. Mr. Rochester was clearly hiding, because all I could see was a sliver of the dim wall of his room.

"Peggy went downstairs," I said. "I'm Andromeda."

"Who?"

I hesitated. "You hired me. To exorcise your house of the Evil Eye."

"The what?"

Did he not know what was in his own house? "The spiritual activity in your house."

"Wait, *who* are you?"

"Andromeda. The debtera you hired. Sir, I wanted to talk to you about curfew—"

"Lock your door by ten if you don't want to be eaten alive. Now get the hell away from my door." He slammed it shut, and then I heard his footfalls recede.

I took a steadying breath.

Remember where you were this morning, Andi.

You woke up in a stall with a bunch of goats. You chased a sleaze-bag off with a rock.

A slightly irrational employer is nothing.

I took a third and final soothing breath, and then went back downstairs to finish my dinner.

CHAPTER

3

━━━◦∞◦━━━

I didn't care what Peggy or Mr. Rochester said. Manifestations were their most active at night, and I wasn't going to waste an opportunity to assess them. I wanted to have a better idea of what I was dealing with when I was given the silver required to construct protective amulets to cleanse them.

I stepped into the quiet hall a minute before ten to wait—well, quiet except for the vague sound of music drifting up the stairs, muted strings plucking a tense and melancholic tune to match my anxious mood. I'd never been this nervous with Jember, but then, it had rarely been me doing the work, only observing. Besides, anticipation was always worse than the actual Waking.

The only way to truly know what I was dealing with was to experience it without my amulet's shield. With that in mind, I gripped my amulet and whispered a quick prayer of protection before hanging it on the inside doorknob to my room and shutting the door.

There was a strange, deep sounding of a bell. The great clock across from the stairs hadn't rung all evening, and yet now it called up to me, full of dread and warning. *Three . . . Four . . .* Each bell interrupted the echo of the last. *Seven . . . Eight . . .*

The eerie music and bell tolls were replaced by the howl of the wind as it slammed into me like a dust storm, knocking me one way, then another. My limbs went numb within seconds, but not enough to deaden the sensation of freezing needles stabbing into me at high speed. I shifted my feet wider to brace myself, blocking my face with my arms, my dress whipping around my legs. Just over the howling, I could hear bangs and scratches, moaning, the creaking of wooden boards.

The Waking had begun.

It was amplified, which made sense for the severity of the curse. Still, I was *freezing.* I needed to work quickly, take in as many Manifestations as I could so I'd know what sort of amulets would be required. Already my mind could see and feel the strokes I'd need to cut from the silver with my welding pen. It was like a box of white powder thrown onto a black board, the patterns of each Manifestation's life force sticking to invisible glue to form a clear design. *Line, line, curve, line, dot, line.* Or, *normally,* they were clear—now there were hundreds, overlapping, jumbling up. Far too many to distinguish one from another.

But I could focus on one. Pick the easiest to start on tomorrow. From there they were all connected, and cleansing the first Manifestation would make it easier for me to take care of the next.

All the candles had been blown out by the wind, so the meager moonlight through the windows at the end of the hall and downstairs were my only source of light. But I saw vague shadows of what looked like a horde of rats at the bottom of the stairs and the first-floor ceiling. Waves and waves of small, dark creatures scampering around and over each other, leaving no view of the wood underneath. Likely not actual rats, but until I knew for sure I wasn't going to venture that way. Besides, the stairs were where the wooden creaking was coming from, the wood visibly shifting and cracking. Breaking.

I bent down and touched a deep crack on the first step, my fingers stopping on the outside of it, as if the space between were a barricade. It was the solid stair, the cracks lying on top like a mirage.

This Manifestation wasn't even tangible. In other words, it was weak. This would be the one to start with.

And thank God I found it quickly, because my skin had shifted from burned and raw to numb, and it scared me a little. I'd never been hurt by a Manifestation this way—but then, I'd never been without my amulet. I needed it back around my neck, and quickly.

I rushed back to the door, fighting to stay on my feet. I tripped—or something tripped me—and hit the floor hard, as if the wind itself had deliberately thrown me down. I gasped, the wind knocked out of me, but I'd at least caught myself just short of my face slamming on the ground.

But whatever had tripped me was still there, and I kicked at it, yelping as it grabbed my foot. I stumbled to my feet, looking around in the dark. The Something grabbed me more firmly this time, and I quickly stomped to get it off and rushed to my room. But as soon as I shoved the door open it grabbed me again, this time wrapping around my ankle to hold me still. It felt familiar and terrifying, and when I looked down the moonlight flooding from the window in my room revealed a hand coming from the ground, long fingers curling around me.

"Get off!" I cried, kicking hard to break its grip, but another replaced it, then another on my wrist, leaping out like spiders from the wall and floor. As soon as I got free of them, I felt fingers dig into my hair, gripping at the roots, and pull me backward. My back slammed against the wall, and more hands scraped at me to hold me there. I was a mere foot from my door, to freedom, and couldn't get to it.

But I fought, anyway, because that's all I knew. I kicked and hit at the Manifestation until I smashed enough fingers to break their hold. I ran into my room, slammed my door shut, and immediately put on my amulet, hugging it to my chest. I secured the lock and shoved the large chair in the room in front of the door. All at once my limbs felt weak, and I lowered myself to the floor, curling up in front of the fireplace.

I was frozen to the core, and it wasn't all due to the wind.

Dear God . . . what had I gotten myself into?

CHAPTER
4

———— ❧ ————

My first Waking had been terrifying. It was before Jember worked for the church that moved us away from this far more dangerous town, and a one-room cube of wood and mud with a tin roof was no place to leave a five-year-old by herself all night. So Jember had taken me with him to see a client. I'd sat through the Waking, staring through trembling fingers as he worked, and for weeks afterward I'd had nightmares of a Manifestation made of long fingernails, crawling up the wall like a scorpion.

Eventually I got used to monsters. Eventually I learned that the world was scarier than anything the Evil Eye could manifest. A merciless upbringing had left me literally scarred, whereas no curse could lay a finger on me.

But after my first night in this house, I knew I was wrong. My God . . . how could I have been so wrong?

I don't remember climbing into bed, but I awoke buried in my blanket, shaking. From the cold or from lingering terror, I couldn't tell.

The wind. The stinging cold. Those violent hands. Everything had felt so real, now all reduced to the memory of a nightmare.

I was almost too nervous to leave my room, but I was there to earn my keep, not huddle in bed all day. I dressed underneath the covers, then forced myself out into the open. A chill shot through my leg as I placed my foot on the ground. If I was going to survive the next few weeks here, I'd have to ask for warmer clothing. After my interaction with Mr. Rochester the night before, I doubted I'd get it.

I would ask Esjay. He seemed to be the only person with sense in this house.

I paused at the door, watching the hearth blaze. Someone had been in my room. I appreciated the heat, but the idea that someone could unlock the door and come in while I was sleeping scared me a little.

And I'd barricaded it, too. Wait, had I? Because the chair was in its original spot near the fire, as if I hadn't touched it.

I rushed into the hall, only glancing at Mr. Rochester's shut door before heading down the stairs. The steps were in perfect form. There was no rat horde, or hands either, thank God. All the spiritual activity in the house seemed quiet.

Still, I hadn't signed the contract. There was still time to run. *Run back to what?*

I needed the money. I had nowhere else to go except back to the street. But the thought of spending another Waking in this house petrified me, despite the amenities that came with living here. My first Waking all over again, amplified ten times over.

From now on I would stick to cleansing the house during the day.

I don't know why, but when I turned the corner into the dining room I half expected to be greeted by a corpse. The memory of the last corpse I'd seen popped into my head. Jember had made me dig a hole—what he'd called "a character-building sport"—and when I followed him back later, I saw him dump in something very human-shaped wrapped in rough cloth. The curiosity had worn off quickly enough that I'd never gotten around to asking, and Jember wasn't the type to kill and tell.

But there was nothing dead on the other side of the wall, unless one counted Peggy's dead-eyed glare as she exited the kitchen.

She put a steaming bowl on the table. "Come eat, child," she said, as if I was already late. I took my seat without a word. It was some sort of tan mush. Porridge, probably, though not done well. Whoever had made the spread last night clearly hadn't cooked this morning. But it was a blessing I had food at all, and it was nice and hot.

"Peggy." Emma leaned in the doorway, her cheeks red, her breath a bit heavy as if she'd been rushing around. "Have you seen Edward?"

"Did you check the stables?" Peggy responded harshly.

"He's not there." Emma's eyes were wide. "Do you think he—?"

"He's there," Peggy snapped, her sharp reaction jolting me a little. "Of course he's there. And if not, he's somewhere else. Go, get on with your day."

Emma hesitated, her eyes glistening a bit in the firelight. And then she disappeared around the corner again, her hurried steps disappearing down the hall.

One thing was certain—I would have to do everything in my power to avoid dealing with Peggy. Stabbing my employer's housekeeper was most likely grounds for immediate termination, no matter how detestably she carried herself.

I ate my mush with a cup of water, and then followed Peggy down the hall—but a few safe feet behind, because her hands were in her apron pockets and I hated that I couldn't see them. It was silly when I thought about it—Peggy wasn't going to attack me. She was rude, but obviously not a killer. And even if she was, I had quick reflexes.

You're in a grand house, Andi. Get your mind off the streets.

Peggy turned a corner, and I rushed to catch up, nearly bumping into another woman. She looked a little older than me. Her head was shaved, and her skin was dark and smooth, radiant against her simple yellow dress—not at all equipped for the cold. She was tall and athletic and beautiful. I wondered if she was Mr. Rochester's wife.

But if she was a rich lady of the house, Peggy would've acknowledged her when she passed her in the hall, especially since she looked as if she was trying to hold back tears.

I opened my mouth to comfort her . . . then remembered the last time I'd tried to comfort someone and instead rushed to catch up with Peggy. It was seven years ago, when seven of my peers decided they didn't like me being kind to a girl they'd already deemed not worth their time. I'd paid for it with a beating and a knife to the face.

"*Whose life is more important to you?*" Jember asked. "*Yours, or that stranger who will never think of you again?*"

"*God loves us both,*" I'd replied, struggling to see him through swollen eyes.

"*Your empathy has created poor survival habits.*" Jember handed me a bottle of alcohol to disinfect my wounds. "*Next time I'll let them kill you.*"

There was no next time. I never tried to protect anyone but myself again.

That wasn't about to change now.

"Wake up, child," Peggy snapped.

I blinked away the memory, and we were in front of an open doorway.

"He wants to see you," she said. "Don't keep him waiting."

I stepped inside. Sunlight bathed the room from the large windows, rows of tall bookshelves cutting stark shadows into the light on the floor. Mr. Rochester sat in an armchair facing the blazing fireplace, leaning forward with a large pad of paper on his knees. He drew with a grey pencil, a red one tucked in his mess of soft curls, which were long enough to reach the bottom of his chin. His skin was the color of wet sand, but there was also something pale about his complexion, almost ill. It lacked the golden glow of someone who'd seen the sun anytime recently. But his cheekbones. Like blades. He stared at the wall for a while, as if deep in thought, then looked back down at his paper. Some sort of bell or metal at his wrist jingled with the movement of his hand.

I looked at the wall he seemed to be drawing. It was a fireplace backed by red and black paisley wallpaper. Over it was mounted a large portrait, littered with darts and scratches, of a white man with a thick sandy-blond beard, holding a swaddled baby. The man looked sad, and a little angry, as if he knew his portrait was marred by darts. I felt bad for the baby.

I knocked on the open door. "Sir?"

"Who is it?" he asked, without looking up.

"It's Andr—"

"Right, yes." He pushed a wayward curl at his temple behind his ear. "Come in."

His voice was light and casual, not at all like the person I'd met the night before. I stepped into the room and Mr. Rochester continued, without looking at me, "I must get my subject down on paper before she notices. Help yourself to cherry tarts and coffee."

Cherry tarts for breakfast? Odd, but I was still hungry after that mush. I sat on the puffy fabric chair on the other side of the small round table and took a tart, then glanced at the wall again. All I saw was the ill-tempered man and the baby, and yet he had said "she." Who exactly was he drawing?

I peered at his drawing and gasped. On top of the fireplace stood a woman wearing a red kaba, the ornate bridal cape and crown fit for royalty. Blood gushed from her mouth, staining her white dress—the only use of the red pencil other than her kaba. The rest of the drawing was shaded in eerie tones of grey.

I looked at the lack of woman against the actual wall, and then back to the drawing. A chill ran down my spine. "Are you seeing . . . her . . . right now?"

"Only in my memory."

"Does she appear often?"

"Every day. I call her the Librarian, because she loves to rearrange my books." He grinned. "Spiteful, tidy woman." He drew one last line and held the pad at arm's length, his wrists jingling sharply at the movement, then turned the drawing to me. "What do you think?"

"Why is she bleeding?"

"I used to ask, and then she would leave threatening book passages open the next morning for me to read with breakfast," he said, gesturing to the table beside us. "I no longer ask."

"I notice you didn't include the portrait in your drawing."

"Yes, well. I don't draw monsters."

I hesitated. That had to be a painting of his father . . . didn't it? "Why not take the portrait down, then?"

"Target practice." He signed and dated his work and then tucked it beside the chair, exchanging his pencil for a tart. Finally, his eyes met mine, and a gentle, almost relieved expression slipped to his face. It was as if all the rudeness and anger I'd seen in him hinged on this one human interaction.

And then his eyes shifted lower and widened. "God. You have a massive scar on your face."

My cheeks flared with shame. Perhaps I'd read his expression wrong, because the eye contact hadn't changed him one bit. *Still as rude as last night.*

"You make a terrible first impression, you know," he went on, and took a bite of his tart. "Weren't you supposed to arrive yesterday?"

"I did arrive yesterday." He paused and blinked at me, so I added, "We spoke before bed."

"Hm. I don't remember that."

"You were . . ." *Fussy. Like a baby.* "Tired, sir."

"Call me Magnus. I don't like the formality of titles. It makes us such strangers, and I don't like strangers in my house."

I paused. "I am employed by you, sir. I don't think—"

"I like the brown of your eyes," he said, with wonder in his voice. "Tilt your head toward the light?"

"Tilt my head?"

"I just want to see the highlights."

I hesitated, then turned my face halfway to the fire, hoping he'd look at my eyes and move on from the topic.

"Umber undertones," he murmured. "Yes. Like steeped tea . . ."

"Is there a reason you wanted to see me?" I asked, settling back in the chair and looking him firmly in the eye.

"I can tell you're annoyed just by looking in your eyes." He sounded almost . . . pleased about it.

Is there something wrong with you? was at the tip of my tongue, but I needed this job, and insulting my employer wasn't the way to keep it.

"Aren't you cold?" he asked suddenly. "Here."

He pulled off his sweater—it was the color of rust, bright compared to what the rest of the household wore—and I froze as he put it over my head. I sat speechless for a moment, his sweater swallowing my torso, and then hesitantly put my arms through the holes. The knit was still warm from his body and smelled like cologne and nutmeg. It was an oddly intimate experience.

Magnus didn't seem to notice my discomfort as he went on. "Peggy was supposed to provide you with proper clothing." He scratched his head, discovering the red pencil tucked in his hair. He laid it beside the other with a fond grin, as if he were crossing paths with a friend. "Oh well, I'll take care of it."

"Thank you, sir."

"Get used to calling me Magnus, or I'll replace you with someone who will. Saba!" He called, and I winced against his sudden volume. "Saba, come here!"

After a moment the woman with the shaved head appeared in the doorway. Now that I was seeing her again, she looked a little like Magnus. Their cheekbones, maybe, and the shape of her eyes. His sister? But then why was she treated so poorly?

"Saba, see if you can find our guest something warmer to wear."

The woman shuffled away, and Magnus turned his attention back to me. "So, down to business. Let me tell you a little about my situation. My mother married my father and cursed him with the Evil Eye. My father then had the nerve to get himself killed three years ago and pass it on to me. Because of that, I had to move from my comfortable mansion in England to live in a giant icebox with a handful of tiresome adults in order to keep the general population out of danger. I'll be twenty-one soon, and Esjay thinks it's important that Thorne Manor is cleansed before that time, since I'll have to take over my father's business upon my birthday. In summary, adults are useless, and you have seven months to do three years' worth of work. Do you have any questions so far?"

"Is every Waking in your house so . . . violent?"

"It's an unfortunate thing. But it's the reason we have a curfew in place. Anyone out in the halls after ten o'clock knows the risks."

"How can it still be so bad after three years?"

He sighed heavily, as if he was sick of hearing about it. "Every time we lose a debtera I feel like less and less progress is made. The servants' quarters are cleansed, some of the bedrooms, the dining room and kitchen. But that's nothing compared to the number of rooms that are left."

I folded a tart into a napkin while he wasn't looking, then slipped it into my pocket for later. "What did you mean you 'lose' debtera?"

"I'm sure Esjay told you you're not the first."

"How many have you had, exactly?"

"Oh, you know . . ." He hesitated, his cheeks growing rosy. "Eleven."

I almost dropped my next tart in my lap. "Eleven debtera in three years?"

"Including you. But that's a nice even number to stop on, don't you agree?"

"You mean odd."

"What's odd about it?" He put down his cup with a *clink*.

"Let's get to the point. I know why you sent me your résumé. Do you know why I chose yours out of the pile?"

"It was the next in line?" I said dryly.

"You're unlicensed. Which means you're seeking a patron, correct?"

Magnus checked all the right boxes for a proper patron. Wealthy. Well connected. Someone who would vouch for my ability in exchange for successfully cleansing his house. With his support I wouldn't need a license to get more work. But he rubbed me the wrong way as if he was born to do it, and if there was any other option I wouldn't be sitting here now.

He raised his thick eyebrows at me, and I had no choice but to nod. "You picked me solely because I'm unlicensed?"

"Esjay used to be in charge of the hiring, but you can see how that's gone so far." He rolled his eyes. "So, I looked at the top of each résumé until I found one that didn't list a license. The others have nothing substantial to lose or gain, whereas the two of us have *everything*. You need this job as much as I need your skill, making this the perfect partnership."

"I . . . suppose that's true."

He looked very satisfied with himself. "Now it's your turn. Tell me about yourself."

"Myself?"

"Esjay said you studied with Jember, which seems to be an impressive accomplishment. How many years did you train?"

"I've been around the craft my entire life, but couldn't officially begin my mentorship until I turned sixteen."

"That seems a little late to begin learning such an intricate skill."

We learned the hymns before then, but never amulet work. Strange that someone who had employed ten others before me didn't already know that. "It takes a certain amount of patience and maturity to construct amulets, and silver is too expensive to waste on the unsteady hands of children."

"Silver's not that expensive," he said, waving his hand carelessly. "And don't worry, I have plenty of it here for you, so you can mess up to your heart's content. As long as the Evil Eye is gone at the end of it, I don't care how many attempts it takes."

I wanted to dump my coffee on his expensive rug. "Yes, sir."

"Magnus." He paused, shifting to lean his elbow on the arm of the chair, his hand blocking his chin and mouth as he studied me. "I get the feeling you were never hugged as a child."

I choked on my coffee. Not just because it was an incredibly rude thing to say, but because he was right. Jember had nerve damage that made skin contact painful, so we rarely touched. On top of that, he considered too much affection to be a poor survival habit. So my experience with hugs was limited.

I wiped my mouth on the oversized sweater sleeve. "What does that have to do with cleansing your house?"

"You're just very formal. Tense."

"Should I not be formal at an interview?"

He shrugged. "You already have the position. So, tell me: Why did you choose to become a debtera?"

"I don't think anyone chooses to serve the church. God puts the desire in you."

"An extremely uninteresting answer, Andromeda." He raised his cup to his lips. "Try again."

My muscles flexed slightly as I leveled a firm glare at him. "I'm not here to amuse you. I'm here to cleanse your house of the Evil Eye. Do you want my help or don't you?"

"I don't know. What makes you better equipped for it than the ten debtera before you?"

"You selected me by my résumé, or else I wouldn't be here."

"Weren't you listening? I didn't read your résumé." He looked around for it briefly, then shrugged. "Esjay tells me it's very impressive, despite the lack of licensure. But you don't really expect me to let a stranger stay in my house without knowing a bit about her? Normally the debtera you trained with would offer a character reference, but I take it Jember didn't supply one while throwing you out."

I stiffened. There was no way he could've known Jember had thrown me out. "What are you talking about?"

"You're unlicensed, which means he either refused to finish training you or you quit. Why?"

"That's irrelevant."

"Not really."

I took a breath and wished for the hundredth time that I had the financial freedom to storm out of there. "Let's just say we didn't see eye to eye on things."

"If I was being trained by the best debtera alive, I wouldn't care if he had different views than me. Come, it had to be something else. Were you just fed up? He's brutal to deal with, I hear, even if you aren't his mentee."

"Depends who you ask."

"I asked every debtera before you. Are you telling me you're tougher than all those grown men?"

"Women usually are."

Magnus laughed. "Finally, some honesty in this house. That's good, because I need you to be frank with your response to my next question."

"Yes, sir."

"Magnus."

I sighed. "Yes, Magnus."

"What would you do if I asked you to kill me?"

I felt paralyzed. Breathless. "What?"

He leaned toward me. "Would you do it?"

There was something in his expression that unsettled me. Like anticipation, like . . . hope. But before I could answer, his light brown eyes lit up. "Ah, your clothes."

He stood—oh God, there were bells on his ankles, too?—and crossed to the door, where he accepted a stack of folded clothes from the downtrodden woman from before. "Thank you, Saba. Here, Andromeda, go get yourself suited up against the cold, and then I'll give you a tour of the house."

CHAPTER
5

───◆───

When I stepped out into the hall, dressed in wool stockings, a dress more fitted to my waist than I was used to, and a sweater, Magnus was waiting for me. He gazed at the walls as the Manifested hands pressed their doughy prints against the walls and ceiling, like a mob trying to get out.

"Good morning," he said to the hands, before turning to me. "Ready for a tour?"

I eyed the walls warily. I'd felt those hands last night. Whatever they were doing, it had nothing to do with wishing someone a good morning.

"I'm ready." I handed his sweater back to him and he put it back on before leading me down the hall.

Random items falling off walls in one room. Strange ripples on the floor, like drops of water, in the next. A room that just seemed unnaturally covered in soot.

Everything appeared to be average Manifestations. But after last night, and knowing ten debtera came before me, I knew better than to think that way.

"You should put these on for this next hallway," Magnus said, picking up a pair of rubber boots from the corner and handing them to me. Then he grabbed a large black umbrella and opened it.

I shuffled in the large boots to keep up as we rounded the corner to the next hall. It was covered in glistening white, feathery flakes drifting down from the ceiling.

I hugged myself and stood a bit closer to Magnus to stay under the umbrella. The snow floated around us as we walked, the inch-deep layer crunching beneath my feet. I wanted to reach out my hand, but I wasn't sure I should touch it. As beautiful a Manifestation as it was, it was still part of the curse.

We left the wet umbrella and boots at the opposite end of the hall and continued on, stopping in front of a large closet.

"All the supplies you could ever need are in here." Magnus unlocked the closet and opened it to reveal stacks upon stacks of thin silver disks, all about the circumference of my face. On one shelf there was a basket full of spools of different-colored thread, and beside that a welding pen. "Just ask me or Peggy if you need access."

I tightened my jaw to keep myself from gaping. There must've been hundreds of disks. I'd never seen that many at once. I could fill my satchel and live a good life until I was old and grey.

You can't steal his silver, Andi. He's paying you too much for you to go and become a thief. And besides, God will see you.

I examined the welding pen without bothering to pick it up. It looked expensive, but only based on aesthetics, because the tip was slightly too thick to be of any use. I'd stick with mine. I shifted all the thread from the basket to the shelf and began filling it with silver disks instead.

"Are those all right?" Magnus asked, looking at the thread I'd put away.

"They're perfect, for when the time comes," I said, examining each disk for imperfections before I put them in the basket. "I don't need them for simple Manifestations."

"Which is the simplest room, would you say?"

"The stairs." I tried on the pair of sleek black metal welding goggles beside the ridiculous pen. They even had an optional magnification lens with the twist of a gear. *Keep.* "It's not physically present, only visual. I suppose you could call it an illusion. Normally that means it has a weaker hold than Manifestations that actually make contact with the physical world."

"I've always wondered, what's the difference between the one you'll make for the stairs and the one you're wearing?"

I glanced down at my amulet. "This one is an all-purpose shield. It protects me from curses and deters Manifestations. The ones I construct to cleanse the house are specific for each Manifestation, essentially expelling them back to where they came from."

"Hm." Magnus crossed his arms, leaning his shoulder on the wall to face me. "How can you tell which amulet goes with which room?"

"I visualize it, like a map in my mind, if that makes sense."

"It does." He paused. "No one's ever explained it to me this well. It's actually fascinating when you understand how it works."

"I think so, too." A small hammer and jar of nails were the last thing I added to the basket before hooking it over my elbow. I usually didn't get to explain my craft to anyone, and I was actually enjoying the conversation, but I wasn't sure how to continue it.

"You know, you don't have to work quite yet," Magnus said. "We can't sign the contract until Esjay arrives tonight."

Well, I *had* been enjoying it. Now I wasn't sure I liked where it was going. "I like work."

"Yes, but there are so many other things we could do to entertain ourselves. Plus, until the contract is signed, it's unpaid hours. Esjay would say that's unethical. Although, didn't you say you got kicked out for being unethical? Maybe you don't mind."

He was fishing. I didn't honor it with a response. God knew me and I knew myself, and that was enough. He was right about one thing, though: I didn't want to work for free. But this place needed to be cleansed badly, and *now*. "Who makes the rules here, you or Esjay?"

Magnus was speechless for a moment, just looking at me. "In that case," he said, suddenly, "I'll leave you to enjoy your work."

He turned on his heel, the bells on his ankles growing softer and softer the further he journeyed down the hall.

I headed back to the stairs, looking at where the cracks and shifting had appeared last night. They were still as a frightened lizard. But there was a presence, barely echoing off my amulet, so subtle I could almost mistake it for my gentle heart.

I sat in the middle of the stairs, setting the basket beside me, and put on the safety goggles. I closed my eyes for a moment, and the chalk marks in my mind became clear. *Four edges, each a diamond shape. Rows of crosshatching along the inside. A basic amulet design, but tedious. Perhaps an hour to construct.*

I removed one of the silver disks from the basket and flicked the geared flint on my pen, igniting the small torch where most people would find a simple writing tip.

This was my favorite part.

Starting with the edges, I moved the torch point through steadily, removing excess silver in large pieces. And then it was time to line the diamond shapes up. I handled the pen a bit slower so I could feel when the stroke lined up with the chalk blueprint in my head and sliced off the necessary silver.

I double-checked the edges were even, then clicked the magnification up on the goggles to start on the crosshatching. The Xs of the hatching had to line up, each be the same size. An easy technique, but I still couldn't be lazy about it. This was the part that could mess up the entire amulet if I made a stroke outside of the blueprint.

The evil didn't respond to the metal itself, but as I welded away at it, shaping it into the very thing that particular Manifestation despised, the cracks began to voice their protest as rumbles in the forming amulet.

I paused every so often, just to relax my eyes from the magnification and flex my fingers.

Almost there. Just a few more adjustments—

"Andromeda!"

Magnus knew I was working. He had hired me to do just that. Whatever he needed would have to wait.

The amulet was so close to completion it pulsed in my hand, and I had to grip harder to keep it still.

"ANDROMEDA!"

My hand slipped, singeing a black line I hadn't meant to be there. I rubbed the line with my thumb, but it was deep enough to stay put.

I'd have to start over now. A brand-new disk. Another hour of work.

I dropped my spoiled work and climbed the stairs.

I found Magnus in his room glaring at a sport coat laid out on his bed. He turned to me, the bells on his wrists tinkling as he threw his hands up in frustration.

"Where have you been? I've been calling for an hour."

I paused, weighing the pros and cons of correcting him on the time difference of an hour versus minutes, but it didn't seem worth it. "Exorcising your house, sir."

"Magnus," he corrected. "I need your help."

"What can I do for you?"

He picked up the jacket, a black wool with silver-threaded paisley on the sleeves. "What do you think of this?"

I pursed my lips. "You called me away from my work for a jacket?"

Magnus looked at me as if I'd spoken nonsense. "This is just as important."

"You ruined an hour's worth of work—"

"How did I ruin anything when I've been in my room the whole time, minding my own business? Just answer the question and I'll let you get back to your beloved amulets."

I took a deep breath, though it didn't stop a vein in my temple from twitching. "It's nice."

"Yes, but for me?"

"I . . . don't know much about men's fashion. What is it for?"

"It was a gift from Kelela."

"Kelela?"

"Esjay's sister."

"Oh."

"They're coming over for dinner tonight, and she'll probably expect me to wear it." He paused to study the jacket, holding it at arm's length. "I don't know. Do you like it? I don't know if I like the color. It's so . . . black."

"Everyone in the house wears dark colors."

"Do they? And it's supposed to be slimming, but for some

reason it makes me look sickly." He held it against himself and stood in front of the full-length mirror.

"I think you should wear it, even if it's only tonight. She cared enough to have it made for you. Let her see you in it."

He looked at it mournfully, as if he'd rather do anything else than wear it. "Of course. You're right."

"I'm going to get back to work now," I said, leaning toward the freedom of the hallway.

"You will be there tonight," he said, hanging the jacket up. The lack of a question in his voice made me tighten my lips. "What are you going to wear?"

"It's one o'clock in the afternoon. I have hours before dinner to decide."

"I can help you choose. It's only fair, since you helped me."

Yes, I helped. Unwillingly. "No. I'd prefer to get back to work."

"Peggy said you didn't come with much— Wait." He threw open both doors of his closet, grinning wildly. "Pick something from here. And then Saba can alter it for you. She's really amazingly fast with a sewing machine."

I gritted my teeth at the mention of that spiteful woman. She had no right to discuss what I did or did not have. "Did you hear what I said, sir? I said *no*. Don't you know what 'no' means?"

He blinked at me. "Magnus," he corrected quietly.

I wanted to strangle him with the very jacket he hated. "I have to get back to work."

He rushed after me, stopping short in the doorway, as if there were an invisible line keeping him in. Good. I might've hit him, otherwise. "I'm very bad at this."

"This?"

"Talking to people. Having . . . friends."

"You hired me to exorcise your house. Save yourself the effort," I said, and stormed down the hall.

I returned to the stairs, and with the added agitation, finished the amulet in forty-five minutes. It might've been a new record, though my eyes and hands didn't thank me for it.

The cracks on the stairs had left without much of a fight. I hammered two nails into the wooden railing, hung the amulet, and stepped back to look at my work. One amulet down . . . God only knew how many left to go.

I could've cleansed another Manifestation but instead I spent a little time constructing an amulet to counteract the cold in my bedroom. By the time I was done it was a comfortable enough temperature to bathe and change for dinner.

There was a knock on the door.

"Who is it?" I asked.

No answer.

I grabbed my small knife, holding it down by my hip to keep it hidden as I cracked open the door. Saba stood there with folded clothing in her hand. I opened the door wider, hiding my knife behind it.

"Magnus said you were fast, but I didn't think you'd be *this* fast."

She smiled and held out the clothing to me.

"I told him I didn't want his clothes."

Saba shook her head and unfolded what she was holding to present me with a long-sleeved white dress, with blue and green forming the traditional design of a cross along the collar and down the center. I touched it, realizing then that it wasn't traditional fabric, but a tight wool weave. The lining was soft and a little fluffy—not a fabric I was familiar with, but then, I'd never touched such fine fabric in my entire life.

"Did you just make this?"

She shook her head and pressed her hand to her chest.

"It's yours?"

She nodded.

"That's . . . very sweet of you, Saba. It's beautiful." I stepped back from the dress. "But if Magnus sent you to give it to me, I already told him I don't want it."

She pursed her lips, her eyebrows quirked as if to say *Are you serious?* and, shaking her head one more time, she held the dress out to me again.

"Thank you." Her eyes had dark circles and looked a little red. I had no doubt she'd been crying. I didn't believe Magnus had nothing to do with this dress, but that didn't matter when there was a clear possibility Saba could be punished if I didn't take it.

Who cares what happens to her, Andi?

And, after all, it was just a dress. A dress I needed, if I was to attend dinner as he had ordered. It would be foolish not to accept.

I stabbed my knife into the wall behind the door where she couldn't see and took the dress from her. My fingers brushed hers, and I felt a chill go through me. "Your hands are so cold. Do you want to warm up in my room a little? It's warmer than the rest of the house."

Her pleased expression dropped and she backed out of the doorway, giving me a polite bow before rushing back down the hall. I watched her go and then locked myself in my room again to examine the dress. Well made, the colors vibrant, the white perfect as milk. And it smelled like honey and almonds. It was Saba's, but had it *ever* been worn?

I took off what I was wearing and put the dress on over my

wool stockings, admiring it in the full-length mirror. Saba was taller than me by at least half a foot, but it fit perfectly, looser along the body, more fitted in the sleeves. It was a tad itchy in my warm room, which meant it was probably perfect for the cold air of the rest of the house.

But that didn't mean I was going to leave this room any sooner than necessary.

CHAPTER
6

———

The aroma of rich meat and spices made me light-headed with hunger before I'd even reached the bottom of the stairs. I hadn't had lunch, I realized. My body was so used to starving I hadn't even noticed until now.

As I headed down the stairs, I heard Esjay and Peggy greeting each other, Peggy's voice friendlier than I'd ever heard it. I wondered if she was faking it, or if she really was a cheerful person who just disliked poor people.

They were standing in the foyer, along with a girl I'd never met. She looked as clean and sharp as Esjay in her fancy green wool coat. She had ample curves, somehow thick and delicate at once. Her hair was long and wavy . . . and blue. But the color didn't look odd on her—it suited her deep skin perfectly, enhancing her beauty rather than distracting from it. It was almost intimidating how pretty and put together this woman was.

I was getting the sense that the weapons of this world were different from the one I was raised in. There it was a matter of stealth, knives, fists. Brutal, but straightforward. Here, the animal with the grandest display won the dominance. *You don't have to be big to take up space*, Jember always used to tell me, which was easy enough for a tall person to say. But someone must've given this woman the same advice. She had claimed her territory simply by entering it.

I was more thankful than ever for Saba's dress.

She was the first to notice me standing on the stairs, and too many emotions flashed over her face to keep track of. Surprise, scrutiny, skepticism. And something else. Something like— well, *disgust* seemed a harsh term, but it felt the most appropriate.

She didn't think any better of me than Peggy did.

"Andromeda." Esjay held out his hand to me, as if to welcome me into their circle of snobbery.

"Where did you get that dress?" Peggy demanded, looking me up and down.

"I didn't steal it," I said, and she had enough humanity to become red-faced with embarrassment before storming away.

"*You're* the new debtera?" said the woman in the green coat, pressing her hand against her chest. "Are we just hiring children off the street now?"

"Kelela," Esjay chastised. "Andromeda is of age. She's a professional."

"Really? Because her eyebrows are crying out for some hot wax."

"*Kelela.*"

"Sorry, brother. I suppose it's a nice change from all the old men we've had to entertain before." She looked over, attempting a smile that barely passed as genuine. "Are you named after that beautiful princess who was chained to a rock?"

Esjay looked politely curious, but Kelela was testing me.

Laughing at me. She knew I wasn't beautiful, or anything close to royalty. I was nothing, at least according to her. Thankfully, I'd probably never have to deal with her again after tonight, so I took the high road and said, "I'm named after the plant."

Not that that was true, either. I didn't know if it was the woman who bore me or Jember who'd given me the name, but it didn't matter—it was only a name. I could move to another town tomorrow and change it, and no one would care.

Kelela raised her eyebrows. "Lovely."

All around us, the floors and the walls began to creak, carrying a messy rumble with them, like a cart full of pots and pans being rolled over rocks. My amulet rumbled too, and I tracked the Manifestation with my eyes from the inner wall to the outer. There were distant shatters, like pottery or glass being shaken from their proper spots. Then it was gone. It would be a tricky Manifestation to get rid of if it was going to come and go so quickly.

Kelela kissed her teeth. "You've been here all day and *still* haven't done anything about that?"

I narrowed my eyes, but before I could answer, Magnus's voice came from around the corner. "Are you done with the hellos? I'm starving."

He didn't stand to greet us or even look up. "Lovely to see you, Kelela. Esjay," he said, managing to sound more genuine than his actions suggested. "How's the weather today?"

Esjay pulled out the seat to the right of Magnus, and Kelela settled herself down, like a roosting hen trying to get comfortable. "You live in one of the hottest places in the world, Magnus."

"Then why is it so cold in here?" Kelela asked. "When we have such a capable debtera on the premises?"

The number of insufferable people who could fit in one house was beginning to feel unrealistic.

Before I could pick a seat Esjay pulled the chair opposite Kelela out for me. The last thing I wanted to do was sit beside Magnus or across from his elitist girlfriend, but it felt rude to decline when it was clear Esjay was the only one in the room who meant well.

"Thank you," I said, taking my seat.

A bowl was passed around to wash our hands, and then everyone reached into the big plate of food at the center of the table. Luckily dinner was nothing like the mush I'd had this morning. Instead, it was more of the delicious food we'd had last night.

I vaguely heard the three of them chatting, but all I could focus on was the injera. I tore off a large piece of the flatbread, still hot from the oven in my hand, and my mouth watered instantly. I tore a smaller piece to scoop up some tibs and spiced rice, stuffing it in my mouth, nearly fainting as I chewed. The beef was tender, hot butter running down my throat with the first bite, and just the right amount of heat in the spices to set my tongue tingling. There was no crunch of sand or dirt, only seeds and spices. I sighed contentedly as I took my time chewing. Last night I'd been too hungry to truly enjoy what I was eating. It had been a necessary lifesaver, then. Tonight, it was a heavenly experience.

"I'm glad you like my food, Andromeda," Magnus said, a slight grin on his face.

"Poor girl," Kelela added, her tone melting with disingenuous sympathy. "You eat like you've never tasted food in your life."

"It's a compliment to the chef," said Esjay, swallowing before continuing. "Peggy sure can cook. I feel like this is the best meal I've had all day."

Peggy had made this? Not likely. She had made the mush this morning, but she wasn't capable of this. She was a dull, soulless human being, and it was clear she couldn't season food if you paid her.

"You're either younger than we think or malnourished," said Kelela suddenly, without questioning it. "You can't be any older than eighteen."

I took a moment to swallow my giant mouthful—no one was going to shame me into not eating everything on this plate. "I can, actually," I said simply.

"Still, you're incredibly young to be a working debtera. You can't possibly have had enough experience to be any good."

Esjay placed his hand over his sister's briefly. "Andromeda has an excellent résumé, Kelela. If she had been on the official list she would've been the first debtera I would've contacted."

He smiled at me, as if bestowing a compliment.

"Not on the official list?" Kelela squared her gaze at me, her shock as fake as her hair color. "So, you're unlicensed?"

Poor sweet Esjay, with his cursed good intentions. All he'd done was given Kelela more ammunition to use against me. "My skill speaks louder than a piece of paper could. Magnus can vouch for the stairs I cleansed this afternoon."

"I have yet to see anything remarkable," Magnus said, knocking a candle off the table like an attention-starved cat. I felt a vein in my temple tic.

"You've started work already?" Esjay asked, wiping his hand on his cloth napkin. "We haven't gone over the contract."

"I read it over last night," I said, looking down at the candle Magnus had knocked over. It was still lit, somehow, but the flame stayed on the wick, rejecting the hardwood floor. I suppose it wasn't the weirdest thing I'd seen in this house. "The terms are fine."

"You must *really* need this job," Kelela said.

Magnus smirked, and looked off at the wall.

Esjay seemed the only one to miss the sarcasm. "What an honor it must've been to be selected to train with Jember."

Not selected so much as bought was the honest answer, but it was more information than these rich snobs deserved. "A true honor. He's the best there is."

"I'm dying to meet him and ask him a few things. I keep trying to invite him for dinner but can never seem to get ahold of him before or after church."

Why would you want to spend any amount of time with that heartless addict? Another honest answer I wasn't going to share. "Evenings are when debtera do most of their work."

"He refused to cleanse my house," Magnus said. "Why do you think that is? I mean I know why, but I want to hear what you think."

I don't know. We don't see each other. "He's not really a fan of long-term jobs. They require too much socializing."

"That's not the reason," Magnus mumbled.

"I heard him sing in church the other day," Kelela said. She looked smug about it, as if it had been a private concert instead of a regular service. "He doesn't sound shy to me."

"He's not shy," I said. "He just doesn't have patience for people."

"Especially you, apparently."

"Little sister," Esjay warned. "Be nice."

"Who made your amulet?" I asked her, eager to change the subject. "It's poor work. I'm surprised something in this house hasn't killed you by now."

Kelela lifted her amulet quickly to examine it, while I stuffed my face with rice.

I knew pettiness was a poor survival habit—one I would have to put aside, despite this blue-haired irritation across from me. And I would. After dinner.

"I found an interesting quote circled today," Magnus said. "'I have been so long master that I would be master still, or at least that none other should be master of me.'"

"So poetic," Kelela gushed.

I pursed my lips at her response. "It sounds a bit like a threat."

"It's a quote from Bram Stoker's *Dracula*," Kelela said. She leaned her chin in her hand and grinned at me. "You don't read much, do you? Oh, I'm sorry. *Can* you read?"

Ridiculous snob. "I actually read a few languages. One of the benefits of being raised in a church."

Kelela gaped ever so slightly, just enough that I knew I'd won.

"Kelela," Magnus said, standing to stretch, "let's find somewhere to digest."

Kelela pulled her glare from me, circled the table, and took his hand without giving me another glance.

I vaguely heard Esjay say something, but my ears were throbbing with the sounds of my elevated heart. If the other debtera didn't leave because of the workload, *this* was definitely why. Everyone in this house was either oblivious or insane.

You could leave now, Andi. They won't even notice you're gone. No amount of money is worth all this.

"Andromeda," Magnus said. "Join us."

I wanted to knock Magnus over the head with something. Just once, to get it out of my system. He wasn't that big. Taller than me, but not much wider. No real core strength, from what I could see, judging by the way he'd slouched in his chair all evening. I could take him down, easily. But hitting him was risky, seeing as he was the one paying me.

This is your only option for a patronage. Grin and bear it until the job is done.

I followed Magnus and Kelela out of the dining room. We headed down the hall, ending up in a game room. But instead of engaging in billiards or darts Magnus went straight to the couch beside the fireplace. Kelela sat beside him without question. I, on the other hand, took one of the two armchairs across from them, if only so a coffee table could act as a bit of a barrier between me and the two irritants in the room.

I guess Magnus didn't care much for coffee ceremonies, because hot coffee was already brewed and laid out on the table. Then again, the ceremonies were about togetherness, and he didn't seem to care much for that either. He picked up a deck of cards from the table as Kelela poured.

"Our new guest should be served first," he said, shuffling the deck.

There was a brief moment of suffocating tension in the air before Kelela handed me the small cup of coffee.

"So, what do debtera do, other than bind curses?" Kelela asked, and, for once, there was almost a light of humanity in her eyes. "Do you tell fortunes?"

"Debtera don't practice black magic," I said.

The light was extinguished almost immediately. "Maybe they do tell fortunes, but you got thrown out too soon to learn."

Magnus cut the deck with one hand, shifting the top of the pile to the bottom with a quick spin, keeping his eyes on the cards as he did it. "What would you want her to say, Kelela, if she *could* tell fortunes?"

"That I'll have a rich husband, of course," Kelela said.

"Your brother is rich enough."

"I'm twenty years old, I can't stay under his care forever. I need a kind, rich, generous husband." She hugged Magnus's arm as she said it. "Who dresses well and adores me."

"That's an easy find," Magnus said. He kept his eyes on his cards, but there was a slight smile on his lips.

I leaned back in my chair. Their flirting was tedious. Annoying. And maybe a little uncomfortable, if I was honest with myself. I was half tempted to get up and find Saba—she would make for far more pleasant company than this. But I couldn't abandon the first dinner party of my employment. The next one, I could make up some excuse. But for now, I just had to grin and bear it.

"You're too sweet," Kelela said, running her hand down his arm. That was annoying, too, though I couldn't quite place why. "Don't you love this jacket, Andromeda? I had it commissioned. Magnus loves wild patterns."

"It's nice," I said.

Magnus raised an eyebrow, and I snickered before I could stop myself.

Kelela eyed me suspiciously. "Even without it he's the most handsome man in the country."

I shifted in my chair, tempted to stand and leave but determined to stay put. "That's a bit of a wild claim, don't you think?"

Finally, Magnus looked up, his gaze direct. "Do you not find me handsome, Andromeda?"

"I haven't noticed, sir."

Magnus had been holding the cards between his thumb and

middle finger, pressing on them with his index, and at my words he pressed too hard and the cards scattered on the floor. He gave me a look that was part glare, part marvel.

On the other hand, Kelela looked relieved. "That's very professional of you, Andromeda. Esjay would say it's unethical to—"

"What do you mean you 'haven't noticed'?" Magnus demanded.

"I mean beauty is of little consequence," I said.

If it were, you wouldn't hire someone as plain as me to save your household . . .

"And besides, it's subjective," I added. "What's beautiful to you may not be beautiful to me."

"What do you find beautiful, then?" he asked, kicking the cards away from him. His gaze was so steady now . . . "If not I?"

"The way you were cutting the deck a moment ago," I said, nodding my head at the cards. He raised his eyebrows with interest, so I went on, "The speed and precision. It was simple, but confident. There's beauty in that sort of skill."

"Like crafting your amulets."

And all of a sudden, it was like we were beside the supply closet again, understanding passing between us.

"The previous debtera took much longer to construct each one," he clarified.

"And yet," I said, teasing, "you have seen nothing remarkable."

Magnus smirked. Kelela gripped his arm, glaring like she wanted to kill me.

"What do you find beautiful, sir?" I asked.

"Magnus," he corrected, and for some reason the lack of chastisement in his tone made my face grow . . . warm. "What do I find beautiful?" A grin tugged at the corner of his mouth, his gaze steadier than ever. "Eye contact."

"Magnus," said Kelela, standing quickly and taking his arm. "Will you draw me? You haven't drawn me in so long."

"I drew you three days ago," he said, but let her lead him without a fight.

I waited until they were walking away toward an armchair where Kelela could pose before quietly rushing out of the room.

CHAPTER
7

———— ❦ ————

I'd started menstruating on my twelfth birthday. I remember because the cramping in my thighs and stomach was so excruciating, I'd literally begged God not to let me die. I didn't know any other way to deal with it—topics of a sexual nature, as a cultural rule, weren't discussed outside the home without drawing shame, and so there was no woman in town I could go to for help. All I could do was wait for Jember to get home, foolishly sticking a glass bottle neck inside myself to catch the blood so I wouldn't ruin every piece of fabric in the cellar.

Jember never batted an eye at creepy Manifestations, but when he saw me cowering in the corner, he turned grey. He made me remove the bottle, grabbing my chin too tightly, the rare touch of his gloved hand catching me off guard. "Nothing goes up there," he said. "Do you understand? Nothing and no one."

He gave me one of his pills for the pain, the drugs knocking me out until morning.

No one, he'd said. I had no idea what that meant back then. Jember was the least sexual human I'd ever met. He couldn't make skin-on-skin contact but didn't seem to want to touch anyone over clothing either. He never commented on appearance, never looked at women any sort of way, never talked about romance or desire. And because he was the only example I had to follow, I never pursued romantic feelings either, even if I felt them a little. Eventually they didn't matter to me. Eventually I was so involved in God's work, I never gave the idea of a relationship a second thought.

Until tonight, that is. When I watched Magnus and Kelela cuddle on the couch and felt a twinge of something I'd been missing.

Not jealousy—that created an entryway for the Evil Eye. But something deeper and worse, because I'd been denying the emotion for so long.

A longing to be loved.

I didn't have to ask who it was when I heard a knock at the door, since the tinny jingle of bells came with it. I hugged my comforter around my shoulders to cover the simple nightgown Saba had given me. When I shoved the chair I was using as a barricade out of the way and opened it, Magnus was there in a soft, fluffy robe and slippers, holding what looked like an ornate jewelry box.

"You left early tonight," he accused.

"I was tired," I said, hugging my cape close.

"I expect you to be with me every evening after dinner. *Especially* if there are guests."

"Right, that is one of your rules."

He grinned slightly. "You're a surprisingly slow learner, Andromeda."

"Quick learner," I said, my mind too tired to keep an annoyed bite from peeking through. "Slow follower."

We were quiet for a moment.

Without a word, he held the box out to me.

"What is it?" I asked, leaning away.

"A peace offering."

I had to remind myself I was in a grand house, not on a street corner. Rich people didn't just hand you stolen things in order to keep the authorities off their scent . . . did they?

I took the box and opened the lid, and what was inside was better than jewelry. Chocolates. The expensive, gourmet kind, handmade with care. Two rows of four sat neatly in their designated grooves, their shiny gold wrappers resting on the red velvet lining of the box.

You could only find these in big cities, made by people who were trained in bigger cities.

"For me?" I held them tighter. It felt like a sin, holding them, but dropping them would be even worse. "I can't take these from you."

"When I turn twenty-one, I'll own the largest chocolate company in the world," he said, shrugging. "I've been crying chocolate tears since birth."

I closed the decorative box gently. My face felt warm. I couldn't have been . . . blushing? Over eight pieces of chocolate? *Get it together, Andi.*

"I didn't know your father was a chocolate maker. That must've been fun, growing up."

"Yes, well, he left when I was five, so . . ." Magnus cleared his throat. "After you left my room this afternoon, I had Esjay pick these up from my private supplier. I didn't tell him they were for you. I . . ." He tugged on the belt of his robe with both hands, twisting it. "I didn't want him to think I'd almost chased off yet another debtera."

"You don't have to worry about chasing me off."

"Yes, of course, the patronage."

"That. And I've dealt with people more difficult than you my entire life."

He laughed a little—an awkward, jolting sound—and then sank back into his concerned grimace, like he hadn't had much practice at happiness. "I doubt that very much."

We were quiet.

"Thank you for the chocolates si—um, Magnus," I said, tracing the raised embellishments on the box with my finger.

"Thank you," he repeated, as if he'd never heard the words. Then finally, for the first time since I opened the door, he ventured to look up at me. His gaze was shy, but hopeful. "You're welcome, Andromeda."

He rocked on his feet, and for a second I thought he was going to leave, but he just looked me in the eye for a little longer before dropping his gaze again.

"Good night," he said, and left the doorway abruptly.

"Good night," I said, my jaw so slack he'd closed his door by the time the words had left my mouth.

CHAPTER

8

———

Last night had given me hope. Magnus was difficult, but at least he had a heart and conscience. At least he was human. Perhaps working here wouldn't be as miserable as I thought.

I left my room with renewed energy, and found Emma standing at the bottom of the stairs.

"Oh, thank the Lord Jesus." Emma tapped on the rail, looking over her shoulder, as if someone might catch her conversing with me. "I know you have a lot of things to take care of, but this room is a bit of an emergency."

I bit the inside of my cheek to avoid contradicting her. To people with Manifestations in their house, *every* room was an emergency. But it wasn't as if I had anything better to do.

"Lead the way," I said.

Emma smiled, relieved. "It's just down here," she said, gesturing down the hall but walking beside me. "So, how are you settling in?"

"Really well, actually."

"Really? You haven't broken any of the dozens of rules?"

Emma laughed. The rules were more tedious than funny, but I smiled so she wouldn't feel alone. "They're nonsense. A waste of your time, if you ask me." She hooked her arm around mine, and I tightened my muscles against the urge to pull away. "The only rule you need to know is that Magnus is mad as a hatter and should be avoided whenever possible."

"He's a little eccentric," I said with a shrug.

"He's mad, just like his father was," Emma confirmed. "Peggy said the curse makes him that way, but *I* would be equally mad to spend enough time with him to find out for sure."

We walked over a rug I could've sworn hadn't been in the hall yesterday, rounding a small table resting on it I was *positive* hadn't been. An obsession with redecorating wasn't quite enough to dub one "mad," but it was certainly a little . . . strange.

"I suppose there's two rules," Emma went on. "Stay away from Magnus and don't go out at night."

"I'm clear on that one."

"That one is the most important." Her step faltered, and when I looked at her, her brows were knitted into deep lines, her eyes tearing. "People go missing in this house if they're not careful."

"Go miss—"

Alone.

The word tickled my ear, like a whisper, and I tripped to a stop. "What?"

"Go missing," Emma repeated. "Disappear."

"No, I mean—"

You are alone.

A chill crawled over my already cold limbs, the words drawing my eyes to the closet we'd stopped beside. My amulet throbbed like an aching heart.

"This house gives me goose bumps," Emma said, rushing me along. She led me into one of the rooms I'd seen on the tour—empty, save for being littered in soot.

"This is it." She held out her hand to the fireplace, which Tom was busy cleaning with a rough brush. "The bane of my existence."

"A dirty chimney?" I asked, and saw Tom's shoulders shake as he chuckled.

"You don't understand," Emma said, "it's constantly dirty. And when it's dirty, it smokes. And we have to clean it, knowing it'll be soiled any minute, any day."

"There's nothing in the room, why does the hearth need to be lit?"

"They all need to be lit, at all times. The house is too cold, otherwise."

I'd felt the proper strokes for the Manifestation on entering the room, but approached it anyway. This one wasn't making my amulet pound, so it was clearly not much of a threat. A nuisance, at most.

I knelt in front of the dirty fireplace, and Tom leaned back on his heels to give me space. I'd never actually looked inside one before . . . to be honest, I wouldn't have been able to tell anything was wrong if I couldn't sense the strokes.

"It's unpredictable," Tom said, scratching one of his sideburns, his soot-covered hands smudging black down his jaw. "Sometimes it happens when the house decides to rumble, sometimes it goes off on its own. No shake, no sound, no warning. The only sure way to not get covered is to clean it as soon as it's done spitting, but—" He looked up at Emma, giving her a reassuring smile. "There aren't many of us in the house, so it can't always be helped."

"Not many of us?" Emma said, pushing her hands so hard

into her apron pockets I was sure she'd tear them. "It's you, me, Peggy, and Andromeda—*if* she stays. Poor Edward has disappeared."

"He left," Tom said, with a weary sigh.

"None of the horses are missing. He didn't pack any of his things. And do you really think a frail old man walked out into the desert alone? He disappeared, just like the others."

"Where do they disappear to?" I asked.

"Tom thinks they leave because they just can't stand being here," Emma scoffed.

He raised his eyebrows at her. "Better than thinking they're being held somewhere, only to be set free when the curse is broken, like some foolish fairy tale."

"Well, let's ask Andromeda what she thinks."

They both looked at me for answers, and I wanted to climb up the chimney and disappear, myself. Instead I said calmly, "I'll look into it."

"There, you see?" Tom stood up and kissed Emma, leaving smudged handprints on her face where he stroked her cheeks. "Why do you worry so much? Let the professional take care of things."

Emma murmured something I didn't catch, because a billow of black powder shot out from the bowels of the hearth. It swelled around the invisible shield of my amulet, engulfing me in darkness. I watched the dust skim by my shield and grinned . . . it seemed a wildly inappropriate reaction to a Manifestation, but I couldn't help it. Sometimes simple joys were all a girl had.

Somewhere in the cloud, Emma screamed in frustration and then both of them were coughing. I let the black cloud settle some before going out into the hall where the two of them stood, doing their best to wipe their faces with their dirty clothes.

This would be an easy amulet, but I was honestly more interested in the closet we'd passed on the way here. So, I pulled the door shut and said, "I recommend staying out of this room for the time being. We'll have to make do without the extra fire for now."

"Peggy won't like that," Emma said.

"Well, she's welcome to become a debtera and cleanse it herself."

Emma and Tom looked at each other, their slightly shocked faces breaking down into smiles. "I told you she was the right one," Tom said, hugging Emma around the shoulders.

"All right, don't boast about it," said Emma, though she was grinning. "Come on, this soot is stinging my eyes." And they headed down the hall, I assumed toward their room.

I waited until they turned the corner to go back to the closet. I looked at the closed door and listened. And there it was—a breath, like a whisper, from behind the door.

I opened the door and was greeted by spiderwebs. Not just a few cobwebs here and there, but an entire closetful of active webs, stretching from wall to wall, ceiling to shelf, shelf to broom . . . spiders living their lives on them as if this was where they belonged.

There were all kinds. Some with long spindly legs. Some smaller than my bitten-down fingernails. Some with red backs, some brown and furry. A few, I saw, glowed pale white from within the darkness.

I leaned into the doorway, the spiders and their webs shifting away from the invisible protective sphere my amulet provided. Some of the webs didn't move. I snatched one from my face, shoving it to the side. This closet had been so rarely used, actual spiders had mingled with the Manifestation.

I stepped inside the dense cross-stitching of webs, stepping carefully. The real ones were easy to spot, since they were the ones undeterred by my amulet, and I shoved them out of the way easily until I made it to the center of the closet.

Something rustled the webs ahead of me, like a puff of breath and a hiss.

Alone.

For a moment I held my breath, listening. There was a dull tap, and I jerked my gaze up to witness a giant spider crawling across my shield overhead. But that wasn't what I was listening for.

Alone, the Something said again, this time beside me.

The spiders . . . the Manifestation . . . the *house* couldn't have spoken to me. Still, the word unnerved me enough that I took out my pen.

You will always be alone.

I froze just short of igniting it.

There was no possible way it was reading my mind. Manifestations didn't work that way. No, it was projecting a common fear. Most of the people who approached this closet could probably relate—

No one loves you.

"That's not true," I said, immediately feeling like an idiot. "God loves me."

No one, the Something said.

I opened my satchel for a disk of silver, muttering, "Stupid Manifestation."

No one loves you.

"You said that already."

He does not love you.

I froze before burning the first stroke. "Who is he?"

I waited. I don't know why I didn't just work while I had

silence, but the voice was so quiet I didn't want to miss what it would say.

The breath moved the webs, which—oh God—had eaten away at most of my shield without my notice and were right in front of my face. One of the large glowing white spiders, its body translucent enough to display its viscera, reached out one of its spindly eight legs to me, the tip of it just short of my nose.

He will never love you, it said, the airiness of its voice making me tremble.

"Who?" I asked, my throat tense.

I saw the spider's fangs flash in the meager light from the hall. *Your father.*

I felt something on the back of my leg and ran out into the hall. I brushed spiders and stray webs off me, taking a moment to catch my breath. If I hadn't felt something, I might've still been frozen there, unable to cope with those whispered words.

I took another deep breath remembering those words . . . *He will never love you.*

And then I shook my head to clear it.

It was likely the Manifestation wasn't talking about me at all. Magnus was the one who was cursed—maybe it was specific to him, or even his own father. And it wasn't as if I had an actual father. Certainly no blood father I cared for. Only Jember, if he could be called that, and he didn't have a paternal bone in his body.

Still . . . the specificity of it unnerved me enough that I slammed the door shut, rushing off toward the safer soot-covered room to cleanse it instead.

CHAPTER
9

⟋⟍

When I entered the dining room, Magnus was sitting alone reading, his legs propped on the table. So it would just be the two of us—a relief and a stress combined. Magnus was a handful on his own, but at least I wouldn't have to deal with Kelela, as well. One arrogant brat was more than enough.

I sat in my regular chair, wincing at the screech of wood on wood as I scooted it closer to the table.

"Evening, Andromeda," he said, keeping his eyes on his book.

"Good evening."

"Give me a moment and I'll look at you."

Odd how much that sounded like a threat.

"Oh, Magnus," Peggy fussed, entering through the kitchen, holding two plates piled with something tan and red. "Feet down, child."

He pulled his feet onto his chair, resting the book on his raised knees.

"Thank you," I said as she laid a plate in front of me. It was a pile of long, pale . . . *things*, with a red sauce smothering it.

"Put your feet on the floor like a gentleman," I heard Peggy say, though I was still trying to figure out what I was about to eat. Worms? But they didn't seem to have any insides— "You're not a cat."

Magnus hissed at her, and I smirked and looked up.

Peggy's face was flaming red. "Feet. Down."

Magnus finally obliged, sliding his feet off to slap onto the floor.

She nodded in satisfaction, set his plate in front of him, and left the room.

He sat there, quietly, until we could no longer hear her footfalls. Then he slid his book down the length of the table, away from our food, and replaced his legs on top. And, as promised, he looked at me. "That woman would starve me on principle," he said, picking up a small three-pronged tool.

I followed his example and picked up mine. "May I ask what this is?"

"You've never eaten pasta before?" Magnus sat upright, planting his feet on the floor, my ignorance seeming to make him forget he was trying to be defiant. "I fell in love with it after spending a summer in Florence."

I'd meant the tools we were holding, and the word "Florence" didn't mean anything to me, but I supposed it didn't matter. I watched him stick the tool into the center of his pasta and twist. The pasta swirled around it, creating a small bundle.

I tried my best to copy his motion, but twirling it with one hand was trickier than it looked.

Magnus took a bottle of wine out from under the table and uncorked it, pouring it far higher than one serving.

"How was your day?" I asked, to interrupt the silence. I knew from living with Jember so long what that much alcohol meant—physically, mentally, emotionally, it didn't matter what. Something was hurting.

"It's sweet of you to ask," Magnus said. He took a swallow of the red liquid. "Unless you're just making small talk, which to that I say: 'Oh God, *must* we?'"

The corner of my mouth twitched into a grin. His strangeness was growing on me, I had to admit. "What would you like to talk about?"

"I don't know," he said, waving his hand vaguely. "What's your favorite thing?"

"Pertaining to?"

"Pick something."

"This sounds like small talk to me."

Magnus choked on his wine and coughed for a moment.

I reached over and patted his back. "Are you all right, sir?"

He cleared his throat, wiping his mouth with his sleeve. "The honesty that comes from your mouth is just astounding."

"You can't be so used to being lied to."

Magnus chewed on his lip. "Peggy means well. My social circle back in England was *violently* against my inability to pass as White, so she's very protective. Not to mention I had no parents."

The pasta I tried to pick up with my hand slipped back onto the plate. "I'm sorry."

He tried to speak, then abruptly held up his finger as he finished chewing his mouthful of pasta. "Oh, don't be. I had plenty of wealth to keep me warm. And besides, seeing as I was to inherit my father's company anyway, Peggy allowed me to abandon school and tour the Continent. Six months in Spain, eight months in Germany. Then I came here to see my *father,* but he was extremely unaccommodating, so I stayed with Esjay for a month and moved on."

His tone made me pause. "I don't think your father meant it personally. He was protecting you, I'm sure."

"Don't assign my father character traits he never possessed." He looked uncomfortable for a second, then abruptly said, "Anyway, after that I traveled anywhere the food was good."

"I can relate," I said, pasta slipping off my tool as I attempted to lift it to my mouth. "Most of my decisions are based on food."

He grinned. "I'm not surprised. Food here is an experience."

"If you enjoy the experience, why don't you host coffee ceremonies?"

He took a thoughtful sip of wine. "They take too long. I don't have the patience."

Well, at least he was aware of it.

"Life isn't about instant gratification," I said, trying and failing to lift more pasta.

"You poor thing, have you never used a fork? Let me show you."

Magnus leaned over to my plate, and my heart tripped as I moved my hand away before his hand could touch mine.

He picked up my—what had he called it? Fork?—his thick brows lowering over his eyes like a shadow, and began twirling pasta. "Are you afraid of me, Andromeda?"

I smirked before I could stop myself. "Who could possibly be afraid of you?"

His twirling slowed. "You're afraid of something."

He held the fork out to me, but for a long moment I couldn't think to take it. I wanted to run. Hide behind the wall. Put on an extra shirt. Anything to hide what he was seeing . . . anything to hide my soul.

I never could summon the will to take the fork from him, and so he laid it on my plate with a glassy *tink*. He leaned back into his own chair, his mouth twitching—whether from a smile or a grimace, I couldn't tell. "I thought I would like having company for dinner, but you're just a little storm cloud, aren't you. Don't you know how to have fun?"

"Fun?" I repeated, still a bit disoriented.

"Yes, fun. What do you enjoy?"

I blinked a few times to be sure I wasn't imagining this entire evening. I had emotional whiplash, not to mention I hadn't even tasted a bite of this impossible-to-eat food. "Is there a point you're trying to make, sir?"

"Point? I'm making conversation."

I gripped the arms of my chair, digging my nails into the cold wood, and took a deep breath. Part of me knew he was right, the other was sick of his constant, invasive questions. But he had gifted me those chocolates. He was trying. I could at least meet him halfway. "I enjoy constructing amulets."

"How old are you—fifty?—that all you enjoy is work?"

"You asked. I answered."

Magnus held up his hands. "No need to get defensive. I've just never met someone who doesn't have, you know, hobbies."

I locked my jaw, shutting myself up before the words could flow out of me.

I was good with a knife because I had no choice. Quiet on my feet to stay out of sight, to avoid adversaries I knew I couldn't overpower. Every skill I'd learned was to increase my chances of survival. But how could a boy who spent hours drawing pictures and playing music simply because he enjoyed it ever understand my point of view?

Magnus leaned over to my plate again, lifting my fork.

"May I?" he asked, and held up the pasta toward my mouth. I froze for a moment. Was he really trying to practice gursha *now*, when I felt so conflicted and annoyed? On the other hand, a sweet gesture of friendship was a nice distraction from this conversation.

I accepted the mouthful of food. I lingered to enjoy the slightly sweet and nutty smell of his skin—or his sweater?—compared to the savory flavor in my mouth, but embarrassment knocked the sense back into me and I moved away to chew.

The sauce was tangy, acidic, strong with garlic, but the pasta was slippery and difficult to chew, wanting to slip down my throat whole instead of staying beneath my teeth. So, I suppose, they were a bit like worms, only without the taste of protein and a healthy pop. Strange, but not awful. I'd definitely had worse, not that it mattered when you were hungry.

"Do you like it?" he asked.

I took a moment to swallow. "It's difficult to eat."

He grinned, leaning back in his chair. "It's fun."

"'Difficult' and 'fun' are the same to you?"

"No." He paused, his wineglass poised at his lips. "Absolutely not. I despise hard work."

I don't know why, but that made me grin a little. "Unless it's for pasta."

He choked on his wine and coughed, slapping his chest. I leaned forward to help, but he waved it away. "Blazes, Andromeda, I almost died," he choked out, wiping his mouth on his sweater again. "You could've warned me you were this funny."

I felt a blush of satisfaction warm my neck. "And you said I have no hobbies."

"See, we're making progress. Now I know you can't stand being touched, you're secretly funny, and you don't like pasta."

"I don't *dislike it*."

"You pull away."

His voice was oddly concerned when he said it, and I felt my face heat up. I didn't want to talk about my lack of basic human skills, or why I didn't possess them. I wasn't sure why it suddenly mattered, but for whatever reason, I didn't want him to find me strange.

And I certainly didn't want any pity.

"There's nothing wrong with being careful," I said. "And I meant the pasta."

"Careful or anxious?" He raised his eyebrows. "And I've seen you eat food you like."

"*Careful*. I trust people when they prove trustworthy." This conversation was becoming unmistakably passive-aggressive, and it was annoying . . . well, partly. Part of me found it intriguing—exciting even—enough to want to see where it would end. In fact, thinking about it made me smirk. "Give me some injera and I'll finish this off within a minute."

Magnus broke into a grin as he leaned his elbow on the table, his cheek in his hand. He looked at me . . . not at my scar or my barely managed frizzy braids, but directly into my eyes, the same way he'd done last night.

I felt myself blushing and looked away before I could fully gather what those eyes were conveying.

"That seems anxious to me," he said. My gaze shot back to him quickly. He pressed his fingers against his cheek gently, rhythmically, his grin the slightest bit defeated by his words. "Which is fine. I'm anxious, too."

"About the curse?"

"No. After."

"What happens after?"

"I don't know." He slumped back into his chair, his fingers laced over his stomach. "I always feel that if I was free of the curse . . . well, people wouldn't feel the need to stay with me. They'd leave. And I'd be . . ."

"Alone," I said, shivering. I closed my eyes for a moment, forcing the whispers of spiders from my mind. "I know exactly how you feel."

Magnus was quiet for a second. Then, suddenly, he shoved his chair back with a loud screech and went to the kitchen. I heard a bit of knocking around, and then he came back holding a small basket. He set it in front of me, removing the cloth on top to reveal injera.

Instantly my stomach growled.

"Leftover from lunch," he said.

"What is this?" I said, breaking off a piece without waiting, pushing down any visual signs of contentment. "A reward for entertaining you?"

"A reward? No." He had a playful look in his eyes that was infectious enough to break my stoicism into a slight grin. "I just wanted to see you finish your pasta within a minute."

CHAPTER
10

⸎

As soon as I stepped into the hall my amulet pulsed.

It was eight o'clock—two hours before the Waking, before the Manifestations should've been wildly active. But the closer I came to Magnus's room, the more dread twisted my stomach. I moved closer and put my ear to the door. There was a vague slopping sound, like water lapping on a rock. I turned the knob, but when I pushed it wouldn't open. I tried again, putting my shoulder into it, and the door budged slowly, like something was pushing against it. I shoved one more time and stumbled as the door gave, my leg splashing into water up to my knee.

No, not water. Thicker than that . . . *redder* than that.

I gaped at the bedroom, at what seemed to be blood filling the room from the floor up, like the swiftly rising tide of a river. Magnus was still in his bed, fast asleep. I slipped in through the crack I'd managed, the shifting of the liquid shutting the door behind me.

"Magnus!" I called. He didn't even twitch. "Wake up!" I waded across the room through the quickly rising blood, the shield of my amulet pushing the blood away from my body.

His chest was moving steadily, so I shook his shoulders, hard. Not a twitch. There was no way someone could sleep so heavily. Not naturally, anyway. Was this . . . part of the Manifestation?

I'd never seen paralysis like this. But then, I'd never seen a room fill with blood.

I climbed onto the bed and scooped his dead weight up by the shoulders to get his face away from the blood that was now working to consume the bed. And only when I pulled him to my chest and his body touched my amulet did he jolt awake with a frightened yell, shoving away from me.

He panted on the opposite side of the bed, blinking and staring as if he was doing his best to remember me. "Is it happening again?"

"We have to get out of this room," I said. When he didn't react, I grabbed his wrist. "Hurry!"

By then the blood was soaking the sheets, and Magnus jolted again, finally looking down at the scene. "It's happening again," he murmured, looking at me for help. "Oh my God."

"I can't lift you. Can you walk?"

"Yes, but—"

"Come with me." I tugged him off the bed toward the door, and he followed without question. The blood was to our waists, and the sloshing and rising had worn down my shield significantly. I pulled at the door, but the pressure of the flowing blood kept it shut. Magnus joined my side without having to be asked, using his foot against the wall as leverage. It budged a little before slamming right back.

"Oh my God," he said again, more panicked this time.

"Calm down," I said, more for myself than for him. I'd never been buried in blood before, but I imagined it was just like any Manifestation. As long as my amulet could last—

I looked down at myself. My shield reached only about five inches beyond me in all directions, but it was enough to give me an idea.

"Count to ten and then pull as hard as you can."

"We can't wait, it's rising too quickly—"

"You have to trust me, Magnus. Just do it."

Magnus was trembling—I don't know if it was from the freezing blood or fear, but his eyes were wide. "One . . ." he said weakly, "two . . ." and he positioned himself to pull the door.

"Three," I counted with him. I dropped down into the sea of blood, blocking out his *four*.

My amulet kept my face clear of drowning. I reached forward with my free hand and felt for the door. If I could use the clear space my amulet provided to relieve some of the pressure from the lower part of the door, it was sure to open more easily.

At least I hope.

It had to be *seven* by now . . . *eight* . . . *nine*—

My count was off, and the door shot open sooner than I'd prepared for. I didn't have time to think about it, wedging my foot and arm behind the door, catching the wood in my hands as it flew back just in time before slapping into my face. That jolt had been enough to break my shield completely, and I held my breath and closed my eyes as blood enveloped me. Magnus's legs knocked into me as he shifted, the door pressing away from me, opening more and more with the small crack I'd given him as leverage.

The more it crept open, the more I crept toward the hall, pressing my shoulder into the door. I gasped for breath as I emerged from the room into the hall, spitting out blood that ran down my face and hair, while the sea stayed within the confines of the doorway. I got to my feet to gain more balance and rammed my shoulder into the door. Magnus eased out his leg. I rammed again, and his upper half leaned out, and he gasped as I had, though his breaths were a little more panicked. I continued until he was clear of the door, standing in the hall with me, holding the door against the liquid mass.

"We're going to let go at the count of three," I said, and he didn't argue. "One."

"Two," he counted with me. "Three!"

We tumbled back, the force of the rising blood slamming the door behind us. The floor knocked the wind out of me, and I gasped a few times to gather my breath. We lay on the ground, our cold, sopping-wet clothing sticking to us. I wiped my face quickly to keep the blood out of my eyes, giving myself a moment to catch my breath. I suddenly realized we were holding on to each other, and I let go of him quickly.

"We're okay," I said, feeling stiff and cold, and his grip wasn't helping. "Let go."

He did so, immediately folding into himself and shivering. We lay facing each other. For some reason that felt intimate, so I rolled and splatted onto my back.

"Is there an amulet for this?" he asked, panting.

"There's an amulet for everything."

I shoved myself to my feet and hurried down the hall, leaving a red trail behind me. I grabbed the entire basket of supplies instead of trying to sort through everything in my dark room. When I slipped to a stop back in front of Magnus's room, he was standing eying the door, as if it might burst open at any moment. But when I sat down with the basket, so did he, hugging his wet clothes to him, teeth chattering.

It was so cold I had a hard time keeping my pen steady. Magnus went in another room and brought out a heavy blanket and an oil lamp and, after a moment, I could continue. Soon droplets of blood started escaping from our bodies, away from the forming amulet. First in drops, then in splatters, skittering across the ground and under the door of his room. Inside, the blood roared like a stormy sea, and there was a gurgling sound, like the unplugging of a drain.

The blood retreated from us like a panicked mob as I drew close to finishing, taking its wetness and stains with it, leaving us whole as if we'd never been touched by the Manifestation.

I opened the bedroom door, holding the blanket on my shoulders like a cape, feeling no strong presence except for Magnus standing behind me. The room was spotless. I found a place where the amulet wouldn't easily get damaged and nailed it to the wall.

"It should be safe to sleep in here now," I said, gripping the blanket close to swallow me in warmth.

His tired eyes shifted above mine. "You still have blood on you." His eyes widened slightly as he was speaking. "You're bleeding."

I stepped back faster than he stepped toward me, touching my forehead. There was a bite of pain as I touched it, and a little throbbing after, but not much else. The cold of this place numbed everything.

I snatched his hand away from my face and gave it a small push back in his direction. "I'm fine."

"You're bleeding," he repeated, as if justifying his reasoning for invading my space. "Saba can take a look at it."

"I've had worse," I said, and turned away before I could see the pity that graced most people's faces when I said that. "Good night, Magnus."

"How did you know I was in trouble?"

I paused at the door, drumming my fingers on it before turning around again. "My amulet pulses." I felt something warm beginning to run down my forehead and stopped it up with the heel of my hand. Maybe the wound was worse than I thought. "When it encounters the Evil Eye."

"Like a heartbeat?"

"I suppose."

"You saved me, Andromeda." Magnus sat on his bed. He looked a little dazed, still. Disoriented. "I owe you. I've been drowned alive once before already, and it was unpleasant enough that I never wish to repeat the experience."

"Drowned alive?"

"This isn't the first time the house has done this. I stayed in a different room, then . . . I think that room is still stained red." He looked up at me, almost in earnest, as if the room he stayed in was the most important detail of the story. "The Manifestation paralyzed me, like it did tonight. I couldn't leave, couldn't scream for help. And if . . . if you know how it feels when you're drowning, your lungs feel tight from lack of air, and you think your head might explode. Well I felt that way, all night. My lungs burning, longing for air. Until the morning when the blood receded . . ."

My throat burned with a sob stuck inside. It was far too easy to sympathize. I'd grown up with that drowning sensation. A few times, when Jember had been preparing me for "the real world," he would choke me and make me figure out how to make him let go. More often than not, it ended with me blacking out. And then he'd lecture on using my body weight to my advantage and not being afraid to force my thumbs into an attacker's eye sockets.

Of course, Real World Prep days normally ended in us stealing baklava from the corner bakery. I doubt the Evil Eye gave Magnus sweets whenever it finished drowning him.

Magnus had been tugging absently on his sweater, poking his fingers in the weaving and stretching holes in it. "It didn't even have the decency to kill me," he muttered.

I went to the bed, hesitating before resting my hand on Magnus's shoulder.

The castle was worse off than I thought. I should've figured, seeing as ten licensed professionals had come and left before me. It was clear I was in over my head. I needed advice. Help.

For once, Jember, please be cooperative.

Magnus looked up at me and then opened the drawer beside his bed and took out a handkerchief, holding it up to me. "Are you sure you don't want Saba to take a look?"

"I'm fine," I murmured, wiping my forehead clean before pressing the now-damp cloth to my wound.

"What can I do to even the score?"

"It's my job, sir."

"Saving my life isn't your job. You could've left me to suffer. Or constructed the amulet from outside the door, out of harm's way. I am in your debt now."

He stood up, slow enough that I could've backed away . . . close enough, that I should've.

"Name your price, Andromeda," he said.

I looked up into his face, which looked down at me. Challenging me. He wanted to see if I'd give in and ask for something in return for saving him, and as petty as it felt, I wouldn't do it. I was used to being challenged and used to intimidating in return.

But for some reason, all I wanted to do was comfort him.

"There is no debt," I said.

"You want nothing from me?"

I couldn't answer that. Not with a general yes or no. Money, but he was already paying me. Food and shelter, mine. I could ask for more chocolates, but those didn't mean anything. Just a response for the sake of responding.

He was asking something deeper. Something he could personally give, that would equal the life I'd given him. In that way, it was a far scarier question than what it seemed. A question I could never answer, even if I knew what to say.

"Well, if you have no requests . . ." Magnus stepped back and opened his drawer, taking out a small wooden box. He took out a wad of bills, not even bothering to count it before holding it out to me.

"No," I said, stepping back. "I didn't save you to be rewarded."

"Call it a bonus for a job well done."

"U-um . . ." It was stupid, really, for me not to take it. I had six cents to my name, and here I was refusing money on principle. It felt strange to acknowledge the money in front of him, but I only had to look at the different-colored bills to count it. It was more than I made in a week. There had to be a mistake. "I haven't been paid my weekly salary yet. We could just say you paid me early."

"For God's sake, take it," he said with a heavy sigh. "You'll be paid your salary tomorrow, as agreed upon in the contract. Besides, I'm sure you could find something better to do with this than I could."

Even touching the money felt shameful. He was paying me for the wrong reasons—I couldn't stand the idea of being paid for doing the right thing. But at the same time, refusing such a generous gift was extremely rude. I hid the rolled bills in my fist. "Thank you . . . I should let you go to bed," I added quickly, just as Magnus was about to speak, and stepped back toward the door.

"I can't let you leave my room bleeding. What kind of host would that make me?" His voice was quiet, hopeful enough that all I did was nod. And then he went into his private bathroom. I heard a cabinet open, some things being shifted, and then he came back with a bottle of clear liquid.

He was in my space again, but I didn't try to leave. My heart was pounding, but not from fear or adrenaline. His gaze was so direct, penetrating. It seemed impossible that his eyes were always downcast when guests were around, that maybe, secretly, he was scared to know people. Because now he was nearly pinning me with just a look, only a hint of shyness in his brown eyes.

But, as if reading my thoughts, he shifted his gaze to my throbbing forehead. He took the handkerchief—my muscles twitched when it left my hand, I'd forgotten it was clenched there—and wet it with the clear liquid from his medicine cabinet. Without warning he pressed it to my cut. I winced, closing my eyes briefly, my hand slapping on top of his to remove it from—

His hand . . . was at the back of my head. *Cradling* it. Me. I swallowed, taking a deep breath. His touch was comforting in a way I'd never felt before. Was I . . . *allowed* to like the feeling of my employer's hand? Even if it didn't mean anything—which it didn't. He was just helping me. And he was only a year older. If he wasn't my employer we would be peers.

He checked his work and then tore a small piece of gauze he'd brought out, applying a bit of sticky medicine to the back of it. I bit back a grin. His concentration face made him look sweet, like a young boy, as he laid the gauze over my cut, carefully smoothing it with his thumbs so that the medicine spread beneath it, making every corner stick in place. It was a nice change to his weary, annoyed countenance.

"Thank you," I said.

He dabbed the edges with the handkerchief, removing excess medicine, and then his focus was on my eyes again. He blinked when I stepped back, as if waking from a trance. "Thank you for making me feel useful."

A blush rose in his cheeks, extending through the tip of his nose. It made him look so sweet—God, stop, what was I thinking? I dropped my gaze quickly.

"Good night, sir," I said, turning away.

"Magnus."

I paused at the door to look at him, meeting his gaze. I should've told him to stop staring at me. It was socially rude. Odd, to be honest. But his look wasn't invasive, wasn't lewd. It was just a wordless request, a boy longing for connection.

And, after tonight, I think it was a connection I needed as much as he did.

"Good night . . ." I grabbed the doorknob, stepped out into the hall. "Magnus."

CHAPTER
11

———

I awoke with a stomachache and a mind full of dread.

Not over the roomful of blood. No, I'd had hours to wrap my mind around the concept. Or the fact that my amulet had barely protected me from it. That was more concerning, but Jember was sure to know of a way to make my amulet stronger.

That is, if he was willing to help me.

I rolled out of bed and dressed in the clothes I'd arrived in that first day. If I hurried I could catch Jember before he left church for the day—he worked all night, and if I didn't catch him before he went to sleep he would be twice as ornery. At least at church there was a chance he would marginally behave in front of the priests.

I took some money from my hiding place behind the wardrobe and tucked it into the hidden pocket in my satchel. Then it was time to pray that Tom or Emma would give me a ride.

The servants' quarters had none of the wide-open doors like the rest of the house, none of the sun streaming through large windows like gossamer kissing wood. It was a narrow, low-ceilinged hall. Cold, in the figurative sense as well as literal. The doors of vacant rooms locked on either side of me, like tombs. I was thankful that voices drifted from the only open door—part of me had been afraid I'd have to search the whole house for them.

"Why can't we just go?" Emma said. "We have enough money saved to get back to London, and there are plenty of friends we could stay with while we get settled with new jobs."

"A few more weeks and we'll have enough to make a life of our own."

"At what cost?"

I stood in the doorway, but they weren't looking in my direction, or else I was just better at blending into the scenery than I thought.

Tom raked his hand through his hair. "Give Andromeda time, I'm sure she'll—"

"We're out of time, Tom. Edward has vanished, just like the rest of them. All we have is each other."

I cleared my throat. The pair turned to me quickly, Emma nearly leaping out of her skin.

"Good morning," I said.

When I tried to look at Emma she turned away to adjust the blanket on the bed.

Tom sighed, pinching the bridge of his nose. "What can we do for you, Andromeda?"

"Would you be able to drive me into the city?"

Emma jerked around, her face dropping as if gravity had given up on it. "You're not leaving us, are you?"

I tried to give her a reassuring smile, but I'm not so sure how convincing it was. I wasn't looking forward to this trip any more than she was to me leaving the house. "Just have to pick up a few things from the market."

"Sweet Jesus, yes!" Emma grabbed a small purse from the side table. "I need an escape from this treacherous place."

There were two specific entry gates into the city within the questionably sturdy stone wall that surrounded it—one on each opposite end of the wall. It was fifteen feet high, easily climbable, and would've been the way I'd taken in if I didn't have company.

Tom steered the horses down one of the two dust roads wide enough for this giant coach, at a crawling pace to avoid all the shoppers. Superfluous coaches with cushioned seats weren't a novelty to this city anymore. But I'd lived here for seven years, ever since Jember was hired for this position with the church, and I had rarely seen one parade through the streets like this. Usually they were only on their way out.

About a mile from the center square where the church stood, the two main roads ended and became one large circle around the inner section of the city. Here there was an expansive goat market, a station where travelers could leave their animals, and where the rich left their coaches. There were already a few camels, donkeys, and horses in the stalls. I got out of the coach just as Tom climbed down from his perch. He handed the boys who walked up to us some money, and they began unhitching our horses without a word.

Tom held out his hand to Emma, who took it and used the other to press her wide-brimmed hat wider. Despite her face being completely shaded, she grimaced. "It's already so hot. We shouldn't stay long."

I eyed their clothing choices, as I'd done before we left, but it was a little too late to say anything. Although they weren't wearing their wool, it was a similar style that seemed too heavy and constricting for the climate. The waists of Emma's dress and Tom's pants were right up against their bodies like they were tempting sweat. The truth was it was barely hot yet, but anyone would feel stifled so bound up in fabric, no matter what the weather.

"How long is 'long'?" I asked.

"Well, we want to make the visit worth the long drive." Emma looked at Tom to agree with her. "I could probably stand an hour."

He nodded. "That's long enough for a little breakfast. We'll need that energy for when Peggy rails on us."

An hour. When the drive round trip was twice as long. Illogical, but the least of my worries at the moment. "An hour it is," I said. "I'll meet you back here then."

I didn't go straight to the church. Instead I went to the goat market and bought some tej from the herder—the wine he made was stronger and better, not to mention less expensive, than anything the regular food market had. I had a feeling I'd need some liquid courage today.

For a moment I just marveled at the honey wine before indulging in a gulp. Sweet, then bitter, a little spiced, burning. It made me a little light-headed. Last time I'd lived with Jember was the last time I'd had any . . . it tasted like home.

And at that thought, the wine turned to poison in my mouth.

I put the bottle in my satchel and rushed into the protective net of roads. While the two main roads and marketplace were dust, the rest were cobblestone alleys, no wider than to allow either one cart or two adults walking comfortably side by side. And, on either side of the streets, a line of ten-foot-tall squared-off buildings made of concrete and cement, separated only by either the bright colors some had been painted or a perpendicular alley to continue the net.

The city had been designed to withstand war—if the enemy managed to get through the wall's defenses, they'd be met with a labyrinth to navigate if they ever wanted to reach the epicenter. But of course, wars had bypassed it completely, to the disappointment of the architects, I'm sure. Now the only people available for the labyrinth to confuse were tourists and drunks.

I wove through the streets quickly, trying not to seem rude as I greeted people without stopping.

Only when I reached the main square did I slow down.

The church was the oldest building in the city, weathered redstone raised on a platform of a dozen stairs. As regal as Thorne Manor, but more elegant and dignified. Even without the platform it was three times as tall as everything else, four flat walls attempting to reach the heavens.

I pulled my netela out of my satchel and covered my head, securing the scarf around my neck, before heading up the stairs casually so as not to draw negative attention.

The soothing rhythm of chanting grew with every step, opening up into an echo as I removed my sandals and stepped inside out of the sun. The colorful paintings of saints on the walls and pillars of the entryway greeted me with kindness and scrutiny in turns. Incense nipped and tickled my nostrils. A large white curtain blocked my view of the sanctuary, simultaneously blocking me from being instantly noticed. Everything was just as I'd left it.

It wasn't my home anymore, in the physical sense, but my mind felt more peaceful than it had in weeks.

The main sanctuary took up most of the first floor. Painted pillars surrounded it, creating a small walkway around the perimeter with a few rooms along the walls, their doorways blocked by heavy white curtains. In between each pillar was a large vase, all full of either water or various herbs, and I alternated between hiding behind those and the pillars. There were a handful of people standing in prayer in the direction of the altar, where Jember sat on the stairs constructing an amulet.

He wore his official debtera attire: a white turban—made slightly larger by containing the dreadlocks he refused to cut— and white robe striped with red, green, and yellow along the hem. And his official Jember attire: red leather gloves, a tall black boot on his left leg, and a peg leg made of dull metal on the right. His beard was unkempt, but his clothes were neat.

Mixed feelings rose up in me, watching him work. The first was that I'd missed him. But if I hadn't been witnessing him cutting intricate patterns with expert speed, that feeling might've been the last. It was the only admirable thing about him, really. His work.

Which was why not too far behind it was anger, an emotion I'd need to quell if I was going to stomach asking him for help.

I tried not to move, not only to respect the ritual, but to keep Jember from seeing me before I wanted him to. It was only a few minutes before he began a chant, the signal for the praying people to drink the small cup of holy water on the floor in front of each of them. I leaned a bit farther around the pillar to see what sort of Manifestations the amulets were for—a mistake. Jember glanced in my direction, not missing a note of the chant he was singing.

Maybe he didn't see me.

Right, Andi. Maybe the desert isn't hot.

That meant there was no surprising him. I had to be ready to approach him as soon as the ritual was over. No greeting, no small talk—Jember didn't have the patience for that. I would have to be clear and quick.

Finally, the prayer was finished, and each worshipper made the sign of the cross on themselves, touching forehead to chest, shoulder to shoulder. Jember wrapped each amulet in a simple cloth before handing it to each person in need, which they accepted with a bowed head and nothing but the sound of their footsteps as they left.

I slipped out from behind the pillar to prepare, and because I was curious about what sort of amulets he had made. For house hauntings, debtera had to go directly to the source. But if someone was having sudden bad luck, or sickly livestock, or their crops weren't doing well, a basic amulet for that purpose would usually deter the influence of the Evil Eye.

Those were the first types of amulet designs I learned to construct, even before Jember actually had a mind to teach me. It was the ritual that made them take a long time, not the construction itself.

I waited until the last person was leaving before stepping up to the altar. "Jember, I need your help."

He didn't bother to look at me as he gathered his things. "Just give me the name." His voice sounded strained.

I bit my lip. I'd had specific instructions—extremely specific, with equally graphic consequences if I were to disobey—from Jember while he was throwing me out: Don't bother him unless I was in danger. Couldn't find food? Figure it out. Nowhere to sleep? Not his problem. But if anyone threatened or tried to hurt me? That was the one and only issue I was allowed to bring to him.

I was pretty good at staying out of danger, partly because I'm small and know my physical limit and so try to stay out of people's way. But mostly, because I never wanted to have to go to him for help. I didn't want to give him the satisfaction of seeing him on his terms.

But I didn't have a name, and it didn't feel right giving one just to make him stop and listen to me, especially since whomever I named might end up dead by the afternoon.

"It's about a job," I said quickly. "This Manifes—"

He walked away without a glance. His legs were far longer than mine, so even with his limp I rushed to catch up.

"I just need to know if I cleansed it correctly," I said.

He still didn't stop. He was almost to the room at the back of the hall where—as an unlicensed debtera—I wasn't allowed. It was where the priests changed from their street clothes into their holy robes before services.

I ran in front of him to block the entryway. "Jember—"

"Don't bother me, girl."

Instead of allowing me to move of my own free will, he shoved me with the spine of the book he was holding against the side of my face. I stumbled to the side, grateful he hadn't full-on hit me, but angry at myself for not grounding myself better.

And then he disappeared behind the curtain of the room and I stood there for a moment in shock. A shock that was quickly turning to silent rage, like my head might burst like a pressed tomato. I wanted to call his name, but I felt ridiculous standing in the hall, begging for him to listen.

I took a deep breath. There was only one option. Well, two. I could do it the long, quiet way—wait until he was finished with everything and meet him at home. That would probably be another hour or two, and I might not get the information I wanted. Then there was always the quick way, which was . . . questionable. But I didn't have an hour or two to wait around.

So I took a deep breath . . .

I hadn't screamed so wildly in so long, it nearly shocked me to silence again as it echoed off the stone walls. But, immediately, I heard the desired reaction from the couple of priests on the other side of the curtain in the form of vague frightened exclamations and frantic footsteps. None of them left the room, so I screamed again.

Then, I saw Jember's bloodred glove peek through the curtain before he shoved it aside, his eyes glinting wild like those of an agitated lion. He still wore his turban but had shed his robes, leaving him in his white pants and undershirt—the same shirt he'd been wearing since I was five, so worn thin in places it looked on the verge of spontaneously tearing. He gripped his maqomiya, the long prayer staff grinding into the floor like it was trying to drill through it, and I couldn't fight the wince my body had long been conditioned to perform at the sight of it. I backed away a few steps, even though my mind rationalized that Jember hadn't disciplined me in years, and never within the walls of the church.

Not where the priests could see, anyway.

"Have you lost your mind?" he growled, approaching as quickly as I retreated.

"If I say yes will you listen to me?"

"I could lose my position if they find out it was you out here screeching like a—"

"There's a dangerous Manifestation that almost—" My bare foot faltered on the uneven stone floor and this time my cry was genuine as Jember caught the front of my loose netela, twisting it to bind it closer to my head, blocking me from escaping.

He used the fabric as a leash, half dragging me into a closet, then shoved me ahead of him. There were no candles inside, but there was enough light coming through the doorway that

I could catch myself against the shelves with my hands before I slammed into them face-first.

"I'm shocked, Andi," he said, slight amusement in his voice. "What would God say about your underhanded tantrum back there?"

I ground my teeth and shifted so I was on the side wall instead of completely boxed in. "God is merciful. Unlike you."

Jember shifted with me, half a snarl visible as the sun lit the side of his face. "I am merciful," he said, all the humor gone. "You can walk out on your own two legs or I can beat you unconscious and drag you down the front steps."

I'd pulled my knife, but now knew it wouldn't be necessary. I couldn't really see his face, but he was gripping the hand that had grabbed my scarf with his other, as if he'd punched a wall. He'd overreached, accidently touching my neck. For him, touching human skin was unbearable, even through those gloves. *Like shards of glass going through to the bone*, he'd said one day when I'd asked what it felt like.

It was due to his missing leg, which was due to the Evil Eye in some way. But asking him specifics was partly the reason I now winced at the sight of his maqomiya, so eventually I'd decided a little mystery in my life was best.

That being said, I should've been numb to his pain by now. I shouldn't have cared. I wished I didn't. But God, it still hurt my heart to see him wince.

Focus, Andi. He doesn't care. Why should you?

"Why are you determined not to help me?" I said.

He rested his painless hand on the horizontal handle on top of his staff, leaning his chin on his knuckles and taking the weight off his peg leg. "Why is an unlicensed debtera worried about Manifestations?"

It was a logical question, but still stung like an open wound. "I wouldn't be here asking for help if you hadn't thrown me out."

"Yes, you'd be married like the rest of the girls your age, irritating your husband right now instead of me."

I scoffed. "You didn't raise me to take much stock in marriage, what did you expect?"

"I expected you to make a decision based on good survival habits. You chose the street rather than a safe home and steady income." He dropped the hand he'd been soothing, gripping it into a fist and standing upright again. I should've found a safer place to stand during his respite. "You have three seconds to decide whether or not you walk out of here."

"I'll walk," I said. He wasn't going to beat me just now, despite his threat. He'd been up since the early hours constructing amulets. He was much bigger, and strong, but I'd always been faster. We both knew without it being said that he didn't have the energy.

Still, if I pushed him much more, a small dose of rage-adrenaline might be all he needed, and I had no desire to wake up behind the church with my eyes swollen shut.

"The room flooded with blood," I blurted quickly. "And it's done it before." Jember lifted his staff off the ground, and I took the opportunity to rush out into the hall. "He said the last time it happened it drowned him alive."

Jember knocked the staff against the stone wall, testing its strength. "He saw the Manifestation, *assumed* he'd drown, and the fear made his body mimic symptoms."

I paused. "That's possible. But—" I stumbled sideways and pressed my hand to the side of my head, nearly biting off my tongue. Sharp pain radiated through my scalp and I blinked a few times to clear my vision from the impact, only for it to be clouded again by tears. Stupid eyes, tearing. Traitors. "So it wasn't a dangerous Manifestation? Nothing to worry about?"

"You cannot drown and also be alive." Jember was in no rush to pursue me, walking, tapping the staff against the wall. "How did you secure a client without a license?"

I backed up to match his approach. This time I wouldn't be caught off guard. "He considered no licensure a benefit."

His eyes narrowed slightly. "In order to pay you less?" I could tell his mind was running through all the options of my circumstance, and it wouldn't be long before he landed on the correct one. Would he help me if he knew I was working a job he himself had refused?

"He paid me enough. I haven't starved to death, have I?"

He'd nearly herded me out to the main sanctuary, but suddenly stopped. "You can't keep this up much longer without a license. And you don't have the skill level to pursue a patronage."

"Whose fault is that?" I felt my face get hot, hate for him rising up again. "You said marry a stranger or live on the street. You gave me no choice but to take matters into my own hands."

"Are you looking for a new mentor?"

"What do you care, old man? You left me to die."

I stumbled back, the wind of the maqomiya's rush tickling my nose. I winced as it splintered against the wall, bracing myself against the opposite one to avoid the end that snapped and skittered across the ground. We were silent as it rolled and finally came to a stop. I never saw it, only heard, because I was glaring at him as he glared at me. Hate knotted the back of my throat, trapping my voice . . . hate to cover the pain, that mingled with fear, that tainted my longing.

His leg was hurting, I knew, because he didn't come after me.

Instead he gripped the ruined staff and watched me hate him, without giving me a reason to contradict myself.

Jember was truly heartless. I'd always known it, but now it felt confirmed. An empty shell of a human being. God, the thought of it made me want to weep, but I fought back the urge. He didn't deserve to see human emotions felt on his behalf . . . he didn't deserve to know that I wished—longed—for him to feel something for me in return. Something human, unprompted by necessity.

I winced, but the broken staff didn't come at me again. Instead he dropped it at my feet.

"Stop acting like a child, Andromeda," he said, his voice dark. "*You* chose this. Don't blame me for your poor survival habits."

He turned and left me longing for and hating him, the urge to cry building by the second.

I swallowed the tears back before they could cloud my eyes and rushed out of the church, the saints watching me go in concern and disappointment.

CHAPTER
12

As soon as I made it back to my room with my bag of supplies, I heard the quick stomp of feet accompanied by the harsh jangle of bells. I turned just in time to see Magnus shove the door wide and plant himself in the doorway.

His jaw was clamped tight enough that I could see the muscles there flex, his cheeks burning red.

"What am I paying you for?" he demanded. "What good are you to me if I don't know where you are?"

His hair was a frizzy mess, his green and blue Nehru-collared shirt just long enough to hide that he hadn't decided on pants yet. I looked away from his bare legs quickly—I didn't mind Jember pant-less, since I'd grown up with it, but for some reason seeing Magnus made me blush. I put the bag down on my bed and began sorting through it, careful to keep my new underthings out of sight. "I went shopping."

"You should've said something."

"Don't tell me you missed me."

He was still scowling, although he seemed to have calmed down from a moment ago. "You are the only human of substance in this house. I've been bored out of my mind for days."

"You've entertained yourself for three years, one extra day should be nothing."

He leaned his shoulder on the doorjamb. "Did you at least bring me something, for all my pain and suffering?"

"I should've brought you pants."

He looked down at himself quickly and rushed out of the doorway. I took the opportunity to put my underthings away while he was gone, but soon enough his socked feet came storming back.

"And another thing," he said, entering the room as he buckled his belt, "why is it so hot in here? Did you open a window? I can't stand the heat."

I rolled my eyes. "You complain too much."

"No one else seems to have a problem with it." He sat on my bed and looked up at me, raising his eyebrows. "So? What did you bring me?"

"Nothing. You're a brat." I folded the fabric bag, but Magnus took my hand to keep me from moving to put it away. His hand was cold, but soft. Smooth. I had the urge to rub it to warm it up, but kept still. "Do you have something to say to me?"

"At least tell me next time if you're going out." He released my hand, then gripped my blanket. "Look, sorry I fussed. I woke up and thought you had—I mean—" He stood up quickly, using his fingers as a comb as he walked toward the door. "Just explain yourself next time. It's common decency."

"I would never leave you before the job is done," I said, and he stumbled to a stop in the doorway.

He hugged himself, standing between the warm of my room and the cold of the hall, and then turned on his heel and walked back in. "So, what did you buy?"

"Just a few essentials."

"I could've gotten those for you. Next time just give me a list and I'll send someone."

"I needed to get out. It was a nice change of scenery."

"You used your bonus money?"

I smirked. But he looked so confused, I couldn't help it. "What else would I use?"

"You don't need to use your own money on things like this. Not when you live under my roof."

"I prefer to be independent."

"Is that why you got yourself thrown out of your training? To be independent?" When I didn't validate his rude questions with answers he tilted his head at me, like a confused puppy. "Why did you get thrown out, anyway? You never said."

"Because it's none of your business."

"Were you sleeping around with the priests?"

I gaped, glaring at him, then threw my pillow at his head. He barely caught it, stumbling into the hall. "You don't have to be so insufferable all the time, you know."

His eyes went wide. "Am I insufferable?"

His reaction implied this was new information, which was strange. Did no one have the nerve to stand up to him? "And disrespectful."

He nodded, hugging my pillow to his chest and leaning forward a bit, as if listening intently. "What else?"

There wasn't a hint of sarcasm in his question. I hesitated. "Impatient."

"That's true. Would you like higher pay?"

"No, Magnus—" I took a deep breath. "I want you to do better."

"You are the first debtera to complain about my personality."

"To your face."

"You think so?" He paused and looked down, wiggling his toes in his socks. "I was . . . a little panicked . . . when I saw you were gone. I thought you had left forever. I wonder if the others left because they couldn't handle me, as well."

"I can handle you, Magnus, even at your worst," I said, taking a step closer. At my movement he met my gaze again, his eyes full of hope, and something steady and pleasing like contentment. "But that doesn't mean you can get away with being a brat all the time. You're a good person, I know. It would just be nice if you'd show it sometimes."

"I can be good. Can I get you anything?"

"Was that a genuine question?"

He looked at me as if I had to have been joking. "Yes. I want to guarantee you never leave me again."

I smirked. "That would've almost been nice if it wasn't so self-serving."

"You're irreplaceable, Andromeda, I hope you know that."

"Tell me, and I'll know."

Magnus paused, as if shocked that I would make such a demand. "You're irreplaceable." He dropped his gaze suddenly, rubbing at his face and scowling at his feet. "But I'm still paying you to do a job. So no more taking off."

"Yes, sir."

"Hearing you say 'sir' drains the life from me. You will kill me before old age does."

"Magnus," I corrected.

"Yes?"

I bit my lip to keep myself from laughing.

He opened his mouth to speak, then just cleared his throat instead. Then, after a moment, "Did you miss me, at least?"

I could feel my heart pounding in my throat. It was strange, to feel pleased and nauseated at the same time. "Not particularly."

He raised an eyebrow. "Vicious girl. After all my efforts to be nice to you."

"What efforts?"

"I said you're irreplaceable, didn't I? Not to mention I inconvenienced myself to walk down the hall and put on trousers."

"You're my employer, you should be wearing them in the first place."

"I mean—" He paused, a sheepish blush spreading across his cheeks. He picked up my bottle of tej, twisting the neck in his hands. "Yes, you're right. As Esjay says, we wouldn't want a lawsuit."

His reaction was . . . adorable. But admitting that, I could feel my own blush flaring up, so I quickly buried the word somewhere to keep myself under control. "You mean pantlessness is an ongoing problem for you?"

"*One* other time is not 'ongoing.'" He uncorked the bottle, recoiling before it'd even made it to his lips. "Oh God! This orange juice has gone rancid."

"It's honey wine," I said, taking the bottle from him and cradling it close. He coughed, then dry heaved like a cat with a hairball. I rolled my eyes. "That's what you get for not asking before taking a sip."

"It's putrid." He swallowed with effort. "I feel a little tipsy just from smelling it."

"Oh, hush. That's not how alcohol works." I took his arm to

escort him to the door, and he placed his hand on top of mine, heat and life burning their soothing mark on me. "I'd like to get a little rest if you don't mind."

"Of course, Andromeda," he said, patting my hand, "whatever you need."

I raised my eyebrows at him. "Thank you?"

He stepped out into the hall. "Would you like to eat together? In a few hours, when you're awake?"

I nodded.

He leaned on the doorjamb, drumming his fingers on it before taking a deep breath and looking at me. "I really am . . . *so* pleased you're back."

And then he left me, too abruptly for me to respond, as was his custom. Awkward man. Awkward, difficult . . . funny . . . sometimes sweet . . . absolutely adorable man.

I was blushing, but this time I wouldn't stop it, even if there had been someone there to see.

"I'm glad to be back, too," I called to his still-open bedroom door, then shut my own door for a nap.

CHAPTER
13

A knock on the door woke me from my nap, and when I opened it Saba was beaming at me, holding a fancy box in her hands.

"Hi, Saba," I said, scratching my scalp. "I really hope those are chocolates."

She raised her eyebrows as if to say *I really hope you're kidding,* and opened the box to reveal bottles and jars, creams and oils.

I gaped. And then let out a sound I hadn't heard from myself in a long time.

It was the excited squeal of a little kid.

"Are these yours?" I asked, and I couldn't begin to hide my eagerness.

Saba shook her head, her grin widening.

"Mine?" I asked, even though I knew . . . still couldn't believe it. But knew.

Saba prompted me to take the box, but I hardly needed prompting, rushing to rest it on my bed so I could sit and sort through it. Soaps, lotions, scrubs. Oils I could've never afforded before this job, not unless I saved money for months. I would've never in my life dreamed of even touching the bottles with my fingertips, let alone having the chance to use what was inside them.

Saba set a small wooden tub on the floor and put some water over the fire to heat. Then she began taking down my hair, examining it as she went. She took a pair of silver shears from the box of oils and showed it to me.

"Yes, thank you," I said. "I need a trim really badly, I'm sure."

Saba squeezed my shoulders and then grabbed a comb and got to work. I sat quietly, nothing but memories filling my head.

"The last time I had my hair cut," I said, "it was at the beginning of my debtera training . . . Jember had to shave it off. The priests didn't want the threat of lice, I suppose."

I mostly remember crying in the alley behind the church, while Jember sat behind me with a straight razor. Not because it hurt or because I was attached to my hair, but because of why it had to be done—because a few men who would never interact with me were worried I would potentially bring bugs into the church.

Because they thought I was dirty.

But this time was different. With each *snip* of the shears my head felt lighter. As a servant, Saba probably had to do this sort of thing all the time, but I could tell she wasn't doing it because it was her job. She was doing it because she . . . *cared*.

When she was finished snipping and combing, she mimed taking off clothing. I hesitated, then locked the bedroom door before peeling off my clothes and placing them on my bed, though I kept on my amulet—after that first Waking, there was no way I was taking it off again.

Saba handed me a jar and demonstrated a circular rubbing

motion on her own arms. I nodded, and she helped me sit in the tub. Inside the jar was sugar, from the smell of it, mixed with fragrant oils. The water she poured over my head was hot but not scalding, and then I took some of the concoction in my hands and started scrubbing. It was . . . I'd never felt anything like it. Definitely less abrasive than sand, and the silky after-feel of the oils was, in a word, heavenly. Meanwhile, Saba had started scrubbing my scalp with the oils sans sugar, and I nearly had to pause what I was doing to take it all in.

If I had to rank the best feelings in the world, having my scalp massaged would come in at a close third, right behind having a full stomach and the ability to easily empty my bowels. It was miraculous. I closed my eyes to better remember the full sensation of the oil warming with the friction of movement, the comfort of rhythmic circles on my scalp, the satisfaction of fingers finally being able to run through the length of my hair without any trouble from tangles.

By the time I was done I felt lighter, as if ten pounds of hard times and grit had been stripped away.

I honestly didn't know if I had ever been this clean. But if I thought about it too much I was bound to cry.

Saba rinsed me off with a few buckets of cold water, which would've felt much worse if my room hadn't been heated with an amulet. She made me dress again, then sat me in front of the mirror to style my hair into albaso braids—thicker and thinner braids alternating on the scalp, releasing midway in a burst of curls at the back of my head. Curls. Actual curls instead of frizz. It looked sweet. *I* looked sweet. And healthy, and . . . better than I'd looked my whole life.

There wasn't much she could do for my unextraordinary face, and maybe I was stupid to refuse the makeup she offered.

But there was only so much of a cleanup job I could take before I disappeared into someone else's ideal. So far, I felt like myself, only cleaner.

It felt good. I hoped people didn't take this for granted, feeling clean, looking presentable. I certainly didn't. It'd taken a few hours, but was worth every minute. It might've been the best thing that ever happened to me.

"Thank you, Saba," I breathed. I touched the ends of my hair, the split, damaged ends replaced by relatively soft strands, then looked at my friend's pleased expression in the mirror. "Can you believe it? I didn't talk that entire time."

Saba gasped and hunched over my chair, shoulders shaking. I leapt up and leaned my knee on the seat to see what was wrong, a grin abruptly replacing my grimace. She was laughing. It was a joyful experience to watch, and I joined in without questioning the impulse.

"You might just be my favorite person," I said, grabbing her—oh my—surprisingly hard shoulder. "You've got solid muscles. I assume it's from Magnus making you do all the hard work around here."

Saba rolled her eyes, but with a slight, forgiving grin.

"I should get back to work before Magnus loses his mind again," I said, leaning forward. I paused. Would Saba be comfortable with a hug?

No. I wasn't going to overstep the boundaries of the only friend I'd ever had. Besides, I didn't have much experience with hugs, and had a feeling I would mess it up.

"Let me help you clean up first," I said, to which Saba held up her hands and shook her head. She grinned and handed me my basket of supplies, then shooed me out of the room and shut the door behind me. I found myself staring at my own closed door.

Everyone in this house was so strange. But at least Saba was the good kind.

I made my way downstairs. Between that trip to town, my nap, and that much overdue makeover, I'd spent most of the day not working. Then again, it wasn't as if I'd ever taken a day off before.

There was a strange sound as soon as I made it down the stairs and around the corner, like the countering plucks of an instrument. I'd heard it before, my first night here—a night so terrifying, I'd nearly forgotten it had begun with beautiful music. I followed the song to find Magnus playing a small piano. It was elaborately decorated, just like everything else he liked. The rest of the room was draped in white sheets, and with the curtains flung open letting in the rich sunlight, dust floating in the rays like magic, it almost looked ethereal. The room was cold, just like the others, but somehow it didn't feel so cold today.

I put my basket down and leaned on the piano, watching him for a moment before saying, "Your piano's broken."

Magnus glanced up, then did a double take and fumbled over a few notes as if he hadn't expected to see me. Or, more likely, he was shocked that I was actually put together. I let out a breath of laughter and he blushed, giving me a sheepish grin before turning back to his music.

I don't know why I laughed. It's not like I found startling him to be funny.

"You look nice," he said. It sounded like an incomplete thought. Instead of finishing it he played with the edge of the page, folding and unfolding.

"Um, thank you. Saba cut my hair for me." And it was better conditioned than it'd been in years, but he didn't have to know everything. "She seems really devoted to you. I hope you pay her well."

"Oh, Saba gets whatever she wants. What's mine is hers."

I doubted that, but with Magnus it was better to deal with one issue at a time. "I mean a salary for her work."

"She isn't paid a salary. She has access to my fortune, same as I do. One of the benefits of being a longtime friend," he said, resuming the quick, canonic notes. "And this is a harpsichord, by the way. Not a piano." He played on for a moment. "You're worse than any specter in this house. Do you mean to intimidate me, Andromeda, with all your looming and interrogation?"

He'd ended our conversation very deliberately, but I couldn't find it in myself to be annoyed. I'd get my answers eventually. "I doubt that's possible, Magnus."

I liked the way he smiled when I said his name. At least, I imagined that's why he smiled. More likely it was because he couldn't play and also turn the page quick enough, which was what he was struggling with now.

He glanced up at me again. "I suppose you can't intimidate an equal."

"I'm your employee. There's really nothing equal about our relationship."

"You're doing me a great favor. And in exchange, I'm doing you one."

"You hired me. You're paying me."

"Yes, but you didn't have to take the job. Besides, we are equal in more ways than that." We were quiet, the music taking over the room. "I need you to turn my pages."

"'Please.'"

"Please, what?"

I rolled my eyes. "You mean, 'Please, Andromeda, will you turn my pages?'"

"Well, will you or won't you? I'm getting to the end and I'd rather not stop."

"Say 'please' and I'll think about it."

His fingers tripped over themselves, ending in a *plunk*. And then he lifted his gaze, hesitantly, like nerves were getting the better of him. But his gaze was getting the better of me. I liked when he looked at me, but this was too steady, too invasive. I wasn't about to let him figure me out before I could gauge him.

He's not your enemy, Andi.

Still, my voice came out slightly tight as I demanded, "Why are you staring at me?"

"Because I can," he replied, almost casually.

"I'd prefer you didn't."

"I can't help it. You don't . . ." The longer he hesitated, the more uncomfortable his expression became. ". . . *vanish* when we look at each other."

My muscles froze for a moment, but it wasn't due to the cold. "Vanish?"

"Every time I look someone in the eye, the next morning they're gone. All of their things still in their room, like they never existed. Simply . . . vanished."

I chewed on my lip for a moment. "Everyone in the house should be wearing an amulet."

"They won't wear them. Peggy's old, and really superstitious of anyone who isn't Protestant. When I tried to tell her that I thought I was the cause of the disappearances, she thought I was having a mental breakdown. She knew it was the curse, but she wouldn't believe it was me directly. That's when I came up with the rule list. If no one was going to listen to me, I could at least keep everyone away."

"Why not just add amulets to the rule list?"

He shook his head. "They won't wear it. Not even Esjay and Kelela could convince them."

"It makes sense now," I said, gesturing to his wrists. "Why you wear the bells."

He nodded. "So people hear me coming."

"I thought you just liked irritating everyone."

Magnus grinned up at me again. I sort of loved that grin. "Saba's been my only real friend in three years. I have a hard time connecting with people when I can't look at them . . . I like to see people's eyes."

His gaze drew me in like a beacon. It was difficult to think when he was looking at me so fully.

"What are you playing?" I said quickly, looking down at where his music sat.

"A Bach sonata." His face first lit up, then cringed. "Very badly. His pieces are extremely law-abiding, and I've never been good with precision."

I had no idea what he was talking about, but he seemed to have forgotten about hypnotizing me with his eyes, which was the end goal. "It sounded wonderful to me."

"Do you know Bach?"

"I don't know any foreign music."

"Oh good. Then you won't know the difference when I butcher another one."

My laugh sounded choked from trying to stifle it, and I buried my face in my arms until I could regain my composure—which only took a few seconds, but still. "Maybe if you practiced music as much as you drew you wouldn't be so disappointed in yourself."

Magnus had a mask of offense over his amusement. "God, Andromeda. Stop making me reflect on my own failures. What a cruel punishment."

"Then practice more."

"I'd rather not work that hard."

"Then be content with mediocrity."

This time when he gaped at me it was real. He played with the edge of the page again. "You truly are terrifying sometimes. Not in a horror sort of way, but . . . you make me feel things brutally. And think things deeply. And you make me sweat a lot. Nothing is easy with you. And, to be honest, after a lifetime of people kissing up to me . . . I actually quite like this change."

I felt heat rising up my neck. I don't know why. It wasn't exactly clear that his speech had been a compliment. "You're a strange man."

"A compliment, coming from you." That hopeful, boyish grin widened when I smirked at him. He patted the piano bench. "Would you like to sit down?"

I paused, then slowly slid around the instrument and lowered myself to the bench. Magnus held a lot of heat, as men tended to naturally do, and I found myself sitting right up against him, arm to arm. He was taller than me up close. Don't know why I was noticing that now.

Anyway, it was nicer than standing. Here the sun hit my back, taking the edge from the cold.

I felt him lean closer and something touched my hair—maybe his nose, since I was looking at his hands folded in his lap. "You smell nice," he said.

"And you sound surprised. Did I stink before?"

"Everything around here smells like this dank house. I never noticed."

I swatted his music book off its stand, like an angry cat, smirking the entire time as he scowled at me. "What do you mean you 'never noticed'?"

His scowl slowly crept into a smile, as if he wasn't used to doing it genuinely. "I mean how a person smells is of little consequence."

I couldn't remember what had been said afterward in that previous conversation, so we paused there while I tightened my lips against a smile. I was enjoying this exchange a little too much. I turned back to face the—what had he called it? Hopsicar?—running my finger along its decorations. "Thank you for my creams and oils," I said, changing the subject to something that made me feel less . . . giddy.

"Thank Saba, she's the one who knows about those things." He looked down at me. "Now, would you *please* turn my pages?"

I smiled. The warmth of his body sent overwhelmingly sweet tickles through mine, even through my sweater. "Only because you asked so nicely."

He reached down and grabbed his book from the floor, opening it up to a song, bending it back to break the spine a bit. "Do you read?"

"Music? No. Jember taught me hymns orally."

"Then I'll nod when I'm ready, shall I?"

I nodded in response, leaning forward in preparation.

And he began.

This one was like oil pouring on the floor—slow, flowing, but somehow unpredictably messy. Not his playing, but the melody. The meaning of it. Like a romance in the midst of turmoil.

"I'm in the way," I said, as his warm arm brushed past me for a high note.

"You're never in the way," Magnus said, and somehow it felt like more than the truth.

He nodded and my heart skittered, as stupid as that seemed, not resuming a steadier pace until I'd successfully turned the page and listened to him continue without a hitch.

"Is page turning always this stressful?"

Magnus laughed, missing a few notes. He was getting better at laughing, I think. It sounded more natural. "Why do you think I get someone else to do it?"

"Evil Eye Manifestations are much easier."

"For you, definitely. You've done the most cleansing out of any of the other debtera."

I started to turn the page, but Magnus made a *tut*-ing sound at me, like shooing a cat off the table. "You nodded!" I said.

"The other way, it's a repeat."

"What's a repeat?"

"Back to the beginning!"

My arm shot to the other page to turn it, but I yanked too fast and the book toppled off onto the keys. Magnus jerked his hands out of the way and laughed. Not in malice or sarcasm, but an adorably genuine one, like a little boy hearing the greatest joke ever. And it was catching, his laughter igniting mine.

I think . . . I could've survived on that laugh alone, if surviving in this world didn't require money.

I shoved him in the arm. "I told you I don't read music."

He wrapped his arm around my shoulders, hugging me, and I felt my breath catch before forcing myself to breathe normally. "You did wonderfully for your first try," he said, still grinning from his laughter, and picked up the music book from the floor.

His arm had to leave me to do it, and I missed it as soon as it left. He paused in getting up, looking beyond me.

I turned to see blood leaking down the walls from the ceiling. It was much easier to construct an amulet when the Manifestation was currently taking place. I had to cleanse it before it went away.

"It doesn't hurt anyone," Magnus said as I stood. "Stay."

Magnus's words made me pause. I looked down at him still sitting on the bench, and he had that hopeful look, same as the night he'd given me those chocolates. That look unnerved me like no other look ever had. It didn't want anything other than human interaction, eye contact, some sort of friendly affection. I was the only one who could give that to him, and part of me felt selfish for denying him something I took for granted every day. But cleansing this house was the only way to save him, so he'd never have to rely on one person so fully again.

Then again, another part of me felt selfish for a different reason . . . for not wanting to save him. For wanting to keep that beautiful, hopeful look to myself.

A sound of disgust for myself slipped out, and I watched his face drop, and all of me wanted to erase the last few seconds and start over without that impulsive sound.

"Magnus," I tried, "I—"

"You're right." He stood quickly, but he wasn't looking at me anymore, and something about losing that contact with him made my throat tight. "Cleansing the Evil Eye takes priority. I'll leave you to your work."

And he left. Just like that. Didn't hesitate, didn't look at me. And my tight throat wouldn't allow me to call his name.

CHAPTER
14

———— ❧ ————

Magnus had holed himself up in his room for the rest of the day, so the next morning I dressed and went straight to where I knew he would be—the library. The curtains on the tall windows were drawn, with so little light seeping under that if I lived in this room I would've thought it was still night. Magnus didn't look to be here, but a used plate sat on the small table and enough candles were lit to be dangerous in a roomful of books, so he couldn't be far.

A book flew from the shelf and slapped open onto Magnus's chair. I touched my knife on instinct. "Magnus?" No answer. I suddenly felt silly. Books jumping off shelves was normal in a cursed house . . . I assumed.

It had to be the work of the bloody woman, from the drawing Magnus had been working on my first day here. The Librarian, he had called her. Didn't she leave him messages through books?

I went to the chair and picked up the open book and the stack of books beneath, sitting and placing them on my lap. The top book was open to a passage circled in dark ink—no, not ink, I realized, as I smoothed the page and it smudged on my fingers, showing red in the firelight. It was as if the Librarian had touched her bloody lips and drawn with her finger.

Don't provoke me—wretched, headstrong girl! Or in my immortal rage I may just toss you over . . .

It had to be a message for me. A threat, just like the night of that first dinner. But, just like the last one, it seemed to be nothing but words—a threat that would never be carried out. I shut the book and put it on the small table beside me, the bright white words *The Iliad* staring at me from the black cover.

I looked at the book that remained on my lap, a sketchbook open to a sheet nearly filled with rows of hands in different grasping positions.

The next page I flipped to was more of the same—rows and rows of hands. The next made me pause. Kelela, from the shoulders up. Five different versions, different hair. All of her profile. All a bit sketchy, without much detail, but all exceptionally good.

And beautiful. Not more or less beautiful than she was in person. A perfect representation of her.

It was irritating, to look at such a beautiful drawing. No. It was irritating to look at such a beautiful drawing of *Kelela*.

I can't believe I'm jealous of a silly piece of art.

The next page made me pause longer.

My ears felt hot. A couple, embracing in the shadows of the bookcases. Like the others, it was sketchy and unfinished, but it wasn't too hard to tell what was happening.

"What are you doing?" Magnus stormed toward me, catching

himself on the chair with one hand beside my head as he slapped his sketchbook shut with the other. His fingers were spread, as if barring the surface area from being accessed, his palm pressing the book into my thighs.

"What are *you* doing?" I warned. I'd drawn my knife on instinct, leveling it with his throat, then thought better of it and put the knife away quickly. I could beat Magnus easily, knife or no. Besides, he was harmless. This confrontation wasn't deserving of a knife.

His eyes were wide, like he suspected the weapon. "Trying to kill me?"

I lifted my chin defiantly. "Of course not. I don't get paid if you die."

"Well then," he faltered, "do you mind? I don't go looking through your things."

I should've told him to move. I didn't. "I didn't know it was private. I'm sorry."

Magnus drooped slightly, as if he'd expected a different reaction out of me. "What do you think of my drawings?"

I thought they were excellent. But for some reason I couldn't bring myself to say it. "You draw a lot of hands."

"I draw things I care about."

All of the drawings of Kelela appeared in my mind to taunt me, and I winced. "Does Kelela know how often you draw her?"

"I only draw her when she asks, so yes."

"What about that scandalous one of you two kissing? Does she know about that one?"

He smirked. "Is that Kelela? You can't see her face. It could be anyone, really, if you use your imagination."

My pulse raced, and for a moment I allowed myself to imagine that maybe he hadn't drawn Kelela. That maybe he had drawn . . . me. But reality won out. "I don't think she'd appreciate you drawing her that way."

"I think you're cross," he said, leaning closer, "because you want to be the one I'm kissing."

I slapped him across the face, so hard I turned his head. I held my breath for an instant, as if my mind had just rejoined my body. It was as if . . . he had heard my thoughts.

"Retrospectively . . ." Magnus shifted his jaw a few times to check its balance, removing his hand from his sketchbook to rub his face. "I deserved that."

It was all instinct, I should've said. I was used to having to protect myself. But he didn't deserve an explanation, let alone an apology.

I put the sketchbook on the table and tried to rise from the chair, but Magnus didn't back away to accommodate me. I scowled up at him. "You're in my space."

"*Your* space? That's my chair you're sitting in."

"Let me up, Magnus."

He smiled, teasing me. "What's the magic word? You know that one you keep telling me to use . . . ?"

I knew what Jember would do. Knife to Magnus's throat, his magic word would simply be "Move." Maybe even with an ornamental swear. And then Magnus would have three seconds to obey before Jember dug out his esophagus.

But all I could manage was to release a heavy breath, like my body was swearing without the aid of words. Because he was right about one thing—I wanted nothing more than to drag his warm body into this chair, to see if his lips tasted like the honey and nutmeg he kept near his coffee.

But I wasn't allowed to want that, was I? He was my employer. Besides, he was infuriating.

It was strange to make eye contact with our faces so close, but I forced a firm glare to show him I was serious. "You can't bully me."

Magnus's brows creased. "I'm not trying to bully you."

"Then move," I said, scooting forward, despite his effort to barricade me. Usually I could intimidate him, but he stood firm, and my face came that much closer to his. "Or should I hit you harder?"

"I welcome it," he said, his voice dark. "Your palm was the most human contact I've had all year."

His words made me freeze, tears pricking the backs of my eyes. To want someone to touch you in any way possible . . . even if it hurt you. It was a twisted, sad way to think.

But then . . . I hadn't been raised with touch. I'd been raised to avoid it whenever possible. So I had to empathize; imagine being raised with that luxury and then having it stolen away.

I couldn't be upset with him. He was tactless and rude, but he was a product of his condition, as well. He was unchecked, but also unnurtured. His poor behavior wasn't all his fault . . . and my poor behavior wasn't helping.

Gently, I laid my hand against his still-red cheek and kissed him.

It was the far extreme, and maybe it was as wrong as hitting him. I didn't care. His soft lips pressed hard against mine at first, as if he'd lost his footing, but then I heard the crumple of stuffed leather as he adjusted his grip on the back of the chair. Even when his lips lifted away from mine, they never quite left me, his uncertainty as adorable as it was unbearable. He pressed closer and the warmth of his body sent my heart racing—

And then he jerked back, stumbling toward the fire. He caught himself on the mantel just as I reached to catch him. But

I stopped just short of touching him, instead hugging my own arms, holding myself steady.

"Why did you do that?" he asked. Angrily. *Painfully.*

My heart hummed like a mouse's in my ear, but I managed to look him in the eye. His expression was more conflicted than his tone suggested. How could I tell him *why?* What answer could I possibly give that would make sense to either of us?

Thankfully, he didn't wait for me to figure it out. "I don't deserve to be kissed."

"Why not?"

"I am . . . a monster, Andromeda." The heat of his face near mine froze me still. I suddenly realized I wasn't looking in his eyes anymore. I was looking at his smooth skin, warm and umber in the fire and dim, the curve of his neck calling to my fingers to run the length of it. "But, then again, if affection is your contribution to my humanity, then by all means . . ."

His whisper was like molten silver, beautiful and dangerous at once.

My heart pounded. My stomach hurt. Sometimes I hated how sick empathy made me feel. Or maybe I just hated that I was thinking of that drawing, of those lovers in the shadows of the bookcases . . . of how the two of us could be living that moment now if we stepped away from the fire just a few feet . . .

Despite my annoyance with myself, I had to bite my lip to keep from tasting his again. I backed away to a more appropriate distance. "You're a heathen. You just like to stir people up."

He raised his thick eyebrows. "Did I stir you, Andromeda?"

I blushed, and Magnus—the little demon—smiled.

"S-stop that," I said.

"*You* kissed *me*, remember?"

I snatched up his sketchbook and shoved it into his chest. My force showed in the shock of his expression.

"Peggy is rude," I said, scrambling for anything I could to change the subject. "If she doesn't start treating me and Saba like her equals, I can't work here anymore."

Magnus's expression dropped into confusion, followed by distress. "I'll take care of it."

"Good. I'm . . . I'm going to leave, now."

"You really shouldn't get too attached to her." His voice stopped me as I spun on my heel.

"What do you mean?"

"As soon as you cleanse the entire castle Saba will leave. At the rate you've been working, that shouldn't be too long."

I spun slowly back around on my heel to look at him. "Is she your caretaker while you're cursed?"

"You could say that." He closed his sketchbook and hugged it to himself. "She's the most important person in the world to me. I love her like family. But I'm telling you not to get too attached."

"Are you trying to tell me who I can and cannot make friends with?"

"I'm telling you you'll regret it if you do."

I opened my mouth to speak, then changed my mind and left the room. It wasn't worth it, arguing. It's not like he could stop me from keeping the only friend I'd made here. The only person in the house I cared about.

Except, no. That wasn't true, and the thought of it made my stomach flutter in excitement.

Because, if I was honest with myself, I cared far too much for Magnus, too.

CHAPTER
15

—⁓—

I managed to avoid Magnus for two days straight after that. I had no choice. That kiss had been . . . surprising. Mortifying and wrong, and yet, somehow it felt like the truest thing I'd ever done. I wanted it again . . . and again . . . my God, what was wrong with me?

I had kissed my employer, and the more time we both had to forget about it the better.

I waited until I could hear him playing Bach to head to the library. It was about time I cleansed the Librarian, although I could tell she was going to give me a hard time. She was an extremely interactive Manifestation, which was normally a sign that she wasn't going to give up her position easily. But from what Magnus had told me, it seemed she could only interact through the books. So, at least I wouldn't have to worry about this evil spirit murdering me with the fireplace poker.

I peeked in the room first to make sure it was vacant. Just entering the library with my basket I felt the atmosphere move, as if the Librarian could see what I was about to do. I ignored it and sat in the chair by the fire. The sooner I started, the sooner I'd be done, and this one would probably take about two hours and two amulets—one to lock it to erase the threat of interaction, one to cleanse it completely. The less time I wasted in here the more likely—

I heard a thump, and from the corner of my eye saw when the book fell to the floor.

Time to work.

I worked quickly but carefully. I didn't want to have to start over. Ten minutes in, a book plopped onto the ground and skidded to a stop at my feet. I ignored it. A few minutes later another one landed on top of the first. I folded my legs beneath me and kept working. That kept happening for the next twenty minutes, until my amulet was pounding and I could identify the page of the top book without leaning over.

Something bright red, something that wasn't on the other books, caught my eye. I paused, venturing a quick look at it.

I glanced at the top of the page, where the title sat beside the page number in the header. *Jane Eyre.* I'd never read that one, but from what I heard it was a romance. A significant one, apparently, because a paragraph was circled in red, wide and uneven as if by a finger.

When we are struck at without a reason, we should strike back again very hard; I am sure we should—so hard as to teach the person who struck us never to do it again.

The room was cold to begin with, but I suddenly felt frozen.

I heard a drop of water drip from somewhere onto the sphere of protection my amulet created. It sounded muted and distant, but somehow close all at once. I watched the drop of liquid slide down the outside of the invisible shield, leaving a red trail behind it.

I swallowed to keep my throat clear and strong. "You can't threaten me. We both know you don't belong here."

It dripped again and I looked up, freezing but trying not to show fear as I looked into the face of the Librarian. She leaned over me, her skeletal hands resting on the back of my chair, her full lips dripping a thick, deep red.

I looked away quickly, hesitating before striking the flint on my pen again. "You can't hurt me," I declared, and proved it by pressing on with my work.

It felt like ages, but was probably only a minute or two, when the sound of dripping finally stopped. The anticipation of the vile liquid made me wince, ready for it. I released a breath.

And then something flapped by my head, just skimming my scalp before passing and tumbling onto the floor beyond me. I looked up briefly. A paperback book. If there was a message meant for me, it was an ill-chosen prop, the spine not heavy or broken enough to stay open. But hard, sharp pain at the back of my head quickly followed it, something heavy knocking my shoulder and dropping beside me in the chair, scaring me to my feet. I held the amulet and my pen with one hand, grabbing the back of my head with the other as I backed into the fireplace. My scalp throbbed when I removed my hand, and I—God help me—stared at the red smudge on my palm that the stinging and throbbing told me was more mine than the dripping from earlier. My trembling hand dropped from my view slightly as I gaped at the heavy book occupying my chair.

It wasn't open deliberately, like the initial pile was. No, this book was sending a different message, same as the paperback.

A message that might kill me if I didn't work quickly.

Another book vaulted off a shelf toward me, and I ducked and dodged away. I hid beside the chair, shielding my head with my arm just in time for another book to fall on my head. I shoved to my feet, running out the door to hide beside the doorway, just as another book came flying out the door, the spine breaking against the wall across from me.

I stood against the wall, panting. The books had stopped . . . but I couldn't feel much from the Librarian either. It was as if, as soon as I'd left the room, the chalk marks in my mind had been smudged, all feeling from them fuzzy. So then . . . there was no way to cleanse the library from the safety of outside the door. I had no choice but to get back in there.

I took one last deep breath and rushed back inside.

My heart was pounding. My head was throbbing. My amulet was pulsing, like it hadn't been outside of the room. I should've analyzed the situation before rushing in, because the onslaught began immediately. I ducked, a dictionary just missing my head.

The Manifestation can't touch me herself.

I blocked two paperbacks with my forearms in front of my face.

That's why she's using the books. If I can just—

A heavy impact on my shoulder made me stumble—but in the right direction. There were two bookshelves against the wall, with no more than two or three feet in between them.

If I can just barricade—

I ducked under a book and ran to the fireplace, my body knowing what to do without even finishing the thought. I shoved the items off the small round table between the chairs— something shattered on the floor, but there was no time—and picked it up by two of its legs. Two books slammed me in the hip and arm, as if trying to make me drop the table, but I grimaced and raced it over to the small space I'd found.

It just fits—

I growled out my pain as a book hit me, sharp end in the back, and turned around quickly to swat another one away with my forearm.

Now to guard the front—

I dodged around a book and skidded to a stop, the heat of the fire at my backside as I grabbed the arms of one of the leather chairs and pushed. It must've been solid wood underneath all that stuffed leather, or else it had just been in the same spot so long that it was stubborn to move—

I gritted my teeth against the books that fell on my lower back and leg, putting my entire body into pushing the chair. It started to move, but my momentum was thrown off by a heavy book to the side of my face. I fell to the hardwood, grabbing my stinging temple. I panted, drained. My head was ringing. Through my blurring vision I saw a gigantic atlas lying beside me.

Another book followed it, and I held back just in time before biting my tongue off.

Get up, Andi. You can't just lie here and get murdered by books.

I tried to push myself up with my other hand, a dizzy spell and another book to my side nearly putting me back on the ground. There was the distinct tickle of liquid running down my face, creeping down my temple. I licked my lips, tasting the salt of my own tears to join the blood on my tongue. The hand at my temple came away red, and I grasped for the chair.

"Oh my God," I gasped. "Help me . . ."

And then I heard muddled pounding. There was a rush and a shadow of something coming toward me, though it seemed to be taking the ground instead of the air. I panicked briefly, shielding my head and face with both arms. Instead of an impact, a metal-lic clang echoed, scaring me out of my cower.

Someone stood in front of me, feet wide apart and ready for action, whatever was in their hands blinding me as it reflected in the firelight. I swiped my wrist across my eyes to clear my vision, my heart suddenly racing faster.

Magnus stood in front of me, a metal serving tray in both hands. My heart swooped in excitement as I watched him use it to swat an incoming book out of the way.

"You made her angry, Andromeda," he said. "I think she likes you even less than me."

I chuckled, despite the life-threatening situation.

I tried twice to get up, the third time mastering it just in time to lift my hand in defense against a book. Magnus smacked it out of the way for me, but I was too disoriented to protest as he herded me into the little corner nook between the edge of the mantel and the wall, his body blocking me in, the tray held over our heads. It blocked out most of the light, and I had to blink to adjust.

"Get ready to run," he said. "I'll cover you."

I wiped the remainder of the blinding tears from my eyes with the back of my hand, so I could really look at him. He looked tired, his eyes dark, his brows grave and creased with an-noyance. I wondered if he had gotten any more sleep than I had.

I flinted my pen. "Do you mind standing there while I work?"

"Standing here?"

I heard the tinny clang of a book hitting the tray, but it didn't stop me from carving a few strokes into the silver. This arrange-ment was working perfectly. "And blocking the books while I work. I promise, I'll make it up to you."

"Are you out of your mind? We have to get you out."

A book hit the wall beside us, and my breath caught as Magnus leaned closer. I couldn't press my back any closer to the wall, as if that was any logical way to escape what I was feeling, anyway. His body did more than warm me, now. Everything in me wanted to continue what we'd started the other night.

But I had work to do. And he was infuriating.

"Magnus," I said firmly.

"Andromeda?" he asked, almost too lightly, with a hint of teasing that drove my nerves up the wall—and, my God, was that a good or bad thing?

"I know you're fond of this Manifestation, but they all have to go at some point."

"Not at the cost of your safety." He wrapped an arm around my waist, and for a moment I thought my knees would collapse beneath me. "Consider it a settling of my debt. A life for a life."

"You don't owe me your life, Magnus." He positioned himself in front of me, taking small steps, using his body to try to prompt me in the direction of the door. I stopped him with my hands flat against his chest. "Just stand in front of me. It won't take long."

"She's eventually going to get around to throwing an entirely too large atlas, and this dinky tray won't be able to handle that."

He moved his fingers on my waist for a moment and I raised my eyebrows at him. "What are you doing?"

He looked a bit discouraged, shifting to poking my neck and underarms. "You're not ticklish? I'm trying to tickle you and loosen you up enough to move you— Ow!" He cradled the hand I'd just slapped to his chest.

I escaped backward, ducking under a book. "If you're not going to help me then get out of the wa—"

Magnus had dropped the tray and rushed at me, taking hold of my shoulders, forcing me backward—he was bigger, and with his momentum I had no choice but to go along for the ride or else fall flat and vulnerable on my back. If I were in the wild, I'd send my knee into his groin, but this wasn't desperate enough for that. I didn't want to hurt him. Still, his method angered me.

"I didn't ask to be saved!" I tried to break his grip, but he held my upper arms in such a way that they weren't of much use. "I don't *need* to be saved!"

"This isn't worth getting your face smashed in by a dictionary!"

"Yes, you are!" I gaped at my own words, but I'm not even sure Magnus noticed.

We stumbled through the doorway, and I dropped my silver and pen. I gripped his shirt to balance myself, just as he released me in preparation to catch us against the wall. But, somehow, we were able to trip to a stop before impact. For a moment we just stood there, panting.

And then the sound of a throat clearing dropped my heart into my feet.

When I looked over, Tom was standing in the hall, holding a basket of firewood, grinning like he'd just learned a scandalous secret.

"U-um—" I shoved away from Magnus, wishing I could melt into the wall. "Magnus was, um, protecting me while I worked." My face burned, and I quickly knelt to gather my things to hide it.

"That so?" Tom said, and I could hear the amusement in his voice.

I examined my pen. No damage, thank God. "You could've broken my pen, Magnus," I said, just to be talking about something—*anything*—else.

Magnus scoffed, and I noticed he'd turned his back completely on Tom. "You could've been concussed by Tolstoy, *Andromeda*."

I could barely keep a straight face, so focused on picking up my dropped silver—which wouldn't be of any use now, with the edge nicked like that . . .

As if I cared about nicked silver. As if I wasn't just trying to distract myself from my present predicament.

Tom adjusted his grip on the basket. "I'll, uh, leave you two to sort it out," he said, winking at me as he walked by.

I stood, waiting until Tom disappeared in a room down the hall before saying, "I hope you're happy. Tom must think the worst of us."

"I am happy," Magnus said. "And I hope he does."

I stormed up to him, and he winced as I grabbed the front of his sweater and pulled him down to be more level with my gaze, although I still had to look up a little. "Why couldn't you have just done what I asked and stood in front of me while I worked? Don't you *want* to be cleansed?"

"Are you mad because I saved your life without your permission or because Tom thought we were being intima—Ow!" I'd shoved him away, his back colliding with the edge of the doorway. He scowled. "Why are you taking this out on me? There are plenty of rooms to cleanse, just pick another one."

"You're protecting the Librarian."

"What?" He gaped, gripping his wild curls with both fists. "I'm protecting *you*, you incredible little snapping turtle."

"Don't call me a snapping turtle!"

"You're snapping at me right now!"

I yelled out my frustration. "Just stay out of my way so I can work."

"Is that why you've been avoiding me for the past two days?" he asked, but I was already walking away. "Or are you just ashamed to admit you enjoyed kissing me?"

I halted, my face flaring red as I turned back to him. "Don't flatter yourself."

"To be fair, I do better when I'm prepared."

"Good for you," I said, unamused.

He let out a small laugh. "Just so you know, today I'm prepared."

I gripped my fists and had to swallow to keep my voice even. "Don't mock me, sir."

"Never," he said, and for once in this conversation he sounded completely levelheaded and sincere. He took out a handkerchief and wet it with his tongue, pressing it to my bloody temple. I would've forgotten about it; it barely throbbed. "And don't call me 'sir.'"

"Or you'll replace me?" I'd meant to turn on my heel and leave him alone to pout. Instead I looked him in his brown eyes brimming with curiosity. "During my interview, that's what you said. That you'd replace me with someone who would call you by your name."

"I don't remember that. I do, however, remember saying you're irreplaceable. I wish you'd remember that instead, too, my little storm cloud."

I sighed and looked away from him, pushing away his handkerchief. "I am not your 'little' anything."

"Why not?"

I raised my eyebrows at him, feeling very much like Jember, despite our lack of shared blood. "What do you mean 'why not'?"

"What's keeping you from being mine?"

My hands trembled, and I hugged the silver to my stomach to make them stop. "Yours?"

"Yes, Andromeda. Be with me."

"M-Magnus, I—" I looked to make sure Tom wasn't in the hall, that he couldn't see the way I blushed. "I can't. I work for you."

He let out a small breath and grinned. "Is that all?"

His relief constricted my lungs because I knew there was only one solution. "Please don't fire me," I said, and my voice sounded so small and tight to my own ringing ears.

His cold hands held my face, soothing my burning cheeks. "If I fired you, I'd probably never see you again. I want to see you every day of my life."

"Magnus," I groaned. I held his hands holding my cheeks, my vision blurring the slightest bit. "This isn't as right as it feels. There's a clear power imbalance."

"I agree," he said, leaning closer. "But I shall do my best to submit to your dominance with the grace of a gentleman."

I laughed, but it was quickly stifled by the gentle press of his lips to my forehead. "I'm waiting for the ax to drop . . . I never get what I want so easily."

"The ax, my dear," he said, wiggling his eyebrows as he ran his hands down my neck, over my shoulders. "Is that we will argue fiercely almost every day."

"In that case, I'm having second thoughts." I smirked at his frown, rising up on my toes, my lips a breath away from his. "You sound like a headache."

His nose brushed my cheek as he tipped his head, and a thrill went through me. "It's odd, everyone seems to sing my praises but you."

"They're lying." The last of my voice was muted as his lips took mine.

This kiss wasn't like the last one. It was certain and sweet . . . it felt like a promise. Not a promise of pain. A promise to look after my heart. To maybe—someday—even love me.

A promise to not throw me away.

CHAPTER
16

——✦——

Dinner was torture. The food was delicious, of course, but I couldn't fully enjoy it with half my mind on Magnus. He was so quiet . . . and sad. I hadn't seen him since the library, but that was only two hours ago. Two hours ago we'd pledged our hearts to each other, and now . . . something was wrong.

All I wanted to do was find out what it was, to comfort him, to . . . to touch him. He was in his regular chair at the head, which put him in just the right position for the two of us to hold hands on the table.

God help me. Could I show that kind of affection in front of others without having it be misunderstood as insolence toward my employer? But his skin was calling to me, and I think he needed the touch as much as I did. Fighting the magnetic pull to be near him was uncomfortable.

Why are you doing this to yourself, Andi?

Beautiful wasn't a word I'd ever use for Magnus if we were strangers passing on the street, but knowing him was like encountering the beauty of a snake. Feared and misunderstood, through no fault of his own. Slender, almost delicate looking, but with undeniable strength beneath the surface. Frightened, hiding and lashing out in turns. It was a brand of beauty not meant for everyone. He had no charm to speak of and all of it at once, made of unruly hair and awkward pauses and shy smiles.

But that didn't mean anything. It was irrational. Those weren't reasons to fall in love with—

"What's so funny?"

I looked up from my food at Kelela sitting across from me. She had long, golden box braids tonight, decorated with thin golden chains and golden flowers made of beads. I'd been proud of my hair makeover, but she looked stunning. Radiant. The most unwise thing I could do would be to compliment her.

She had a curious expression on her lovely face, but an untrustworthy one, like she intended to use my response to shame me in some way.

"Funny?" I replied, keeping my tone level. "I don't remember laughing."

"You were smiling."

Were you, Andi? "I'm just enjoying the food."

"Peggy is the best," Esjay chimed in. "I really need to get her recipes for our personal chef."

"And I'll need to learn them too," Kelela said. "Or at least all of Magnus's favorites." She grinned at me. "Good advice for you in the future, Andromeda—the way to keep a husband happy is through his stomach."

It was a seemingly innocent comment, but the implication twisted my gut.

"You don't need to learn to cook," Esjay said, "that's why you hire someone. Focus on your studies."

"Yes, brother," she replied, but I could see the victory in her expression. She knew she'd rattled me.

"Oh, you're engaged?" I asked, trying to keep my tone just as light despite my slowly tightening throat. "Magnus has never mentioned that."

"Why would he mention it? Men don't care about things like weddings, do you, Magnus?"

Magnus made a vague sound, though I couldn't tell if it was a yes or no.

It felt like a betrayal either way.

"I need a more comfortable chair," he said, standing abruptly. Kelela was on her feet and at his side in a matter of moments.

Esjay reached out to me before I could stand. "Andromeda, could you stay behind for a moment? I have just a few things to discuss with you about the contract."

"The stupid contract again, Esjay?" Magnus mumbled. "Hang it. I should just give her everything. What do I need money for anyway?"

"You're tired, Magnus," Esjay said quickly. "Kelela, help him to a more comfortable room."

She didn't really need to be told—she'd had her arm around his waist, leading him away before Esjay had even finished.

"Why don't we sing a little?" said Kelela as she helped him into the other room. "I remember seeing a book on your music shelf with a song I really like."

"I'm sorry about that," Esjay said, when they were gone. "Peggy said he was fine this morning. Did you happen to notice what changed his mood?"

I shook my head, even more confused than he was.

Esjay sighed. "I wish Kelela wouldn't keep bringing up the

engagement. They are promised to each other, yes, but . . ." He shook his head. "I just don't want her to get her hopes up."

"In case Magnus is never cleansed?" I asked.

"Yes. I don't doubt your skill, but we've been through ten debtera already. There's always the possibility that no amount of professional help will be enough."

"I *will* cleanse this house," I said.

"I believe you."

"And yet you won't let Kelela learn to cook his favorite foods."

There was a pause, long enough that it felt as if I'd given too much away. As if the word "love" was hovering at the front of my brain again, and he could read it like a sheet of paper.

"I started off as enthused about it as she is," he said. "But things are different now, and she's better off with an education that can take her places. That's a sure thing. Marriage to Magnus isn't."

"She seems hell-bent on marrying him, regardless."

"She's young, and I indulge her to dream. But she's going to France soon, to stay with our aunt . . . and dreams can change by the circumstance."

Kelela was leaving? I'd been here for weeks and hadn't heard a thing about France. Kelela seemed the type who would brag about something like that. It had to be a last-minute plan, seeing as their dreams of marrying her off to a wealthy chocolate heir weren't working out.

Still, a flash of hope sparked inside me . . . and I quickly doused it with a dash of common sense. "There's nothing about the contract you actually wanted to discuss, I assume?"

He shook his head and I headed to the music room. I don't know why, since all I really wanted to do was finish my work and never look at Magnus again. Because I . . . I had kissed him.

And he had kissed me back. He'd said he wanted to be with me. Knowing he was committed to someone else.

I found him sitting on a sheet-covered couch, holding a cup of coffee. Kelela was across the room, searching the bookcase. I sat on the couch across from him. I probably could've used some of the coffee on the table between us, but my stomach was fluttering so much I didn't think I could keep any down.

"I looked Tom in the eye today," he said, his voice quiet and frightened.

I glanced at Kelela, who had her back to us, still searching through the small library of music, then whispered, "When he caught us in the hall today?"

"I was so distracted, I didn't hear his footsteps. I should've looked away. I knew better."

"He must've heard your bells. I'm sure he looked away in time."

"Maybe." He sounded unconvinced.

My gut sank into knots. I didn't have much choice, did I? I would have to go out into the halls during the Waking if I was going to keep Tom from . . . vanishing. If that's really what was happening.

"Let me deal with everything, okay?" I said. "That's what I'm here for."

"You're such a godsend, Andromeda. I hope you know that." Magnus sipped his coffee and then leaned forward on the couch, forearms resting on his thighs. "I'm struggling tonight."

I swallowed a painful lump. "I'm sorry."

"Is there a cure? With an amulet?"

"I've never known an amulet to work on depression."

"Is that what this is?" he asked, staring into the blackness in his cup. "Depression?"

"Maybe you should cut the evening short."

He shook his head. "Esjay and Kelela come from so far to see me. I'm grateful for the company." The coffee rippled as he moved to set it down on the table, and I reached across and grabbed the cup to steady it. My hand rested against his. His skin was soft, his fingers trembling, and more than anything I wanted to toss that stupid cup out of the way so I could hold his hand. I felt foolish for wanting that.

"Stay, Andromeda." It was more of a question, tonight, than a demand.

"Of course." I pulled my hand away, taking the coffee cup with me.

"I found it!"

Kelela's too-loud voice jolted me upright, and I nearly spilled the coffee, steadying it just in time.

"This is the song I was talking about," she said, holding out a music book to Magnus. "You play, I'll sing."

Magnus took the book, with less enthusiasm than I'd ever seen him handle music. "You'll have to give me a moment to figure it out."

"Oh, it'll be so easy for you," Kelela insisted, pulling on his arm to make him stand. "You're the most talented musician I know."

"I'm the only musician you know," he said, but followed her without a fuss.

Regardless of what Esjay said about France, they were promised to each other. They would be getting married, probably as soon as the castle was cleansed. I needed to calm down. Soothe my racing heart. Behave like an employee, a friend, even, but nothing more.

Because Magnus would never—could never—be anything more to me than that.

So that was it. I would focus on my work, on making money, on earning my patronage. No more spending time with Magnus, no more emotional involvement. Besides, it was a poor survival habit, loving people. I was far better off on my own.

As soon as they were settled at the instrument, the first few notes ringing from it, I left as quietly as I could and headed down the dark hall. I'd barely gotten to the stairs before I heard him call my name, followed by the sound of footsteps—and bells—pursuing me.

"You said you would stay," he said as he followed me down the hall.

My heart ached from sprinting so hard in my chest. "I thought you'd want time alone with Kelela."

I quickened my pace when I reached the stairs, but Magnus stepped in front of me.

"I *asked* you to stay."

And I wanted to. So *badly*. But how could I? So, instead I said, "Congratulations on your engagement."

He froze. I wanted him to deny it, to ask me what I was talking about. Instead he just looked guilty.

I took the opportunity to get around him and rush up the stairs.

But still, those bells pursued me. "What did Esjay tell you?"

"You sound shocked," I said bitterly. "Why, was I not supposed to know about it?"

"It's not what you think—"

"Yesterday you said you wanted to be with me, and today I find out you're engaged. It's *exactly* what I think."

I grabbed the doorknob to my room, but his hand was suddenly on top of mine, keeping the knob from twisting, pulling back as I pushed forward. His other hand rested on the doorjamb to keep himself steady. He was actually as strong as his height suggested when he put his mind to it.

"It was a verbal agreement I made when I was fourteen," he said. "A fancy, really. I was young. I didn't know what I was saying."

"Esjay seems to think it's legitimate."

"Esjay never minds his own business."

"That's because his business is minding yours."

I wanted to hate the feeling of his body shielding me with warmth. I wanted to hate him for kissing me. But, God, I didn't.

"At least give me a chance to explain," he said.

"Explain what? That you're using me for your own pleasure while being committed to Kelela?"

"I'm not committed to Kelela."

"You're a liar." I pushed against his pull, managing a small gap before he slammed the door shut again. I felt my heart pumping, irrationally, my adrenaline kicking in from being cornered in a small space. It didn't matter that Magnus could never scare me, would never pose a threat, whether he intended to or not. Soon my good survival habits would prompt me to put a stop to it more violently. "Back away from me, sir."

"Again with 'sir.' Andromeda, it's me—"

I spun to face him. "You are my employer, *sir*. Nothing more."

His grip loosened, his hand trembling against mine. "What can I do to prove I want you?"

Before tonight I would've blushed. Felt unworthy of the sweet attention I was being shown. Now I knew the attention meant nothing.

But his expression was knitted with pain and desperation and—oh God, why was he looking at me like this? I had to repeat to myself that he was a dirty liar, that he wanted Kelela, that he had *drawn* her. But he was so close I could feel his breath caressing my face, and I wanted his lips, I wanted them—

As if hearing my thought, he kissed me. I bucked anyway, shoving hard against his chest, trying to pry his hand from the back of my neck, to turn my face away from his. But when a verbal protest finally made it to my lips it didn't sound like a protest at all.

I grabbed his sweater, dragging him closer so quickly we slammed against the door. But he didn't stop kissing me, and I didn't want him to. For a moment, our souls spoke to each other a single truth, shutting out all the anger and shame. In that moment we both wanted each other, deeply and honestly.

But then the moment was over, and reality stepped back in . . . and honesty had nothing to do with it.

I pushed his face aside to catch my breath. Magnus let me, thank God—maybe because he knew his fantasy was over.

"You flirt with me," I said, my voice shaking. "You kiss me. And the whole time you're engaged to someone else."

"But you want this too, don't you?" he said, and I felt like a thread about to snap.

I shoved him in the chest, and he stumbled backward. "I may be poor and ugly," I said, "but I have human rights, same as anyone. I will not be a fancy to you like your engagement was. I will not be used."

"Withholding details isn't lying, Andromeda. Everyone does it, even you—blazes, *especially* you. But none of that means I used you. I would never use you."

"You already have." I braced myself against the door as he approached, halting him with my words. "Don't touch me."

"Why, will you bite?"

"If I have to."

He let out a short, breathy laugh, his gaze so steady I felt naked beneath it. "You are remarkable."

I took an even breath to calm my nerves. "I'm going to bed."

"Not like this," he said, reaching out to me. "Not angry with me."

"I am a human being with free will. I am going to bed."

"You know I'm a tactless fool sometimes." Magnus sighed heavily, as if he were in pain. "Stay with me, Andromeda. Forgive me and stay."

"I can't forgive you if you never actually apologize."

I shut the door in his face, just in time to partially block out his annoying "I didn't apologize?"

I leaned my back against the door, covering my mouth to mute my trembling breath. I couldn't believe I actually thought . . . but of course it had all been in my head. I should've known better—anything that felt that good could never be true. God, I was an idiot. Any man who could kiss one woman while being committed to another, no matter how tenuous the commitment . . . How could I believe anything he said ever again?

And yet his voice, right up against the wood of the door, muted but somehow still ringing through me . . . "I'm sorry, Andromeda. Please, believe me. I'm sorry . . ."

I hated that his pleading softened me. That he held such power. That I wanted nothing more than to open the door, forgive him, kiss him again and again.

Instead I threw the lock and buried myself in blankets to block out his pleas.

CHAPTER
17

I hadn't had much time to devise a plan, and the one I did come up with was rocky at best: Stand outside Tom's room just before the Waking begins. Cleanse whatever Manifestation comes to make him "vanish." Don't get eaten alive by the house in the process. Magnus had said the servants' quarters were cleansed, and so I wouldn't have to worry about any other strokes getting in the way.

At three minutes to ten I put my knife in my pocket, and grabbed the fireplace poker just in case. I had my amulet on, of course, but after the terror of that first Waking I didn't want to take any chances.

As soon as I opened the door a shadow flew at me. I cried out from shock, but I was used to keeping my head enough to at least swing the poker in the right direction. Now the light of my fireplace allowed me to see Saba standing in front of me, pushing the door shut with one hand . . . gripping the poker I'd just swung with the other.

That honestly would've been stranger if I wasn't living in a house with hands coming out of the walls.

"I can't cleanse the Evil Eye from my room," I said. Saba ignored me, locking the door instead. "Tom might be in danger. I have to get to his room. That requires leaving mine—Saba, stop it!"

I'd pushed past her, but she pushed back harder, and it only took one hand pressing on my stomach. I panicked for a moment—*How is she this strong?*—but it only took that one moment, that bit of hesitation, for Saba to overpower my momentum and forcefully guide me back to my bed.

I fell onto the bed, glaring up at her. "What are you doing? I *have* to go out there."

She shook her head firmly.

"Yes." I got up and she blocked my path. "Don't you care about Tom? About Magnus? This is the only way to save them."

I tried to get around her, but she intercepted me, wrapped her arms around me, holding me close. For a moment I struggled, but she was far too strong. Her body was firm, but not in the same way it would be if she had hardened muscles. It was unnatural.

Even through my sleeves I could feel her cold arms. So cold, and yet she never wore a sweater, as if she couldn't feel what her arms were feeling.

"Let go?" I asked, and I felt her chin move at my forehead as she shook her head.

I took a deep breath. If I relaxed, if she felt I'd calmed down, she'd let go. Then I'd draw my knife on her. God forgive me, but I'd have to. Just to keep her away long enough so I could get out of the room.

Ten o'clock struck on the great clock downstairs, and the wind immediately began rushing. Screams, moans, knockings, though none as intense as that first night.

I had to get out of this room. *Now.*

A few more deep breaths and my heart rate was getting close to level. I wrapped my arms around Saba's waist, leaning the side of my face against her chest, hugging her back. Tricking her was more accurate. I'd never been great at crying on demand, but I could try. *Again, God, please ignore any underhanded activity you see here tonight.*

It worked sans crying, because after a moment Saba's hold relaxed slightly, her hug feeling more natural around my neck. The room was quiet except for the moaning spirits and howling wind outside, except for the snap and crack of the fireplace, except for my own heart pounding in my ear. My *own* heart, I realized . . . just mine. No counter or synced rhythm from the chest I was leaning against. Still. Nothing.

And suddenly I could no longer relax.

Saba felt me tense and tightened her grip, but I didn't fight back this time, my brain working through too many thoughts.

She wasn't acknowledged as a servant by anyone in the house but Magnus . . . by anyone but the Evil Eye's host. And she wasn't affected by the cold. Literally heartless. It all made sense. Well it did, but didn't.

Saba was, in some way, a result of the Evil Eye. Despite having no traits of a Manifestation, her survival depended on the curse. And so there was no way she was going to let me cleanse it without a fight.

Magnus had told me not to get too attached to her, but I'd never expected this to be the reason.

"Whatever you are," I said, and felt her jolt, "whatever you had been, please know I feel deep compassion for you. But I have to end this. Too many people have disappeared, and it needs to stop. Let me go, Saba. I don't want to hurt you."

Saba's response was to tighten her grip like an iron clamp.

My stomach turned. I'd fought plenty of times on the street—for food, for my life, for ideal shelter. I had the scars to prove it. But to hurt a friend . . .

Just do it quick, Andi.

I snatched Saba's forearm with one hand, digging my fingers in and reaching for my knife with the other just as I kicked her in the shin. Saba stumbled back a few steps, and I heard the *shinkt* of a breaking plate, a sharp, warm pain rising up my fingers that the rest of the cold house might've numbed. But I ignored the pain and focused on my knife, pointing it toward Saba and her missing—

My blood felt cold.

. . . her missing . . .

I turned to my shoulder slowly, where I still held Saba's arm, despite the fact her body was five feet away. Where my sliced fingers had gone through the top of her arm, through the hollow middle, and rested on the bottom, my blood dripping off the end of the shattered appendage.

I looked quickly up to Saba, as she stood still, her right arm missing and hollow at the forearm, making her look like a beautiful, sad porcelain doll.

A distant scream echoed up the stairs. Oh God. Tom.

I shrugged the broken arm off my shoulder, letting it drop to the ground. It immediately started feeling its way back to its body, crawling on all fingers like a giant spider. Saba approached to retrieve it. It was now or never. I rushed forward, stabbing Saba in the knee and twisting, breaking off her leg with a subtle *click*. She lost her balance, stumbling to the only knee she had left, and I dodged to get around her.

Something grabbed my leg, tripping me. The impact on the ground sent my head spinning and my knife skittering into the shadows. I slammed my foot on the ground, breaking the fingers of the dismembered hand from my ankle, and launched myself at Saba, managing to tackle her to the ground before she could get her leg fully attached to her body again.

In the streets I would've punched her, but I couldn't afford to slice open my right hand, too—my welding hand. So instead I reached over for the metal shovel, having to knock over the entire bin of tools to get to it. Saba grabbed me with her good arm, her strength keeping me from the shovel, even with one hand, and I made the mistake of looking at her. And feeling a twinge of guilt at the fear widening her eyes.

"Then let me go, Saba," I pleaded, for her welfare and my own conscience. I didn't want to feel my friend's body break beneath my force, even if there were no signs that it hurt her.

She shook her head vehemently. Her goal was clearly to protect herself. Part of me respected that. I'd been doing it all my life.

But her intention meant that, for the moment, I could no longer see her as a friend—if ever again, but I'd deal with those emotions another time. For now, my good survival habits were urging me to remove the obstacle blocking me from what I needed.

So be it, then.

I grabbed her arm with both of mine and pinned her. Managed to grab the shovel and broke her arm at the shoulder with the narrow end. Stood, and did the same thing to her last leg. Then swiped them under my bed, so they'd have further to crawl to get to her body.

"I'm sorry," I said quickly, barely able to look at her terror-stricken expression. I snatched up my satchel of supplies and raced out of the room.

I ran in the direction the pulse of my amulet led, down the stairs and around the corner, ignoring every other Manifestation I passed—all except for the horde of rats, which ran over and under my feet, making it hard to keep up my speed. I was hot and sweaty from the struggle in my room, so I barely felt the cold. I squeezed my fingers into my sweater to get rid of excess blood, though my heart pounded heavy and painful in my fingertips. I put on my welding goggles, smudging warm blood on my face that quickly turned cold in the air around me.

My amulet pulsed to the point it echoed through my body painfully, and when I turned the corner I saw why.

In the meager light of the dying embers, I saw Tom's body crumpled on the ground, a dark puddle slowly pooling beneath him, his eyes staring at nothing.

And standing over him, looking straight at me, the reflective green eyes of . . .

Oh God . . .

A hyena.

Without a shadow of a doubt, this was no mortal beast, no Manifestation. It was the curse itself. The Evil Eye incarnate.

I only knew that because Jember had cleansed one—the only debtera in the last twenty years, maybe even fifty, to successfully do it. But he'd never taught me how he had cleansed it. All he'd said was if I was ever offered a job to do so, to run in the opposite direction and never look back.

It suddenly occurred to me where Jember's leg and humanity had gone, and the reality of my imminent fate hit me like a fist to the skull.

"Please, God," I prayed, grasping my amulet for comfort, but its pulses were so heavy, so painful, they felt like screams of terror.

The hyena stepped over Tom's body, the tinkle of bells with every step, the mane on its hunched back standing on end.

I took out my silver disk and got to work.

You have no plan, Andi.

The hyena padded closer, its growl mingling with the crackling of the embers.

Did you expect the Evil Eye to just sit still and watch you work?

At least, thank God, my amulet shield reached three feet. I sat down and got to work.

Seven strokes in, I heard the scratching of sharp nails against the hardwood stop in front of me, felt the hot breath cloud my oxygen . . . heard the growl dangerously close to my face. I glanced up, just to make sure the amulet was doing its job. Three feet really wasn't much when a bloodthirsty demon hyena was standing by.

And then I jolted up from my work. The hyena's head was leaning forward at the three-foot mark, and then it backed away and rushed forward, slamming its head on the same spot again. Again. And again. It was making short work of my shield, already a foot closer than when it had started.

My heart raced. Oh God. There was no way I could finish the amulet at this rate.

But what other choice did I have?

I got back to work quickly, ignoring the slams of the hyena's head against my shield.

But the more the hyena pounded, the worse the rumbling in my amulet became, until I had to pause, nauseated.

Keep going, Andi.

I wasn't nearly done.

God help me. Give me strength . . .

I'd paused for too long. By the time I'd flinted my pen I felt the hyena's hot breath on my face. I pulled my legs in closer. Did I have any shield left at all—?

Something grabbed me, dragging me around the corner, and I screamed and hit at it, dropping my barely half-baked amulet to the hardwood floor. But with one hand sliced open my fighting didn't do much good. I closed my eyes briefly as my back hit the hallway wall, thankful I didn't bite my tongue off from the jolt. Two strong hands gripped my arms, pinning them to my sides.

I glared at Saba, now eye level with her. "Let me go."

She shook her head.

"Don't make me break you again. I'll do it if I have to."

Her grip tightened, and I had to force myself not to wince.

She shifted her body to block me as the hyena padded slowly out of the room we'd just been in. But I barely saw it, barely had time to feel fear or determination before Saba opened the door across the hall from us and threw me inside.

"Saba, stop it! Let me out!" No light came through, save for the meager bit beneath the door. My hand landed on a wall, and I followed it to another wall, to . . . another wall. All the while the hyena's presence felt weaker and weaker, less and less, until I could barely sense even one stroke. "Saba!"

The last wall led me to a door, but by then it was too late. Locked. I banged on it with my good hand. "Saba!" I jiggled the knob, kicking the door as I did. I reached in my pocket for my knife, cursing myself for not snatching it off the floor before running out of my room.

I screamed out my frustration, then lowered myself to the

ground to search for something to help me. There had to be something I could use to pick the lock. What kind of person had empty closets in their house?

And then I realized, I couldn't feel the hyena's presence at all. I had failed.

CHAPTER
18

〜

Somewhere in the fog I heard my name. Felt a shaking, like an uneven cart. Something touching me, soft yet hard.

I groaned, an unnatural grogginess making it difficult to open my eyes. When I finally managed, even the indirectness of sun rays on the ceiling made my head hurt. Someone sat over me . . . their head on fire.

I blinked and my name came out of the fog. Blinked again, and the fiery creature transformed into a hysterical Emma, her red hair glinting golden highlights in the sun.

"Andromeda, bleawait unt!"

"Where are we?" I tried, my words slurring.

"Tongath vabee! Blea, you habbu eat!"

"What?" I fought to sit up, and felt her hands on my shoulders, assisting me. Immediately the room began to spin.

I lifted my hand to grab my aching head, the sharp smell of some herb invading my sinuses, clearing my mind. I opened my eyes wide to make them focus.

My bed. My room. Wait, it was coming back to me . . . the Waking. Saba breaking like clay.

Oh God. The hyena.

I leapt to my feet, my knees buckling, and caught myself with both hands. A small spot of red began to spread on my bandaged hand, and I watched it without being able to feel it.

"Andromeda," Emma said, helping me sit up. She patted my cheeks, searching my face for signs of sanity, I was sure. "Are you all right?"

I didn't remember ever getting out of that closet. But then again . . . I looked at my sliced fingers, which were individually bandaged and wrapped. I could barely feel them. I felt lethargic. The aftershock of a sleep aid, or some kind of painkiller, I was sure of it. I'd never consented to that, and it put my nerves on edge.

My guess was Saba. Which was sweet, considering what I'd done to her. And even so, she'd saved my life last night. Or stopped me from saving—

"Oh God," I murmured. "Tom."

"Yes, Tom." Emma nodded, her relieved smile quickly dissolving to tears. "Please, help me find him, Andromeda. I think he's vanished."

"Vanished . . ." Memories were flooding back to me now, and that one slapped me right down my spine, making me tremble. The image of him lying mangled on the floor, his empty eyes staring at heaven, was scarred in my mind. No, he hadn't vanished. And, unless Saba had cleared away the body, like she'd cleared away the evidence of our struggle last night, I knew in which room his body would still be lying.

I pushed myself up, slowly, Emma at my side. I was still dressed from last night, so that would do. Remembering my knife, I looked for it briefly on the floor before spotting it sitting neatly on the side table as if it had never been used last night. Careful not to use my left hand too much, I strapped my knife on my waist without bothering to hide it.

I looked at her, but had no strength to manage a smile. "Let's go find him."

Emma hooked her arm through mine to help me down the stairs. As much as my head was still throbbing, movement was helping my body adjust, as if working the drug out of my body. By the time we reached the bottom of the stairs I had enough autonomy to grab her shoulder.

"Let's split up," I said, and her eyes widened in horror. "It'll take hours if we don't."

"This house scares me," she whimpered.

How could I tell her that the image she might see if she went with me would scare her more?

"Open the windows, let the sun in as you go to make you feel better," I said. "Half an hour we'll meet back here."

She nodded, and rushed in the direction where I knew she'd find nothing. I went the opposite way, to the room where it happened.

It looked off. I tried to think back to how it looked last night, and every day before. Yes. The large tapestry had fallen off the wall and was lying in the middle of the floor. No . . . not fallen. It was arranged like a rug.

I pushed the small table on top aside with my shoulder and good hand, and then stepped off and threw the woven thing aside. Instantly, I recoiled.

Tom was where I had left him, but he wasn't. His body had sunk partway into the floor, as if resting in a shallow pool—

only glimpses of his thigh, his hand, his face, surfacing. Except the medium wasn't water, it was solid stone and cracked hardwood, and his body was like a fossil, petrified within. His skin was grey with death or hardening, his expression frozen in that blank stare to God.

I quickly covered him back up where he had been hidden, but for a moment after I couldn't move. That tapestry had been purposely moved from the wall to the floor to cover up the evidence of what the Evil Eye had done.

I got up and rushed out into the hall—moving too quickly made me light-headed, but that was the least of my worries. The random table and rug in the middle of the hall didn't seem so random anymore. The small wooden table was heavier than it looked, but I shoved it over with my shoulder and kicked away the rug. The shocked, fossilized face of Edward stared back at me . . . the man whose kind eyes had greeted me that first night and had undoubtedly vanished that first Waking.

I threw the rug back over him and rushed to the wall, shifting over a tapestry. Nothing. I rushed down the hall, shifting every piece of wall décor I came across until I snatched away a basket that seemed to be hanging too low and found a hand reaching out to me as if begging for help.

I stood in the hall, trembling.

Emma had been right, in a way. The house was holding victims hostage, but I had a feeling there weren't going to be any happy reunions after the Evil Eye was cleansed. The house was consuming them. Sucking the corpses dry and—my God—regurgitating the victims' blood? I dry heaved at the thought of it, and then looked down the hall.

"Magnus?" The hall was quiet, and so my voice sounded far too loud, even without yelling. I didn't hear the hopsicar, so went straight to the library. Magnus was drawing in his regular chair. He paused to throw a dart at the portrait of his father. It stuck firm into the canvas, joining a cluster of darts just below the man's belt.

"Castrating your father?" I asked.

"A perfectly therapeutic way to spend the morning." Magnus slapped his sketchbook shut and left it on his lap, giving me his full attention. He was grinning, seemingly clueless as to what had happened the night before. I would've been grateful for that, except that now I had to explain my gruesome findings.

"You slept in, Andromeda," he said, shaking his pencil at me in chastisement. "I honestly didn't know it was possible."

God bless him, he was so cute, raising his thick eyebrows at me with such sweet curiosity. I felt overwhelmingly pleased to see it.

"The drugs made me do it," I said stupidly, sitting beside him. He immediately reached over and took my hand. I accepted it, squeezed it too tight. His lies should've mattered to me, but they didn't. At the moment there were bigger things to worry about. "I have to talk to you."

His eyes widened as he saw my bandaged hand. "God. What happened?"

I took a deep breath. "People in the house aren't vanishing. They're being killed."

The color fled from Magnus's face. "Killed? By the Evil Eye? But I thought—" He looked as though he might vomit. I didn't blame him. "I'd been taught that that's what eye contact with the Evil Eye's host did. But there are never any bodies found, and I can never remember what I did the next morning. So, I . . ." He tugged and poked at the weave of his sweater. "I assumed that maybe I wasn't killing anyone after all."

"There are bodies. The house is just consuming them. Haven't you ever noticed the décor looks off?"

"I let Saba arrange the furniture how she wants." He froze. "You're not saying she—"

"No. No, she's just covering it up. Because . . ." I swallowed. "Because she's part of the Evil Eye, isn't she?"

Magnus blinked at me. "What do you mean? There's nothing wrong with Saba."

I shook my hand from his, every deceitful thing he'd done slipping back to memory. "I don't appreciate being lied to any more than you do, Magnus."

He blinked at me, his brows lowering. "I'm not sure what you're trying to say."

"Are you playing dumb?"

"No, I just didn't catch what you said—"

I leaned over the table and tugged his ear, raising my voice over his frantic protests. "Then I'll repeat the question for you—"

"Okay, I heard you," he fussed, prying my fingers from his ear.

"She has no heartbeat. Her skin is cold and shatters like pottery. No one in the house but the two of us seems to be able to see her. What *is* she?"

It only took him a moment to say "Will you shut the door?"

Who's left to hear us? I almost blurted, but there was no point in rubbing salt in Magnus's wound. I took a deep breath and rushed over to shove the door closed, then dropped down into the chair beside him again. "Talk," I ordered.

"She's a victim of the Evil Eye," he said, still rubbing his ear.

"A victim?" My wild confidence began to crumble. "So she's . . . dead?"

"Yes. Reanimated, but not truly alive."

I froze. "B-but—" My dear friend Saba . . . *dead?* "But why? How?"

He sighed heavily, like he was weary from the question. "I don't know if I can say."

"This is life or death, Magnus. You have to tell me." I reached across the small table and grabbed his hand to draw his attention to me. "Please. Tell me."

Magnus didn't look at me. That's usually all he wanted to do, but now . . . "Don't hate me because of it."

"Because of . . . ?" When he kept his silence, I turned his face to look at me. "Tell me."

He swallowed. Took a deep breath. "Who do you think she looks like?"

I paused. "You, I thought, the first day. Your sister, maybe?"

"Close."

I paused even longer this time. "This isn't making sense, Magnus."

"After a victim of the Evil Eye is buried, there's a short window of time in which the body can be exhumed, and the Evil Eye can reanimate for its own purposes." He stared at the fire for a moment. "My poor excuse for a father did that . . . to my mother."

I gripped the small table, my fingers pressing into the wood like they might splinter it. "What?" I gasped. My fifth attempt.

"The Evil Eye waited until I was born, at least, before unleashing its curse. It had its billionaire and an heir . . . two generations of wealth." Magnus sat quietly, swallowing a few times. "My mother was the first victim of my father . . . the first person to make eye contact and die."

I got up, curling my good fist in and out restlessly. "Saba is your mother."

His mother. Which would make her at least twenty-two years older than she looked.

We were quiet for a moment. My sliced hand was beginning to throb, but the knot in my throat hurt worse. I tried to swallow a few times, then gave up, instead going to the fireplace and spitting the nasty taste into the flames.

"That's why you said that when the Evil Eye is cleansed, Saba will leave. It's because she's connected. A servant to it. She dies when it's expelled."

"She's my friend," Magnus countered, offended. "I never knew her as my mother, but she's always been my friend. She obeys the Evil Eye because she can't help it, because she has no defense against it. Sometimes she . . ." He slouched further in his seat, hugging his sketchbook to his chest. "She cries while she's carrying out commands. She doesn't want to do them, but her body is forced to obey. It makes me sick to see her that way."

"Magnus . . ." I knelt in front of him, my hands resting on his knees. The fire made the tear streaks down his cheeks glisten. My voice still felt tight as I said, "I feel so guilty. I was holding back. I could've been cleansing the house more quickly this whole time."

"I'm glad you're not rushing it." He leaned forward, dropping his sketchbook on the floor beside him. "I'm not ready for you to leave."

He traced the curves of my ears with his fingers, his palms cradling my face. I closed my eyes. His hands held the perfect amount of warmth. I could sit here all day if my body would allow it. If my mind would allow it. I still didn't trust that this wasn't wrong.

Either way, there were more important things to think about

now, so I stood up out of his reach. "I have to tell Emma about Tom."

Magnus chewed his lip. "You really think that's a good idea? Disappearing is a kinder fate than death."

"Kinder for whom? She's holding out hope that after the Evil Eye is cleansed everyone will be released. I need to tell her whatever necessary to make her leave this place."

"Don't mention death, at least." He stood, touching my cheek. "She already has nothing left."

"She has breath in her body, doesn't she?"

"Hard truths aren't for everyone, Andromeda. Sometimes the only mercy is to lie. We're not all as strong as you are."

I hesitated. Took a deep breath. "I won't tell her. But I will encourage her to leave. And live."

"You're better than all of us." He kissed my forehead, lingering just long enough that for a moment my breathing faltered. "So, what's the next step?"

"The next step?" I looked at my bandaged hand, determination blazing through me. "We get rid of this hyena."

CHAPTER
19

⌇

I was glad I'd taken Magnus's advice, because Emma took the news that Tom had "vanished" as well as could be expected. I let her cry on my lap for a few minutes and then let Peggy take over, although I doubted the woman had a tender bone in her body. Emma couldn't travel, crying like this, especially not alone—I didn't want her to be a target for harassers or thieves. But I assured her she could sleep in my room tonight, and that I would take her to the city as soon as she was ready.

But I couldn't linger. I needed to see Jember as soon as possible, and this time I wouldn't be polite, wouldn't adhere to any narrow time limit. I would bother him all day if I had to—this time I was getting answers, whether he liked it or not.

When Saba and I reached the stable door it was already open, and Emma had started hitching up the horses. She wore trousers and a white shirt, though they fit too well to have been Tom's. She had on a flat hat that would've been too big for her if she hadn't stuffed all her hair inside, the lip of it sticking out enough to block the sun from her face . . . the same hat Tom had worn the night I met him. There was a large shoulder bag sitting beside the coach.

She could maybe pass as a fourteen-year-old boy if she was lucky, but maybe that would be enough.

"Are you sure you're up to it?" I asked.

"Anything is better than staying here," she said.

I let her climb into the coach, trying to distract myself from her crying as Saba finished preparation.

It was closer to lunch, now, than breakfast. I jumped down the short distance from the perch and paid the stable boy, waiting for Emma as she slowly climbed out. It was obvious she'd been crying, her face red and puffy, and I took the liberty of tipping down her hat to hide it.

"You have enough to live on?" I asked. I didn't want to specify money in this public space, but she seemed to understand, patting her vest pocket and bag.

"Enough to reach England. And I have plenty of friends and family to help me from there."

Her face was already rosy from the heat. I wasn't sure she'd last a day without boiling.

We were quiet for a moment.

"I really respect what you're doing," Emma said suddenly. "Finding your own job, your own way in life. Women don't have that option where I come from."

Women here didn't have many choices either. No one did unless you had money. Starve or survive, those were our options.

I shrugged. "I just do what's necessary to survive."

"I suppose it's about time I do the same."

"Do you have protection?" I asked. She allowed me a glance of the gun she had in her pocket. "God be with you, Emma."

"And with you." Emma took my hand and nodded. She looked both certain and uncertain at once.

I watched her go for a moment, then looked up at Saba, who had joined me.

It was time to go—my good survival habits didn't like me standing out on an open street for too long.

We snaked through the crowded marketplace, passed fruit and nut vendors shouting, customers haggling over meat, before passing over into the labyrinth.

This time I didn't bother going into the church—by now Jember would be sleeping after his busy night. I led Saba to the back alley of the church, blocked off from the maze behind it by a wall along all sides but the front, to where a cellar door was embedded in the dirt. The chain and lock weren't on the outside handles, which meant Jember had locked it from the inside. He was definitely home.

I looked at Saba. "Will you be okay waiting outside for a few minutes? No one ever comes down here, I promise."

They really didn't. Law enforcement held no power over the church—or rather, the people seemed to respect the church over law enforcement—and so the portion of my childhood I spent under the church somehow felt freeing in more ways than one. Perhaps that's why Jember had chosen to live beneath the church, literally. No one would dare commit a crime in the vicinity. It was the safest place in the city to be.

Despite that, I knew there were a couple booby traps around the door. Just because it was safe didn't mean Jember trusted anyone.

"You may not want to touch anything," I added.

Saba gave me a reassuring smile, waving me toward the door. I knelt in front of a small grate beside it, a forceful tug with both hands making it squeak against its metal chamber before yielding to me.

I grinned.

Lazy old man, still hadn't gotten this fixed.

I peeked in to make sure the way was clear, then slid in through the small opening, legs first, landing on a crate right below, and closed the grate behind me.

There wasn't much light, other than the little bit of daylight peeking through the grate. I got down from the crate, dust puffing up at my movement. I muted a cough with the bend of my elbow and used my welding pen to light the first oil lamp I could find. If I were still living here, this entryway would've been clear. Now it was cluttered like a storage closet, with books and boxes, vases, a bicycle. Our small cooking pit was completely blocked by wooden crates, a caked layer of dust and dirt confirming that it'd probably been that way for weeks.

If the door hadn't been locked from the inside, I would've thought no one lived here anymore.

Looking down, I could see a path from the bedroom to the stairs leading up to the cellar doorway that was a little less dusty than the rest of it.

I picked up the oil lamp and shoved my way through the junk, pushing aside the curtain over the door at the back wall. The light of the lamp shone like a yellow path to the bed centered against the wall. I took a deep breath, then let my body deflate, my annoyance overtaking my relief. The silhouette of Jember lay on his back, and when I put the lamp on the dresser I saw that he was in nothing but his white pants and red leather gloves, peg leg missing. He'd never eaten any better than I had, but I guess older bodies processed food differently or just needed less of it, giving him a relatively fit chest and arms and a slight gut. Glass bottles and jars littered the bed, and there was a paper bag of pills on the side table that were most definitely illegal.

"Jember," I called from the doorway, and only when he didn't respond did I move closer, clapping my hands. "Get up, old man."

Nothing. My heart suddenly picked up, and I couldn't help but be annoyed with myself for it. He wasn't dead, and I shouldn't care if he was. But I was used to caring, and old habits were hard to break.

I went to the bed and laid two fingers against his neck, but there was no time to regret that decision, let alone scream, as Jember's gloved fingers closed around my throat. My knife was in my hand by the time he'd slammed my back onto the mattress.

"Go ahead, girl," he said, his dreadlocks falling in my face as he leaned over me. "Make me let go."

Even though he had my other wrist pinned, I could still slice his arm. There was a good artery there.

But that was exactly why I wouldn't.

I felt the tight burning of my constricted windpipe. I had seconds to decide what to do before I lost strength. Blacked out. And then he'd win, like he always did, and I'd have a headache and sore throat for the rest of the day.

Without his wooden leg, he only had one leg supporting his weight. I kicked it out from under him, shoving him onto his back. I pressed my knee into his arm, aiming my knife at his face with both hands. He caught both hands with his only free one, pushing up against me.

"Why didn't you cut my arm?" he grunted. "I gave you the easiest opening."

"Artery."

"You're soft."

"I'm not soft, I just need you alive." I shifted my meager weight more on top of the knife and lowered it closer to his face. "Surrender, old man, before I give you one less eye."

"Your threats have gotten more realistic." He glanced at the knife. "I surrender." I let up on my pressure, allowing him to drop his defensive hand, but I kept the knife pointing at his face, in case he changed his mind. "Tell me, how do you check a man's pulse?"

"By sticking a knife in him," I said.

"Then why do I have to tell you this again? Never put yourself within grabbing range of someone, especially someone bigger than you." He waved me away and I got up and put my knife away. "What the hell happened to your hand since I last saw you?"

"Oh—" I looked at my still-wrapped fingers, which were beginning to throb from all that activity, despite the medicine. "I cut myself on . . . some pottery."

"Was it pottery or wasn't it? You sound like you have no idea." He scraped his fingers through his beard, giving me a skeptical look. "We both know this isn't a sentimental visit. What are you doing here, girl?"

I folded my arms across my chest and backed up another step to gather up my courage. *Just say it, Andi.*

Instead, "This place is disgusting" slipped out of my mouth.

"That's because you're not here to clean it."

"You don't have another mentee by now?"

"Haven't found one with enough potential to be worth my

time." Jember coughed out a laugh, then groaned as he forced himself to sit upright on the end of the bed. I heard his joints creak. He was almost thirty-eight but pain had made him seem older to me. He winced, massaged the puckered and rounded-off end where his knee used to be, then swallowed two of the illegal pills without water. All his energy must have been sheer adrenaline.

Living on the street so long, you learned how to turn it on and off when you needed to.

I wanted to be mad at him. I wanted to hate him. I couldn't.

"How are you even surviving?" I said. "You don't get paid by the church unless you train debtera for them."

Jember let out a long sigh, his posture drooping as he glared at me, as if he were already sick of me after only a few minutes of interaction. He yanked off his gloves and dropped them on the bed, shaking out his sweaty hands, then opened the drawer beside him and took out a pipe. "I really thought I'd made it clear last time not to bother me."

I snatched the thing out of his lips before he could light it. "Your body is a temple for God's glory."

"My body is mine, and yours is yours." He snatched it back but didn't light it. "Unless I decide to finally kill you and use your fat as cooking oil."

And he said *my* threats were unrealistic. It had worked for the few months—months of living in constant anxiety, until I learned that Jember was too lazy to ever follow through. Now it was just tradition.

I smirked. "Good luck finding any fat on me to burn."

Jember laughed a little, ending it with a heavy breath. For a moment neither of us spoke. For that moment, I felt like I was back home. Finally, he said, "You must be truly desperate to come to me for help."

I swallowed. "You said to come to you if my life was in danger."

"Who is it? Just give me the name."

"It's . . . more of a what than a who."

The color left Jember's face, and I felt myself trembling at his expression. Concerned? Terrified? I'd never seen those emotions from him, especially not at once.

"You're at Thorne Manor, aren't you?" he said, his expression finally slipping into anger. "Have you lost your mind?"

"What do you care?" I snapped. "You're the one who did this to me."

Jember threw one of the bottles beside him, and I winced as it shattered against the stone wall. He tried to get up, then remembered he wasn't wearing his leg. We both knew he didn't have the energy right now to hop on one leg.

For a moment we were quiet. Hate and guilt mixed in my gut.

"I know you're smarter than this," he said finally.

"I needed work."

"Needed wor—?" He pressed his fingers into his temples, taking a deep breath. "You know ten experienced debtera have already been through there, don't you? Wasn't that enough of a hint to stay away?"

"They told me you refused the job," I said, forcing myself not to cry, even with tears burning the backs of my eyes. "Why?"

He looked at me like it was the dumbest question he'd ever heard. "What do you mean why?"

"You're the only debtera alive who has experience with a hyena. Magnus probably would've paid you more than he's paying me."

"I've told you a thousand times, it's dangerous to take a job purely for money. Wearing an amulet doesn't mean you should deliberately tempt the Evil Eye."

"But even without the money, he needs our help."

"So?"

"How can you be so selfish?"

"Selfishness is a good survival habit."

For a moment we didn't speak, but the room was loud, regardless. My heart pounded in my ears, my throat was tight with a trapped sob. "All I need to know is how to cleanse it."

"You're not going back to that house."

"You don't get a say in my life anymore."

"Then you don't get to ask for my help."

"Fine," I said, grinding my teeth. I opened my satchel. "It's not a favor, then. I'll pay you for the information."

Jember opened a drawer on the side table and took out his amulet. It was bigger than mine, on a heavier chain, most of the silver wrapped with black iridescent thread. He held up his amulet in my direction, warding off the money as I took it out from the secret pocket. "I'm not taking your tainted money."

"*This* tainted money?" I said with a smirk, and dropped some on the dirt floor.

His glare was as cold as the castle I'd left. "Pick that up."

"God knows you need it, old man."

He put on his amulet. "I never accept money from a household that hasn't been cleansed yet, and neither should you."

I rolled my eyes. "Nothing bad has happened to me."

"Your bandaged hand says otherwise."

I froze, the memory of the beast chilling me all over again, even in the heat of the desert, and suddenly I had no desire to tease him anymore. I picked up my money quickly and put it away. "You're the only debtera in the past twenty years to have successfully cleansed a household of a hyena—that's why the church recruited you. But you've never talked about how to cleanse it. Please, Jember. You're the only one who can help me."

Jember sighed and hung his head, resting his elbow on his knee to rub his forehead, while I held my breath. After a moment he sat up again. "It can't be cleansed like other Manifestations, only removed and barred from its host, then released to find another one. So, you know what you do?"

"What?"

"You leave it the hell alone."

I groaned in frustration. "Why did I ever think you would help me?"

"I *am* helping you. You want to live? Get out now. Leave the castle to rot. When the family dies the Evil Eye will go off to find another greedy victim to infect. End of story."

"You ruin my career prospects and then think you can—?"

"Ruin? I did you a favor."

"If you don't tell me how to cleanse it, I'll read every scroll I can get my hands on. I'll find another debtera to ask. Either way, I'm going back to that house to finish the job."

"Andromeda, wait."

I'd already turned, already stormed toward the door, but his voice halted me. I spun on my heel to look at him. I shouldn't have cared about what he had to say. I should've kept going without looking back.

Jember was scooting off the bed, and I went to him without questioning myself and dragged his leg out from under the bed. The wood was rough and a little chipped, the leather straps and pads worn. The metal end was still sturdy, just a little scratched, but if the wood gave it wouldn't be of much use. I held his leg out to him by the peg end. I should've left him and let him do it. He'd been doing it for weeks without me.

"You going back just to spite me?" he asked, taking his leg from me. "Because I know you're smarter than this."

"I'm going back to save someone's life."

"This is not going to end how you want it to," he said, strapping his leg on. "I can attest to that."

"Then help me. The two of us together can fix this."

Jember chuckled bitterly. "You've always been unrealistically optimistic. You certainly didn't get that from me." He took off his amulet and held it out to me. "You want to act like an idiot and go against a hyena? You'll need better protection."

Neck pain might be an issue if I wore his heavy chain for too long. But this was the same amulet he'd used to face the Evil Eye before. This was the only help he would offer me, and it was all I needed. I could deal with a little aching.

I hesitated before reaching for it. He held it out of my grasp, his eyebrows raised.

"This is not for you to take. I'll let you go back, on the condition that you construct yourself a hyena-proof amulet."

I gaped at him for a second. "What? But you never taught me how."

"And, technically, I'm still not going to." He held it out to me again with a slight grin. "But you're smart enough to study this and figure it out."

"That could take days."

"Days to construct a better shield or seconds to die without it." He waved it at me obnoxiously. "You have three seconds before I revoke my gracious offer."

I took the amulet immediately, although I wanted to hit him over the head with it rather than study it. I'm pretty sure God would look the other way, seeing as it was Jember.

"Where am I supposed to stay, if not the castle?"

"Here, if you can keep your head down and mouth shut."

I smirked. "That was almost kindhearted of you, Jember."

"Or you can annoy me some more and sleep on the street again." He pushed himself up to stand, stretching. "Actually, I need to run some errands. Give that back. You can study my old amulet, for now."

I handed him the amulet with both hands on the heavy chain. "I have to tell my friend I won't be back to the castle for a while, so she doesn't worry. She's right outside." Jember froze, so I added, "Don't worry, you don't have to say hello."

"Didn't intend to." He grabbed a turmeric-colored shirt, with enough holes that it almost looked artistically done, and sniffed it before pulling it on over his amulet.

I took the key from the dresser and unlocked the chain, shoving the doors open. Saba was leaning against the wall across from the church, as casually as if she lived here instead of in a grand house.

Jember stumbled to a stop on the steps, and I checked to make sure his peg leg hadn't gotten caught in a crack or something. And then he swore—a gross, vulgar word.

I glared down at him. "You can't say that word right behind a church."

He said it again.

"Jember, *stop*." I looked at Saba to apologize, but . . . she was looking at the ground, her brows lowered . . . her eyes glassy.

"Saba?"

I'd never heard Jember's voice tremble, and my head shot up to look at him, just to make sure it had come from him. "You know each other?"

"Don't tell me—? God. You *can't* tell me." He said that gross word again, then slammed the cellar doors shut.

"What's gotten into you, old man?" I demanded through the doors.

"Get her away from here," he said, his voice muted from the other side. "Right now."

"U-um—" I looked at Saba. A tear had broken free down her cheek and my breath faltered for an instant. But I led her toward the side of the church anyway. "Stay right here. I'll be right back," I told her, and raced back down the alley.

"She's gone now," I said to the door, which opened immediately.

He stormed up the stairs, snatching the key back from me and locking the chain without a word.

"Wait a second," I demanded of his back as he left, "what was that all about?"

Jember turned on me, glaring as if I'd said something disrespectful. "Let me guess, that was the pottery you cut yourself on?"

He didn't wait for an answer before leaving me alone in the alley.

So he knew. Of course he knew. He'd faced a hyena, that must've had a servant of its own.

It took me a moment before I could gather myself from all the emotion and go back to where Saba was waiting. She'd dried her tears, but still looked distressed.

I had too many questions, but decided it was better to go with the least insensitive, first. "Are you okay?"

She started to nod, but didn't get very far, her eyes distant.

"Jember's offered me the opportunity to learn how to make a better amulet. One that can withstand the power of the Evil Eye. So, if you could let Magnus know it might be a few days until I can come back . . . Saba?"

At her name she blinked, her gaze snapping to me as if waking from a dream. She gave me a sad smile and nodded.

"What happened?"

She shook her head. Paused. And then she took out a charcoal pencil, leaning on the stone wall of the church to write something. She folded the paper up and handed it to me. It had been her shopping list on one side, because I saw remnants of bullet points and items among the folds. But on the front, in darkly scribbled letters, were the words *For Jember*.

Her expression was so earnest, I decided to keep the rest of my questions to myself. They would keep until I saw her again. "I'll get it to him."

I could tell her grin didn't come easily, and then she turned and walked toward where we'd left the coach.

CHAPTER 20

I held Jember's amulet in my lap, shifting my eyes over it like reading a scroll. The basic markings to see through illusions. Ones to build up a shield.

But, even though this was one of his older amulets, it was still more advanced than mine. Most of it was a confusing array of strokes and dots. The color combinations of the wrapped threads didn't make sense to me. There was no pattern to it.

I picked up the little chalkboard, chipped and cloudy, from when I was little and still learning to write. I started with the strokes I knew, working until the construction deviated from my own amulet. From there it was chaos. It wasn't enough to see them and make a rough copy—any imperfection in the construction would render the amulet useless for what I needed it to do. But trying to sense the strokes was like too many voices echoing in a cave. Unfocused. Indecipherable.

One at a time, then.

This way was tedious, and gave me a little bit of a headache, but it was better than no progress at all. Jember wouldn't let me practice on a slab of wood until I mastered the strokes. And it had to be absolutely perfect before he would give me a disk of silver—*one* disk, because the church didn't believe in supplying too many at once for something so expensive. If I had known I'd be staying here, I would've brought a few from the castle. As it stood, I'd just have to get in enough practice to not mess up.

Easily done.

The cellar door creaked open, and I finally looked up and rubbed my eyes.

"Had to pretend to be fascinated by the archbishop's new horse for the past half hour," he said, wiping sweat from his brow. "Massive beast. We could eat meat for a year."

I raised my eyebrows. "You could stand to eat such a beautiful creature?"

He looked at me like I was crazy, raising his eyebrows right back. "People shoot lame horses all the time. Why waste all that good meat?"

He had a point. And a young horse probably hadn't seen much hard work yet, so the meat might be more tender. My mouth was watering at the prospect of a dream. "It won't be lame for a while if he just bought it."

"Who's to say?" His tone sounded vaguely underhanded. He took a small brown package from his pocket, groaning a little as he sat beside me on the bed. He quirked his brows at my work. "Hm."

"Is it wrong?"

"You tell me."

I lifted his amulet level with my chalkboard, comparing the two. "It looks right."

"Then why'd you doubt yourself?"

"Because you said 'hm' like you disapproved."

"You want to die, girl?"

"Of course not."

"Then start over." He swiped his sleeve on my board, wiping away all my work before I could stop him, then took off his own amulet and handed it to me. "And this time be sure."

He opened the brown paper and held it between us. I grinned and snatched up my triangle of baklava. Warm and flaky and crispy and dripping precious gold. I took a big bite, leaning my head back so the honey running out would get in my mouth instead of my lap.

I hummed a joyful tune, licking my lips.

"Glad you're enjoying it," he said. "Because it's your lunch."

"Well, that's okay, I can—" I could buy us some groceries with my bonus money. But he'd hate that, out of principle. Anyway, with the kitchen a mess there'd be nowhere to put them. I was used to getting by on little. I would "survive."

"Living in that castle hasn't stretched your stomach yet? Surprised."

"Oh!" *Speaking of the castle* . . . I fished out the folded note from my pocket and held it out to him. "Saba wanted me to give this to you."

There was the slightest hesitation before he took it, but no hesitation whatsoever when he opened his drawer and dropped it in.

I chewed on my lip. "Don't you want to read it?"

"While I was out, it occurred to me," he said, licking honey off his fingers, "you'll need a special thread for the hyena's amulet."

I raised my eyebrows. "So you *don't* want to read it?"

"Do you want a patronage or don't you?"

"I'd prefer a license, but it's a little—"

"Too late for that," he said at the same time I did. "Our concern now is that thread. It's woven with pure gold, very rare. The
church doesn't keep it on hand and, for obvious reasons, I never
thought I'd need it again. So we'll have to go shopping."

I felt my nose crinkle. I was surprised I knew what the word
"shopping" meant, Jember had used it correctly so few times
growing up. "Food and medicine are one thing, but you expect
me to steal *gold*? They'll notice it's gone."

"No, they won't. No one frequents where we're going."

I stood up and paced a little. "I have money now. We can just
buy it."

"The closest place that sells it is half a day's journey. Besides,
what would be the fun in that?"

Seeing the spark of mischief in Jember's brown eyes made my
heart kick off with excited anticipation. And, God forgive me, I
only felt the slightest bit of guilt as my lips slipped into a grin.

The sun was setting by the time we left on our errand, but the
moment we exited the city gate and began walking west I realized
it didn't matter that the market was shutting down for the night.

"You didn't say we'd be robbing a grave."

Jember let out a breath of a laugh. "But I did say they wouldn't
notice."

Twenty minutes later, we stood in front of the stairs that led
down into a tomb. Jember leaned on the small shelf-like handle
of his maqomiya, then removed a long candle from his pocket
and held it out to me.

"How did you find out the thread was here?" I asked, flinting
the candle to life. "You haven't faced a hyena in twenty years."

"I've been shopping in here before." He led the way down the stairs, through a crudely constructed gate, and into the dark.

The candlelight didn't have much range, but it illuminated enough that I could see the stone walls and low ceiling of the tomb. The echo of our footsteps told me it was most likely multiple rooms, and my ears were proven right when Jember led us through two more doorways.

Jember handed me the candle and leaned his staff against the stone wall, and I followed his lead as he sat in front of a stone coffin.

"Hold it close."

Already, with the candle close to a carved line, I could see something glint. He took out a needle and stuck it down into the small slit, prying up a small glimpse of the thread. He repeated the action a few times, until there was enough of a loop sticking out from the slit to pinch with my fingers.

"No," Jember said, when I tried.

I sighed and settled down to watch him loosen a little more. "Can I help you?"

"Just hold the candle steady."

It was another few minutes of silence before I said, "How much of this do I need?"

"A meter."

"The candle won't last that long, at the rate you're going. Let me help you."

"If the thread breaks it'll be useless to you. Don't be in such a rush to die."

"I'm not going to die." He scoffed, and I bit back the urge to drip hot wax on him. "What do you care, anyway?"

"I've invested fourteen years of my life in keeping you alive."

I don't like to see my investments wasted— Ah." The end of
the thread revealed itself and he wound it around two fingers.
"Won't be much longer now."

It was work-related, and so I knew I could trust his word.
And sure enough, the rest of the thread came up more easily, as
if guided by the end he was winding. The candle was barely half
used by the time he cut the end of the thread with his knife.

"That's a little bit more than a meter," he said, handing it to
me. "Enough to knot the end."

I tucked it into my pocket. "Thanks, Jember."

"And when we get home—"

"I work on my amulet." I grinned and shrugged. "No rest for
the weary."

"Or for any debtera, for that matter," he said, and I almost
thought I saw him grin too. "Get used to it."

Our gazes shot to each other's at the shuffle and tap of footsteps on the stair, and the quiet voices with them. Immediately I
blew out the candle and we held still, quietly watching as a lantern's light illuminated the main gateway—though my back was
facing the door, so I only saw an edge of light from the corner of
my eye. I prayed to God that it was people coming to visit their
dead loved ones, or even priests.

But Jember's quiet swear sent my heart into my throat. "Grave
robbers."

We were grave robbers, but it seemed the least important
detail at the moment. "Maybe we can sneak out when they're in
a further room," I whispered, knowing my words were simply
wishful thinking. If it were a parade involving the entire city in
the middle of a sandstorm, you would still hear Jember's peg leg
in the midst of it.

"The one with the lantern is smaller."

Smaller. Meaning I would be the one to have to kill him while Jember took the other. Kill, because doling out threats and injuries only created reasons to look over your shoulder for the rest of your life.

I took out my knife, my palm feeling sweaty around the handle. Killing wasn't on my list of favorite activities. I'd only done it once, and only because I would've been violated otherwise. But I'd cried for days afterward, thoughts of my panicked aim solidifying in my memory along with the haunting image of having to stab my attacker three times to finally kill him. Jember usually handled the killing, and rarely in front of me. And since moving into the cellar of the church, we hadn't dealt with that issue as much.

When it came to physical confrontation, I would much prefer to hit and run. But, because of his injury, Jember wasn't as fast as I was. If he was going to hit anyone, he had to make sure they couldn't get up again and come after him.

I froze at a heavy slam and a panicked shout. A shatter. A cry of pain.

Jember swore again, and I felt the brush of cloth as he stood, heard him step around me. My heart raced with adrenaline. I was ready to jump up for whatever came after us—if only I could hear what was coming, my pulse sounded so loud to my own ears.

The robbers' lantern approached, but it was held by the tall, athletic figure of a woman, with the familiar face of an angel.

I gaped. "Saba!" I ran to her and wrapped my arms around her solid waist and she rocked me, her head against my hair. "Am I glad you showed up."

"You . . . followed us?" Jember's voice was tight, and when I looked at him he was gripping his staff enough to make his knuckles white, even in the lantern light.

Her embrace faltered, and then she stepped toward Jember. He held up his staff to keep space between them.

"Spying for your master?" he demanded.

She shook her head quickly.

"Jember," I said, taking my friend's hand, "Saba's on our side."

He scoffed. "That would require thinking of others. Is that a trait you developed *after* death?"

I shoved his staff out of the way. "Jember. Stop."

"Don't follow us again." And he rushed past her and up the stairs.

I looked at Saba apologetically and she shook her head, her eyes sad despite her smile.

"*Did* you follow us?" I asked as we exited the tomb. When she nodded I raised my eyebrows. "Just now, or all day?"

She chewed on her lip and gave me a sheepish look. She drew a circle in the air with her finger, traveling it in one direction, then mimed walking with her index and middle finger in the opposite direction.

"You came back?" I laughed and hugged her again. "You saved us back there. We're both grateful, even if Jember won't admit it." I held her at arm's length and looked up at her. "But you should go take care of Magnus. I know how he hates to be alone."

She kissed my forehead, and handed me the lantern. Taking one last look in Jember's direction, she ran out into the desert toward the castle, swallowed by the darkness of night.

CHAPTER
21

I'd never run toward death so quickly as when I saw the bleak castle lying before me. I could honestly say I was happy to be back. Happy the amulet hadn't taken as long as I thought it would. Happy Jember had helped me with zero to little trouble. Happy to be back near Magnus. Happy . . .

Simply happy.

"Magnus!" I called.

"Welcome home, Andromeda," his melodic voice purred, and my heart pounded.

I threw the door open, my breath retreating from my body.

Magnus was half sunk into the floor before me, half mangled bones and flesh, his face distorted in shocked rigor mortis.

I screamed but no sound came out. Instantly I knew something was wrong, that I wasn't supposed to be here. I screamed again and something hard hit me in the face.

I blinked, panicked breaths shaking my body. I was lying on my side, in my dim childhood room, staring at Jember beside me.

He sat on his half of the bed, back against the wall, finishing up an amulet.

I was too fatigued to touch my temple, even though I could swear a bruise was pulsing there. It was better than the dream. *Anything* was better than that. "Thanks for waking me."

His only response was a grunt.

For a moment I watched him work. He didn't need to see to loop the black and red thread through the tiny welded cuts, the needle like an extension of his hand. He threaded it through, knotted it, threaded the next one. Like a weaver at a loom. I tried to count the loops through my slitted eyes. Fifteen? No. He worked too quickly, and I was already agitated.

I closed my eyes again, although with no intention of sleeping. Instead I spent a while thinking a prayer to drive away the images of Magnus that had lodged themselves to stay . . . images of what might happen if I couldn't save him.

I convinced myself they weren't realistic. The Evil Eye wouldn't kill its own host. It would never—could never—be his fate.

. . . could it?

The wooden creak of the drawer opening made me spasm, but it was only after the crinkle of paper that I opened my eyes. I watched Jember open Saba's letter, with her list on the back of it. Slowly. Too slowly. I held my breath.

He let out a breath of laughter and grinned, and my breath relaxed. But, without much pause in between, he leaned forward and covered his eyes with his hand, murmuring a swear. He stayed that way for a moment, and then sat up and fished a notepad from the drawer.

We'd never used much paper growing up, and so he wrote on the archbishop's pack of stationery I'd stolen three years ago—off-white with an elegant, intricate gold-leaf cross. He wrote more slowly than he threaded amulets. Occasionally pausing. Frequently crossing out what he'd written. He didn't waste the sheet, filling it with words and crossed-off words before flipping it over and doing the same. He paused to read it over.

"Go back to sleep, girl."

"What did Saba say?" I asked, if only to shove away the image that wouldn't let me go.

"None of your business."

"How do you even know each other? You said you never went to the house—" I froze, then jolted up, my grin unbridled. "Saba's older than she looks. If she were alive, I think she would be about your age."

"I know—" Jember looked at me quickly, his slightly wide-eyed expression confirming he knew that I knew. "Shut up."

"You two were a couple!"

"I'm putting you outside," he threatened, though it was a little less effective with the blush rising over his face.

"You love her," I sang, dodging off the bed when he reached for me. "Admit it."

Jember's eyes were burning, and if he had been wearing his leg he would've come after me. "Why don't you do what you came here to do," he growled, pulling out the chalkboard and holding it out to me, "and work on your amulet."

I didn't move. I didn't trust that if I got into grabbing distance he wouldn't drag me onto the bed and beat me within an inch of my life.

And that truth bubbled up anger in me. "There's nothing wrong with loving someone."

"You've known me for fourteen years. Do you think I'm capable of love?"

My throat was suddenly tight, whether with a pent-up laugh

or sob, I couldn't tell. I swallowed . . . and again. "No" finally slipped out through thin air. "You are heartless."

The silence between us was so thick I wanted to drown in it.

"You're not staying here past tonight." Jember waved the board at me, and I took it without question. "Work."

I worked deep into the night, graduating from the chalkboard to wood, etching so many versions of the amulet I almost never wanted to look at wood again. And every time, Jember would tell me to start again.

Pride and arrogance were faults. Knowing your ability wasn't. I was good at amulets. Really good. And I had an excellent amulet to study. It had never taken me three days to master an amulet. Ever.

There was a reason Jember was denying me silver, and it had less to do with my work and more to do with payback.

"I'm ready for silver now."

"No, you're not," he murmured, dozing on his back.

"You didn't even look at this one. I'm ready."

He opened his eyes to look. Long enough to humor me, but not nearly long enough to see if there were any imperfections. "Start over."

I felt my heart pick up painfully. "I've done it a dozen times."

"And it still isn't right?" The question was sarcastically rhetorical, and it made my face hot. "Hm. Okay."

"You're not being fair, Jember. You're the one who wants me out of here by the morning, but you're not even trying to help me." I thrust my wooden amulet into his face to make him look at it. "It looks exactly like yours. I'm ready for silver and you know it."

He snatched the amulet but kept his glare on me. "Who cares if it looks like mine? Does it *feel* like mine? The slightest imperfection makes a difference."

"You haven't even looked at it."

Finally, he looked at it, his eyes shifting, reading it, soaking it in. And then he snapped it in half and threw it through the doorway into the next room.

"Why did you do that?"

"Don't lose your temper with me, girl—"

"It was flawless and you know it."

"You want to get back to that castle so badly you're willing to risk your life with poor preparation. Why? What's there waiting for you?"

I looked away so he couldn't see my blush. My heart . . . that's what was waiting there. Held by a boy with hopeful eyes. But all I said was, "A patronage."

"Not if you're dead." He took his amulet from the bed and shut it into the drawer. "You're going to get your silver. But first I want you to make a copy of your amulet."

I paused. "Mine?"

"From memory. You wear it every day, you must know how it feels by now."

True. It was like a second skin to me. I could feel it from inside the drawer, although the strokes mingled with Jember's. I took a heavy breath in an attempt to calm myself and then snatched up another piece of wood from the other room.

As complex as it was, it took only an hour to replicate mine. When I held it out to him, he looked at it briefly, unimpressed.

"Now construct mine," he said.

I didn't complain this time. Actions spoke louder than words, after all. But, as I worked, I suddenly realized that he was right.

I couldn't quite define every stroke in my mind. Some of them were looped, and I couldn't quite figure out which way. Some had tiny nicks on one side that the others didn't. Jember was my mentor, the best of his generation. But I hated to admit he was right.

If I couldn't even construct his amulet while the strokes were mingled in the air with my amulet's, how was I supposed to seal the hyena while all the chaos of the Waking was going on around me?

I paused and shook the strokes out of my head.

Try again, Andi.

By the time I'd copied his amulet, thread wraps and all, Jember was sleeping soundly. How long had it been? It had to have been nearly morning.

I widened my eyes and paced a little, fighting to keep myself awake now that my mind wasn't occupied.

Meanwhile, Jember was asleep . . .

I looked at the drawer, chewing on my lip. I stretched my neck and back, then carefully opened it and took Saba's letter out.

I still love you, it said, in small, rushed print, and excitement sprinted my heart. *Can we forget everything and just spend my last days here together?*

I stared at the words for a moment. Last days here? She meant . . . when she vanished along with the Evil Eye. The thought of it left needles in my stomach, but Jember shifted and I was forced to quickly put the letter away.

I touched his shoulder to wake him gently and held the amulet in front of his face. He took it from me, while I did some more stretches.

"Looking at my physical amulet was hindering you from sensing the strokes," I heard him say.

I turned to him just as he held the thin wood over the candle by the bed.

"It was perfect," I said, "admit it, old man."

"I admit nothing." He let the wood burn a little before dropping it in the dirt, and my eyes lit up as he nodded his head at our shelf of amulet supplies. "Go get your silver."

CHAPTER
22

Jember refused to come with me to Thorne Manor, so I had to spend a good chunk of the morning bribing anyone who would listen to take me anywhere close. This merchant was at least a little more generous than the last—I only had to walk a mile this time. But even more disappointing, Jember hadn't given me a letter to bring back to Saba. Part of me hoped she wouldn't ask about it.

But the journey had given me plenty of time to think. If I was going to cleanse Magnus, we would have to find a way to release the hyena. Which meant we would need a well-thought-out plan . . . and a willing volunteer.

Esjay could help with that, I was sure of it. Of course, he wouldn't be the volunteer, but he probably had connections, someone who could help. My first thought was Kelela, but there was no way she'd volunteer or he'd allow it. Which was a shame, because I would've loved to see her sweat a little, for once.

I was only a few yards from the castle when the door swung open. Peggy stood in the doorway, hands on her hips. I sighed, wiping sweat that threatened to drip off my chin.

"Where have you been, child?" she scolded, blocking the entire entryway so I couldn't get in.

Momentum had been the only thing keeping me from needing to sit, and now between the heat and lack of water on the trip I felt like I might collapse. "I sent word to Magnus that I'd be a few days."

"You did no such thing. What you did was take the coach without permission, then send it back to us with nothing inside but a few bags of supplies. We thought you'd died out in the desert somewhere."

"Did you mourn me, Peggy?" I gathered a bit more strength and shoved past her into the house. The cold felt good for a moment, but I'd need to get a sweater on quickly. My body didn't seem to like the extreme heat exhaustion followed by the bitter cold, and I suddenly felt nauseated.

"And I'll bet you convinced Emma to run away with you," Peggy went on, following me to the stairs. "I read the note she left on her bed. Ungrateful girls, both of you."

"Emma's husband is dead." The conversation was over as far as I was concerned, so I rushed up the stairs before her look of shock could turn into a response.

I looked at Magnus's bedroom door, then rushed into my room. I didn't want to greet him covered in sand, as silly as that sounded. I dropped my sandy clothes in one corner to consolidate the mess, then scrubbed myself clean, my impatient heart thumping in my temple. My hair might've had some sand left, but I was too eager to worry about it, braiding it into a crown.

I heard rushed footsteps, and then my doorknob jiggled, followed by a knock on the door. "Andromeda?"

"Magnus!" I slapped my hands over my mouth. *Too eager, Andi.* "U-um, just a minute."

I dressed in my wool skirt and sweater quickly, blushing as I pulled on my stockings. Magnus would've barged right in while I was naked. Thank God I had locked the door.

When I opened the door Magnus was right there waiting, beaming like a little boy. "Welcome home, Andromeda."

Images of my dream flashed in my head and I closed my eyes to be rid of them. I jolted, feeling a cold hand against mine, opening my eyes in time to see Magnus bring the back of my hand to his lips and kiss it.

"I didn't expect you so soon," he said. "Your present isn't here yet."

"You didn't have to buy me anything."

"Of course I did." He reached out his hand and my breath caught. The warmth of his hand near my face was . . . overwhelming. A tingle went through my scalp as his fingertips admired my braid. "Esjay and Kelela are bringing it when they come for lunch. They should be here any minute."

The mention of Kelela made my stomach ache. I stepped out of his grasp. "That will be nice for you."

"This is better," he said, though didn't close the space between us. He leaned his head on the door and grinned. "I missed you."

"You shouldn't say that."

"You can't still be mad at me."

"You're engaged, Magnus." He scoffed, but I held up my hand against him speaking. "You must be content to be acquaintances. A friendly, *working* relationship."

"Don't be ridiculous," he said, leaning closer. "Look me in the eye and tell me you're content with that."

I closed my eyes, taking a deep breath before looking him

square in the eye. "I am content to maintain the dignity of not giving myself to a man who is spoken for."

Magnus groaned as if my words had physically hurt him. "I want you, Andromeda."

"No," I said sternly, stepping back.

"And you want me."

"I don't. Not like this."

Magnus huffed in frustration, pushing curls out of his face. "Even if I was engaged—which I'm not, by the way—that is not a legal union. I could break it off whenever I like."

I saw Peggy heading toward the door—Esjay and Kelela must've arrived—and lowered my voice. "Then break it off."

"There's nothing to break, Andromeda," Magnus said, and I shushed him and dragged him into my room. "That's what I'm trying to make you understand."

"If it were only Kelela being spiteful, I would believe you. But Esjay is also under the impression you're engaged. What reason does he have to lie?"

"In what galaxy is a verbal promise from a boy whose voice still cracks legally binding?"

"You promised her and then never took it back. It's your integrity in question."

"I'll take it back at lunch, then, if that will make you feel better."

"Don't bother," I said, scowling up at him, my heart, soul, and lungs burning from pent-up tears. "You were never going to act unless I said anything. You were content to have both of us."

Magnus leaned the side of his head on the doorjamb, helplessly, his palm out to me in supplication. "I want *you*, my darling—"

"I'm not your darling."

"Only you."

"Then you shouldn't have lied to me about being engaged."

I pushed past him and headed downstairs, but Magnus followed close behind. "I'm going to tell Kelela."

I spun on him and pinched my fingers together, wishing the action operated his mouth, that I could shut him up without words. "No more, Magnus," I said, low and vicious. "This conversation is over. We're going to have lunch with Esjay and Kelela, and I don't want to hear another word about it."

"Right, that would be embarrassing. I'll tell her in private afterward, then."

"No, you won't."

I went to turn around, but Magnus grabbed my arm, holding me still. "Say you don't want to be with me and I'll stop fighting for you. But you can't keep moving the goal post."

"You lied to me and used me, and I'm supposed to roll over and accept that treatment because you try to make it right *after* you're caught?" I pulled away, glaring up at him. "This conversation is over."

Magnus cut me off before I could go further, standing on the stairs in front of me to make us eye level. "Tell me you don't want me." He took hold of my waist and I grabbed his wrists without purpose, my heart suddenly unable to make him let go. "Say you're only here for a patronage, that you don't care for me at all, and I'll leave you to your work." He cradled my face and I closed my eyes to press back tears. "Because if you dare leave me a shred of hope, I will fight to have you with the last drop of blood in my body."

I heard a whimper escape me before I could stop it, felt Magnus's soft thumbs wipe tears from my cheeks. "I don't want to lie to you, Magnus."

"Then don't." His lips blessed my forehead, my salty cheek, my nose, each kiss sweeping my breath and pulse into madness. "Say what you want from me. Whatever your answer, I'll take it like a man."

"I-I came here in the first place—" I took a steadying breath as he kissed my temple. "I came here for your patronage, Magnus. That's why I'm here."

It wasn't a lie if it was true. And it was, even if it wasn't the only truth. Maybe I was as wrong as Magnus for withholding the rest of it . . . that I wanted him. That I would give anything to be with him. That I love—

A sudden sob escaped Magnus's throat, his hands at my face trembling. "You don't want me?" he whispered, and he might as well have stabbed me in the chest.

I swallowed, speaking slowly to control my voice. "I'll never be able to find more work without your patronage."

"This is your answer?" He nodded without waiting for me to confirm, almost absently, as if his heart wasn't in the action. "I will do my best to obey you . . ." He grabbed hold of the rail to steady himself, and I balanced between the desire to comfort him and the thought of holding back so as not to make the situation worse. But as he hung his head and cried, pain shot through every inch of my gut, and then it was I holding his jaw in my hands, tasting his tears as I kissed his face.

"Don't cry," I begged, in vain. He lowered himself into a crouch, his head between his knees, holding the rail for support, and wept. And I was too cowardly to stay to see it.

I rushed back up the stairs to my room, locked the door, and buried myself under the covers to cry.

Not a good survival habit, Andi.

At least, that's what Jember would say. But I was in a safe place, and I was alone . . . oh God, so alone.

I kicked off the blanket and went to the barrel of water in the corner, dunking my face into it. Despite my room being warm, the water was cold enough to shock me into calming down. I held my breath until I was more concerned with my lungs than my heart, and came up panting, my chest burning.

I'd never cared about boys before. Why was this one any different?

I dried my face and made my way back downstairs. If I was going to be here only for the sake of working, I had to abide by Magnus's rules.

I shoved the urge to cry to the back of my mind to join the rest of my childhood nightmares and entered the dining room with my head held high. Magnus sat in his usual place at the table, but on seeing me he leapt to his feet. I should've ignored him, but we locked eyes immediately. His eyes were rimmed a bit with red and his nose was rosy, but otherwise he seemed intact.

Magnus pulled the heavy chair out for me. I dropped my gaze. I don't know why that simple act of politeness was too much for me.

Maybe because he'd never done it before.

"Thank you," I murmured.

"You're welcome," he murmured back.

Again, simple, polite words, but brimming with so much intimacy I could barely stand it. I felt the urge to kiss him emerging through the tiny cracks in my stoicism. Instead, I sat and allowed him to push in my chair.

"You too, Andromeda?" Esjay asked, concerned and a little confused. "Everyone is so depressed today. Don't worry, this isn't the last time Kelela will visit before she leaves."

"I won't miss how cold it is," said Kelela, her tone especially sharp today. It should've been ludicrous, but she looked beautiful in her high pink ponytail and matching pink lips. "Have you done any cleansing at all?"

At this point I knew better than to get upset over Kelela's prodding. Anyway, I had plenty else to be upset about.

"As long as the Evil Eye is still present," I said, "it's not going to get any warmer. But the focus now is to cleanse Magnus."

"Well, that's excellent news." And then Esjay and Kelela went about dinner as if that were the end of the subject.

I chewed on my lip. "So, we'll need a volunteer to make eye contact with Magnus and draw out the Evil Eye."

It was equally fascinating and discouraging to watch Esjay's expression drop as I spoke.

"Kelela," he said, standing quickly, and it was the most severe I'd ever heard his voice. "Don't let Magnus look at you. Bow your head as you get up."

"Esjay," she protested, as if embarrassed by his behavior, but did as she was told. "We only just got here."

Magnus popped up, wiping away stray tears. "Wait, you're leaving?" he asked, a slight squeak of panic at the end.

"It won't be just anyone." I held up my hand, standing. "It has to be a willing volunteer, who's fully aware they'll be in the line of danger."

"That's a death sentence," Esjay said, taking Kelela's arm to prompt her to her feet. "You'll never find someone to cooperate. Come, Kelela." And he guided his sister toward the exit.

"We have to try," I said, following behind him. "With the right preparation and a controlled environment, I don't see why it shouldn't work."

"Of course, try. We've come too far to give up now. No,

Kelela." He opened the front door and made her walk out, despite her protests about being hungry. "Wait for me in the coach." He shut the door behind her, taking deep, slow breaths before turning back to me. "I'm not going to be part of this. I'm sure you can understand why."

It was such a stark change from when I first met him. To go from full support, dining under one roof, offering his own sister in marriage . . . to wanting nothing to do with it at all? It was irritating, to be honest. And it didn't seem just.

"People have died in this house," I said, forcing my voice not to sound harsh. "Not vanished. *Died*. You didn't stop hiring servants when the first one disappeared, did you? All of them knew the risks. Whoever this brave person is, they will, too."

"And it'll only take *one more* dead person to cleanse Magnus, is that what you're trying to say?" It was strange to hear Esjay sound almost aggressive. He opened the door. "If you need anything, let me know. But I don't want any progress reports on this. I don't want details. Just tell me when it's over." He went to leave, then paused. "And tell Magnus I'm sorry. Kelela was going to come over to say good-bye before she left for France, but due to the circumstance I think it's better she doesn't." He hesitated, as if he had more to say. And then he left, shutting the door behind him.

I stood, staring at the door. *God help me*. And then took a deep breath and walked calmly back into the dining room.

"They left," Magnus said, slouching slightly in his chair.

"It's okay." I took my seat again, taking his hand.

"I heard Esjay. They're not coming back." He slouched further, sliding down to sit on the floor under the table. "I think I'm going to die."

I shoved his chair out of the way so I could get to him. "You're not going to die."

"That's right," he added bitterly, digging his knuckles into his eyes, "I *can't* die. The Evil Eye won't let me."

"We're going to get a volunteer, Magnus. Everything will be okay."

"How? No one will come near here, let alone inside to be *killed*." He lay down, pressing his palms to his eyes. "Oh God. The room's spinning. I want to die."

"You have to calm down—"

"Calm down?" he shouted, tears running down the sides of his face. "You rejected me. My only friends on the outside abandoned me. It's only a matter of time before Peggy does, too. You might as well kill me now."

My stomach twisted at the mention of my villainy. "Don't be ridiculous."

"Where's your knife?"

I leaned down and tapped him in the forehead. He yelped like a startled puppy, swatting my hand away. "Stop it, Magnus. I'm not going to kill you."

He was panicked, his breath coming in quick huffs. "Do you have any idea what it's like to be alone?"

His words sent a thin, needle's stab through my stomach and out my spine. Wandering the streets. Checking over my shoulder. Having no one to rely on for . . . weeks at a time. I didn't just have an *idea* of what it was like. I knew. Only, it wasn't a burden I had the luxury to make room for.

"Magnus." I spoke firmly but calmly as I sat down beside him. I stroked the line from his forehead, between his eyes, down his nose, and back again, shushing him gently. "You need to calm down now. All right? Calm. Down. Breathe."

My slow words and soothing touch seemed to do the trick, and eventually his breath eased. Tears flowed freely down his face, but no sobs with them.

"I hope you know what you're doing, Andromeda," he said. "Because no one in their right mind is going to volunteer to die."

CHAPTER
23

━━━━ ⌇ ━━━━

I pulled on the oversized boots, opened the big black umbrella, and stepped into the snowy hallway.

Apparently, snow was common in many parts of the country, the world, but I'd never seen it before. It was mesmerizing, watching the little icy fluffs materialize from the ceiling to aimlessly drift down. I almost didn't want to get rid of it.

But it wasn't real snow, obviously. More obvious when it retreated from me, shifting away and around the shield of my brand-new—apparently more powerful—amulet.

I left the snow and hammered a nail just outside the domain of the Manifestation, hanging my amulet on it and making sure it was still in sight when I stepped back in, feeling the snow crunch underfoot.

I stooped down, the umbrella shading me and the snow below. Spreading my fingers, I pressed my hand into the white fluff. It gave easily with a *crunch*, wet and light, and I was buried to mid-forearm before my palm touched something harder and colder. When I lifted my hand out, I took some of the snow with me, gazing at the fluffy crystals in my hand.

"I wish you didn't have to go," I whispered. I stood and brushed off my hands, then closed the umbrella to bask in it a little longer . . . though I quickly realized the umbrella was there for a reason. I'd be soaked through if I wasn't carefu—

I yelped as something solid and cold hit my shoulder, scattering snow like an explosion that got some in my eye.

"Hey!" My scowl turned into a smile as I watched Saba laughing at the end of the hall. "What was that?"

I wiped the water off my eyelashes and looked down at my shoulder, a splotch of snow sticking where it had hit me. I dusted it off quickly, before it seeped through my sweater. Saba bent over and gathered more snow, pressing it into a ball between her hands. I gaped, realizing what she was doing, and barely had time to dodge as she threw it at me. I slipped and fell onto my bottom, giggling like a little kid.

"Oh, you've done it now."

I pressed together my own ball of snow, using the umbrella as a shield to block Saba's attack, but mine was small and ineffective, Saba barely needing to move to get away from it. I threw the umbrella away to gather more snow, but I'd never be able to move or block in time to—

Snow hit Saba in the chest and she grinned wildly beyond me. It suddenly occurred to me how similar her smile was to—

"Magnus!" I felt myself beaming as he bent beside me to gather more snow. I dropped my gaze to the snow at the last second. "I'm not wearing my amulet."

"I'd say the odds are a bit more even this way, wouldn't you?" Magnus pressed his snowball tightly in his bare hands. "And that's okay, keep your eyes on the prize."

"Beating Saba?" I held up my arms in front of my face just in time to block Saba's attack.

"Not in the face!" Magnus threw his snowball in my defense. "We can't just put ours back together, you know."

Saba stuck out her tongue at us, and I slipped to my feet, laughing. "Get ready to lose, Saba!"

And with that, it was all-out war. My hands were numb, my hair and sweater coated with snow, but I didn't care. This was the most I'd laughed in—

"What the devil is going on?"

Peggy's voice made me jolt around, slipping before I gained my footing.

"Have you lost your mind?" she said, glaring at me as if I truly had. "Why are you throwing snow around?"

"She started it," Magnus and I said together, pointing at where Saba had been—she certainly had a way of disappearing at all the right moments to avoid Peggy. And maybe Magnus thought so too, because we both laughed.

Peggy gave a disapproving look. "Magnus, come out from there, you'll catch your death."

"Wouldn't that be novel?" he said, but stood, holding out both bluing hands to me. I took them and he lifted me to my feet.

I made my way carefully out of the snow and hung my amulet around my neck before turning to look at Magnus. He was rosy and grinning and . . .

And not yours, Andi.

"After you," he said.

My heart was still pounding, but I think my body was beginning to realize it was cold, because my teeth chattered when I murmured my thanks and hurried ahead of him.

There was no denying getting over him was going to be

impossible while living under the same roof, especially while sleeping on the same floor. I would have to amend that quickly if I was going to survive.

"Andromeda," Magnus said, when we'd made it to our rooms, "may I have a word with you after you've changed?"

My heart panicked, and I prayed to God he couldn't hear it. "Of course." And then I rushed into my room and locked the door. I quickly changed out of my wet clothing, toying with the idea of finding a random closet to hide in. But I couldn't avoid him for days like I did after that first kiss.

Don't be a coward.

Perhaps I'd taken too long to consider, because when I finished changing and went into the hall, Magnus was waiting for me, leaning on the wall across from my door.

"You look nice," he said.

I glanced down at my long grey dress and sweater, nearly identical to the ones the snow had soaked through, except this sweater was a little too big for me and covered my hands nearly to the ends of my fingers. "What did you want to talk about?"

He opened his mouth to speak, wincing and closing his eyes briefly as Peggy called his name from the bottom of the stairs. He took a deep breath. "Yes, Peggy?"

"Esjay's coach is here," she called.

"Have a good time."

"I'll be gone past dinner, but I've already prepared it for you. It's waiting in the kitchen."

"Thank you, Peggy," Magnus said, almost too sweetly. I smirked.

"Behave yourself while I'm gone."

"I will," he said, his expression full of mischief, and I had to stifle a laugh.

God forgive us, we managed to hold in our laughter until after she shut the door.

"I thought she'd never leave," said Magnus.

I raised an eyebrow. "Why, what are you up to?"

"An entire day alone with you. And Saba," he added quickly. "Of course. Love her."

"I love her, too."

"Yes, who wouldn't. A maniac, maybe." He fidgeted, and I could see a blush rising up his neck. "Although, I could've warned you she would start throwing snowballs."

"That was incredible." I felt my own blush rising. "More fun than I've had in a long time."

"See? You can have fun without working." He looked at me for a moment with the slightest of grins, and my heart swelled. "We can be friends, can't we?"

"I hope so," I said.

"I promise, I'll do my best not to flirt."

I grinned. "I don't even think you *do* flirt, Magnus. You're just . . . you."

And *"you" is wonderful*, I would've added, but I didn't want to encourage him. Not after I made him weep yesterday. My stomach twisted with the memory.

Magnus played with his sweater. I was surprised every one he owned wasn't stretched out by now. "What about hugs?"

"I'm not much of a hugger." I reached out and smoothed the crease between his brows with my thumb—I shouldn't have touched him at all, but it seemed to happen without any thought. He closed his eyes, taking a slow breath. I wanted so badly to kiss him.

"You're flirting, Andromeda," he said, eyes still closed, leaning forward to relax into my touch. "You must control yourself."

I tightened my lips to suppress a smile. "I just don't like seeing you scowl."

"So, no hugs, but this is acceptable?" Magnus pushed my wet hair behind my shoulder, his fingers tracing tingles over my bare skin. Instinctively I raised my shoulder against it, and he bit his lip, as if to keep himself from laughing.

I looked away to keep my wits. "On second thought, I see what you mean."

"Are you saying I caused this beautiful blush?"

I felt my face grow even hotter but lifted my chin defiantly, raising my brows. "Your ego would love to think so, I'm sure."

Magnus grabbed his heart dramatically. "Your vicious honesty sustains me, Andromeda. Never change."

"Such sweet words," I said with the slightest scoff, but it wasn't scorn that made me turn my face away or tighten my throat with a sob until it burned.

"No good? Then tell me, how would you like your words?"

"As honest as mine."

"Except not so vicious. I am a gentleman, after all." Magnus laid a finger against the side of my chin and turned my head to face him and, despite my inner fight to defy it, I felt myself grin. "Now. What should we do with the rest of our day?"

A heavy bell echoed through the halls.

Magnus looked around, startled. "What was that?"

I raised my eyebrows at him. "Your doorbell."

"Really? Blazes, that was scary." He grabbed my hand as I moved toward the stairs. "Ignore it. Maybe they'll go away."

The only visitors I'd ever seen come to the house were Esjay and Kelela, and after this morning it seemed strange that they would be here. Unless . . . maybe Esjay wasn't as unwilling to help as he'd claimed.

Maybe he'd sent a volunteer.

I gave Magnus's hand an encouraging squeeze and led him down the stairs. Saba was waiting by the door, as if she expected trouble.

"I'll meet you in the game room," I said.

Magnus kissed my hand. "Don't be long."

I waited until he'd disappeared and then opened the door. I recognized the pink hair in a simple bun before the person, and then Kelela stepped inside without waiting to be invited, rubbing her arms.

I gaped. "What are you doing here? What happened to your party?"

"It's not until tomorrow night. Esjay thinks I'm out saying good-bye to friends," she said, buttoning her coat, tucking the collar around her neck.

"Does Esjay know you're here?"

"He knows I'm seeing friends." She gave me a direct look, like she planned to kill me if I ever told anyone those friends meant *us*. "If I do this, you have to swear you'll protect me when the time comes."

"Protect—" My heart felt heavy as a rock. "Kelela. No."

"I've already made up my mind."

"Magnus won't agree to it."

"No one in their right mind would volunteer for this. And I—" She paused. Swallowed. "I love him. I know he doesn't love me the same way, but I can't help it. I've watched him suffer for three years . . . I can't do it anymore."

We were quiet for a moment.

"So, do you swear?" she asked again, and her voice warbled slightly.

Immediately the scripture stating not to swear settled in my head, as it always did in these situations. But this was a great sacrifice Kelela was making, and I could tell just by looking at her she was terrified. She needed to hear it. "I swear it."

We stood there awkwardly for a moment. "So, will this all happen tonight? I couldn't get Peggy to agree to stay overnight."

I raised my eyebrows slightly. "So, the dinner party . . . ?"

"Esjay's idea. But Peggy helping was mine. There's no way I'd get away with this with her in the house."

I couldn't help but grin. So, her evil actually could be used for good.

"He's in the game room," I said. She led the way while I hung back with Saba to exchange wary looks.

"I knew I smelled your perfume," Magnus said, though he kept his eyes on his drawing. "After yesterday, I didn't think—"

"Magnus." I could already hear tears in her voice. She dropped down next to him and wrapped her arms around his neck, making him drop his pencil. "You have to look at me."

"Don't be ridiculous," he said, but squeezed his eyes shut, as if he expected her to try it without his cooperation.

"I'm the only volunteer you're going to get."

"*Stop*, Kelela." He shoved her off, leaning over his knees and pressing his hand to his eyes for extra security. "Have you lost your mind?"

"From the day I met you."

Magnus let out a small laugh that slowly developed into sobs. He cried into his hand, and I wanted so badly to go comfort him, but I stayed where I was.

Kelela rubbed his shoulder. "It's okay, Magnus—"

"It's not okay," he said between gasps. "Do you know what you're asking me to do? If I look at you, you'll die."

"I want to do this for you. I've watched you suffer for three years. I want you to be free." She took his hand, and I had to look away. It was the wrong time and place to feel jealous, to be hurt by a simple gesture. But I can admit, it hurt in multiple ways, the main one at the moment being that I felt ashamed for thinking petty thoughts about her when all this time she was selfless . . . and incredibly brave.

"What do you expect me to tell Esjay?" asked Magnus.

"Nothing," Kelela said. "He'll never know. Andromeda said she'll protect me."

"I don't think she can." Magnus groaned and sniffled, wiping his nose on his sleeve. "God, Kelela, if you die—"

"Then you'll have to live your life to the fullest for the both of us."

He shook his head. "I can't do this to you."

"I've missed looking you in the eye. They're what I fell in love with first, you know. Can't I spend one last day falling in love with you again?"

Magnus dragged Kelela into an embrace, and it was so genuine I had to look away. He . . . he loved her. It was clear. No matter how many sweet nothings he swore were for me, there was no denying the desperation in that hug, as if he were anchoring her soul to this earth.

Nearly a minute passed, it seemed, before they let each other go, slowly. Magnus took deep breaths that were interrupted by occasional hiccups. And then he swiped his hand across his wet eyes and looked up at me. "You'll protect her?"

I felt my heart crack into dust. I tried to swallow, but my throat was too dry. There would be plenty of time to feel stupid about falling for his lies yet again, but just now wasn't it. Besides, how could I feel anything when I couldn't even think? I barely knew what I was supposed to feel . . . all I knew was that I would be a horrible person if I said no.

Think of the greater good, Andi. Magnus will be free. Saba will rest in peace. The Evil Eye will be gone . . . you'll have your patronage.

A sour taste rose up in my throat just thinking about it.

I was back to the beginning, wasn't I? Back to only caring for myself.

Back to being alone.

"Andromeda," Magnus said earnestly. He reached for my hand, but I couldn't bear to take it. "Please?"

A laugh got caught in my throat. A sob, a scoff. I cleared my throat of all those things and nodded. "I will."

And with the last of my strength, I forced back any emotion that could hinder me from surviving—how it felt to be in his arms, to be kissed by him, to lov—

I shoved it all back until all that remained was angered determination.

Magnus closed his eyes and took one more deep breath before turning to face Kelela. He forced his eyes open, staring widely at her, then squeezed them shut again. "I can't do it anymore," he gasped.

Kelela laid her hand on his cheek. "Look at me, Magnus."

He took a deep, trembling breath, and opened his eyes. Lingered on her. Grinned. "Your hair really is pink this week."

"Do you like it?" she asked, flicking her head like it would swish her hair, despite it being secured in a bun.

"It suits you. It's been so long. Andromeda was right, you're really beautiful." His smile crept downward. "And I'm a monster."

He got up and rushed toward the door, tripping to a stop in

the doorway. "Protect her, Andromeda," he said, a fearful anger in his voice.

"With my life," I said without hesitation.

And he left the room.

"What now?" asked Kelela.

"Now you should rest," I said. "Eat something. We'll likely have to stay up all night, so save your strength."

Kelela nodded and stood, looking at the fireplace. "Magnus was right, I've lost my mind."

I didn't know how to respond. The silence stretched between us. "You love him," I said, to fill it. "And you're a good person."

Kelela laughed, and it almost wasn't completely bitter. "You're the only good person I've ever met."

"We're all sinners."

"No, but you're selfless. It's hard to compete with someone so admirable." She tucked her coat closer. Cleared her throat. "I can see why he loves you."

Loves me? I forced myself not to gape, my brows lowering. "I want you to know, I don't encourage him. And when he's cleansed, I promise you'll never see me again—"

"That won't be necessary." She let out a small, bitter chuckle, as if she couldn't believe her own words. "I broke it off with him."

I hesitated, forcing back my hope. "Why?"

"Because I saw you together yesterday. On the stairs." She stroked the baby hairs at her temple. "He was so tender with you. He . . . isn't normally like that." She twitched, shifting uncomfortably, and I was glad she wasn't looking at me so I wouldn't feel badly for blushing so much. "The way he kissed you . . . the way he cried when you rejected him. I had to put the poor man out of his misery."

Nothing I could think to say seemed right.

"He said you won't have him," she said, and when she turned to me her expression was accusing.

"It wouldn't be right," I said, and the words sounded idiotic even as they left my mouth.

"Even with no one in your way?" When I didn't answer she kissed her teeth. "Let me guess, some excuse about being employed by him?"

"I don't expect you to understand."

"Whatever it is, it can't be as big a deal as you're making it. Do yourself a favor and get a little pleasure out of life while you can because we could all end up dead tonight—" At her own words her expression dropped to something more solemn, veiling fear. She cleared her throat. "You'd better keep your word and not get me killed. There are too many Parisian men I've yet to meet waiting for me."

And she lifted her chin proudly and left the room.

CHAPTER
24

───❦───

hatever it is, it can't be as big a deal as you're making it.

Kelela's words rang through my head, driving me crazy through the couple hours I spent constructing a better amulet for her. I mean, Magnus had led me on, knowing full well he was engaged and not thinking anything of it. Then, he'd had no intention of breaking it off with Kelela except that I'd given him no other choice. If I'd valued my dignity less, how long would he have kept us both?

But then . . .

Jember had been careless with my heart since I was five years old, and I'd yet to abandon him. And, well . . . perhaps the engagement had just been the whimsical words of children after all. It wasn't as if he'd gone through the proper arrangements of paying a dowry—and honestly, they shouldn't have been seeing each other before the wedding the way they did, if they were to do it properly. So maybe the engagement wasn't official, and maybe I was the only one making a huge thing of it, and maybe he would've told me if it had mattered, and maybe—oh God, it felt crazy to hope—he did love me as Kelela said and I'd chased him away forever and . . .

And maybe it was too late to ask forgiveness.

I rushed out of my room, checking all the usual rooms until I stopped in the library doorway. It was darker and colder than usual. There were candles lit behind and around the chairs, big metal stands with branches like trees spreading out, with small holders for candles all along them. But the fireplace was nothing but a small flame, and only by the candlelight and the shadows he created did I see Magnus, kneeling in front of it.

I went in and knelt beside him. He didn't look at me. Didn't move.

"You'll hurt your eyes," I said after a moment, "staring at the flames like that."

"I'm afraid the position of Nagging Mother has been filled."

I bit back a laugh. Now wasn't the time. Or maybe it was, and I'd missed the opportunity to brighten his mood.

I rolled my sleeves up to my elbows and crept forward, reaching into the hearth to get the fire live again.

"You don't want to use the tools?" Magnus asked.

"I trust myself." I moved the wood until the flame caught again and began to thrive on its own.

I watched the flames dance, bright and wild like my heart. *Enough stalling, Andi.* "Kelela said she broke it off with you."

Magnus made a small sound of confirmation. "She's a smart woman." A deep silence stretched. "Not sure how I attract such smart, caring women when I'm such a disaster of a man."

"You're not a disaster."

He let out a small, bitter laugh. "I am, a little. You have to admit."

"If you are, then . . . I suppose I like disasters."

Finally, he looked at me. "After how foolish I've been, you still like me?"

"You're not foolish."

"Don't be so generous, Andromeda. I prefer you honest."

"I am being honest." I hesitated, then stood up abruptly, my heart pounding. "U-um, yes. Well. We have a busy night. I should nap beforehand."

But I didn't leave the room. If anyone was the fool, it was I—I couldn't speak, and yet I couldn't bear to leave his side. I couldn't imagine what he must've thought of me, seeking him out only to leave him in a rush.

He stood up beside me, and I wanted to both stay in his soothing presence, in range of his soft scent, and to drop dead.

"You have so many scars," I heard him murmur, and turned to see that he was studying my arms. "You said Jember's training was brutal, but I never expected . . ."

"Life is brutal, Magnus. My training had nothing to do with it." Standing so close to the fireplace made the fabric of the sweater a little itchy, but despite that I pulled my sleeves down over my scarred arms. "Jember would discipline me when I was younger and didn't know any better. But he's never hurt me in a way I couldn't recover from, or that didn't teach me an important survival lesson."

"That he hurt you at all is disgusting. What a wicked thing to do to a child."

"You never got beatings, growing up?"

"Rarely. Certainly none that left me scarred." He looked like he wanted to cry. I gasped, closing my eyes briefly as he ran his soft fingertips along the scar on my face. "D-did he give you this?"

I moved his hand away, suddenly self-conscious as I turned

my face again so he couldn't see it. "Some peers attacked me for defending someone. One of them had a knife, I guess—they were hitting me so much I don't remember exactly when it happened. All I know is that if Jember hadn't shown up I would probably be dead."

"You think highly of him." I couldn't tell if it was a question or a comment. Judging by his expression, Magnus wasn't sure, either.

"No. Well—" I felt myself scowling in thought. "He's a pretty despicable person. If I had to name one good thing about him that wasn't related to his work, I don't think I could. But I care about him. And I'd defend him with my life." I sat down in my usual chair to relieve the itching the closeness of the flame created . . . and to keep Magnus far enough away so he couldn't touch me again. Being near him was more overwhelming than I'd ever anticipated. "And I think he has a heart, even if he doesn't like to show it. It's nice to imagine that he bought me from my parents to get me away from terrible people. That he cares about me like I care for him."

"Your parents *sold* you?" I'd never heard someone sound so shocked to find out slavery was still a thriving business. Magnus collapsed into his chair, as if the weight of the world were on him. "Monsters. All fathers . . . monsters."

"Your father was cursed. He didn't choose his fate."

"He chose to hire someone to kill him and leave me to deal with his mistakes. Even if he wasn't a monster, he certainly wasn't any good."

"You knew your parents. And you have a handful of people who love you, who are working to save your life. You're blessed."

"How can you stay so positive? Your parents sold you off like produce. The man who raised you was abusive. Are you sure you don't need to let off a little steam? It's just us, Andromeda. You don't have to pretend you're fine with the people who have hurt you."

"I can't change those things. What should I be doing, complaining about them?"

"That's what I would do."

"Jember taught me to live by good survival habits. One of mine is well-placed optimism. If I look at all the bad in my life along with the good, the bad would bury the good in a landslide. My spirit, my will to live, would shrivel and die. So, instead, I choose to be thankful for what little good I have. And I choose to hope."

We didn't speak for a moment.

"I've noticed . . ." He rubbed his face, as if what he was about to say was stressful. "You're very stiff when we touch. Another good survival habit?"

"I didn't realize I was stiff."

"Well . . ." He grinned slightly. "Not when we kiss."

I suddenly became interested in a small scratch on the arm of the chair, hoping the firelight would hide my blush. He'd said it as if he intended to kiss me right this minute. And, God help me, I wanted to taste his lips more than anything.

Magnus leaned in my direction, his arm on the small table between us. "If you need me to fight Jember, I will."

I smirked slightly. "He'd definitely kill you. He has no morals when it comes to a fight."

"He's a cad who denied you basic human affection, so it's worth a try."

"Affection isn't so important when you've lived your entire life without it," I said, finally having the stomach to look at him. "And you don't know him, so you don't get to call him names.

He raised me. I turned out fine. So, keep your mouth shut about him."

He raised a sly eyebrow at me. "What'll you give me to keep my mouth shut?"

I felt a vein twitching in my temple. "I'm already cleansing your castle. I don't owe you anything else."

"It'll have to be something on top of that, since I'm also already *paying* you to cleanse my castle."

"I'm tempted to punch you in the face. I can simply *not*."

I straightened my posture the longer he looked at me. There were two chair arms and a table between us, but somehow I felt too close. I should've stood. I should've left. Not because I was afraid, but . . . my God. Why was I trembling like this? This was not what I'd expected at all. "Don't look at me with those sinful eyes," I said, as coldly as I could manage.

"Sinful?" He slouched forward, gazing into the fire for a moment before looking back at me. "Since when is desiring someone a sin?"

"Desiring—" My jaw snapped shut. He couldn't be saying what I thought he was saying . . . "Since when? Since forever. It's called lust."

"Lust might be part of it, but it's too crude a word for my feelings for you."

"Lust should be nowhere near your feelings for me." Anger and hurt swelled up in my gut, and I stood as he opened his mouth to speak, cutting him off. "I was right, after all. You do intend to only use me for pleasure."

"*What?*" Magnus looked up at me, still leaning forward in his chair, that deep and wild look still in his eyes paired with something like nervous concern. "Sit down, Andromeda—"

"No." I took a step back to prove my point.

"Does it shock you? To be desired?"

"I'm not beautiful like Kelela."

He looked at me like I'd lost my mind. "I don't care about that. And since when do you?"

"I suppose I just . . ." I swallowed. Cleared my throat. "I wasn't raised to acknowledge . . . attraction . . . of that sort."

"But do you feel attraction of that sort, even if you choose not to acknowledge it?"

"You shouldn't ask me such things," I said, my face burning.

"As I said, that's only part of my feelings, and the least important at that." Magnus grinned the slightest bit. "Will you sit down, Andromeda?" He gestured to the chair. "Please?"

I sat without thinking, without questioning it. This conversation wasn't going to lead to a noble place, and yet I wasn't doing anything to stop it.

God, save me. What am I doing?

"How can you desire me, Magnus?" I blurted into the silence. Humiliation made me bite my tongue, a stuck sob not allowing me to speak for a moment and, God bless him, Magnus waited for me to get myself together. "How can you feel anything for me after the way I've treated you? I don't deserve it."

Magnus sighed heavily, shoving his hair back as he sat up. I watched him stare at the fire for a moment, and then he looked at me again. "You're a rare thing, Andromeda. A masterpiece. You deserve the world."

"But I'm not," I said, shaking my head, feeling my throat burning with rising tears. "I've shown such unforgiveness toward you over one tiny mistake."

"Your reaction was just." Magnus reached over and took my

hand, and I shifted so I could take his in both of mine. "Kelela helped me see what it must've looked like to you. I'm an absolute blackguard."

"You have to understand, I don't trust easily . . . if at all. I had made myself vulnerable to you. You said you wanted to be with me, and then it came out you were engaged. I felt . . . betrayed. So, I protected myself by pushing you away."

"I'm sorry." He got up quickly and knelt in front of me. "Oh, my little gentle-heart. You had every right. I'm so sorry."

"No, I'm sorry."

"I'm sorrier."

I chuckled, shaking my head. "Are we really going to argue over who's sorrier?"

"Of course we are," he said, grinning. "You act like you've never met us." I laughed as he kissed my hands, first the backs, then the palms. "I'm sorry," he whispered to them, and more than anything I wished he'd kiss my lips. Instead he stood, still holding both my hands. "I think I'm going to play a little music. Would you like to join me?"

"You haven't learned to turn your pages by now?" I teased.

"Am I that transparent?"

"It seems you're completely hopeless without me."

"I fear I am."

I pulled my hands from his so he wouldn't feel them tremble. He was giving me that look again—desire mixed with adoration mixed with upmost respect and, as always, hope. I pretended to study the dancing flames of the fireplace to distract myself from crying.

"Those eyes in that firelight . . ." he murmured. I could feel his gaze on me, and I forced my expression neutral as I sat up straight. "They are my mistress."

All my efforts were crushed, and I let out a short laugh, biting my lip against the urge to cry, my face burning without help from the warmth of the hearth.

"Don't move," he said, and I didn't dare. I sat poised, my heart pounding so loudly I was sure he could hear it. Waiting. Would he . . . touch me?

Instead he retrieved his sketchbook and knelt beside my chair. I broke into a smile. Magnus gave a small sound of chastisement, and I quickly resumed a more serious air. But inside, every part of me was smiling. My heart. My soul. My fingers gripping my knees. Part of me was scared this didn't mean what I wanted it to mean, but I was too happy to acknowledge it fully.

I was plain. I had no family, no inheritance.

But Magnus was drawing me.

Me.

It was a few minutes of silence, with just the pencil scratches and my own breathing as he worked. From the corners of my eye I saw him look at me and then down at the page again, and each time he did the urge to kiss him became unbearable.

Finally, he signed and dated the drawing before handing the book to me.

I gasped.

It looked like me, but didn't. Not in the way I thought I looked. I knew Magnus to be a practical artist when it came to detail, drawing only what he knew was true. He hadn't made me beautiful. It was homely, unextraordinary me, ugly scar and all. And yet . . . there was beauty in this picture I'd never seen in myself before.

"Am I always so fierce looking?" I asked, not knowing what else to say. I'd felt so happy while he was drawing me. Why didn't it show up in the picture?

"Always." He leaned on the chair arm to watch my expression. "I'm glad I managed to capture your soul this time. It's taken a bit of practice."

I looked at him, laying the sketchbook flat against my legs. "Practice?"

For a moment he didn't break my gaze, and then he tilted the sketchbook up and flipped to the previous page. It was me, multiple times. My silhouette. My hands. My profile. Twenty, maybe more, small overlapping sketches.

My breath caught, and maybe Magnus mistranslated it, because he quickly said, "I should've asked, I suppose. But then the moments would've been lost."

"Are there more?"

"Yes."

"In this one?"

He hesitated, gauging my expression. "And others."

I flipped back to the one he'd just drawn and stared at it. Tears burned the backs of my eyes, blurring my view, and I closed the sketchbook and dropped it on the side table so it wouldn't get wet if they fell. I blinked a few times, trying to clear my vision and choked out a laugh. It felt like a strange reaction, to cry and laugh at once, but I couldn't stop either.

"Don't cry. You know I don't know what to do about crying . . ." I felt him leave my side, saw the blur of him kneel in front of me . . . felt the warmth of his hands on my knees. "Is it okay, Andromeda? That I draw you?"

"Magnus," I said, swallowing through the knot in my throat, wiping at my tears so I could see him more clearly. "You only draw things you care about."

He grinned, blushing warm and sweet. "And love, in your case."

For a long moment, I was unable to speak, my heart like a hummingbird's in my throat. I escaped from the chair over the armrest, but he came after me and caught my waist, pulling me close.

"The ancient Greeks believed," he said, "that humans were born with four arms, four legs, and two faces. Then some jealous god tore them apart, leaving them to search the earth for the missing half of their soul."

"That's a terrifying image," I said, trying not to panic. "And a flawed concept. I think, when you're past a certain age, there isn't one person on earth you need to survive. I mean, I did it for weeks on my own."

"It's not about surviving. It's about *living*. I'm not convinced I was truly doing that before you." He leaned closer, and my heart picked up. "And now I know I won't last without you. You are my soulmate, my meaning, the entire point to my existence."

I could barely look at him, so I settled my gaze on his shoulder, hugging myself to stop my trembling. "You're scaring me, Magnus."

"*I'm* scaring *you?*"

I heard the teasing in his voice, but I couldn't laugh, not without breaking down into tears. "That you think you can't live without me. Your heart was beating long before we met."

"Was it?"

His tone sounded so gentle, so heartfelt, it nearly tore my heart open from feeling too much. And that was it. The tears started to flow without my permission.

"My love may be mad and reckless," he went on quickly, "but it's real and honest. Please believe me, this is not a trick—"

"I need a minute," I gasped. "Please." And I rushed between two tall bookshelves to collect myself.

I leaned against the books, resting in the shadows, trying to steady my breath. And then, after a few moments, the tinkle of bells approached. Magnus came around the bookshelf, his movements tentative. "Andromeda?" His face was mostly in shadow, only beautiful hints of it where the candlelight glowed through the cracks. "Was I wrong to confess?"

"You love me?" I whispered.

He strode over and took me in his arms, and it didn't matter that I could barely see him, his hands like anchors holding me to this earth. "You know I do."

"Only me?"

"My darling," he cooed, running his fingertips across my lips, "it's always been only you." And he pressed his lips where his fingers had warmed.

CHAPTER
25

———※———

The plan was almost too simple. Kelela would stand in front of the door to act as bait. Saba would make sure the hyena couldn't get out of Magnus's room. I would cleanse it. Five minutes before the Waking, we took our positions.

Saba and I stood in front of Magnus's bedroom door, with Kelela slightly behind us. When I glanced back at her she was grey-faced. Trembling. But there was a spark of something—of will, of life, of determination. She planned on seeing this through to the end.

And the end would be quick. One hour. That's all the time I needed to seal it.

I heard the sudden shift of a lock and pulled my knife. But it wasn't Magnus's door—in hindsight, a hyena wouldn't be much good at opening one, anyway.

"Stay here," I said, running and skidding to a stop at the top of the stairs just as Peggy opened the door.

"Peggy," I shouted down the stairs, "the Waking is in three minutes. You need to lock yourself in a room."

She looked up at me as if I were a nuisance, before making her way slowly up the stairs. Her room was on the ground floor; why was she coming upstairs? "I need to check on Magnus."

I ran down halfway to meet her, getting behind her to push. "The hyena is going to be released in less than three minutes."

She halted—the opposite of what I needed her to do. "W-what? What time is it?"

"Saba, help me!"

Saba rushed to my side, throwing Peggy over her shoulder without my having to ask.

I don't know if Saba decided to reveal herself or Peggy thought she was being carried by an invisible entity, but she wouldn't stop screaming, and we were under too vital a time crunch for me to do anything but roll my eyes. "Take her to my room—no, the closet. At the end of the hall. Hurry."

"Kelela?" Peggy gasped as Saba passed, and she released a desperate moaning wail, like a banshee. "Oh God Almighty, what are you doing here? Get out of the hallway!"

Saba ran to the opposite end of the long hall, carrying the screaming woman like she weighed nothing. The closet was a petty choice when my room was available, but I didn't want her looking through my things.

"I suppose that isn't the strangest thing I've seen in this house," Kelela breathed. Judging by her terrified shock, I knew she wasn't talking about Peggy.

I took my position again, in front of a further-shaken Kelela, just as Saba shut the door and was running back. I could still hear Peggy shouting curses at me. She had the good sense to do it through the door.

Because the big clock downstairs was striking ten.

Dhong!

I took a deep breath.

Dhong!

A breath.

Eight more like it, and each time I breathed in courage until there wasn't a scrap of fear left in me.

As the last gong echoed, the rush of swirling wind took its place in my ears, and with it sheets shifting, rustling. Then the click and scrape of claws on hardwood, the familiar jingle of bells with each pad.

The chalk marks sprung up in my mind as soon as the hyena's paws hit the floor.

I flinted my welding pen and got to work.

I wasn't even a minute in when the bedroom door rattled. Kelela yelped at the loud bang, and grabbed my shoulder, but I shrugged her off quickly. "Don't touch me, I can't mess this up." Another minute went by. Another bang.

"Can't he break the door?" Kelela asked, slightly frantic.

"No," I said, not missing a beat with my pen.

Another bang. Kelela backed into the wall behind us. "Are you sure?"

"It only has the strength of any old hyena, and these doors are solid wood." I said it to shut her up so I could concentrate, but hopefully it was enough to assure her, too. Because I didn't know. Maybe demon hyenas were stronger than normal ones. Saba was stronger than any human, after all—but no. No. After all that courage I'd breathed in, I couldn't go filling myself with doubt now.

I saw Saba move toward the door from the corner of my eye and glanced up. She looked sick. Her nose and brow were creased in a grimace, like she tasted blood. I pressed my back against the door as she reached her hand toward the doorknob.

"I know it's commanding you, Saba," I said. "But you have to fight the urge to obey."

She shook her head, tears forming in her eyes and breaking away to roll down her face as the hyena slammed against the door again.

"Run down the hall and sit on your hands. Get away from here."

It was a fragile solution, but it was all I could think of with most of my brainpower consumed by getting this amulet right. Why did I let her stay? Because I had the same concern as Kelela—that the hyena might break through the door. But now my greatest fear was Saba releasing it too soon. Magnus had said she had no choice but to obey the Evil Eye. This wasn't something she could fight against for much longer. And I still needed at least fifty minutes before the amulet to lock the monster away was complete.

Saba hugged herself tightly and turned away, heading down the hall before stumbling to a stop. From the corner of my eye I saw her standing there, bent over herself, unable to go further either way.

Another minute of strokes down. Accurate, but I wished I was as fast as Jember. Because now I needed this amulet done sooner. I didn't have an hour. Saba didn't have an hour. The door certainly didn't, if it kept—

Another slam, this time with a dull *crack* of wood, and Saba came toward me.

"It'll all be over soon," I wanted to assure her. "You won't have to obey the Evil Eye ever again after tonight—" But her hand was turning the knob and I only had time to stumble in front of

Kelela before a mass of black shadow rushed at me. It slammed into my shield, darted to get around it. I backed up, herding Kelela back with me, despite her screaming in my ears.

Saba grabbed the hyena by its haunches and dragged it backward.

"My room," I said, shoving Kelela in the right direction, just as the hyena snapped at Saba and got loose. My amulet took the full force as it charged at us, its head shifting an entire foot forward.

My blood ran cold, but only for an instant. That much of my shield gone at once?

Saba grabbed the hyena around the neck, wrestling it to the ground, and I got back to work on my amulet immediately. But I'd only done three strokes before the giant paw clawed Saba's arm, breaking it off at the shoulder. She kept it at bay with her other arm for another two strokes. And then it bit down on her chin, breaking most of her face off and throwing it across the hall.

Kelela and I ran in opposite directions at once. She'd shut herself inside my room by the time I reached Saba's face—thank God she tended to break in larger pieces instead of shattering into shards. The hyena tore at the floor in front of my room, scraping deep lines into the wood like it was trying to dig a hole underneath the door. Instead of handing Saba her face, I got back to work on the amulet. Two strokes. Saba reattached her arm and face and took a few steps toward my room. I ran ahead to block her way.

"Don't do it, Saba." I held out my hands to block her from getting around me. "It can't get inside there without your help. Leave it alone to try, that'll buy time for me to finish sealing it."

Saba gripped her stomach, like she'd been stabbed. Her face was straining, her eyes blurring with tears.

"Don't listen to it, Saba," I shouted, grabbing her arms and shaking her. "Please, you have to fight back!"

She burst into tears, shoving me out of the way to get to the door.

This plan should've been simple. Why was everything going wrong?

I ran and rammed into the hyena's side, my shield knocking it out of the way just as Saba opened the door.

But it was on its feet a second later, ignoring me for Kelela. It ran into my room, and I cringed at the screaming.

"Help, help!" she kept repeating, more and more frantic each time. I pulled my knife, dodging out of the way as the hyena backed out of my bedroom door, snapping its jaws and clawing at the fireplace poker Kelela was swinging at it. "Andromeda!"

I stabbed the hyena in the back so it would turn on me, but—oh God—Kelela ran away from my room instead of back inside, and I had no time to say anything but "Stop!"

The hyena lunged at her, colliding with her shield, but fear sent her screaming and stumbling backward. She fell hard onto the stairs and tumbled down, and I skidded in front just in time to stop the hyena from chasing after her. It knocked into my shield, shattering another few inches of it. I couldn't keep getting so close—my shield was already down to a foot and a half, and if I had to fight and run all night there was no way I'd finish this amulet before the Evil Eye went dormant again.

A loud bang broke through the wind, so distinct that I paused in my work to look. Peggy stood just outside the closet door, holding a gun steady with both her hands.

The hyena tipped its head, shifting its eyes in an almost-eye-roll. It swung around, away from me, and charged at Peggy, despite the gunshots. The bullets weren't stopping it. They weren't even hurting it. Saba ran after the monster, right on its tail. I ran after Saba, not nearly as fast as her, but far more desperate.

"Peggy!" I shouted, my voice cracking, killing my volume. By the time I swallowed and finished, "Get back inside—" her terrified scream drowned out my voice again.

The hyena leapt at Peggy with a force that slammed them both against the back wall of the closet. Saba didn't follow them inside, instead skidding to a stop, nearly hitting the wall as she shoved and held the door shut. And then there was nothing but shrill, tearing screams.

I tripped to my knees, gaping. Panting. My well-developed survival adrenaline zapped from me. Oh God. This wasn't supposed to happen. What—?

My heart pounding in my ears blocked out Peggy's horrible screams, allowing me to engage my survival instincts again.

There's nothing you can do, Andi. Finish the amulet while you can. There's nothing else you can do.

I took a deep breath and ran up to the door, grabbing Saba's arm. "Get away from here. Go downstairs or outside. Hurry, before it's done with her."

Before it's done with her.

There was no time to hate myself for that command.

Saba backed away from me, but too slowly. I shoved her to get her moving, and she finally ran.

I took a few deep breaths and flinted my pen. The screams had stopped. All that was left was the rush of wind, the hum of my flame, and the periodic slam on the door of the hyena trying to come for me, too.

CHAPTER
26

———— ❧ ————

All at once, the slamming and scraping stopped. I froze, my ears ringing from the lack of noise, my pen poised over the silver. The hyena couldn't have gone dormant already.

But of course it had . . . it had taken a victim, even if Peggy wasn't the original target.

I squinted at the amulet, but really there was no point. If it was finished and had done its job, I would've felt the presence of the Evil Eye contained . . . but I couldn't feel it at all. And the amulet wasn't nearly finished.

I let out a yell of frustration, but checked myself before throwing my half-finished work on the ground, opting instead to place it in my satchel. And then I ran to my room to get an oil lamp, lighting it with my pen as I hurried back.

I hesitated in approaching the closet as blood seeped out from underneath the door.

I opened the door, slowly, holding my amulet out in front of me . . . and choked out a gasp. Peggy's torn body was almost unrecognizable, cold and white and covered in tattered wool, lying in the corner. The ground and everything on it was saturated with sticky, wet blood. And in the middle sat Magnus, his face buried in his knees, his trembling arms wrapped around his legs . . . completely naked. His body was smudged with blood that wasn't his, his hair matted with it, his nails caked.

"I killed Peggy, didn't I," he said, his voice wet and trembling.

My stomach lurched just at the mention of it. "You're all right. Just don't look behind you."

Words crumbled on my lips as I tried to speak again. I felt frozen, down to my marrow. None of this was supposed to happen. The plan should've worked.

"Magnus," I barely gasped, and he looked up at me. Oh God. I wish he hadn't.

His eyes were red from tears, but his mouth was smeared red with something more sinister. He coughed, gagged, and suddenly more blood leaked from his mouth, and it was enough to send bile up my throat.

"Kill me," he gasped back.

I took a step back, shaking my head.

"Please, Andi."

"I can't." Or at least I think I said that. It sounded more like a sob.

"You have to kill me," he said, shifting to his knees, his hands slipping in the thick blood on the floor. "It's the only way."

I couldn't answer him. All I could do was run.

I leapt down the stairs two at a time. Saba skidded into view at the bottom of them, distressed.

"I have to go," I told her, even though she could clearly see what I was doing.

She grabbed my arms, leaning down to level our faces, as if to reason with me. I don't know why something as rational as that broke me, but God, it did.

"I'm not going back there," I screamed, my entire body leaning forward, every muscle tight with the strain of it, as if it had never let out so much pain and fear at once before.

Maybe it hadn't.

And it disturbed me enough to put this all behind me.

I rushed out into the desert, but I heard soft, sandy steps behind me and Saba put herself in front of me, a pleading look on her tearstained face.

"Please, don't try to stop me, Saba. I can't stay here."

I tried to get around, but she cut me off again. She gestured, but it was too dark out to tell what she was doing. Even if the moon had been brighter, my mind was so chaotic I couldn't process anything. All I knew was that I was panicking, a leveled panic full of adrenaline, familiar as the back alleys back home. I had learned to perfect that panic, because my survival depended on it. It turned friends into enemies, and my empathy was gone faster than one of Magnus's chocolates could melt in my mouth.

Fight or flight, Andi?

Saba was pushing me toward *fight*.

"If you try to keep me here by force," I warned, taking a few steps back as I touched the knife in my pocket, "your limbs will have to drag themselves across the desert to get to you."

Saba gestured again, but it involved pointing toward the castle. That was enough of an indicator.

Fight.

But before I could do anything, Saba scooped me up over her shoulder.

"No!" I cried, and immediately started kicking.

"*Scream your lungs out,*" Jember had always said. "*Don't make it easy for them. If they get you where they want you, you're as good as dead."*

So I screamed, wordlessly, trying to aim the sound at her ear, and kicked. She had no hair to pull, no flesh to dig my nails into, but I managed to get my knife from my pocket and stab her in the back. I felt the break of pottery, my knife easily piercing through. I cocked back my knife to stab again, but my body went backward instead as Saba dropped me onto my back in the sand. I think Saba had learned from our last fight, because she quickly shoved me onto my stomach and pinned my arms to my sides. This time when she picked me up she held me out at arm's length, facing away from her.

And then she kept walking. My kick couldn't reach her effectively this way, but I kept kicking. Kept screaming. Kept throwing my weight in different directions, forcing her to grip me tighter. My scream was cut off by a sob. God help me. Any tighter and she'd break my bones.

As she stepped through the doorway, Saba shifted to hugging me against her body with one arm, and I took the opening to throw my head back into her face. There was a frightening, though at the moment satisfying, *shinctk*. Something skimmed past my shoulder and cracked on the floor, but it didn't stop Saba's task of forcing me to sit on the stairs.

"You're really not going to let me leave?" I asked stupidly.

Saba was just standing from picking up the quarter of face I'd knocked off when I looked at her. Cracks had spread up her neck, over her shoulders, from when I had been kicking her. There was a gaping hole in her face, but her frustrated glare was still readable as she went about putting the broken piece back in its spot.

My heart was still racing, but enough panic had subsided to make room for embarrassment. "Sorry I broke your face," I murmured. "And stabbed you in the back."

Her response was to brush sand out of my hair, gently and attentively, before lifting me effortlessly and carrying me up the stairs.

I fought the urge to breathe deeply, to soothe my pulse. There was no more panic, maybe, but I needed the adrenaline. I needed the strength. Because as soon as Saba shut me into my room I opened the window. I couldn't see down to the bottom, as if a void were swallowing the castle whole, but it couldn't have been any higher than the wall to the city. I took off my shoes so I could better navigate the stone and lowered myself out, feeling for small cracks to grip into.

It was as easy as I thought it'd be. Crossing the desert wouldn't be, but what choice did I have? Attempting to wrangle one of those horses would only get me caught.

I didn't linger, my adrenaline taking over for me as I ran in the direction of the city.

The alleys were eerily empty, which was good because I felt heavy on my feet, my breath loud to my own ears. I wiggled through the grate at the back of the church and rushed through the still-messy entrance area, straight to the bed. I collapsed onto it, gasping. Jember wasn't home. That was normal, if he was working, but still, it crushed me. I didn't expect Jember to offer any comfort, anyway, but I also didn't come here to be alone.

No Andi. You came here to hide.

I'd abandoned Magnus.

I never said good-bye to Saba.

You're a coward.

I pressed my face into the pillow and cried myself to sleep.

CHAPTER
27

Magnus sat in a puddle of blood. Naked, shivering. Covered in it. When I stepped closer he looked up at me, tears streaming down his face.

"Andromeda . . ."

The voice soothed and scared me, drove me on and killed me at once. "I'm here, Magnus."

"You left me . . ."

"I-I'm sorry. I was afraid." I blinked at tears, and swiped my eyes with the back of my hand.

But when I looked at him again his eyes were glowing a bright, unnatural green. His fingernails crept longer and longer into claws with a grinding that made my bones quake.

"I will give you something to fear . . ." As he spoke, his teeth grew to fangs, tearing through the corners of his lips to spill more blood on the ground. I stumbled back as he leaned forward, as he lunged—

My eyes shot open, my hands aching from gripping the edge of my childhood bed. "Magnus!"

Instead of an answer I heard the cellar door creak. The slap of sandals, a boot, and a slightly more metallic, heavier tap on the stairs. Jember wasn't alone.

I didn't know what kind of mood he would be in—depended on whether he'd been out all night drinking or working. And I probably shouldn't let the other person catch me in here. But I didn't have the will in me to move from this spot. Or care, for that matter.

"Andromeda . . ."

Magnus.

His sweet voice echoed in my empty, cavernous heart, and I squeezed my eyes to force it away.

The footsteps stopped before coming into the room.

"Get me a salt slab," I heard Jember say.

"You mean carve it from the desert?" asked a boy's voice. He sounded tired, and I felt a small twinge of irrational jealousy mixed with relief. A new mentee meant Jember was making a steady living, at least, even if it also meant I'd have to share the room with one more. "But we've already been out all night. And I don't know how—"

"Are you complaining, boy?"

"N-no, sir—"

"I've decided I need five slabs, now."

"B-but—"

"Ten. Another word out of you and I'll split your head open, instead."

The only response was quick footsteps up the stairs.

The poor boy didn't know what he'd signed up for. I let out a breath of laughter before sinking into misery again.

I heard the cellar door creak shut, the chain clinking as he turned the key in the lock. After a minute a weight dipped down the flimsy mattress at my back as Jember sat on the side of the bed.

"Andi."

Jember's voice was gruff, comforting because it meant I was home, but not attempting to soothe me in any way. Not my Magnus. Not my imagination. But it felt like a dream, anyway. He didn't sound drunk. Or smell it. He smelled like incense, sharp and herby, and the subtle undercurrent of sweat. It was strange how much I'd missed that smell.

"Look at me."

I didn't move. Couldn't.

He grabbed my shoulder, shifting me to my back so that I rested against his, and I didn't fight the movement. He was wearing his white long-sleeve undershirt and pants, and of course his ever-present red gloves.

"Someone hurt you?" he asked.

I wiped my blurred eyes with the back of my hand. "No."

"Then what are you crying about?"

I took a trembling breath. "I failed."

Jember scoffed and turned back around to unlace his boot. "You live in some rich man's house for a few weeks and suddenly you're soft."

"I'm not soft," I countered.

"If everyone cried at every failure, the entire planet would be in a constant state of mourning." He yanked on his boot, giving up with a frustrated grunt. "Get this off me, girl."

I sighed, but somehow it wasn't out of annoyance. I scooted off the bed to kneel in front of him. "So, you found a new mentee," I said, tugging off his boot easily.

"I was *assigned* a new mentee."

"How's it going?"

He shrugged, pushing his dreads behind his shoulders. "Eager to learn. But he can't seem to understand how to sense Manifestation strokes, which is literally the easiest part of the job."

"He just needs time. It doesn't come easily to everyone."

"I'll find someone better and replace him."

"No one's ever good enough for you," I mumbled.

"You were. Now look at you. A mewling quitter."

I shoved his boot to the side. "You're the one who told me to quit in the first place."

"Didn't tell you to cry about it."

I pushed myself to my feet to stand in front of him, my eyes burning from the threat of tears. "Can you just help me find a job? And I'll be out of your hair forever."

Jember's gaze shifted, searching my face. "What happened?"

"I failed." It was more of a sob than words. I hugged the amulet to my chest, my vision blurring as I looked at the floor. "He was counting on me, and I couldn't save him. And now he's alone and frightened—a-and—" I swallowed another sob. "I'm a coward. I can't go back there. How can I face him after I let him down so badly?"

"What did you do, girl, fall in love with him?"

And that was it. My body shook, my hands pressed against my face. It burned to breathe. I let loose with uncontrollable sobs, more violent than I'd ever felt before. Maybe my body was just playing catch-up from the rest of my life when I wasn't allowed to cry.

"I'm going to count to five," I heard Jember say, barely audible over my sobbing. "And then I'm going to stop your crying for you. One."

I tried to take deep breaths, but my lungs wouldn't cooperate. "Two."

Smothering was his usual warning when I was about to cry, anyway . . .

He pushed himself up from the bed and snatched up his pillow. "Three."

Then again, he'd never made it to five before.

"Okay, okay," I gasped, forcing myself to breathe, wiping my face.

"Four."

I fixed my posture and swiped my sleeve across my tear-welled eyes, alternatively taking deep breaths and gasping.

"Five." He stood in front of me, holding the pillow with both hands, like he was prepared to use it. I hiccupped. He threw the pillow at my face, and I caught it as it fell, hugging it to my chest. "Don't ever cry over a boy again. Unless he transforms into a hyena and tears your leg off. Until that happens, you don't get to cry."

I sniffled a few times, wiping my nose on the pillow. "I love him, Jember," I whispered. It felt good to say out loud.

I was staring at the pillow, so I didn't see Jember's expression. But, for a moment, he had nothing to say. "Don't cry," he ordered finally. "No little boy is that important."

He took the pillow from me and threw it back onto the bed. From the corner of my eye I saw his hand move toward me again, but by the time I'd looked up he had dropped it to his side.

"Why don't you ever touch me?" I managed through my tight throat . . . although, God help me, it was tight with something more vicious than before. "I mean, I understand, your skin can't take it. But you wear gloves all the time, and we're wearing long sleeves. If you wanted to hug me you could. Or a pat on the back, even. God, I'd even accept a slap at this point."

Jember tightened his lips to a thin line, letting out a slow huff through his nose. "Why do you care, all of a sudden? A few weeks off the street and your good survival habits have already become lax."

"You raised me. Don't you have any affection for me at all?"

"Yes, I raised you." He lowered himself to the bed again. "That's affection enough."

"But you love Saba."

"I never said that, you just assume—"

"Or you did, at one point. You haven't forgotten those feelings, and you haven't seen her since I've known you. So how can you have raised me for so long and feel absolutely nothing for me?"

"Did you hold on to the amulet you were constructing for the Evil Eye?"

He ... completely ignored me. I sniffled, rage throbbing in my throat. "It's in my bag."

"You expect me to get up again? Let me see it."

I pulled out the amulet, unfinished and blood smudged. Pathetic.

Jember took it from me. Flipped it over. Then he started miming the strokes in the air. "Wrong order," he muttered, then continued. He ended with a long, thoughtful stare at it. "Not bad, girl," he said, handing it back to me. "You were on the right track."

"You changed the subject."

"No, I didn't. That conversation was finished."

"I was just hoping that ..." I picked at my nails. Why did I feel so nervous? So lost? "I don't know. That maybe you loved me."

We were quiet for a moment.

Jember pressed on his leg above his knee with a groan, massaging it with his fingers. "Most people start training in amulets when they're sixteen. You ever wonder why you came to me so young?"

"You bought me from my birth parents."

"*Bought* you? When have I ever paid for anything? No, I stole you from the ones who bought you."

"Why?"

"Because your parents sold you to a brothel. And you were five." He shrugged, as if he wanted to be done thinking about it. "Your affinity for amulet construction was just a bonus."

He groaned again, and I saw him wince as he leaned heavily on the bed. I knelt to remove his leg so he wouldn't have to ask.

"I thought empathy was a poor survival habit," I said.

"It is. You've caused me a lot of trouble over the years." There was a spark of humor in Jember's eyes before he took his leg from me and tapped me on the head with the thicker wooden end. I was lucky it was his leg and not something he could afford to break, but still, I felt myself grinning. "You want a bed to sleep in, girl? Then shut up and mind your business."

This had always been my side of the bed. Mostly because it was easier for Jember to get into bed on the side closest to the door, so he wouldn't have to scoot across it or walk around. But tonight, I couldn't sleep.

Tonight? No. It was morning, though the shut door blocked out all hints of light. Magnus was probably awake now, unaware of what he'd done last night, wondering where I was. Meanwhile, I was back in my childhood home. Hiding.

I rolled onto my side. Jember lay on his back, his breath slightly jagged, an unintentional groan every other exhale. I don't think I'd ever noticed how much pain he was actually in. He'd always come home after I fell asleep, wake up before me. Or he'd be so drunk he'd just pass out. I felt ignorant for thinking all this time that he was just a heavy sleeper. That those pills were more of a necessity than an addiction.

I sighed, rolling onto my back again. I couldn't believe I was lying here, wasting my time feeling sorry for myself, when the people who needed me most were waiting for me.

If I cleansed the castle, Magnus would never have to worry about avoiding people ever again. He could join me in town. Among people. Or anywhere we wanted, really.

Saba's soul would be free. I would miss her, but it was selfish to keep her here to be tortured by the Evil Eye's commands.

And—something I hadn't thought of before now—I could afford the best doctors for Jember. Someone who could help him with his pain, maybe make him a better leg. Maybe then he wouldn't be so cranky.

There was no doubt I had to go back. But, this time, I needed a better plan. One that wouldn't get anyone hurt or killed. Kelela had meant well in volunteering, but when it came down to it she'd panicked. The target had to be someone who could stay levelheaded, preferably someone who had experienced the hyena before and knew what to expect . . .

I looked at Jember, but quickly disregarded the idea. He'd never agree to it. And, with his injury, he wasn't fast enough to keep himself from being killed before I could finish the amulet. But . . . I was.

I sat up quickly, my mind suddenly clear.

I was fast. I could keep my head in the midst of stress. Having experienced the hyena multiple times, I knew what to expect. And

Jember was faster at constructing amulets than I was, anyway, so I wouldn't need to keep the hyena busy for long.

I took a deep breath, hugging my knees and closing my eyes. "God," I whispered, "please let this be the right choice."

Now all I had to do was convince Jember to come back with me. Which was the most tedious part of the plan, if I was being honest.

"Jember," I whispered. I don't know why I didn't just yell. I needed him awake.

I shook his shoulder, and he swatted at my hand lazily. "Why are you bothering me before noon?"

"I'm going back to the castle." I kicked the blanket away and rolled out of bed. "Will you take me?"

"Are you crazy?"

"Probably."

Jember leaned up on his elbows with a long groan. "No boy is worth killing yourself over."

"You're the one who said I was on the right track." I threw my satchel across my shoulders, put on my amulet. "I have part of the amulet done, I just have to finish it. Even if it takes a few days—"

"The Evil Eye isn't some stupid Manifestation that follows a pattern. It's a thinking creature that's going to do whatever it takes not to be expelled."

I pulled Jember's peg leg out from under the bed. "All the more reason for you to come with me. Two debtera can do more than one."

"God . . ." Jember let himself drop back onto the bed, pressing his hand into his forehead. "Your optimism is exhausting."

"Are you going to help me? We have to go before the midday

heat." I opened the drawer to grab clothes for him. "Besides, you're the only debtera in twenty years to—"

"I'm not going near that thing."

"But together—"

"You don't get it yet?" He sat up, slapping my assisting hand away. "I'm the *only* one to cleanse a house because I'm the only one who survived long enough to do it. And I barely escaped alive. This is not a fight you're going to win, Andromeda."

"I have to." My words felt desperate. I knelt to attach his leg so he wouldn't see my eyes tear up. "I can't abandon the people I care about."

He shoved me away with his leg as soon as I'd gotten it attached. "Go on, then. Get yourself killed."

I pressed my lips together to keep them from trembling. "That includes you, you know. Do you know how much medical help we could get you with—"

"Stop," he snapped, holding up his hand. "Just . . . stop."

His voice had drifted from anger to something more melancholy, and it tightened my throat.

We were quiet for a minute.

"You're going to go no matter what I say."

I nodded. "I have to."

"You don't have to." He leaned over and opened the drawer beside him. "Do you need money?"

I shook my head, a small ache in my heart. It suddenly occurred to me . . . he wasn't going to come with me. My entire plan hinged on his cooperation.

Instead of money he took out an amulet. The silver was a little thicker than normal, and wrapped mostly with black and red thread, with a few bursts of gold. I'd never seen that amulet before—wait. Yes, I had. It was the new one I'd made, with added attributes. I could almost feel the power echo through it as it moved on the chain. If that couldn't keep away the Evil Eye, I don't know what could.

Although, part of me was annoyed that he'd made me struggle through making my own when he was just going to fix it for me, anyway.

"You save all the good techniques for yourself," I said, smirking.

"Don't be ungrateful" was all he said. I took it from him and hung it over my neck. "This is good-bye."

"Come with me."

"I can't." He shook his head, giving me a sad smile. "And I can't function under optimism and hope the way you do. This is good-bye, Andi. I don't expect to see you again."

"Will you at least take me?" I asked. "If this really is good-bye?"

"Take you on what?" Jember scraped his hand through his beard with a heavy sigh. "It would go against all sane judgment, going near that house." A heavy knock and his name made us both look at the door. His mentee was back—I'd forgotten about him, honestly, but it occurred to me only then that he'd been gone for hours. Hopefully he had the ten slabs of salt, if he knew what was good for him.

I could practically hear Jember roll his eyes with his sigh, and when I looked at him again he swallowed three pills with water then pointed at his boot. "Let's go before I change my mind."

CHAPTER
28

———— ❧ ————

The archbishop's horse, which was kept in a private stable at the edge of the good part of town, was almost too easy to borrow—because Jember had gone to see it before, the stable hand let him right in. I sat behind Jember, leaning forward, trusting more than seeing where we were going. The face masks we'd adapted out of welding helmets caught all the flying salt and sand. I should've really waited until we'd arrived to put my sweater on, because sweat was gathering on every inch of me, the hot wind flying past doing nothing to soothe me.

But the thought of seeing Magnus kept me from minding too much.

Jember expertly stopped a few yards from the door, and I slid off the giant animal, holding the heavy amulet still so it wouldn't slap against my chest.

"Thanks, Jember," I said, taking off my mask and handing it up to him.

He took it from me, but didn't remove his, so his voice was

slightly muted when he said, "I suppose it's too late to tell you not to do anything stupid." The horse looked antsy, stomping and shaking its head, as if telling me not to go inside. I stepped back from its hooves a bit more. How could Jember even control it without reins?

This was it. I only had a minute, maybe less, to convince him to stay and help me. I didn't think my plan would work without him. I chewed my lip. I *knew* it wouldn't. "Why don't you come in and help me? There's no way the Evil Eye can beat us if we work together."

He hesitated. Shook his head. "I don't think so."

"Just come in for a minute, then. The horse must need water and rest after that long ride."

He held up a waterskin, and I could practically hear his eyes narrow as he said, "What are you after, girl?"

This was never going to work if he suspected me. "Nothing."

Great answer, Andi. Not suspicious at all.

Jember sighed. "It's hot out here, Andi. This is good-bye."

I rushed in front of the horse and held its thick neck. "Please come in. Just for a minute."

He reached down and shoved my hands away. "Stop acting like a child before I beat the whining out of you."

"Is this really how we're going to part ways?" I blurted. "After fourteen years of having no one but each other? You have to say something other than threats and 'good-bye.'"

"What do you want me to say?"

"I don't know . . ." I adjusted my bag, trying to sort my anger and this strange, sad feeling of loss. My plan had been to get him to stay, but this . . . this was something else. Something so unexpectedly genuine it scared me. "Something not based on survival habits, for once."

"Fine," he said with a heavy sigh. "I'll miss you. Is that what you want to hear?"

I threw up my hands, barely holding in a scream of frustration . . . frustration concealing something that hurt so much worse. "You truly are heartless. Do you even care whether I live or die?" My blood rushed through my veins, and I gripped my fists to try and take back control. "Am I nothing to you?"

He kissed his teeth and looked away, and that one small sound was enough to make my stomach twist on itself. "You care too much about what people think of you—"

"I care about what *you* think of me," I snapped. "You. Because you're my—" I choked on an unexpected sob. "You're the closest thing I'll ever have to a father."

He didn't respond, but didn't move, either. I wished he wasn't wearing that mask. I wished I could've seen that he felt something. Anything.

Instead I turned away toward the door so he couldn't see my emotion get the better of me. He wasn't going to say he cared for me. That he . . . loved me. Because maybe he didn't. I mean, he'd never sent a note back to Saba. Maybe he didn't know how to feel that sort of thing anymore.

And maybe . . . maybe my new survival habit needed to be that I didn't care.

The creak and screech of wood against stone sent my nerves into panic mode, and for the briefest moment I reached for my knife. But my muscles relaxed when I saw Saba in the doorway. Her eyes were red, dried tear streaks on her cheeks, and she wore the same bloodstained clothes as last night. I tried to speak, but a painful lump blocked my way.

"What happened?" I asked, finally, as she stepped out onto the sand.

She touched my cheek, almost tenderly, as she walked past. I turned just in time to see Jember stiffen on the horse. And, because loyalty made people foolish, I felt protective of him. I ran ahead of Saba, holding up my hands to ward her off. "Saba, don't touch his skin—"

If it had been anyone else, Jember would've pulled his knife. Would've thrown a punch. Or rode away before she could reach him. *Something.* Instead, Saba held the horse steady around the neck with one arm and grabbed Jember's leg with the other.

"Let go," Jember said, his warning even more threatening in the dead muting of his mask. He had two hands free to go for his knife, but he didn't. He didn't try to pull away.

And, I think, if it had been anyone but Saba, they would've let go. For a moment she stared wide-eyed and brimming with tears at the metal leg she gripped. Then she closed her eyes and shook her head, and when she looked up at Jember her gaze was steady, glaring as much as imploring.

To be honest, I couldn't decide who to root for, so I took a few steps back.

He attempted to kick away from her incredible grip, pausing when he couldn't. "Let go, Saba."

I rocked between taking a step closer and another away. His voice had carried an edge I was familiar with. On the brink of something like panic. Like me, he had survival instincts that were switched on when he was restrained.

Saba gripped her heart, her face speaking nothing but anguish as she pointed to the castle.

I gasped. "She's asking for your help, Jember," I translated.

"I don't care," he said, jerking his leg from Saba's grasp. "Don't look at me like that, Saba. You're the one who left, so don't act like I owe you anything now."

Saba gaped slightly, brows pulled in. And then she shoved Jember over, horse and all. The horse squealed as it fell, and Jember's cry of pain followed, along with a string of curses. I let out a single laugh, God forgive me, before realizing the horse had fallen on his missing leg.

I stumbled, trying to avoid getting kicked as the horse bumbled to its feet and ran off a little ways, keeping clear of us as I ran over to Jember. So much for my new survival habit.

Saba had been heading back to the house, but tripped to a stop. She rushed back to us, crouching in front of Jember and reaching for his leg.

"Don't touch it," he said, panting.

Saba's hand trembled, hovering above his leg. She looked at him with such painful understanding it made me want to cry. She reached out, carefully removing the mask and dropping it in the sand beside him. Jember squinted for a moment, but whether it was from pain or the glaring sun, I couldn't tell. Her fingertips touched his chest, tentative, spreading slowly until her entire hand was resting against his heartbeat, the contact, even over his shirt, making Jember wince. But finally—finally—I saw a remnant, a spark in his face of the look Magnus gave me sometimes. Hopeful, pleased, wanting to be adorable and adored, but all too muddled by the familiar anger Jember would never let go of.

"I can't go through it again," he said, cringing with each breath. "Please don't ask me to."

She nodded, tears welling up. But she didn't linger. She grabbed my hand and pulled me inside.

"I don't think he can get up," I protested as she led me up the stairs. If I left him out there alone, he might leave, and my plan would be ruined—or, at least, delayed. He'd need a few minutes to catch his breath, though, which gave me a few minutes to figure out how to convince him to stay. If all else failed, Saba could just drag him inside.

Normally Magnus would be up and about, no memory of what he'd done the night before. But as soon as we made it up the stairs, I knew something was wrong. Saba led me to the end of the hall. To the closet where we'd trapped the hyena. I didn't have to ask. I couldn't bear to, anyway. It was clear Magnus was still in there. That he'd never left.

As soon as I touched the doorknob, Magnus's weak voice said from behind the door, "Go away, Saba."

Immediately, she stepped back, new tears wetting her cheeks. I glared at the door. I would make sure this was the last day the Evil Eye would ever command her again.

"Saba, will you turn away for a second?"

She gave me a skeptical look, but turned her back.

I removed my amulet and placed it carefully on the floor, out of view of the doorway. This was the only moment I had to make eye contact with Magnus. Even if he fought me over it now, it didn't matter—when he woke up later he'd never remember, and everything could go ahead as planned.

I swung the door wide, steeling my nerves. The house had absorbed the blood, leaving no signs of carnage . . . except for the few lumps deforming a portion of the wall and floor of the corner, which I'm sure only resembled part of a human thigh, shoulder, and wrist because I knew better.

"Magnus?" I stepped into the closet and knelt in front of him. He was shivering, his teeth chattering a little. But the house had taken the blood on him as well, thank God, the nightmarish image of last night decreased to something only devastatingly sad. "It's Andromeda. I'm here to help you."

"I was calling for you," he said. "But you left me."

"I-I know." I didn't know what else to add, how to justify it. So, all I said was, "I won't do that again."

"Why didn't you just kill me like I asked?"

"Don't be ridiculous." I swallowed and leaned closer, touching his face. "Magnus. Look at me, please."

His eyes shifted to mine without a word, fully aware of what he'd done, shamed, terrified. But somehow still hopeful, amidst all that.

I pushed sweaty hair from his forehead, kissing his sweet, frightened face. "Will you let Saba carry you? I'm going to help you to bed."

He didn't protest, so I went to retrieve my amulet, putting it back on and tucking it under my top to make it seem like it'd been there the entire time. But when I turned, it was obvious Saba had been watching me, her lips sucked in as if to press back tears. I shook my head quickly, and she nodded in return. After a moment she rushed over and pulled me into a hug, her hard body knocking the wind out of me. She leaned her head against mine, and I finally had the sense to return the hug, gripping my wrists around her waist.

She leaned back abruptly and held my face in her cold hands, pressing her lips to my forehead. I broke into a smile like an impulse. This was no time for smiles, but I couldn't help it. Saba was my friend, but maybe ... maybe this is what it felt like to have a mother.

Saba released me and went into the closet and laid a blanket over Magnus before lifting him effortlessly from the ground. I led the way to his room, tripping to a stop in the doorway. Kelela lay in his bed, covered in a blanket except for her arm, which was bandaged and set and resting on a pillow. She snored gently. I hadn't thought much of her—God forgive me—in all the chaos after she had fallen down the stairs. But now I was in my right mind enough to feel relieved. Her injuries would heal. She would be okay.

It was Magnus I was worried about.

"Let's not wake her," I whispered to Saba. "My room is warmer, anyway."

Saba heated some water, and we gave Magnus a warm bath. And then she laid him in bed, and went back to the closet to . . . do whatever she needed to do. Probably move some furniture or rugs to cover up the life lost. It put a tinny taste in my mouth, so I focused on dressing Magnus. He lightly assisted, lifting his arms or legs when I needed him to, but he leaned his head on my shoulder . . . the only sounds between us his soft crying.

Say something, Andi. Anything. Anything to comfort him, to show him everything would be all right. Instead I just let him cry on me, loving him the only way I was truly good at—taking care of people who were in pain. It was a specific type of love I'd developed because it had been the only way I was allowed to love Jember. And, for me, I'd needed to love someone for my own survival.

It didn't occur to me until after I was tucking him into my bed that I hadn't thought twice about him being naked. I barely remembered what it looked like. I guess it was habit, from taking care of Jember my whole life. There was no room for shame when people needed you.

Speaking of Jember . . . oh God, please. Bathing Magnus had taken longer than I'd anticipated. I hoped Jember had gotten up okay. And I hoped beyond hope that he hadn't left. I hadn't heard him ride away, but maybe setting up the bath had blocked it out.

I rushed down the stairs, stumbling to a stop in the middle.

Jember sat in the doorway, leaning against the doorjamb, halfway in the heat of the outside world and half in the icebox of the castle. He'd removed his leg, and it lay on the floor beside him. I took a deep breath and tried to walk casually down the rest of the stairs.

"What are you still doing here?" I asked as I approached him, my tone not betraying the fact that I was inwardly leaping. "You made it clear you wanted nothing to do with this place."

"I just had a horse fall on me." He nodded at his knee, the tender, bruised, sick-looking skin exposed to the freezing air. "Have to numb up before I can stand that peg."

I looked at my fingers, the ones that had been sliced open during that encounter with Saba. Whatever she'd put under the wrapping that day, I hadn't felt any pain, and the scars were white now. They were never going to go away . . . but I guess I was used to that. "They have medicine here."

"Not for this," he said, leaning the back of his head on the wood.

"It's better than nothing. I'll go ask Saba—"

"No."

"She was anxious about Magnus, that's all. It won't be so, you know, hostile this time."

"I don't want to see her again."

"Why not? What are you afraid of?"

"Mind your own business, girl." He glared up at me. "I'll be gone in a few minutes—"

"You're already here. Just talk to her." Jember picked up his peg leg, and I stepped out of range of getting hit by it. "Tell her what you couldn't in that letter."

He ignored me, positioning his leg to strap it on with a wince.

My stomach began to cramp up with anger . . . unless I was just hungry. I hadn't eaten since dinner last night, and living in this house had gotten me used to regular meals.

"She loves you, you know." I put my foot on top of the wooden part of his leg, leaning my weight on it only slightly. "God knows why."

"Break this leg and I'll kill you."

"No acknowledgment," I said, throwing up my hands in annoyance. "You're too heartless to care about anyone but yourself, aren't you? Most people raise their children because they love them. I'm not even yours, so what were you getting out of it?"

He lifted his leg to knock me off, and I backed away out of his grasp as he held on to the wall to stand up.

"And maybe you could love," I went on bitterly, "before the Evil Eye sucked the soul out of you. Maybe you loved Saba. But that's all over, because now you don't know how. You're just an empty shell of bitterness and anger."

Jember grimaced from his own pain, merely scowling at mine as he pushed himself away from the wall. "Andromeda—"

"I should be the angry one!" I snatched out my knife, pressing the tip to his stomach before he could step any closer, freezing him in place. "You're a miserable old man and you took a five-year-old in to drag her down with you."

There was a tense silence. He moved. I didn't have to. A small stain of red began to spread on his shirt from the tip of the knife.

"Were you miserable growing up?" he asked finally.

The short answer? . . . No. And it didn't shock me to say it.

We had good moments. And when it wasn't good, I made the best of what I could.

But what slipped out of my mouth was, "You were cruel to me."

"I'm not cruel by nature . . . if that eases the pain of it."

"It doesn't."

The silence that followed felt like a needle point creeping slowly beneath my skin.

"You were a sweet little girl. Always wanted hugs and kisses, even when we were still strangers. Do you know how painful it was to break you of that habit?"

My hand trembled. The stain of blood spread further, running out and downward, like a disturbing magnifying glass. "Then why did you do it?"

"Well, first of all, hugging strangers is a poor survival habit."

He had a point, but I wasn't going to acknowledge that now. Not when I needed him to admit that he was wrong. "If that's your explanation, it's not good enough."

"You know why, Andi."

"I want to hear you say it."

Jember laced his fingers behind his head, taking a deep breath as he looked at the ceiling for a moment. He swore and then looked at me again. "Because it hurt, that's why. Every little kiss and nose rub was like a new tear beneath my skin. Loving like you do *hurts*, Andi. So I broke you of the habit, along with any other habit that would make you seem weak to our environment. So that you could survive in the outside world . . . and so that I could survive living with you."

I looked at the knife in my trembling hand, tears blurring my vision of it. "Why didn't you just give me to someone who could love me?"

"No one was looking for another mouth to feed. And I tried multiple times to take you to the orphanage. You kept running back to find me."

"I don't remember all that." I laughed, despite my budding tears. "I was a stupid child."

"No, you were a survivor. Better the devil you know than the devil you don't." He looked down at the knife, then shifted his eyes back to mine. "I might as well tell you I've decided to help you with the hyena."

I dropped my arm to my side quickly, gripping the handle. "You mean you're staying?"

"You think after raising you for fourteen years I'd let you die now?"

"I think you'd let me come close before saving me." I said it like a joke, but neither of us laughed. Maybe because we both knew it was true. Normal. "And you're right. Better the devil I know." I put my knife away, and grinned, but only because it made me feel better about everything. "Come on, Satan, let's go put your horse in the stable."

"It's fitting, since I'll be in hell for the next few days," he replied, but the corner of his mouth turned up the slightest bit. "The archbishop is going to lose his mind."

The creaking of the stairs caught my attention, and I turned to see Saba hugging a folded wool blanket to her chest. Even the air around Jember went rigid when she approached.

Jember folded his arms across his chest. He didn't look pleased to see her. How could he not be happy to see Saba again? Even I was happy to see her, and I'd only been away from her for a few minutes.

"Saba," he greeted.

She nodded, giving him a shy grin.

He dropped his gaze to the floor immediately. Cleared his throat. "I don't think we have anything more to say to each other. I'm just here to help Andi."

Saba bit her lip, and then shook out the blanket, draping it over his shoulders.

"I don't need it," he protested sternly, and I was about to open my mouth to chastise him about being stubborn, but Saba was way ahead of me. She tucked it around him tightly, holding it in her fist by his chest, like she was threatening him. He looked at her then, and for a moment they stood in each other's gaze.

It felt . . . intimate. It was a look. That was all. But I felt like an intruder to newlyweds' first night together.

"You look exactly the same," he murmured. His gloved hand lifted, lingering near her chin. "God . . . why did I let this happen to you?"

Saba slid her hands up the blanket, close to his neck, and I wanted to mentally scream at her to stop. Because, just as I anticipated, he abruptly stepped back from her touch.

And, just like that, the connection, the intimacy, was gone.

Saba looked like she might cry, but she didn't give him long to see it as she rushed past him and headed toward the door.

"Are you moving the horse?" he asked, going after her. "I can do that myself."

She turned on her heel in the sand and snapped her fingers before pointing at him.

"What happened to pointing being rude—?"

She rolled her eyes, moving him easily past the threshold with one hand, and shut the door behind her.

I burst out laughing. "I've never seen someone handle you so thoroughly."

"Shut up, Andi," he said, throwing his blanket at me, probably because it was all that was on hand.

I caught it and rolled it up, throwing it back. "I can feel the connection between you two. Are you sure you don't want a second chance at this?"

Jember was silent for a moment, wrapping the blanket around him again. "Where can I get this off?" he asked, glancing down at his leg.

"Um . . ." I swallowed my frustration so I could think. "Down that hall, the first big room. It's a game room with couches."

He nodded and headed in that direction.

I sighed and went back upstairs to check on Magnus. He was sleeping peacefully. I envied him. It was a sin, but I did.

I lay on top of the covers to watch him sleep. When he woke he wouldn't remember a thing. Not the screams, or the taste of blood. Not the fear and chaos. He'd just be weirdly adorable Magnus and I would be . . . haunted. I'd let a human being be torn to shreds. Maybe there was nothing I could've done about it, but I felt it anyway, deeper than the scar on my face. Magnus thought *he* was a monster? At least he wasn't aware of what he was doing. At least it wasn't him causing the pain.

I, on the other hand . . .

I let myself cry for thirty seconds, and then closed my eyes and shoved the horror of last night deep where the rest of my trauma lived . . . so deep it only lived in nightmares. There was just no room for it anywhere else.

Not if I wanted to keep surviving.

I heard the sheets shift, and opened my eyes to Magnus stretching, like a cat in the sun.

"Good morning," he sang.

"It's the afternoon, now."

"What am I doing in your bed?" he asked, looking around the room. He blushed, gaping. "Did we . . . ?"

I rolled my eyes, but was blushing same as him. "No."

"Good. If we ever do I want to remember it."

I raised my eyebrows. "What do you mean 'if we ever do'? Don't answer that, there's no time. You're not free of the Evil Eye yet."

"Oh." His frown was deep and weary, as if all the muscles in his face were too exhausted to do anything else. "Well, that's okay. You did your best, I'm sure—" He sat up quickly, the color retreating from his face. "Kelela!"

"She's fine," I said. "Asleep in your bed." I squeezed his shoulders briefly. It was always comforting when Saba did it to me, so I figured it would work for him, too. Maybe it did, because he fell back onto his pillow again, grinning slightly.

"Thank God. Well, maybe the four of us can have breakfast together."

"Well, there are five of us right now, actually. Jember has graciously agreed to help me."

Graciously? Sure, Andi.

Maybe my thoughts betrayed me, because Magnus's smile deflated a bit. "Jember? Here?"

"Two debtera are better than one."

"But he's awful to you."

I hesitated. I should never have told him anything. "He's fine."

"Fine?" Magnus kicked the blanket off himself as I shushed him. "He beat you. That's not fine."

"Disciplined," I corrected with a sigh.

It was a good thing I never told him about Jember choking me. That might've given him a heart attack.

"Well, he kicked you out," he said, throwing his hands up. "And he broke Saba's heart."

"It was the other way around, actually."

"I love you, Andromeda, but do you really expect me to believe that?" He stood and combed his fingers through his loose curls, just adding frizz to his bedhead. "He was the first debtera we asked three years ago, and he refused the request to get back at her."

"That's ridiculous. And irrational. Stop riling yourself up."

"I'll ask him, then."

"Asking will only make him angry, and it was hard enough to get him to say yes in the first place."

"Then, by all means, he has my permission to leave." Magnus swung the door wide. "But not before I tell him what I think of him. I'm going to go find something special to wear for the occasion." And he stormed out of the room and down the hall.

I pressed my palm between my eyes, taking a few deep breaths. Was I the only person in this house with any desire to be civil?

CHAPTER
29

⸻

When I peeked my head into the game room, Jember was sitting in the chair facing the door, one leg propped up on the coffee table, the other lying underneath on the cold rug.

He glanced up from the amulet he was constructing. "Is the host awake?"

"He's getting dressed." I leaned my shoulder against the doorway. "Saba gave you silver?"

"Not even the fireplace is penetrating this cold," he said, tucking his blanket closer. "I need to construct a heater if I'm going to sleep in here."

"There are plenty of bedrooms."

"Not near the exit."

"We're not on the street anymore, Jember." We were quiet for a moment. But I guess I had no right to say such a thing. When I first arrived here I was wary of everything, too. "Did you and Saba speak when she gave you the silver?"

"She literally can't speak."

I raised my eyebrows at him, expecting more. "Did you at least apologize?"

"For what?"

I scoffed. "And to think, I actually wanted you two to be together. But you don't deserve her. You don't deserve anyone."

"I know I don't." Jember's voice chased me as I stepped out in the hall.

I paused and slid halfway back into the room, hugging the doorway. "Self-pity doesn't really suit you."

He planted his foot on the floor, leaning forward. "What more can I say to make you stop trying to force us together?" he said, placing the amulet on the table. "She's *dead*, Andi. And my skin can't bear to be touched. So what do you suppose we'd do with each other, hm? Gaze at each other lovingly until the Evil Eye is defeated and she's gone forever? Indulge in feelings that'll only be wasted?" He went back to working on his amulet. "I don't think so."

"So, you admit it. You love her."

"I admit nothing."

I sighed and sat on the edge of the billiards table. "I realize this is my first hyena and I don't know what I'm doing, but Magnus is still my client. I don't mind if you take the reins on certain things—that's why I asked you to stay. But I do expect you to be nice to him."

"I'm in too much pain today to take demands from a child."

"I'm not a child anymore."

"Every time you say that you sound more and more like one."

I scowled. "You have to be nice. This is *his* house. And he already thinks you didn't accept the job to begin with in order to get back at Saba."

Jember halted in his work. "If she had told him the whole truth he wouldn't be so angry. She isn't as perfect as she appears."

"She's his mother, of course he's going to take her side. Besides, you could stand to behave a little less like a villain."

He rolled his eyes, focusing back on his work, though a bit absently. "I'll be nice as long as he doesn't try my patience."

"What patience?" I grumbled, and pushed some of the billiard balls around the soft surface.

What did you expect, Andi? You're lucky he's even here.

I bowed my head, pressing back my excitement as Magnus walked in, Kelela on his arm. She was probably worn out from last night, not to mention her injury. I'm sure he was simply assisting her. But . . . they just looked so good together. So right. They were of the same social standing, and she was so beautiful. She was showing her prowess, again, by stealing a room just by entering.

I wasn't jealous, was I? There was no point, not after Magnus had already declared his love for me. But part of me couldn't help it. I would never look perfect with him. We would never be anyone's ideal.

Magnus's brown jacket looked like—what was it called?—a tuxedo, shorter in the front with two long tails in the back, but the fabric was more textured. His white Nehru-collared shirt went almost to his knees. I liked that he mixed his two cultures in his decorating and his clothes.

Kelela gaped as soon as they walked in the room, her eyes shining in the firelight. "Oh my God, it's Jember! This is such an honor."

Jember paused in his work to look at her, squinting slightly. "Have we met?"

She looked starstruck. "I'm Kelela. I go to your church. I love when you sing the chants, can you sing something now?"

"Are you kidding?" I grumbled, raising my eyebrows at her reaction. Cleansing a hyena had made Jember a living legend, but that didn't make him worth fawning over by any means.

Jember looked as unimpressed as I expected. "Why are you *here?*"

"Oh," Kelela said, smoothing her hair. "I volunteered to make eye contact with Magnus."

He kissed his teeth and put his focus back on the amulet. "What is with you girls risking your lives for this awkward little dope?"

"That does it," Magnus said, helping Kelela sit on the couch across from Jember before leveling a glare at him. "I wore my corduroy jacket for such a time as this."

Oh God. "Magnus—" I tried.

"I contacted you three years ago, Jember, and you wanted nothing to do with this house. What's different now?"

"What's different?" Jember said, as if Magnus should've known, and continued his amulet without actually answering.

"You are a coward and a fiend."

"Let's not hurl names," I said, stepping between them.

"Now that you've slept for a year," Jember said, without looking up, "perhaps we can finally talk about what comes next. Now, where's your guardian, little boy?"

Magnus crinkled his nose like a snarling puppy. "I'm not a little boy, old man."

"Why does everyone your age think thirty-eight is old?"

"I don't," said Kelela, batting her eyelashes.

I rolled my eyes.

"Let's take a step back," I said, holding my hands up between everyone. "Magnus, Jember is here to help me cleanse you. Jember, *please* don't rile Magnus up, he's stressed enough as it is."

"Stressed?" Jember scoffed. "We're the ones doing all the work."

I clamped my hand over Magnus's mouth, muting his biting remark. "We have to work quickly, don't we? So, what's the first step?"

"Depends. Was there a victim last night?"

"No," I said. It was probably stupid to lie to Jember about something so important, but I just couldn't bear to say it in front of Magnus and have him ask questions later. Besides, I had already made myself a target, so details were unnecessary at this point.

"It will need a night to recuperate, which means we only have until tomorrow. That doesn't give us much time, so first thing we need to do is gather anything that can be used as a weapon. Long, with a sharp end, are best."

"No, first we need to eat," Magnus said, stretching. "I'm starving."

Jember raised an eyebrow. "*Starving* is a little melodramatic, don't you think? When's the last time you ate, boy, yesterday?"

"Eating's a good idea, Jember," I cut in before Magnus's scowl turned into mouthy defiance. "There's plenty of daylight left to work afterward. Besides, we don't want Saba's food to get cold."

I looped Kelela's arm around Magnus's to keep him occupied, steering them toward the door.

"I thought you said you'd be nice," I whisper-yelled at Jember.

"There was a stipulation to that," he said, removing his blanket now that the amulet was finished. It was so cozy my wool sweater was starting to make me itch.

I huffed and followed Magnus and Kelela to the dining room.

"I have so many questions," Kelela said, "but my head hurts."

"Is your arm okay?" I asked.

"It's completely numb." Magnus helped her sit in a chair and pushed it in for her as she asked, "Where's Peggy? Did you leave her locked in the closet?"

I choked on my spit as I tried to swallow. Oh God. Peggy. The one thing I never wanted to have to explain. I sat across from Kelela, quickly.

Magnus gaped, then laughed, blissfully ignorant. "You locked Peggy in the closet?"

"Magnus . . . Peggy, she . . ." I couldn't say it. That woman had raised him. And as horrid as she was—forgive me, God, for saying anything cruel about the dead—Magnus would be heartbroken if he knew.

Kelela didn't know what had happened. Magnus couldn't remember. Saba couldn't tell.

So, "She left" came out of my mouth before I could think too hard about it and make it sound like a lie.

Even so, the amusement in Magnus's face was gone. "Left?"

"She couldn't take it anymore, she said," I said, distracting myself with the washing bowl so I wouldn't have to look at him. "She left last night. Didn't say where she was going."

"Well, when is she coming back?"

"Never," Kelela said, rather harshly. She looked ready to kill the ghost of the woman herself. "I guess she didn't want to have to be the next volunteer. What a coward."

"Don't say that," I said quickly. "She reacted how anyone would. You're just braver than most."

"Of course I am." She gaped at me slightly, but I noticed a pleased blush on her cheeks. "Thank you."

"So, she's not coming back?" Magnus butted in.

"No, Magnus." I touched his hand, and he weaved his fingers through mine, making my heart pound. "She's not coming back."

He was quiet for a moment, his body sinking into his chair. And then he stood and left the room, his bells jingling joylessly down the hall.

"I suppose I'll have to tell my brother what happened seeing as this arm won't allow me to travel right now," Kelela grumbled, digging into the food with her one good hand without bothering to wash it, either. She shouldn't have been eating with her left, but it's all she had available—and, anyway, etiquette was never the strong suit of this household. "God, he's going to kill me."

I tore some bite-sized pieces of injera for her so she wouldn't have to struggle. "Do you want a ride to town?"

"No, I'm too achy for that bumpy ride. He'll be here tomorrow morning. I'll wait."

"Won't he be mad that you put yourself in danger like this? And that you waited so long to tell him about it?"

"He'll forgive me. He always does."

Somehow I didn't believe it would work out how she wanted. Looking at her arm, splinted and in a sling, I was developing an understanding of Jember's reluctance to let me do this. It didn't matter how brave or determined I was if I wasn't qualified.

But, with Jember's help, I would be.

I had to be.

Speaking of . . . "I forgot something," I said, stuffing one more fingerful of spicy food in my mouth before rushing out to get Jember. There was no way he could put that leg on himself in the condition he was in.

I tripped to a stop before the doorway on hearing a whispered voice, and peeked inside to see Saba standing a short distance from Jember's chair. He had his arms crossed and Saba was gripping a small wooden box . . . but they were clearly talking, which was progress. Saba approached and sat on the coffee table, opening the box beside her. A first-aid kit. I prayed Jember would let her touch him, if only to help.

And then I backed up slowly out of the doorway to go finish my lunch.

CHAPTER
30

———— ❧ ————

"This is all we have," Magnus said, laying out two swords, three rifles, a case of pistols, and a handful of kitchen knives. He blinked at my significantly larger pile of household items. "What is all that junk?"

It was easy to find weapons in such a huge house. Curtain rods, fireplace tools, plenty of solid-wood broomsticks that could be sharpened into spears or used as clubs.

But I guess if you weren't used to fighting for your life, they could more easily be overlooked.

"You need a little more imagination," I said. "And these"—I moved the knives away from everything else—"won't do any good. We want long-range weapons, only."

"Ever heard of 'knife throwing'?"

"That's a thing?"

"They do it all the time in the carnivals in Prague."

"What's a carnival?"

"It's the greatest show on earth." Magnus grinned and took

my hand, lighting it on fire, a feeling so glorious I never wanted to let go. "When this is all over, I'll take you."

I blushed, turning away to sort the weapons. "I've never been out of the country before."

"We'll be able to go anywhere. Everywhere. You'll love it."

"Well, I mean, I have to see if there's time between clients."

"Oh." His smile slipped away slowly. "Right. Of course. Your job."

"Why work for a patronage if you're not going to use it afterward?" My words sounded shallow to my own ears, but I couldn't stop them. I was doing to Magnus exactly what I hated Jember for doing to Saba.

He helped me sort, though he was sorting differently than I was and messing up everything I'd done. "I was thinking about hiring someone to run the chocolate business. I mean, when I'm twenty-one and it's mine to command. They'll do all the boring business things, and I'll get to sit back and focus on my art."

"Really?" I'd been counting the weapons but lost the number somewhere between twenty-one and twenty-six. "That's great. You should definitely do what you're passionate about."

"I figure you can do art any time of the day and still be able to sell portraits overseas. At night, for instance. Plenty of countries are awake while we're asleep."

I lost count again and stopped trying. "Magnus, we really need to get these things organized."

"And debtera work at night, too. So, you know, we'd be awake at the same time."

"Right. Okay." I raised my eyebrows at him. What did art and exorcism have to do with each other? "Are you going to help me with these weapons?"

"We could be together," he clarified. "And we could be nocturnal."

That made me laugh, and it lifted the seriousness from his expression. He wrapped an arm around my shoulders and pulled me in for a kiss. After a moment I pulled back, breathless. "I want to be with you, nocturnal or not," I said, rubbing my nose to his. "But first things first."

"Right, yes, the Evil Eye," he said with a heavy sigh, as if he were tired of hearing about it. "And then, wedding preparations."

I gaped, then snapped my jaw shut, blinking at him for a moment. "Wedding preparations?"

"Of course."

"What do you mean *of course?*"

"Andi," Jember called from the top of the stairs, "come see me in your room."

"Oh, thank God," I murmured, rushing out of the room and up the stairs. I had been beginning to sweat. A wedding . . . I couldn't even imagine it. I'd never really *wanted* to. Men seemed to need periodic babysitting, but women came already fully capable—unless they were unable to work or wanted children. But I was working, doing what I loved, and I could cook and defend myself. And bearing children was the furthest thing from my mind.

Our ideas for the future vastly differed, but there would be plenty of time to talk about that when he was safe and well.

Like you said, Andi. First things first.

Jember followed me into my cozy room and locked the door behind us. The door had an amulet nailed to it, one I'd never seen before. "What's that for?"

"Extra protection," he said, easing himself to sit on my bed. He was wearing some of the dark grey knitwear this house had chosen as its uniform. It was strange seeing him in dark colors. I'd grown up seeing him in mostly white, with rich colors as accents. The grey didn't suit him. "Because you counteracted the temperature, the Evil Eye isn't connected to this room, thus can't hear us. But I added an extra shield, just in case."

"Just in case of what?"

"The two of us are the only ones who can be in on the plan of attack. If Magnus or Saba get wind of it, it'll get back to the Evil Eye. We need to work with the element of surprise as much as we can."

"I understand. So what's the plan?"

"We need to put up as much defense as possible. If we prepare a room ahead of time—the game room downstairs, which I've already started on—we can create barricades with amulets to keep the hyena inside."

"But it'll break through. We need more defense than just amulets."

"If the hyena's target is inside the room with it—hear me out," he said, and I clamped my jaw shut again. "The target and someone helping to protect them in the room. An amulet shielding the doorway. And then you, outside of the room, constructing the amulet."

How could I tell him I would be the one inside the room without giving myself away?

"We can't lock Kelela in with it, there's no way she'd be able to help defend herself with her injuries. And if she's killed—God forbid—the Evil Eye will just go dormant again and this will all be for nothing."

"If the hyena is focused on the target it won't bother to waste time breaking down the defense at the door. It's important that you're out of danger while you're working."

"I think you should be the one constructing the amulet. You're much faster than I am."

"I'll be gone before then. And you're fast enough."

Tomorrow I'd have to try to force him to stay again, but that was a problem for tomorrow. "Is this how you did it?"

"I didn't have a team of people. Just me. I'd sent the target out of the house for the day, then spent part of the afternoon scattering the limbs of the Evil Eye's servant around the city. But I did lock it in a room with the defensive amulet on the door, and I crouched on top of a high bookcase for extra protection."

My gape tweaked into a grin. "That's brilliant."

"It only *just* worked. If I'd had help maybe I wouldn't be . . ." He gestured to his leg. "And I hadn't had time to construct any more than one shield at the door. I'll show you how, and we can make at least three apiece tonight if you're willing to stay up."

"Of course I'm willing. I'll do whatever it takes. Although, I'm not really comfortable scattering Saba across the desert."

"Me neither. We'll just have to keep an eye on her." He leaned over, his forearms on his thighs, and groaned. "I can't believe I left my pills at home."

"And your mentee, now that we're on the subject."

"What?" Jember lowered his brows for a moment, then raised them. "Oh right. Him." He winced, rubbing his knee. "Maybe he'll get fed up with waiting and go back to his parents. That would be the perfect homecoming present."

"I'll ask Saba to bring you some medicine."

"I'll ask her. You need to get a little sleep for tonight."

I grinned. "So, you two are talking now?"

"Earlier, when she was taking care of my leg . . . I . . ." He shook his head, like he didn't understand what he was saying. "I don't think her touch hurt me."

I gaped. "Really?"

"I'm not sure. It was hard to tell, since I was already in pain."

"Wait." I leaped off the bed, suddenly realizing: "Her skin is made of pottery, not actual flesh. That must be why it doesn't hurt."

Jember's brows lowered—the opposite reaction I was expecting. "That's your optimism talking. You want this to happen. It's not going to happen."

"Why not?"

He got up with a groan. "Because I don't want it to."

"But you love her, don't you?"

"I don't know."

"You don't *know*?"

He shrugged. "It's been a long time, Andi. I don't think I know how to love in that way anymore."

Finally, some honesty, even if it sounded like agony coming out.

He opened my bedroom door, swinging it wide, and left. Ending the conversation just like that. No more plans could be made. No more secrets could be said.

Not without consequences.

When I peeked out into the hall, Jember was out there talking to Saba, and I saw him gesture to his knee. She nodded and hurried to the closet down at the end of the hall. I froze, bracing myself as she opened it, but it had been rearranged to block any proof of what had happened.

"Andromeda!" Magnus called, and I heard pounding on the stairs. When I went to the top I saw him jumping them three by three. "Do you want to play a game with me?"

"Well, Jember wants to observe the house tonight, so I'm actually going to get a couple hours' sleep before the Waking."

His expression dropped. "You'll be up and about during the

Waking? Whose idea was that?" But he was leveling a glare at Jember before I could even respond. "Look, there are rules in this house, Jember. And I'm not comfortable having Andromeda out in the halls during the Waking."

Jember gave Magnus a look that seemed to assess whether or not he had the energy to bother explaining our job. "If you have any more stupid comments, just write them down so I can more easily ignore them."

"Why, because you can't read?" Magnus countered, with far more intensity than necessary—but it was Magnus, after all.

I would've laughed, but now really wasn't the time. Jember had been on his feet all day. He needed more painkillers. By this time of day his patience was thin, which is why we normally slept. And I could tell Magnus didn't like Jember even before he'd entered the house. So, part of me wanted to step in between them in case a fight broke out—though the other part knew better than to step between two people about to fight.

Then again, Magnus would maybe get in a few hits but would ultimately lose horribly—knowing Jember, by way of death. I liked him too much to let that happen.

"The spirits are more active in the evening," I said quickly. "Remember, Magnus? Besides, there's nothing out there but wind."

"You're a terrible father, you know that?" he growled, and I quickly grabbed his arm and pulled him back, while Saba shot him a chastising look. "I wish you'd take that amulet off so I could look you in the eye and save her from you."

"Magnus, stop—"

"Please shut him up," Jember said, rolling his eyes. "He's exhausting." He looked at me. "Be ready to work in two hours."

"I'll be ready," I said, dragging Magnus away. I shoved him into his room, shutting the door behind us. "Jember is here to help. Could you not start fights, please?"

"I hate him like that putrid honey wine," he said, punching his pillow a few times before sitting on his bed. "He doesn't deserve you. Or Saba."

"No one deserves Saba."

He grinned slightly. "That's true."

"Jember has his own set of survival habits. And . . . he has really bad pain because of his injury." I probably shouldn't have revealed Jember's business, but it was too late now. I sat beside him on the bed. "He doesn't mean most of what he says."

"You're too used to defending him. He doesn't deserve it, Andromeda." He huffed and lay back on the bed. "He's a horrible human."

"I know he is, but you don't get to say it."

Magnus blinked at me curiously, and I realized I had raised my voice.

I stood up quickly. "I should go nap before tonight," I said, and rushed out of the room.

"Where is everything?" was the first thing Jember asked after we'd walked through the halls a bit. He only needed to talk slightly louder over the wind as he leaned in close.

"I cleansed it all," I said. "Well, most of it."

He chewed on his lip for a moment, then headed to the closest room—the library.

I followed, then shut the door and the wind behind us. "This room isn't the safest. There's a ghost who likes to hurl books."

Jember narrowed his eyes, but at the portrait of Magnus's father instead of me. "Normally, I would applaud your good sense—"

"Would you really?" I said, raising my eyebrows.

"—in cleansing the Manifestations in order of strength." I dodged away as he attempted to flick me in the forehead. "But in this case, you should've left all the Manifestations intact and dealt only with the hyena. Cleansing it all first gives the Evil Eye too much opportunity to assess your capability."

"Well, I didn't know that," I said with a frustrated shrug. "We never made it to that lesson, remember?"

"That's because you weren't supposed to be here."

A book dropped on the ground and skidded, stopping between us.

"That's our warning to go," I said. "Should we work in the game room?"

Jember didn't move. "Hand me that."

I sighed, but picked up the book and held it out to him. I winced as he cocked his arm back. He threw the book at the wall, the sharp edge denting the canvas right where someone had painted Magnus's father's throat. The book flipped, slapping messily against the mantel then to the ground. Jember murmured something that included a swear and the word *colonizer* as he left the room.

I followed at a safe distance until we were in the game room.

"I have a feeling you know the man in the portrait," I said carefully.

"Never met him." Jember chose the chair by the fire, so I put the basket of supplies on the coffee table before taking the couch across from him. He snatched a disk of silver from the basket. "But that boy has the same face."

"Really? I think Magnus looks more like Saba."

He flinted his pen violently. "That little jackass does not look like Saba."

I smirked at his defensive tone and leaned forward to watch him work, but he waved me away. Right. Don't watch. Just feel. I sat back in my chair again.

"I never wanted you to have to learn this sort of thing," he said, a few strokes in.

"Then why did you start teaching me to cleanse Manifestations in the first place?"

"At first? Because constructing amulets kept you out of my hair for hours at a time." He shrugged. "You were good at it. Excited about it. And I liked teaching you. Besides, when I took you with me to see clients they would always tip you."

"And then I stopped being lucrative because I wasn't cute anymore."

It wasn't just growing older and longer, my face morphing out of its cute little baby features into something more plain and awkward. Jember had stopped bringing me along about the same time I'd gotten my scar. The quick memory reminded me it was there, and my arm instinctively lifted to cover it, trying to make the gesture look casual by pulling my knees up on the chair and folding my forearms on top, shielding my mouth and cheeks.

I don't know if Jember noticed what I was doing, but he said, "That's not true. You stopped being lucrative when you became a little dick."

I let out a breath of laughter. "Kind of like you."

"Yes, but I had already built a reputation. It has a different effect when you're previously an endearing angel." He leaned back, propping his legs up on the table between us. "You'd never been beaten up like that before, so the attitude was understandable. But I like that you grew out of it. You have to find the survival habit that works best for you, and you operate better on optimism."

"Maybe you should try it."

"It's too exhausting. I have to save my energy for things that matter." He sighed and waved the amulet at me. "Are you paying attention? I'm not going to start again for you."

"It doesn't feel done."

"It's not." He raised an eyebrow at me. "If only you weren't so ambitious. Then we wouldn't be here right now."

"Feel free to leave after you've finished with that amulet," I said. "I can handle it from there."

It was stupid of me to say that—if he called my bluff there'd be no one to construct the amulet when the hyena was released.

He sighed and looked at the unfinished silver, not like he misunderstood it but like it was the canvas for some other thought. I didn't dare interrupt that thought, and so we sat in silence for what felt like minutes. "Only four debtera in history have survived their encounters with a hyena. All of them suffered nerve damage from their injuries. None of them could bear to touch another living person again. Three of them killed themselves before old age could take them." He shook his head, as if realizing he wasn't working, and made a few more strokes. "I don't want that for you."

I swallowed, my throat dry as I took in his words. "Why haven't you ever told me this before?"

"Would it have mattered? All children think they're invincible. Besides, constructing amulets is in you, like music. Most debtera are content to cleanse everyday Manifestations, but you've never been. Teaching you to cleanse a hyena would've been too much encouragement."

"I'm good at this, you know I am. And if you had just taught me everything, maybe you wouldn't have to be here right now doing it for me. I know you hate being here."

"You're too inexperienced to know you should be afraid."

"I'm terrified, Jember. I've been since the first night. But there are more important things than fear at the moment."

"Yes," he grumbled, "your insufferable lover."

"We're not lovers," I said, my face burning, then added indignantly, "Anyway, you're Saba's insufferable lover, you know."

"I know." He cursed and leaned back in his chair. "For the life of me I can't figure out why she still loves me."

"Because love is a strange beast. I don't know. Why do I love Magnus?"

He raised his eyebrows as he worked. "Yes, why do you? You used to make more sense."

"Same reason I care about you," I said, smirking. "Every girl wants to marry someone like their father. You've conditioned me to have horrible taste in men."

He laughed, putting the amulet down on the table with a sigh. He was quiet for a moment, the remainder of his smile drifting away into deep, sorrowful thought. Finally, he looked at me. "I was never qualified to take in a child, and you paid the price for that. I'm sorry, Andi."

I didn't expect his words and, for a moment, I didn't know what to make of them. I felt tears pricking the backs of my eyes, but I knew he'd scold me if I cried. I could've easily turned this on him, told him off for everything he'd ever done to me.

But, somehow, I didn't want to. "I forgive you."

"You don't have to."

"I think it's better for my own conscience that I do."

We were quiet for a moment.

Jember broke it with a sigh. "I think we can agree the bond between us isn't based on normal love. We're survivors. We keep coming back together again because we need each other to survive . . . but that's not to say I don't care about you. I do."

My heart suddenly started pounding, and I had to force myself not to smile. That was all I'd ever wanted to hear. "You raised me. That's affection enough."

He looked at me, studied me, as if to see if I was being sarcastic, and then handed me a disk of silver. "I hope you were paying attention."

"Just watch, old man, I'll show you how it's done."

He smirked and leaned back in his chair. "We'll see."

He got to work on his next amulet without waiting for me to finish, and for a while we worked together in silence. Such familiar silence. Growing up, I used to call it *quality together time.* But still, it was marred by a creeping anxiety in my gut.

"Is the fourth debtera okay?" I asked suddenly.

"Hm?"

"Three killed themselves. The fourth doesn't want to, does he?"

"Not so much since I found you." He paused in his work, grinning the slightest bit. "Turns out having someone to live for helps."

I entered my room to find Magnus fast asleep. The drawer where I kept my sleeping dress tended to creak, so instead I took off my warmer layer, wrapped my hair in my satin scarf, and climbed carefully into bed. I left space between us, just as Jember and I had done for years, but . . . somehow lying beside Magnus felt different. It felt . . . final.

But the word "final" could mean so many things. It could mean he was my final destination, my life partner, the man who I might one day call Husband—as distasteful as the concept seemed to me now, I knew in my heart my future would lead to it.

Unless . . . unless "final" meant something a bit more eternal, involving more of the physical presence of God and entirely too much less of Magnus.

No . . . No. It was not my time to die yet, God willing.

I reached out to caress Magnus's cheek. He sighed, murmuring my name quietly.

"Yes, I'm here," I whispered back.

"Did you have fun?" he mumbled, still mostly asleep I was sure, because his face was still pressed to his pillow.

I grinned, only holding back a kiss so as not to wake him. "I did."

"You love working . . ."

I shushed him gently, and he sighed and went back to sleep.

CHAPTER

31

I awoke with my face to a wall. I lifted my hands to push away, but it felt surprisingly flesh-like. Merciful God, how could I have forgotten. Magnus had shared my bed last night. His arms were around me, leaving only a breath's amount of room between us.

"You broke the bed-sharing rules," I mumbled to his chest.

"Good morning to you too, my little sunbeam," he whispered to the crown of my head.

I felt overly warm, and it wasn't all due to body heat.

We lay in bed, basking in the rays coming through my window, but it was difficult to fully enjoy remembering what would happen tonight. That the hyena would be released . . . and my life would be on the line.

No. Death wasn't an option for me. Besides, what could death do to me that life hadn't already? This was performance anxiety. That's all.

The sounds of a coach and horses outside sent me kicking off my blanket and leaping to my feet. I got dressed quickly, but by the time I got to the stairs Esjay had let himself in.

"Peggy?" he called, and my heart went immediately into my feet.

"She left," I said, rushing down the stairs.

Esjay paused in putting on his coat. "What do you mean, left?"

As I approached, I could see he looked more tired than usual. More anxious. But I hadn't really thought out the details to my lie, so I just shrugged. "She didn't want to deal with the curse anymore, I suppose."

Esjay looked at me like I had to have been a figment of his imagination. "She's taken care of Magnus since he was a baby. How could she just *leave?*" And then his jaw dropped, his eyes wide. "Who did you find to volunteer?"

"U-um—"

"Peggy!" he called, poking his head in the dining room before rushing up the stairs. "Magnus!"

"Esjay, you're back," Magnus said, yawning as he came from my room. "You're not here to pick up Kelela, are you?"

"Kelela?" Esjay stopped himself just short of looking at Magnus, not trusting his amulet. "She's supposed to be with friends. Are you telling me she's *here?*"

"We are her friends," Magnus said, his tone indignant.

"She's here," I confirmed, chewing on my lip. To be honest, I was just glad his attention was away from asking about Peggy.

Esjay turned a sharp look on me—a strange change for him, but relatively tame compared to looks I'd seen on the street, and even from Jember. "Where?"

"Magnus's room."

He stormed up the rest of the stairs and down the short distance in the hall, barging into the room without knocking.

And then it was all yelling. "What the hell is wrong with you?" and "You can forget Paris, young lady!" and "What in God's name happened to your arm?"

Magnus let out a weary sigh and held the back of my neck, pressing his lips to my forehead. "I'm going to get dressed. Don't go far."

"I won't," I said, every nerve in my body reaching for him as he left me in the hall. But there was no time for that. I needed to find Jember.

He'd designated the game room as his sleeping space, so I went there first and found him and Saba drinking coffee. Well, Jember was drinking coffee. I wasn't exactly sure if people made of pottery could digest food.

"Saba got ahold of you, I see," I said, gesturing to his neater beard by stroking my imaginary one. "It's a sweet act of love, isn't it?"

"More like a compulsion," he said, raising his eyebrows at Saba as she innocently grinned and shrugged.

"You two must be getting along really well," I said, and Saba returned my sly expression, confirming my hopes. "He's letting you touch his face and everything."

"Who was making all that fuss out there?" Jember asked—to ignore my comment, obviously, since he didn't sound like he cared that much about Esjay.

"Kelela's brother."

As if on command, I heard banging footfalls down the stairs and Esjay's argumentative voice. Jember's brows lowered slightly, and he touched Saba's arm to excuse himself as he led the way out.

Kelela rushed over to me as soon as she made it down the stairs, hugging me around the neck with her good arm. I froze for a moment before returning it, squeezing her around the waist.

"Kick that hyena's ass," she whispered, but Esjay dragged her away before I could respond.

"I will," I called after her, while Esjay shot me a *Why are you talking to my sister?* look.

"I can't believe you let Kelela do this," he said, turning on Jember. "You're the adult here. You should've stopped her."

"She's *your* kid," Jember said, without any remorse.

Esjay released an angry huff through his nostrils, like a wild horse ready to charge. And then he simply ignored the instinct, instead grabbing Kelela's good arm and dragging her outside.

"First thing we're going to do is see a *real* doctor," I heard him say. "Your bone is going to heal all wrong—"

Jember shoved the door shut and headed for the kitchen.

"Will the plan still work?" I asked, rushing up beside him. "With Kelela gone?"

"The important thing is that the Evil Eye has a target," he said, "which she's already provided. She doesn't have to be in the vicinity for it to become active. The two of us will just have to construct some more shields to make up for it."

We spent the morning constructing more shields, while Magnus lounged around in the room and drew, then took a break from each other after lunch. Not that working with Jember was unpleasant—some of my best memories were of us sitting on the bed, constructing amulets. It was as if the act of carving patterns was the only way we could connect. Therapy, in a way.

But he needed time to rest his fingers, so Magnus and I took a short nap and then headed to play some music. I think we'd both decided, without telling each other, that we wanted to spend the entire day together. Besides . . . part of me was terrified there'd be no tomorrow.

Nonsense, Andi. Everything will be fine.

For a moment, all I could hear was the creak of wood and our slow footsteps echoing off the old hollow halls as we walked.

But Magnus jolted and held me close, because there was something else echoing, too. Some sort of slapping sound coming from the game room.

"God, what was that?" he whispered. He grabbed my hand as I moved toward the questionable sound. "What are you doing?"

"Stay here," I said, rushing to the door, but Jember's laugh made me freeze before I could enter the room.

"Are you trying to break me?" I heard him say. "Your skin is hard enough without you using full force."

Definitely questionable.

I peeked into the room and saw Jember and Saba standing on opposite sides of the billiards table, their hands flat against the fuzzy surface in front of them. I felt blessed to witness the full glory of him and Saba playing the slap game. Both at once, they each shot their right hand out, attempting to slap their opponent's left hand. Jember won that round, managing to move his hand out of the way and slap Saba's.

It didn't have an official name, and as I grew older I wasn't really convinced it was a game as much as a method Jember had invented to torture me. We'd played it when I was little, as something fun to pass the time between possible dinner and leaving to see a client. My left hand was usually red and sore by the end. I was fast, my reflexes good, but Jember's slaps *hurt*.

To be honest, I was glad Saba was giving him a taste of his own medicine.

"Andi," Magnus whined, and I waved him away.

Saba slapped Jember again and he laughed and swore, grabbing both her wrists. "Play fair. I need these hands for work."

She gave him a flirty, teasing look, turning one of his palms faceup to trace his fingers with hers.

They were quiet for a moment. It was a sweet silence, that only the crackling fire dared interrupt.

"The first time we made love was on a table like this," Jember murmured, and Saba's smile was instantly uncontrollable, her gaze shy as she dropped it to the table. "Remember that?"

She bit her lip and nodded, searching his face. And then she climbed onto the table, crawling over and closing the gap between them as she kissed him. I had to press my palms over my mouth to keep from cheering.

I'd gotten them together, as stubborn as they both were. This had to be one of the most rewarding moments of my life.

I heard Magnus gasp over my shoulder, and turned around quickly to stifle him before he could say anything to ruin the moment. Hand pressed over his mouth, I walked him down the hall a bit before taking his hand.

"What the living hell was that?" Magnus hissed.

"I didn't want you killing their romantic moment."

"Romantic moment? That scoundrel was kissing my mother!"

I shushed him, dragging him into the music room. "It was beautiful."

"It was horrifying."

I grinned, raising an eyebrow at him. "I thought you were a fan of love?"

"I am," he said, scowling at the doorway. "When the person is deserving of it."

"Everyone's deserving of love, Magnus. And if they aren't, who are we to decide that?" I sat at the hopsicar and pressed a few keys, and he sat beside me. "Anyway, I think they're cute together."

Magnus grumbled.

"Let's only think of nice things now. How about you teach me to play?"

He paused, glancing at the instrument. "Really?" His enthusiasm was palpable. He got up and went behind the back of the bench. "Sit in the center."

I centered myself on the bench and scooted forward like I was told. And then I tensed slightly at the weight on the cushion as Magnus kneeled on it. I looked down to see his knees on the outside of each of my legs. He leaned his face over my shoulder, and I forced myself not to blush. I was wrapped in warmth. Human warmth. Better than any fire.

"This is Middle C," he said, reaching around me to press a key. "That's where both of your thumbs will start."

I put both thumbs where he instructed, keeping my fingers out of the way, but was met with a short chuckle. "What?"

"You need your other fingers, too, you sweet little onion."

If his arms were around my body it would've been a hug. Instead they were on my hands, gently guiding each finger to a key. His hands were so soft, and I suddenly felt self-conscious of my calloused ones.

"Relax, my love," he whispered near my cheek, and it was the worst thing he could've done.

"You're making me nervous," I said, shoving him away with my back.

His grip tightened slightly on my hands as he regained his balance. "We both know you're the scarier of the two of us."

"I can't tell if that's a compliment."

"So small yet so terrifying." He kissed my cheek and lined my fingers up again. "Ready to play?"

I nodded, too content to speak. Magnus slipped his soft hands beneath mine until my palms were against the back of his, each of my fingers curved over his. And then, slowly, he began to play. Slow enough that my hand could stay with his without any effort. Slow, but not melancholy, the notes melding like hot silver into something beautiful, something substantial. It was as if his music was creating life.

And for a moment, I basked in the thought that everything would be okay.

His hand slipped, his fingers streaking the cream keys red. All at once his playing halted, the instrument echoing eerily, the lingering notes turning sour as they hovered.

He jerked his hands away with a gasp.

For a moment, neither of us said a word, silently watching the blood seep its way from every crack of the keys, like from a mouthful of bloody teeth.

It wasn't until I heard liquid drip on the floor that I felt Magnus's breath become heavy.

"Who was it, Andromeda?" he asked. His voice was trembling.

"Maybe this isn't what you think it is," I said quietly.

"The house bleeds after the Evil Eye takes a victim." His hands were shaking as he gripped my arms. He was curled into me, his lips resting on my shoulder. "Tell me. Please. Was it Peggy?"

He said it as if he knew and was desperately hoping I'd deny it. I didn't know what to say. But my silence was answer enough.

A loud sob broke our silence. He wrapped his arms around me, his body shaking erratically. My arms were pinned by his, so the only comfort I could give was holding his head against my neck and massaging his scalp with my fingers. It only made him cry harder.

"She was very brave," I said, talking near his ear so he'd hear me over his crying. "She died fighting, protecting the people she cared about." In other words, Kelela. But now wasn't the time to talk badly about her.

"That—" *gasp* "doesn't—" *gasp* "m-make me fe—" *gasp* "—el better."

I jolted, gripping his hair in pained helplessness, lost on what to do.

His head felt like dead weight on my shoulder. It felt awkward to sit and wait for him to recover, but I couldn't just leave him down here alone, either. My neck was warm and wet, my boney bottom beginning to hurt from sitting in one spot. Maybe this was why Jember had always threatened me with pillows. Crying took a long time. But I had never lost someone I loved. Who was I to rush his mourning?

But maybe I'd need to, because I heard rushed footsteps coming down the hall, and suddenly my adrenaline was running, my instincts knowing they meant me no good.

And a moment later Jember stormed in, looking ready to kill, with Saba's expression full of panic as she followed.

I should've been on my feet immediately, reaching for my knife, but Magnus was leaning heavily on my shoulders.

"Why is the fireplace bleeding?" Jember said, shrugging off Saba's comforting hand.

It never occurred to me that multiple rooms could bleed at once, that maybe the Evil Eye really only did it to show off its latest kill. But this was what I deserved for not telling Jember sooner. Because I was the next target, he had to construct the amulet, and that wasn't something I could tell him minutes before—his mind and fingers needed to be rested enough for it.

But that wouldn't stop him from knocking me unconscious beforehand.

I tapped Magnus's knee frantically to make him get up, but instead he hugged me protectively, as if that would ever do any good. I was blocked in, front and back, and my heart began to pound for a way out.

"The hyena is being released again tonight," Jember said, rounding the hopsicar. "Who's the target, Andi?"

"Stay away from her," Magnus commanded, "or I'll—"

Between the hopsicar and the sweet boy at my back, the latter was arguably the easier obstacle to get through, and Jember grabbed him by the back of the collar and yanked him backward. And, God forgive me, I used those couple seconds to escape on top of the instrument. Magnus yelped and fussed as his back slammed on the floor and Saba rushed to his side.

Jember slammed his hands down, raising a muted scream of dissonance from the instrument. "Tell me you didn't do what I think you did."

What I'd initially thought was anger I now recognized as more. Something like panic. Fear. It shook my resolve a little.

"Jember," I said, slowly reaching for my knife, "calm down—"

He shoved the instrument and I lost my footing, tumbling off. I caught myself—just barely, my hip would definitely bruise— and got back on my feet quickly, knife at the ready.

We both knew I was never going to use it, and so he had no problem storming toward me. I backed away just as quickly.

"Did you make eye contact?"

I hesitated. It was essentially a yes. "At least listen to my plan—"

"Have you lost your mind?" he yelled. His hands were in front of him, imploring, grasping in and out as if he didn't know what else to do with them. "After everything I've done to keep you alive, you go and put yourself at the mercy of—" He yelled out in frustration and covered his face with his hands. His shoulders were shaking a little.

I put my knife away, just as slowly as I'd pulled it. Jember didn't cry often. Sometimes, when he thought I was sleeping and he didn't have any more pills, he would cry a little from the pain. But I'd never known him to show remorse. Tears were never shed over a human. Least of all me.

But when he removed his hands, tears were there, though he wiped the evidence away so quickly it felt almost like an illusion. He'd released the bit of humanity he allowed himself, his good survival habits taking over faster than I could summon the emotion to comfort him.

"You little idiot," he said. "I might as well kill you myself—"

Saba planted herself in front of me. His momentum slowed the slightest bit. I couldn't lie, I loved the power she held over him, as meager as it was.

"I swear to God, Saba, if you don't move—"

"You can't beat her, old man," I said, waving my scarred fingers at him. "And we can fight if you want, but what good would it do? It won't change what I've done."

"Do *you* know what you've done?" he shot back. "Because I don't think you do."

"I'm protecting the people I care about—"

"At the expense of your own life?"

"It was the best way—"

"You know damn well it wasn't—"

"Stop it!" Magnus said, rushing over to me. "Why are you threatening—?"

"I will kill you, little boy," Jember said, and the look in his eye was animalistic. "This is between me and my daughter. Back away."

I wasn't sure which part to react more strongly to, the part where he said he'd kill Magnus . . . or the part where he said, clear as day, that I was his daughter.

Saba had put herself in front of Magnus, just in case Jember tried to carry out his promise right then. And Magnus looked terrified, but he backed up a few steps, thank God, quiet as death.

Jember pointed out to the door. "Game room," he ordered, and I rushed out into the hall. I ran the whole way there, not wanting his rage so close to my back where I couldn't keep track of it. Jember didn't seem to be in a hurry, his uneven steps echoing the expanse of the hall like a still-beating heart trapped in the floorboards. I found a spot in the room where I couldn't be cornered and faced the door, waiting for that foreboding heart to join me. He shut the door, locking us within the protection of the amulet, then leaned against it, arms folded across his chest.

For a moment we didn't speak. He looked pensive, but in a dangerous, unpredictable way.

"How did you know it was me who looked at him and not Kelela again?" I asked.

"Because you lied about it." Finally, he looked at me. "You'd better have a good reason."

"I trust my ability to survive murderous attacks, for one thing."

He paused, as if considering my sarcasm. "I would trust you, too . . . in any situation other than this."

"I'm fast, and strong for my size. And you're the best debtera I know—with you constructing the amulet, I won't have to distract it for long. This is the most efficient way to do this, and you know it."

"That's if it goes smoothly. If Saba doesn't give in to the Evil Eye's commands. If it doesn't break through all our shields. If you can—" He swallowed, scowling at the floor. "—avoid dying."

"I kept Kelela alive, didn't I? I'll wear amulets like I gave her, so the hyena has one more barrier to fight through. We can do this, Jember."

"You didn't give us much of a choice." He took a deep breath, then walked slowly to the chair and lowered himself into it, supporting himself with his hands on the chair arms. He leaned back in the chair, staring at the fire for a moment. "I should've told you I loved you when you were growing up. Maybe then you wouldn't be throwing your life away for the first person to say it."

"But you don't love me," I said, crossing my arms and looking at my feet. "You already admitted it."

"I could've said it for your sake."

I settled down on the couch across from him. "Then it would just be a word. As empty as most of your threats."

"You're right," he said. That made me gape a little, and I sat silently, waiting for him to turn my point into an argument. Instead he shrugged. "Love is an action. It's something you do." He swore at the flames, then finally looked at me, his brows lowered as if fighting against pain. "I guess you're justified in your sacrifice, then."

I went to him, removed his peg leg, and placed it beside the chair. "It's dangerous, but not a sacrifice. Because I'll be okay. *We'll* be okay."

"Keep your optimism to yourself."

Despite everything, I grinned, but it didn't last long. "I'm sorry about you and Saba."

"She's dead, Andi." It sounded so final when he said it. "Just a memory. The kindest thing I can do for her now is make sure her soul finds rest."

"That sounds like an act of love to me."

We were quiet for a moment.

He took a deep breath, wincing a little. "I suppose I should rest before tonight."

"Okay." I waited for him to say more. When he didn't, I stood. "I'll wake you for dinner."

CHAPTER
32

———— ✦ ————

Everything was ready.

Jember and I had made eleven shields—one amulet in the doorway of the game room, the other ten in the hall about five feet apart from each other, creating small pockets of protection in case the hyena got out of the room. The weapons we'd found were dispersed throughout the room and down the hall. Candles were lit everywhere, casting dancing shadows, creating haunting figures where there were none.

"It's not too late to kill me," Magnus said for the twentieth time tonight. He was lying on his side on the game room couch, a blanket pulled up to his chin despite the amulet Jember had made to warm the room. "Look at all the weapons in the room."

I glanced at the clock on the wall. Nine forty-five. "It'll be over soon, Magnus," I said, barely processing my own words.

God. Over for whom?

I rushed out of the room, anxiety making my heart flutter.

Jember sat in a chair out in the hall, beside the open door so the hyena wouldn't see him. He had a lightweight rack around his neck over his amulet, which housed the different colored threads he needed for easy access, and the amulet I'd started in his lap. I'd put a few more in my satchel, just in case he needed to start over, but Jember was used to only getting one at a time from the church. He'd never been allowed to mess up.

"Are you nervous?" I asked, hugging my arms in my light long-sleeved shirt.

"It's better not to focus on how you feel," Jember said, sounding as if he felt nothing.

"Well, I'm scared," I said, the words falling out of me, despite his instruction.

"*You're* scared? You did this to us. Besides, there are more important things than fear right now."

"That's my line." I tried to swallow my fear, but it only sat in my stomach. "Can we pray together?"

Jember cringed. "God hasn't heard me for quite some time."

"He hears you. Maybe you're just not listening when he responds."

"I don't hear a lot of things over this," he said, patting his knee.

"Have you ever thought that maybe the last twenty years were preparing you for tonight?"

He grinned the slightest bit. "Too existential, Andi. Another time, when we're not about to release a demon."

I sighed and leaned in the doorway to see the clock. Twelve minutes to go. "I'm going to pray for you."

He raised his eyebrows. "Why?"

"Because you need it more than I do."

"Your inability to think of yourself first is what got us into this."

"And it's going to get us out." I laid my hands on his shoulders. "Remember in the Bible when Job was sick and had lost his crops, his children, everything? He didn't get well until after he prayed for his friends."

"I think you misread the story."

"Almighty God," I started. "Give Jember wisdom and courage for when it gets scary. Protect him, despite his shaky belief. I know he still loves You. He's just angry because of his pain."

"Unnecessary," Jember said with a sigh, "and we don't have time."

"And when this is over, grant him all the desires of his heart." I took his hand and put it on my shoulder. "Now you pray for me."

"I told you, He doesn't hear me."

"He will." I waited quietly for him to start. "Just speak from the heart."

Jember sighed. "Listen . . ." He was quiet for a moment. "This little girl thinks highly of You. If You won't do anything for me, at least do it for her. Protect her when the amulets fail . . . because if she dies, I'm officially through with You." He dropped his hand from my shoulder and took a deep breath. The prayer empowered me, but somehow he looked a little shaken. He jerked his head at the door. "Get back in there."

I nodded and went in. Saba gave me a sad smile, reaching for my hand. I sat in the chair beside her and took it, clung to it, suddenly realizing it might be the last time I'd get a chance.

And then, all too soon, the clock struck ten.

I stood and picked up one of the swords on the floor, whispering along with the clock's strikes.

"Four . . . three . . . two . . ."

The echo of the last *dhong* was cut off by the rushing wind in the hallway.

Magnus squirmed beneath the blanket and, a moment later, the form of something shorter stood in his place. The hyena shook the blanket off, letting it slide to the floor, then immediately locked its gaze on me.

I held the sword out in front of me. There was no time to question how to use it. The hyena charged at me. It slammed into my shield and I slashed at it with the sword. There was no blood, only a messy, gaping gash, like a poorly butchered piece of meat. But it barely paused, charging at my shield again as the wound knitted itself together. I slashed again and again. Five times, and this time it had to stop for a moment until its eyes were whole again. I took that brief moment to put a little more distance between us.

Saba stepped in front of it before it could go after me again, and it broke off her arm with its powerful jaw and threw it across the room, but she still got it around the neck with her other arm, holding it at bay until it could break free.

We alternated like that for a while. It would charge my shield, breaking some away but getting it close enough for me to slash up its face. I would retreat, Saba would hold it back for a moment, and we would repeat. But I could tell early on my amulet wasn't going to last an hour. Not even close.

My shield was nearly depleted, so I took my amulet off and threw it at the hyena as I ran.

It charged and I bolted out into the hall, skidding and knocking over the candles on the floor, which sent frantic shadows to match my pulse. Not hearing the slam of it on the shield, I turned to see that Saba had tackled it onto the ground. But I doubted she could hold it for long.

"Thirty-five minutes," Jember said, without looking up from his work. "Impressive, but not good enough."

Despite being contradictions, both were true. He had finished welding, and was threading some of the thin lines he had burned through the silver with red thread. There were three colors in total he had to thread, and he was only just finishing up the first. He needed more time, and I wasn't sure I could give it to him.

A slam on the shield made both of us wince. I grabbed a weapon off the floor—a sharpened broomstick—while Jember got up and moved into the next amulet's pocket of protection. The hyena backed down and Saba stepped forward, her face a mask of terror and regret as she reached up to remove the amulet from above the door. It was nailed on, but with her strength she could probably easily break it off.

"Saba, no!" I cried, and when she didn't stop I hit her arm with the broomstick, cracking it. She still wouldn't stop. "Please, Saba!"

I had to hit her again, and her arm dropped to the ground, forcing her to pick it up. And the hyena resumed slamming into the shield. It didn't take much. Three slams and I could hear the shield cracking. The hall suddenly felt too small and I panicked, backing into the safety of the amulet on the opposite side of the door as Jember.

The hyena broke through just as I made it out of that space, its mane standing up with rage . . .

But it didn't come after me. It paused where it was in the doorway, just looking at me. And then it swung its long neck to look at Jember. My stomach dropped into my feet. It must've been able to sense that the amulet was getting close to completion.

"I'm your prey!" I yelled, tapping the ground to get its attention. "Come get me, monster!"

But it was done with me, it seemed. Instead it ran at Jember, so fast it cracked its own head against the shield.

Jember jolted, making eye contact with me from across the

doorway. I'd never seen him so scared, and for a moment my heart was pounding hard enough to weaken me. There were fewer amulets on the wall going toward the stairs—only two. It was a bad side to be on when you were suddenly the new target of the Evil Eye. There was no way I could break through and get to him, especially when there was so much more of the amulet to go.

I swallowed, adjusting my grip on the broomstick. And when the hyena charged at Jember's shield, I ran out from behind the safety of mine and speared it through the neck.

I rushed back behind my shield on the other side of the door, checking on the damage I'd done only after I was safely behind it. It barely reacted, as if nothing had happened, even though the sharp end of the stick stuck through its neck about two feet, dragging heavily on the ground on the handle side. It could barely run now, let alone break the shield, with its head being weighed down. But its focus was on me again, which was all I cared about. We were back on track.

Saba, God bless her, had held herself back for as long as she could, but now she came out into the hall and took hold of the broomstick. I picked up the closest weapon—a cricket bat—and stood ready to swing, waiting for what would happen next. As soon as Saba threw the stick aside the hyena came at me, and I hit it before it could damage the shield. It clamped the bat in its powerful jaws. I yanked the weapon back, the force making me stumble further into the protective pocket.

"Andi!" Jember shouted. "Watch—"

A solid, strong, far-too-smooth arm wrapped around my neck from behind. I gagged, dropping the bat to grab Saba's arm as she lifted my feet off the ground. I clawed at her arm, trying to dig my fingers beneath hers, to let up the pressure enough to catch my breath. She wouldn't budge so I kicked back at her, throwing my entire weight into it, slamming her back against the wall. I heard a crack so I kept going, slamming my heels backward until she let go.

I never thought Jember's Real World Prep training would come in handy until now—when, instead of being short of breath and panicked, I was more clearheaded than ever. I snatched up the bat and swung at Saba, breaking off her arm in one big piece. I rammed it at her stomach, stabbing a hole through it.

Saba's eyes were wide with fear—fear of what I couldn't tell since, out of the two of us, she couldn't feel pain. But there was determination in her expression, too, as she nodded at me. *Do what you have to do*, her expression said. So I pulled the bat out of her stomach and broke off her face. Then her shoulder. Her legs. I kept hitting and hitting until Jember shouted, "Focus, girl, it's breaking through!"

That's when I finally paused, staring at Saba in pieces on the floor, like a broken doll. This was more horrific than if we had just scattered her across the desert. I had to remind myself she couldn't feel it. That if I didn't do it one of us might die before Jember had a chance to finish the amulet.

"Andi, run!" he said, and I didn't question it. I pulled my small knife, prying one of the nails out of the wall and stealing the amulet there, holding it in front of me as I ran past the hyena. Jember let me pass him before following, but I could hear the hyena's head ramming against one of the last two shields between it and us.

"Pick a room!" Jember shouted over the wind as we ran past the stairs. I didn't put much thought into it. We ended up in a small study I had never spent much time in. Neither did anyone else, clearly, because the fireplace wasn't lit.

Jember locked the door behind us. "Near that corner," he said, tipping his chin toward the only one with any moonlight touching it.

I grabbed a paperweight to re-nail the amulet into one of the walls while he shoved a solid wood desk in front of the door. And then he eased himself down in front of me. Between all the running and panic and the solid wood desk, he was panting. He removed his supplies without a word, transferring them to me. First the amulet, then the rack of thread. And then he took up the needle, threading the amulet while I wore it.

"Why?" was all I asked.

"In case I can't finish."

He knotted it off, but his hands were shaking. I took the needle from him to thread it with the final color.

I yelped at a knocking on the door, jolting my heart. Now that we had a moment to breathe in the thick of battle . . . I was terrified. Not of death itself, but of leaving everyone behind where I couldn't look out for them. Of not saying everything. Not doing enough.

"I love you, Jember," I blurted.

"Don't get emotional," he said, taking the needle back to work. "We're almost done."

"I wanted to say it, in case I die."

"You're not going to die. Keep your head, Andromeda."

There was a loud snap as the solid wood door cracked a little.

"You called me your daughter earlier," I said, as the door cracked again. "Did you mean it?"

The door flew open, breaking and sending splinters flying as it slammed against the heavy desk.

"Not now," Jember said, his voice tight.

Again, and the desk legs screeched against the floor.

"Did you?" I asked quickly.

Again.

"Yes, I meant it," he said.

Again, but this time the hyena's snout could fit through the space in the door.

"Then I love you, Jember. You're my father, and you've done what you could. That's all I could ever ask for."

Jember was a despicable excuse for a human sometimes. But he took care of me, cared about me, in his own way. And if I was going to die, I wanted it to be for the boy I loved, for the girl I called friend, and for my *father*, not for a man I resented for withholding love from me.

Besides, his effort to keep me alive was love, if that's all we had.

And that's all we had.

So, I would love him, because love made me braver . . . and I would die brave, if nothing else.

The hyena snaked through the opening and rushed toward us, colliding with the shield I had nailed on the wall. Jember worked, without acknowledgment to anything, as the hyena broke the shield closer and closer. I couldn't tell which amulet it was trying to work against, the one on the wall or Jember's. But it was getting closer far too quickly.

And the amulet didn't feel finished.

"Only a few loops left," he said. "Get ready to take over."

"Let me fight it," I said. "You have no energy."

"With what weapon? Use your head, girl." I looked around quickly, my heart constricting. Oh God. I'd forgotten to grab the bat again after I'd pried the amulet off the wall.

The hyena rammed us and Jember winced as he handed me the needle. He didn't have much shield left. "Finish it. I don't need energy to shield you."

"Shield me?" My heart dropped into my stomach. "Jember, no—!"

The hyena rushed, a dark swift shadow, and I knew in my heart the next time it charged the shield would shatter. There was no time for anything else. I had to finish this.

Two loops.

Jember's body canopied me into the corner, his forearms resting on either wall.

Another.

I heard claws on wood and a savage sound. Jember cried out in pain and my fingers faltered. "No," I begged, but no one was listening to me. He whimpered and huddled over me, blocking out the light, but I could still hear the clawing and tearing, Jember panting over me, my own heart sprinting, splats of liquid on the hardwood.

But I could also sense the last two loops.

Jember screamed again just as I finished one, and his body moved to let in more light. It was only a second, a breath. But I saw the hyena's green eyes glint at me, even as its jaws were sunk securely into Jember's side. It threw Jember across the room, and I leaped up and ran to the desk, climbing on top of it, watching it the entire time. I saw blood drip from its mouth. Saw it charge at me.

One more loop, Andi.

Saw it leap—

I knotted the last loop and screamed as a body slammed into me, arms wrapping me tight. I caught my hand on the desk, staring at a naked chest.

A chest. A human chest.

"You did it," Magnus's beautiful voice whispered, trembling with relief.

I wrapped my arms around him, and then shoved him away abruptly, remembering where I was.

Remembering where *Jember* was.

Saba had put herself together and come in sometime—I had never processed when among the chaos. She had a cloth bundled at the wound on Jember's side, but already I could tell it was soaked. I tore off my sweater as I ran to Jember, dropped to my knees, and pressed it over the wound with both hands.

"Finish the job," he said through gritted teeth.

"The Evil Eye's not going anywhere."

"Exactly. You have to bar it from coming back." His gloved hand grabbed mine, trying to remove them. "There's no point."

"You're not dying." I hadn't meant to raise my voice, and it immediately crushed my adrenaline, the wall that had been blocking everything but survival giving way. I could feel tears burning the backs of my eyes, my hands trembling as I pressed. "You can't die."

"If you're going to leave the area, make sure you get the chest of supplies from home, first."

"Jember, stop. I'm not going anywhere without you." I lay against him, my ear to his heart, my arms around him like letting go would disintegrate me. I felt his hand grip my back, his fingers trembling. As long as they trembled there was life in him, at least, as much as it killed me to feel it.

I looked at Saba, who sat beside him, peeling off his glove so she could lace her fingers against his skin. She saw me watching her and gave a small, sad smile, touching my cheek with her smooth, cool hand.

"You said those same words the night we met," Jember murmured, his breath warm against my hair.

I didn't remember ever trusting Jember so fully, but I supposed the dark memories had crowded the good ones out. His hand on my back twitched, and I held him closer, as if that would keep the life in him for longer. "Tell me the story."

"I was on my way to drink myself to death—"

"Jember, no," I groaned, "don't tell me that."

"You wanted the story . . . anyway, I never got around to it. I saw you walking into the brothel between your parents. You were so small, I remember . . . I don't know what came over me. I slipped in, picked you up, and went out the back window."

"What happened next?" I asked. His voice was getting weaker, but I didn't want him to stop. I wanted to hear his voice for as long as I could.

"We almost got caught because you wouldn't stop talking." I could practically feel his eyes roll in his tone, and I laughed. He was quiet for a moment, and I tapped his shoulder firmly to keep him awake. "When I got you home, you said you wouldn't go anywhere without me . . . then fell asleep on me, just like this. That's when I decided I couldn't die yet. At least not until you could take care of yourself."

"No, you couldn't." I lifted my face to look at him. His eyes were heavy and dark with pain and fatigue. "And you can't now, either."

He moved, but I couldn't tell if it was a wince or a shrug. "You can take care of yourself, Andi. You've been able to for a while now."

"What does that matter?" I practically yelled. "I want you here with me. Stay with me because I'm asking you to . . ." Sobs choked me briefly, blocking my words. "Please stay."

"I'm dying."

"No," I said, panic making my voice tremble. "You can't."

"My blood loss disagrees with you."

Maybe that was meant to make me laugh, but I burst into tears instead. Jember didn't tell me to stop. He just held me while I held him. I heard movement, saw Magnus lie in front of Saba, head in her lap, and reach over to rub my shoulder. He had gotten a throw blanket from the other room, hugging it around his shivering nakedness.

"One amulet left," Jember said. And then he swore quietly and leaned his head against Saba's as she leaned on his shoulder. "I'll try to hold on until you finish . . ."

I saw Saba pull up his sleeve and write with her finger on his bare arm. He sighed in agreement, and then none of us said another word.

Magnus quickly dug in the satchel hanging off Jember, handing me another silver disk with trembling hands.

I stayed where I was to keep Jember's arm around me, just shifted onto my side to get both arms where they needed to be. And I got to work.

The amulet to bar the Evil Eye from returning was really similar to the ones we'd created as shields. It felt almost too easy compared to the other one, almost like a trick. But, as I worked, the temperature was creeping back to normal, the regular chill of the desert night pleasantly warm compared to the supernatural temperature it had been.

And then I couldn't sense any more strokes.

"Finished?" Jember murmured, even though I was sure he could sense it, too.

"Yes," I said, but I wished I wasn't. I wished it had hours and hours to go. I wished Jember wasn't injured. I wished the four of us were leaving here together . . . "I'm finished."

"Good girl . . ."

His muscles relaxed a little more. He was no longer trying to stay.

We stayed that way for what felt like an hour, at least, though it couldn't have been that long . . . until I could no longer feel Jember's fingers tremble on my back, until his muscles went slack against me . . . until his heart sounded like nothing in my ear.

By then I had prepared myself for the end. I felt . . . calm, almost. When I sat up to look at him, it just looked like he was sleeping. It was only the blood soaking his clothes and pooling beneath him, and Saba's freely flowing tears that told me otherwise.

But no, not freely anymore. Just streaked, dripping from her soulless nose and chin . . . like rain running off a statue. She was frozen as she had been sitting—cross-legged, her head against Jember's shoulder, her fingers laced through his.

Both of them, still. Both of them, lifeless.

I made a cross from my forehead to chest, shoulder to shoulder. And then I kissed Jember's cheek and carefully removed the amulet from around his neck and put it on.

Magnus had stood up before I did, pressing against the opposite wall, staring at the two of them. When I joined him he dropped his gaze, as if embarrassed to be looking. "I'm so sorry," he murmured.

"He's not in pain anymore." It was dim in the hall, the candles burning low, but it was obvious Magnus was pale. He'd tried to wipe the blood from around his mouth with the blanket, but some was still smudged and dried there. "Are you okay?"

"Are you?"

"I'm not sure how to feel." I looked at Jember and Saba again, linked even in death, and . . . it was so tragically beautiful. But maybe the fact I could feel that instead of numbness was a good sign. "We should . . . clean up the blood."

"Not now." Magnus grabbed my shoulders with blanket-covered hands. "Give yourself a minute to mourn, at least."

"There's no point in crying."

"What is that?" He lifted my chin so I'd look at him. "Another survival habit? You don't need to suppress your humanity anymore, Andromeda . . . as if I'd ever let you live on the streets again."

I let out a breath of laughter, but it felt strange, considering the circumstance. The emotion was weighing on me, but I couldn't cry. I had to keep a clear head. How could I ever bear to clean my father's body if I—

"What's that smell?" Magnus inhaled a few times, quickly. "Smoke?"

It only took that one word to strike my memory. I'd knocked over candles earlier . . . and the Evil Eye was no longer making the wood immune. "Fire!"

I ran to the hall we'd started in, Magnus on my heels. Bright flames had enveloped the far end of it already and, with the amount of wood in the house, it wouldn't be long until it reached us.

"My sketchbooks!" Magnus cried.

"Forget the books." I dragged him in the opposite direction. "We have to get to the stable."

"Wait, I need clothes—"

"You can't go upstairs, the house is on fire."

"My first public appearance in three years can't be in a *blanket*."

I tripped to a stop on seeing the open door where Jember and Saba still sat, for a brief moment considering bringing them.

They're dead, Andi. They would have to be buried here, with the rest of the memories.

But Magnus must've had my same initial thought, because I had to drag him back before he could get to the office.

"I can't leave Saba here," he begged, forming tears making his eyes glisten. My eyes were tearing too, but for a totally different reason. The smoke was spreading quickly, and there wasn't much time before the fire would follow.

"She's gone, Magnus. It's an empty shell." I grabbed the back of his neck with both hands and dragged him down to my eye level. "Listen to me. If we don't get out of here we'll be dead, too. Do you know how to ride a horse?"

"I haven't ridden in three years."

"Good enough." I took his hand and we ran outside to the stable.

We'd lingered too long. The near-moonless night was now glowing red, flames shattering the windows, licking the stone castle black. The horses must've sensed something was wrong, because when we threw the stable door open they sounded upset, although I couldn't see anything. I used my pen to light the closest lamp, and the room was suddenly haunted by elongated shadows of panic.

"Stay back, Andi!" Magnus shouted, rushing up to a stall and opening it wide for a horse before rushing to the next one. I don't know if it quite knew what to do with the information now, but it would if the fire got any closer.

I grabbed Magnus before he could unlatch another one. "I'll do this. You get a horse for us."

I released the other horses—seven in total—then went to help Magnus, who had gotten reins onto the archbishop's horse but was still strapping the saddle.

"We don't need one," I said.

"Are you out of your mind?" He yelped, wincing at the sound of something inside the house crashing down. "I'm already wearing a blanket for a skirt, I don't also want a sore backside."

"A sore backside is the least of our worries right now!"

Magnus tightened the saddle, then gave me a boost onto the horse, climbing up behind me and taking the reins. We rode away from the heat into the natural cool of the desert night, the other horses following our lead, the flames cleansing all the memories and pain of that castle just as well as any amulet.

EPILOGUE

I gripped Magnus's hand, barely processing it as I stared at the doors to my childhood home. It had been a month since I'd last been here. A month since Magnus and I left the castle behind . . . a month since I'd lost a father and a friend.

Magnus adjusted the lay of the amulets around his neck—the very same ones that had cleansed him of the Evil Eye. "You can't be serious, Andi. This is where you lived?"

I couldn't bear to answer. Instead, I crouched in the dirt, wedging my knife into the keyhole, and released the lock with my hand before twisting the blade with both hands. The lock popped open, along with a row of metal thorns along the edge of it—a booby trap, designed to release when anything that wasn't the exact shape of the sole key tried to turn it.

I grinned. *Welcome home, Andi.*

Magnus started coughing as soon as I opened the double doors. I couldn't blame him—the air inside was thick with dust, so much so I was sure that attempting to light a candle would set the atmosphere ablaze. His eyes were wide as he said, "We can't go in there."

I could picture Saba giving me a knowing, feisty look at her son's protests. She would've followed me in without a second thought. God, my sweet friend . . . I'd never had such a mutually supportive relationship. I was glad she was at peace, but I missed her presence keenly.

"You lived in a cursed castle for three years but you're scared of a cellar?"

"True love shouldn't judge, Andromeda." He pulled a handkerchief from his pocket, covered his mouth and nose. "I'm with you. Lead the way."

Everything was as I left it, with the addition of about six more layers of dirt, and a few rats. It smelled like rotting produce. Dancing dust and shadows looked like ghosts come to protest our intrusion. But there was nothing to fear here . . . only memories. Those could only hurt you if you let them.

"It's a literal storage cellar," he said, between coughs.

"True love shouldn't judge, Magnus," I teased.

I went into the bedroom, directly to the side table where I knew there would be an oil lamp. Rats and insects scattered at the invasive light. My heart was suddenly in my stomach, pulsing and aching and making me nauseous, but it wasn't due to the new occupants.

Jember's indent was still in his side of the bed. His clothes were still on the floor and folded on the shelf on the wall. I knelt down to open the supply chest, and the familiar scent of incense, trapped inside the chest all this time, tickled my nose. I grabbed Jember's debtera robe from the top of the pile and buried my nose in the fabric.

"I miss you," I whispered into it, and for the first time in a month tears began to well out of me.

I felt Magnus crouch behind me, rubbing my arms. "Maybe we shouldn't do this today."

"It's okay." I wiped my tears quickly and shut the chest. "This is long overdue."

I moved to the bed, a puff of dust rising around me as I sat, but I barely noticed Magnus's coughing as I opened the dresser. *His pipe. His pills. His . . .*

I took out the stationery, the letter Jember had been working on still on top. A grin slipped to my lips. "I have to read this." I waved Magnus to sit beside me. "I know you never liked Jember, but do me a favor and don't interject with insults."

"I wouldn't do that to you." He gave me a sheepish grin when I raised my eyebrows. "I'm grateful for his sacrifice. I don't know what I would've done if . . ."

I pressed my thumb to his brow to smooth the furrows there. "Don't think of it, Magnus. We don't have to anymore."

He shifted behind me, hugging me close. "Distract me, my darling. I promise I won't interrupt."

I was suddenly aware of my father's familiar handwriting in front of me, and I cleared my throat a few times to get rid of a tickle.

Saba, I don't know why you still love me. I am the reason you're dead.

His words chilled me, and I had to take a few deep breaths to soothe myself.

I was afraid choosing a job solely for money would attract the Evil Eye. It was a cowardly decision, and we've both suffered greatly for it. Apologies are not enough.

There were a few sentences crossed out—petty words of frustration, felt in the heat of the moment, that I knew he didn't mean—so I left those out as I continued, "'The debtera you hired is my—'" I choked on a sob. "'My daughter.'"

For a moment I couldn't go on. Magnus held me closer, but it didn't stop tears from stinging the backs of my eyes.

She's brilliant, you're in capable hands. But she's all I have in this world, so send her back in one piece, will you?

"Send her back, my ass," Magnus grumbled into my hair, holding me closer. "I'm keeping her."

I burst into laughter. "Magnus!"

"Sorry, you're right, I promised. No more interruptions."

As much as I owe you your last request, I don't know how to love in a way that isn't led by fear. If that's confusing, ask Andi and I'm sure she'll explain how I break her heart on a daily basis.

"I forgive you," I said to the letter, as if Jember could hear me through it, then went on.

Please don't contact me again. Andi will lay your soul to rest soon, and you'll forget all about me. But I don't think I could bear losing you twice in one lifetime.

I flipped the page over, and over again, but there was nothing left but crossed-off words and absentminded amulet strokes.

"I'm glad he never sent this," Magnus said, and when I looked at him his expression was somber. "They were meant to separate—neither of us would be alive right now if they hadn't. But no one should have to be alone at the end."

We were quiet for a long moment.

I chewed on my lip. I couldn't do a proper funeral. Jember wouldn't have wanted one. Saba had already had one, twenty years ago. I was a month too late, but I had to do something.

I went to the supply chest, thankful to find a single disk of silver. I took my welding pen out of my pocket. "Can you bear the dust for a little longer?"

We sat on the stairs so Magnus could get fresh air without going outside, and I got to work on an amulet. I didn't really know what I was doing. The dead generally didn't have need for amulets—for them, it was too late. But this was what I knew. This was what Jember had taught me, what had saved Saba. It was the only way I knew to honor them.

I worked as if a fire had been ignited in me. The amulet came together quickly, and by the time I was finished my hand was cramping but I didn't care. I nailed the amulet to the wall and stepped back to stare at it.

Jember and Saba had both wanted this—to finally be at peace. Their souls weren't here anymore, but it made me feel better to leave something behind to cover them . . . to protect them.

To be with them where I couldn't go.

We carried the chest between us to the coach. Then we sat inside, silently gripping hands, waiting to leave the church behind.

"Are you okay, Andromeda?" Magnus asked gently, as I laid my head on his shoulder.

I shifted to my knee to lean up, kissing his lips. His hand skimmed my jaw, the pure love in his touch pushing away the remainder of my sadness and regret.

"Yes, Magnus," I whispered to his lips. "I'm definitely okay."

ACKNOWLEDGMENTS

There are so many people who made this dream possible! First, I'd like to thank my God and King, Jesus, and my family for their never-ending support. Thank you to my agent, Lauren Spieller, for scooping me up from the trenches (on my birthday of all days) and for putting up with my shenanigans—pairing up with you has been a gift, and I'll forever be grateful for your genius notes and wisdom.

To Tiffany Shelton, my Jamaican sister from another mister, who really understood my work—thank you for leaving me in the capable hands and sweet spirit of Vicki Lame, queen among editors, whose patience and knowledge know no bounds. Huge thanks to artist Palesa Monareng and my cover designer, Kerri Resnick, who is a mastermind. Thank you to my publicist, Meghan Harrington, and I can't forget Jennie Conway, holding everything together. In fact, I have to thank the entire Wednesday Books team, because you all have made my first publishing experience so incredible—Eileen Rothschild, Sara Goodman, Elizabeth Catalano, Lisa Davis, Lena Shekhter, Devan Norman,

DJ DeSmyter, Alexis Neuville, Brant Janeway, and Angelica Chong. In all my life I have never worked with such a competent, hardworking, extraordinary group of people, and I feel #blessed.

And last but not least, thank you to all my Ride or Die writer friends and critique partners, especially Ayana Gray (from the trenches to the shelves, baby!), Emily Thiede, Amber Duell, and Maggie Boehme—never have I met such kindred spirits. Shout-out to the ladies of The Muse critique group, Team Peppermint, and The Monsters and Magic Society. I couldn't have survived this process without any of you!

Turn the page for a sneak peak into Lauren Blackwood's
next thrilling fantasy, *Wildblood*

Available February 2023

CHAPTER 1

Bunny is getting strong for fourteen. It takes my whole weight to hold him down tonight, hands and chest on his back, knees braced against the dirt floor. My muscles shake from the effort.

"You are loved," I whisper, even though I can't quite reach his ear like I could a year ago. "Come back, my little Bunny."

Maybe he can't hear me—enough rain to drown the island pours from the sky, splashing through our glassless window as it slides off the tin roof, and he screams loud enough to wake the whole jungle, even a mile off.

His wild blood flashes near my face—a small, bright yellow crackle like lightning—but his blood science has never burned very hot, so I ignore it. I focus on keeping him pinned, even with his kicking and cries. I stay on the side of his good eye, so when he wakes he knows me.

Huddled on their floor mats, our ten hut-mates sleep through it, or at least they try. It's the second time this month Bunny has raged. No one asks why anymore. A Wildblood's science flares out of control with overuse, and everyone just waves it off as Bunny being a reckless kid. But I don't think recklessness has anything to do with it.

"I'm getting my promotion tomorrow, Bun," I whisper, my voice harboring an edge of panic. "To team leader. Remember? Everything will be okay now."

Even mindless, Bunny knows I'm a bad liar. Everything won't be okay. Not if he keeps overusing his science and making his blood go wild. Not if he rages and I can't bring him back . . .

His screams shut off like a faucet. My ears ring in their absence, but I don't let up on my pressure. Not until his muscles soften, until he whines my name to make me stop. And then I lie there on his back to catch my breath, relieved to feel him breathe evenly, even if I can't.

He fishes for my hand in the dark, and his body only relaxes once he's found it. I squeeze tight, shifting to lie beside him.

"You scare me, Bunny," I say, and pat his back with a force between a soothe and a smack. "You can't keep raging like this."

"I have to rage, Victoria," he murmurs, closing his one beautiful dark brown eye. "Rage is all I have left."

Rage is all I have left . . .

I should be so lucky.

Ad in the *Wilmington Gazette*,
4 June 1893

THE EXOTIC LANDS TOURING COMPANY
Providing the greatest adventure of your life since 1872

The jungle, with its monstrous inhabitants, has long been something to fear and considered nigh uncrossable . . . **BUT NO MORE.** Whether you need to cross the island for business or pleasure, our skilled tour guides will provide a safe and pleasant experience you'll remember for years to come. The **QUICKEST WAY** to the other side is through!

Enjoy our Rare Beauties and experience the jungle in a way never before possible with the Exotic Lands Touring Company.

A COMPANY YOU CAN TRUST TO KEEP YOU SAFE

CHAPTER 2

Victoria.

I wake to a whisper.

The jungle always whispers, when the rain isn't there to block it out.

The storm cleared out sometime before dawn and the sounds of gulls and breeze through the branches find their way in the open window.

Bunny makes it a point to sleep in on our days off, but he needs it more than ever after last night. I, on the other hand, have a list of things to get done, even if the only work-related one is finally asking for my promotion.

Finally? I was owed it when I turned eighteen last week. The boss promised.

Like when he used to promise he'd never punch you in the face and punched you in the stomach instead.

Carefully, I pull Bunny's sleeve up, and immediately deflate.

Tiny cuts litter his arms, closed but still pink, some of them not quite scabbed over yet. He's been picking again. Just enough to expose a little blood, to use his own blood's energy to play with his science. It's why he's tired all the time—stealing energy from the body takes its toll. It's why he rages so often.

I take a deep breath and get up carefully so as not to wake Bunny, dress quickly.

One problem at a time.

The ground is still wet from last night, making the sandy stone of the square look like the bed of a drained lake. But the sun is already warm, and it'll be dry before noon. Beyond the square, a much-too-long mile off, lies the thick jungle.

Vibrant, damp, the breezes rustling its leaves. *Victoria*, it hums through my body. Part of me wants to answer that call, escape what I must do.

Escape. Poor choice of word. No one escapes the Exotic Lands Touring Company, unless one would call deciding how they'd like to die "escaping"—shot trying to climb the twenty-foot wall between us and civilization, or dead somewhere in the jungle in any number of ways exceedingly worse than a shot to the head.

I've been here since I was six, and in that time, only five people have tried running. Maron, Wiles, Liz, Benji, John. I remember their names, if not their faces. They each chose the wall, because the next day we had to look at their bullet-nested bodies in the square. Each time, the boss wouldn't let us take away their bodies until they stank of rot in the mid-day's scorching sun. Just once I wanted someone to choose the jungle . . . no bodies involved. No memories. No rage burning in my belly. I could imagine the only reason I never saw them again was because they'd made it to the other side, alive and well and living free.

Me? I'd choose the jungle in a heartbeat. And I do, without the risk of running—I spend twenty-seven days a month on the road that runs through it, and I'd spend more if I wasn't forced to take days off. Unfortunately, no one ever travels on Sundays. I'd do anything in my power to get away from the boss and Dean, and volunteering for tours is the only thing in my power.

I should take more days off—what's happening to Bunny could very well happen to me if I'm not careful. It could happen to any of us. But I *am* careful. And my science has always had more endurance than anyone's.

No, I'm not worried about raging.

Though I'd prefer that to what I'm about to do.

Do it for Bunny. When he's safe, and away from here, you never have to take another day off again.

I turn away from my view of freedom and walk toward the office, leaping over scattered puddles. The main office is about a half mile from our huts and hidden behind a lumber fence—as if the jungle isn't angry enough in the first place about us clearing a bit of its majesty away to build on. But the boss doesn't want clients seeing where we live. It ruins the touring experience, he says.

There are about forty Wildbloods in the company—half here and half on the other side of the jungle road. For the moment, Bunny is the youngest in the camp; the oldest of us, Jim, is somewhere in his fifties. He had a head injury a few years back and can't seem to keep track of details anymore, so we decided fifty-three sounded fair. I pass some of my fellows hanging laundry on flimsy clotheslines, reading, kicking a ball around. No one says good morning or wishes me luck, even though I'm certain everyone knows what I'm about to do given how many gossips there are among us.

Not that I expect them to—no one has trusted me since I was twelve years old and used my science to bust a guard's eardrum, sending blood gushing from his ear and everyone running away screaming. It was self-defense. The man would've beaten me for something as simple as getting too close to the trees, but that didn't matter to them. To them, an inability to control your science was close enough to raging to shun me—a danger to everyone who should not be associated with. As if raging is contagious and not just an unfortunate quirk of one's own body.

What they don't know—or just can't stomach—is that what I did to that guard was 100 percent in my control. I meant to do it. But I was young. I didn't know it would hurt him so badly. That there'd be so much blood. That he'd be deaf in that ear for the rest of his life. But it was me or him. He'd meant to beat me, and if any of my injuries had been lasting, the boss wouldn't have had use for me anymore.

I may be the most powerful Wildblood, but out on the relatively uneventful journey by road that doesn't matter much. The boss only allows me to go on as many tours as I do because of my looks. What he doesn't know is that on tours I wear baggy men's clothing and a wide hat to make sure no one ever sees the Rare Beauty they're getting.

I glance up at the armed guard strolling atop the stone walls. Unlike my peers, he waves as if he knows me. He's a wall guard, so I don't know his name—and with the sun glaring I'd never recognize him even if I did. I wave back, the gesture meaningless and empty. I don't want to say hello to a man who can and will shoot me if I step out of line, but better to obey and not cause a scene. Not now, when I'm so close to what I need.

Someday, when Bunny is safe, I'll defy that threatening wave by simply not responding to it.

I arrive at the office and look up at the painted wooden sign over the door. THE EXOTIC LANDS TOURING COMPANY WELCOMES YOU, it reads. Seems a flock of birds disagreed and decided to drop their breakfast on it sometime this morning, so the L and S are whited out, making it THE EXOTIC AND TOURING COMPANY.

What's exotic about Jamaica, anyway? Having never lived anywhere else, I can't say. The English seem to think it's accurate, despite having occupied the island for centuries. Strange that it isn't normal to them yet.

Now that I'm here, my stomach aches. Like every organ in me is trying to knot itself small enough to hide. I don't want to do this. After avoiding the boss for so long, it feels like a betrayal of myself to walk into the snake pit again.

God, I don't want to do this.

But Bunny needs me.

I swallow back the urge to cry then grab the doorknob, pressing my eyes closed for a moment.

Good morning, sir. I want to remind you that you said you'd promote me to tour leader when I turned eighteen. You already prepared the contract on my last birthday. I have it with me. If you'll just sign here . . . Thank you, sir.

I take a breath.

The bell on the door chimes as I push it open and step into the reception area. No one is there to occupy the ten seats arranged about the room, but even if clients were waiting Louis would find some reason to scowl at me from over his typewriter.

"Mr. Spitz can't see you now," he says. As usual, he doesn't give a reason. He's already sweating in his neatly pressed shirt and jacket as he peers over the desk at my feet. "Good Lord, girl."

My feet aren't that dirty—I avoided all the puddles—but I wipe them carefully on the mat anyway. "I can wait."

"You're going to, whether you can or not," he says, going back to his loud typing.

The boss never meets with clients this early. Louis has no reason to keep me away. And besides, unnatural sounds, like the slamming of those keys, grate on my nerves. Give me insect wings and birdsong and water dripping through leaves any day.

The opposite end of the small reception area has another doorway, leading to a hall laid with hardwood floors. Ten feet down, the boss's office door sits to the right; ten more feet to the left, his bedroom. My body is trying to revolt, but I don't have time to lose my nerve. All I need to do is get to that first room.

"Did you see that birds disrespected the sign?" I ask.

Louis immediately looks up, like I swore at him. "What?"

"Shat"—I spread my hands as if smearing the stuff on the air—"all over it."

He eyes me suspiciously. "Still legible?"

"Um, well . . ." I can't lie if I look at him, so I pretend to fix a stack of pamphlets on his desk. "Maybe. I mean, if you know what it's *supposed* to say."

"If it isn't one thing, it's another," he grumbles, shoving up from his desk. He stomps away, heading outside.

As soon as he clears the door, I rush down the hall.

I halt before knocking.

Voices.

So, he really is with a client? This early? Strange.

I sigh and stand against the opposite wall to wait, teetering a bit before stepping toward the door again. If their consultation just started there's no point in wait—

I scramble backward at the shifting of wood against wood, pressing my back against the wall.

A young man halts in the doorway, and I see his eyes light up right before I drop my gaze to the floor. I hate when they do that. Gawk. Because I'm light-skinned Black. Because I'm somehow more desirable because my great-grandmother or great-great- or great-great-great- or maybe all of them were raped by some slimy slave owner who thought no better of her than a dog.

Or maybe I look away because this young man has skin the color of blackstrap molasses, eyes black as ackee seeds, dimples in his cheeks without even trying . . . and because I don't feel sick like I do when other men look at me.

From the corner of my eye, I see him remove his bowler hat. "Morning, miss," he says, then moves away quick with a small jerk, shoved casually by the man behind him. I look up in time to see that man sneer at me, eyebrows raised, like he wants an explanation for why I'm bothering his friend.

I'm used to that look, too.

Out of all the many races of people who live on this island, there's one thing for sure they have in common—everyone hates a Wildblood.

I watch them walk away, the beautiful one looking over his shoulder at me, and I feel myself blush at his unmannerly curiosity. Both are Black, which is strange for clients, but I have no time to wonder about that.

The boss's hacking cough carries into the hall and anxiety swims in my head.

I'm here for a reason.

I turn my attention to the office and my blush is replaced by heated loathing.

Dean has his arms crossed and is leaning against the desk, glaring at me. His skin is almost as pale as the boss's—if the boss didn't get so red in the sun—like a tree with the bark shaved off to a nutty cream inside. His gray eyes hold the same hateful, questioning expression the man from a moment ago had, tangled with panic.

I relish that panic.

We were both taken from our families younger than most, both Black, both light-skinned. Level ground, until you consider his science is next to nothing compared to mine. Level again, when you consider he's a boy and can pass as white to the whites when his hair is cropped short. The boss will always favor Dean above me because of that. Let him have it—I built a figurative altar to God the day he became Dean Spitz, lone adopted son and heir to the boss's company and fortune, and the boss finally stopped summoning me to compete for the coveted position.

But the thought that laying eyes on me can stir fear of losing his beloved inheritance, that I can torture him just by entering a room . . . I'm not a vicious person, but I hate him enough to enjoy this.

Maybe that *does* make me vicious.

But he isn't the one making my heart twist with anxiety, pound painfully in my throat.

The boss drinks his morning cup of rum, reading one of the papers on his desk. Even standing in the doorway of the room he's in makes my skin crawl. But I can't turn back now.

Louis calls my name, chastisement in his voice, but the door to the office is still open so I knock without his permission.

"Come in," the boss says, without looking up from his paperwork.

I try not to look at Dean's hateful expression as I step inside. Quickly, before I can back out. Before I'm eaten alive by nerves.

"Good morning, sir," I say in a steady stream, just like I've been rehearsing to myself all week, "I want to remind you that you said you'd promote me to tour leader when I turned eighteen—"

"Isn't it your day off, Victoria?" the boss says more than asks. *Warns* more than states.

"Yes, sir." My head hurts. I take a deep breath, collecting myself. "B-but, um, you did already—um, you prepared the contract on my last birthday. I have it with me." I take the contract out of my pocket, holding it out to him. "If you can just sign here . . ."

Dean tilts his head, raising his eyebrows slightly. *Well played.* Tour leader isn't anywhere near as prestigious as protégé, but it's a degree of freedom, a pay raise, guaranteed opportunities to get me out onto the jungle road and away from this suffocating place.

And for all those reasons, I know Dean is going to make sure I don't get what I want.

But, for now, he doesn't make a move.

The boss looks up from his papers, removing his reading spectacles. My muscles tighten painfully under his gaze. He smiles, but that's never meant anything. "I'm afraid I've already promoted someone today, Victoria." His voice is coarse from years of cigar smoking, and frighteningly calm from years of trampling on the hopes of children. "We won't need another leader for some time."

I swallow, my courage dwindling. This is not the response I was expecting. "I get very high reviews on my client surveys, sir. And you promised me."

Dean scoffs, and I hate him even more. But he's right—I used the *P*-word. To the boss that has as opposite a meaning as his smiles.

"This client is too high profile for your lack of social skills, and the tour will be off the marked path. It requires men who can stand that sort of rough environment."

My courage surges a little. "That's me, sir. I lived in the jungle for a year, you remember. I know all the dangers, how to navigate—"

"As a feral child," the boss says, and it's his turn to scoff. "Not an experienced tour guide."

"The important thing is to remember the way. I do."

I don't. That was a long time ago, and I barely remember anything before coming here. But it's better than what Dean can do. *Anything* is better than what Dean can do. He hasn't stepped foot on the jungle road for a year and has *never* wandered beyond it. And who knows, maybe certain landmarks will spark my memory.

Besides, the jungle will guide me if I continue to respect it and ask politely.

The boss has another coughing fit into his handkerchief before sighing. It only started happening in the past few months, the coughing. I told him all that smoke in his lungs would kill him one day.

God, I hope it does.

"The *important* thing," he says when he's finished, "is to make a good impression. As you know, Dean is taking over ownership of the touring company, since I have no children of my own. And the best way for him to be an effective leader is to know all the ins and outs—that includes leading tours."

I gape before he's even done speaking. "*Dean?* But sir—"

"Do you have a problem with my decision?"

My stomach turns. His tone is no longer calm. For a moment I think of the loaded gun he keeps in his desk. He's never used it on me before . . . but then, I've never questioned his decisions.

"N-no—" I stutter, then press my lips tight to shut myself up. It's over. I feel my heartbeat ticking in my wrists, and I can't be sure intelligible words will come out of me next time I speak.

"Enjoy your weekend." The boss shoos me away. "Shut the door on your way out."

I nod instead of trying to speak and turn on my heel.

The words *Bunny is counting on you* hammer in my mind to the pounding of my heart, and I stop myself before heading down the hall, taking a deep breath.

You idiot. Get away while you can.

I ignore my own sage advice and burst back into the office.

"Dean's science is pathetic," I say, my voice coated in desperation. "And he's never wandered off the marked path. How can he lead a tour to the center of the jungle? He'll get everyone lost, or worse—"

The boss presses on the arms of his chair to help himself stand, and it's like there are three gates between us and one has been thrown wide open. He's stocky, the remains of a retired boxer—a skill he's demonstrated on me enough times that I don't want him to open that second gate. But he does, by stepping around the desk toward me, and I have to adjust my breath to seem calm. If I back away, he'll never give me what I want.

Be brave. Bunny needs you.

The coaching barely helps as he comes closer.

"You foolish little girl . . ." he chides.

Please don't touch me . . . please please please . . .

When he's close enough, he takes my chin in his hand.

The third gate has been breached.

I freeze, bracing for that caress to turn into a fist. I'm taller by a few inches, but his presence is massive and consuming and I can't breathe . . . Lord, have mercy, I can't breathe . . .

I glance behind him at Dean, though I don't know why I expect he's going to intervene for me. But he could say *something*. Admit that I'm right, at least. Or do something other than grip the desk as if he's about to be beaten instead of me.

But it's been a year since I could trust him to do right by me.

"I know the jungle better than Dean," I try again. Or I think I do. The boss's touch is so repulsive, his presence filling me with so much anxiety, I might die right here and now.

"That's not the point," he says, his voice calm enough to

make my stomach turn. "What would it look like if a quiet little girl who can't even speak without stammering was leading the pack? Who would hire me again, with my reputation tarnished? No, you're a follower, girl—and good at it, too. Let's not change a system that isn't broken. Besides, these are the most prestigious clients we've ever served."

My stomach swims. The one thing I know I have to offer is the thing I'm also dreading.

"Then I'll help make Dean look good," I say, silently thanking God my words cooperate.

I'd felt the beginnings of the boss's clamping grip tightening on my chin, but he pauses. Whatever I fill this pause with will mean victory or destruction.

"I'm the most powerful Wildblood," I say quickly. "And I've faced the dangers of the deepest part of the jungle. Give me my promotion, and I'll make Dean look like the best tour leader you've ever had."

I'm surprised I didn't falter during my speech. Deliberately working with Dean. Closely, as a team. After the way he betrayed me? Being torn apart by rabid dogs would be a kinder punishment. But if I can swallow my emotions and pull it off, Bunny will never have to go on another tour again.

The boss releases me slowly, and I let out a small breath of relief, wanting more than anything to tear all the skin he's touched away and burn it with my own lightning. "Now there's an idea."

Behind him, Dean stands upright, shocked and fuming. "The clients requested strong guides, not antisocial little girls."

I use those fumes to fuel my own fire. "My brand of strength is more useful in the jungle than the strongest man in the world. Besides, don't these prestigious clients deserve the best protection and service Jamaica can offer? My blood science will provide that."

The boss paces, stops abruptly. "One condition. The client has to come back singing Dean's praises and *unaware* that you were assisting."

That's two conditions, but I'm too relieved to care. "Yes, sir," I say, holding back a smile—but I do hold out my unsigned contract. He grabs his quill and signs it without question, high on his own ego. Or just high, probably—the office reeks of ganja.

Dean, wisely, says nothing.

"I want to be paired with Bunny, if that's okay," I slip in, seeing as the boss is in a good mood.

"Ask your tour leader," he says, and falls into more coughing, no longer interested in looking at me as he heads back to his desk.

I take a second to swallow before I look at Dean. He's more pissed off than usual, if that's possible, but thankfully not stupid enough to start an argument in front of the boss—not with his own promotion on the line.

"He's your responsibility," he grumbles.

I nod. "No problem." And I leave quickly, before the boss changes his mind.

I trip to a stop around the corner, just out of view. My legs tremble, and I have to grab the wall to keep myself upright. My lungs ache as I release a heavy breath, taking a few deep ones to give my nerves a moment to settle.

I did it. I actually did it.

Well, almost.

One more trip, first.

Don't screw this up, V.

The sound of creaking wood alerts me to Dean, even if his footsteps are as quiet as mine. "What do you want, Dean?" I ask, walking toward the waiting area quickly—Dean wouldn't dare try anything in front of Louis, who reports all "hooligan behavior," as he calls it, to the boss.

But I barely make it a few feet before a strong hand clamps around my wrist, his touch, his presence igniting my fighting instinct immediately. He tugs me around, and I lift my open hand just as he lifts his fist.

I feel my wild blood spark like an ember within my gut, feel the warmth of my irises shifting to a glowing red with power, but shove my energy back under the coals just as quickly. It's not worth the trouble to fight back. Not when I've already gotten what I wanted. I drop my hand, my eyes cooling to light brown again. My hate-filled stare is stronger, anyway I know, because he twitches while his fist lingers in the air, passively.

His science really is pathetic when compared to mine. I know it, he knows it. Which is why I know to threaten him with it, seeing as, if he had the mind to, he could easily beat me bloody with that callus-hardened fist. He wasn't so much taught how to fight as forced to learn by boxing with the boss twice a week. It's why most of the bones in his face have been broken at one time or another, one cheekbone lower than the other, his nose twisted. The boss never promised not to punch *him* in the face.

We both know our strengths. All I need to do is pull a drop of blood from his pores—more easily his gums, since they're softer—and fashion it midair into a needle to drive through his eye, maybe all the way into his brain. He's gripping one of my wrists while the other is cocked away, fingers closed off from summoning his science, which puts him at a deadly disadvantage against my open hand.

I've won the round in the office *and* this one in the hall.

Overall, it's been a satisfying morning.

"Don't you ever," he says, low, because the door is still so close and wide open, "embarrass me in front of the boss again."

"You don't need my help to embarrass yourself," a braver, stupider Victoria would say. For Bunny's sake, I say nothing. When he's safe and off the island, living a life where he doesn't have to stress over long journeys and using his science, maybe I'll find some way to get back at Dean. But there's too much riding on this trip for me to make trouble now.

He releases my wrist, and I hide my trembling revulsion in my pocket.

"You'd better not mess this up for me," he says, then storms back into the office and, blessedly, away from me.

Terri LaShae

LAUREN BLACKWOOD is a Jamaican American living in Virginia who writes romance-heavy fantasy for most ages. When not writing, she's a musician and a tiramisu connoisseur. She's the *New York Times* bestselling author of *Within These Wicked Walls* and *Wildblood*.